What people are saying about

Luisa Buehler

The Station Master: *A Scheduled Death*

"Cutting-edge cozy. *The Station Master* is filled with long-buried secrets, elaborate twists, and nail-biting suspense. Buehler and Marsden just keep getting better and better."

J.A. Konrath, author of
Bloody Mary: A Lt. Jack Daniels Thriller

The Lion Tamer: *A Caged Death*

"…a curious heroine, a handsome husband, a dashing ex-lover and a skeleton or two…engaging…romance and mayhem vie for her attention–much to a reader's satisfaction and delight!"

–Sharon Fiffer, author of The Jane Wheel Mysteries

The Rosary Bride: *A Cloistered Death*

"…a stylishly written novel evocative of Barbara Michaels and Teri Holbrook. Luisa Buehler presents a fascinating cast of char-acters, an engrossing tale of old wrongs, long-kept secrets, and murder."

–Denise Swanson, author of the bestselling
Scumble River Mysteries

Other Books by
Luisa Buehler

The Grace Marsden Mystery series

The Station Master: A Scheduled Death (*Book Three*)
The Lion Tamer: A Caged Death (*Book Two*)
The Rosary Bride: A Cloistered Death (*Book One*)

Luisa Buehler

The Scout Master:
A Prepared Death

Book Four

A Grace Marsden Mystery

Echelon Press
Publishing

THE SCOUT MASTER: A PREPARED DEATH
A Grace Marsden Mystery

Book Four

An Echelon Press Book

First Echelon Press paperback printing / October 2006

Echelon Press
9735 Country Meadows Lane 1-D
Laurel, MD 20723
www.echelonpress.com

ISBN 1-59080-475-9
Library of Congress Control Number: 2006928243

PRINTED IN THE UNITED STATES OF AMERICA

10 9 8 7 6 5 4 3 2 1

As always, a loving thank you to my guys.

∂   ∽

I am grateful to the host of people who gave generously of their time and talent when I needed clarification and information. Scraps of notes and bits of conversation with many people grew this book until my editor demanded a paring of the prose. Special thanks to Alex Matthews, author of the Cassidy McCabe series, for allowing Cassidy to treat Grace. Sarah Stone, who guided me to sources and information on Wicca. Debby Preiser, Oak Park Library, who tracked down an elusive copy of *Animal Inn* by Virginia Moe. To Gloria Onischuk, proprietress extraordinaire of Under the Ginkgo Tree Bed and Breakfast for allowing Grace's family to party at her home. To Christine Cederborg of Elmhurst Kiwanis Club for accompanying me into Robinson Woods in a foolhardy but necessary research trip. Dick Tresselt, Scoutmaster Troop 16, Oak Park, whose innocent comment three years earlier gave me the idea for this book. The boys, especially Kit, Frank, Mike and Adam, of Troop 562, Woodridge, IL, and Paul Riggs, former Scoutmaster who ran a troop that was the total antithesis of the one depicted in this book. He taught me my knots while I volunteered in the troop for only 'one hour a week.'

ॐ   ॐ

A scout is trustworthy, loyal, helpful,
friendly, courteous, kind, obedient,
cheerful, thrifty, brave, clean and
reverent…except when he's a killer!

The shock-still silence grabbed my attention as no shout could have. Moments before, Robinson Woods had reverberated with the incessant noise only pre-pubescent boys made. I'd been a step-mom for only one month, but I'd grown up with four brothers. Throat gripping silence was never golden, rather a violent shade of purple, or a bright slash of crimson, but never golden.

Harry and I had arrived at Robinson Woods two hours ahead of the designated pick up time for scouts participating in Troop 265's community service project to clean up the woods. Since meeting Will for the first time last month, Harry had immediately taken to his newly discovered parenthood, unwilling to give up any time he could spend with his son. Our early arrival today marked another 'method to his madness,' as Harry thought he might be able to lend a hand since he'd been a Scout in the U.K.

We'd left the car near the troop trailer and walked into the woods. A few minutes later, deeper into the woods we heard the cheery shouts and yells of the boys happily scouring the ground for trash and treasure. Then silence.

"Put it down and move away," Edward Bantonini, the scout leader commanded. The two boys carefully lowered the hinged box they struggled to carry. The thick undercover of leaves accepted the box greedily as its shape settled into their mass. The arrival of the scouts, carrying the box between them, pallbearer style, had caused the abrupt silence.

The youngsters backed away toward the rest of the scouts who'd formed a semi-circle around their leader and the wooden crate.

"It's heavy, something's in there," one of the boys reported. His buddy nodded.

The box looked about four feet in length and eighteen inches in width. The leader motioned the group around to the other side. The whispers began, questioning the boys. "Where'd you find it? Did you look inside?" They grew silent as their leader knelt before the box.

I'd already thought of it in terms of a 'casket' and now my heart thumped against my ribs in anticipation. Most of me wanted him to call the Forest Preserve Police and turn it over to them, but that tiny part which usually lead me astray, wanted him to open the box now. Harry moved. I reached for his hand but he kept moving.

The scout leader stood when he saw Harry. His dark eyes registered recognition and he extended his gloved hand. "Mr. Marsden, right?"

"Yes, Harry Marsden." They shook hands. "My wife, Grace." I smiled at him and his open stare caught me off guard. Sometimes when people noticed my lavender colored eyes they stared a little, but his look stayed riveted to my face. I shifted to stand behind Harry who stepped forward. "Looks like an interesting item." Harry motioned. "Were you thinking of opening it now?"

The boys crept forward, anxious for the answer.

Edward Bantonini's face flushed. "I'd hate to call in the squirrel police to open a box of rocks. On the other hand, I'd hate to open something that could be dangerous or that would give these guys nightmares."

He showed a mix of mostly good sense with a modicum of hastiness. Of course, with Harry on the scene a second man could tip that scale.

It did.

"If your concern is something biological, the box isn't sealed and it's wood. If anything had been in there it would have leaked out by now." Harry brushed the debris from the top and used his handkerchief to clean off the written area. "The sides of the box look rotted enough to have been out here for ten years, but the markings on the top are even older."

Edward read aloud, "Property of the United States Army."

Comments of 'whoa', 'cool', and 'awesome' escaped from the scouts' mouths.

"This is a munitions crate from World War II. I don't believe there's any unexploded ordinance inside; possibly a few weapons and ammunition, which would be dangerous enough."

The boys stood slack-jaw, staring at Harry. I sensed a bit of showboating for the scout whose cornflower-blue-eyed stare never wavered from his father. One of the older boys, a Life Scout according to his insignia, stepped forward from the crowd. "Should I take the troop back to the trailer?"

The boys immediately shouted in protest, many faces turned to Harry as their leader in this adventure.

"That won't be necessary, thank you, Brad. I think Mr. Marsden and I can take a look and determine our course of action."

I pulled a length of yarn from my jacket pocket and braided three inches before identifying the dread pulling at my heart. I didn't want them to open it here, didn't want to run that risk. My thoughts had rejected munitions and headed directly to dead body. Since last year, my life gravitated to dead bones with a story to tell. I didn't have a good feeling about this crate. I prayed for guns.

"Those are the conditions. Anyone not clear on that?"

Edward Bantonini took the silence as a 'yes'. I'd missed the conditions, but the boys stepped back and tightened the group.

Harry and Edward stood on the far side, their backs to the boys. They pried the lid up at each end, preparing to lift it toward them, and carefully staying to the side. I walked toward the front of the crate. Harry motioned me behind him.

The lid lifted easily and both men held it at a forty-five degree angle to block the boy's view. I held my breath and leaned around Harry to look inside. It wasn't munitions.

❧ 2 ❧

Small bones lay cradled on a blue velvet pillow. Two cloth toys nestled around the skeleton. A rhinestone collar, caught by the light, twinkled between the third and fourth vertebrae.

My startled gasp tempted the boys forward, but Brad held them in check. I reached for Harry's hand. "A cat. Someone's buried their pet." I heard the relief in my voice and looked at Edward Bantonini. Sweat beaded across his upper lip; he swiped his mouth with the sleeve of his jacket.

"Looks that way. Thank God." He turned to the boys in his charge. "Okay, fellas, no guns just somebody's cat that got a fancy burial." He smiled at the boys. "I think we've had enough excitement for one outing." The boys gathered around the makeshift coffin and peeked in. Their expressions ranged from indifference to sadness, but not one looked fearful.

"Are you going to bury it?"

The simple question received a number of answers.

"Yeah, we could give it a proper burial."

"Yeah and George could play taps."

"If George *could* play taps."

Further comments dissolved into laughter. Crisis over, mystery solved, time to move on to other adventures. The boys turned to Brad. A lanky youngster with carrot colored hair spoke for the group. "You promised to show us the rock with the face. Can we go now?" The boys voiced their approval. Brad looked to Edward Bantonini for permission.

"Go ahead, Brad. Have the boys drop their trash bags at the trailer and we'll meet back there in forty-five minutes. That should give you time to find the face." Edward looked at the boys. "May the face be with you," he intoned seriously.

A few boys giggled; several looked confused. Will looked at his dad as if to say, 'what now?'

Brad answered in the same tone. "Thank you, sir." He faced the boys. "Patrol leaders, prepare to leave. Two boys stepped forward.

"Turtle Patrol, ready."

"Roadrunner Patrol, ready."

Brad picked up his plastic sack. "Anybody not ready?" He waited and nodded. "Let's go. Single file until we reach the fire lane."

We watched the boys walk away through the woods, their voices carrying back to us over the crisp air. I'd never been in the woods this late in the year. Normally, the dense foliage would have swallowed up and muffled the noisy boys.

"I hope forty-five minutes gives me enough time to figure out what to do with this." Edward pointed at the crate. "I don't know who would handle this. I can't leave it out here for someone else to stumble on."

"Why don't we bury the cat and take the crate out to the parking lot? We could help you carry it," I offered.

"Before we move anything let me snap a few photos." Harry pulled a camera from the inside pocket of his jacket. I knew he'd wanted pictures of Will on his first scout outing.

"You want to take pictures of a dead cat?" Edward Bantonini sounded two-parts incredulous and one-part mortified. He stared at Harry and swiped at his upper lip covered with renewed perspiration.

Only a few people knew that Harry's career before we were married had been in His Majesty's Service. Scout leader Bantonini would have no way of knowing that Harry's mind worked from the premise of foul play and guilty until proven harmless and innocent.

I think Harry sensed that his son's future with this troop might hang in the balance. He cleared his throat and used his 'man to man' voice. "The cat is incidental. It's the crate that may be of interest to the authorities. This is a munitions crate. They're supposed to be numbered and accounted for at the base. Could be vital to a cold case theft the Army might have on its books."

Bantonini looked ready to believe. Harry's next comment pulled him over completely. "Would be nice for the Boy Scouts to give the U.S. Army an assist." He smiled that inner circle-guy secret kind of grin and Bantonini grinned back.

Harry photographed the sides and top of the crate, zooming in on the stenciled words. At his signal, Edward and I lifted the lid and Harry snapped photos of the interior. I noticed something silver and shiny caught between the lip of the wood and the inside of the hinge. I pulled at it gently; it came away in my hand. Three links of some sort of bracelet. I slipped the metal into my pocket.

"I have a shovel in the troop trailer. I'll get it."

"Good. Do you have a towel or something to lift the skeleton out?"

"How about latex gloves from the first aid kit?"

"Excellent. I am dealing with the 'be prepared' people."

Bantonini looked pleased by Harry's praise and hurried off. I looped my arm through Harry's. "How do you do that?"

"Do what, darling?" His blue eyes widened in mock surprise.

"Turn him from thinking you're a nutcase to some kind of secret agent…" My voice slowed as I realized why he'd think that. We both burst into laughter.

"Well if the shoe fits," Harry said between fits of laughter.

"You don't wear those shoes anymore, remember? Right?" My laughter slowed when he didn't answer. My deep-seeded fear that you never really 'retire' from that life moved closer to the surface. "Right?" I repeated with a tinge of panic.

Harry heard the tone and understood. He pulled his arm out from mine and slipped it around my shoulders. "I am one hundred percent retired. My most clandestine op is sneaking cannoli out of your dad's kitchen."

I leaned into him and turned my face up. "Oh, wait till I tell."

"I'll share," he offered, then brought his lips down over mine. A sweet minute later, Harry lifted his face and smiled. "*Mmm.* Lovely." We hadn't heard Bantonini return. It's not like we jumped apart when we realized he was there, but I felt Harry's shoulders stiffen and I flushed. Bantonini looked flushed, not from embarrassment, maybe exertion from the walk.

"Here." He handed Harry a pair of gloves and a towel. "I'll dig the hole." He walked a few feet away and started the small excavation. He glanced at us, an odd look on his face.

Harry pulled on the gloves and spread the towel on the ground in front of the crate, carefully lifting the pillow cushioning the skull with one hand. He managed to remove the skeleton atop the pillow intact. I looked down at the bones, which looked even smaller set against the backdrop of the large green towel. I wondered at the ages of the children who buried their beloved pet in such a manner; it would have taken at least two to carry the box.

"Hullo, what's this?"

I looked at the bottom of the box where Harry pointed. A flat octagon-shaped piece of metal glinted dull blue. Harry pinched it up between his fingers. "Some sort of license tag." He rubbed his thumb over the quarter-size bit of metal to remove the dirty film. "Cook County 55-48," he read. "Can't make out the rest."

I took it from his hand and performed the cleansing trick I'd learned from my four brothers. A little spittle on the object, swirled around with your finger, then rubbed hard with the end of the towel. The I.D. number appeared miraculously. I handed it back to Harry.

"Will's going to find his step-mum fascinating." Harry grinned. I shrugged "Same 'be prepared' crowd.

Harry added the toys to the blanket and then photographed the empty interior. "That should do it." We lowered the lid. He gently folded the towel around the skeleton and carried it to what I hoped would be its final resting place.

Bantonini had dug a more than adequate hole for the remains that Harry placed in the dirt. "Sorry about the towel." Harry brushed his hands together to shake off the dirt.

"No problem. It's from my bathroom; I never liked it." He finished tamping the ground. "Perfect timing. We should be meeting the boys at the trailer. Parents will be arriving soon. I want to thank you for your help, with the crate and everything."

"Not at all. I'm sure you had it under control." He smiled at the leader and motioned for him to lead. Three more cars sat in the lot. Two of the parents lounged against a car chatting, apparently accustomed to waiting for their sons. The third parent remained in the car listening to music, her head bobbing.

We reached the trailer in a dead heat with the boys. They came from the east side of the lot. Several boys rushed toward us, indifferent to their waiting parents, calling out in excited voices. "Mr. Bantonini, we saw it, we saw it."

Harry and I exchanged glances. *Saw what? Not another pet burial.* The boys didn't look frightened, but their shouts were upsetting the adults. Brad brought up the rear with Will limping next to him.

Harry shot across the parking lot like he'd been launched from a cannon. Much to his credit, he didn't scoop him up in his arms, although I'm certain he had to fight the urge. Instead, he walked next to him, slowing his pace to match Will's. Brad moved away and joined the other boys. I couldn't hear their conversation from this distance, but Harry calmed down.

The boys gathered around Brad and their voices rose again. "Tell him, Brad. You saw it too." The carrot top boy, whom I heard called Tim, demanded.

Edward Bantonini stepped forward and raised his hand high above his head, his thumb holding down his pinkie leaving three fingers extended; the universal Boy Scout signal for quiet and attention. The boys squelched their comments, some in mid sentence. "We've had an exciting day, an unusual day. Let's do troop business first and then we can move on. I need all the trash you collected sealed in the bags and marked with your patrol name. The trash will be weighed and sorted. I'll know by next meeting which patrol picked up the most trash and if anything was worth salvage."

More parents had arrived and most now stood at the back of the circle of boys. A few of the dads who'd been early leaned toward newcomers, probably filling them in.

"I have a feeling I know the answer to this, but each patrol needs to vote for the most unusual thing they found and report it to the troop meeting this week."

The boys started talking at once. Edward held up his hand and the group fell silent. He continued as though no one had spoken. "The entire troop will vote for their favorite and the winning patrol's name will go on the Community Service plaque in our display case at St. Edgar. Everyone's picture will be in the Pioneer Press. Okay, line up here in front of the trailer with your bags so I can take the picture."

Brad herded the boys toward the trailer and arranged the photo, handing one boy a shovel and placing his own Aussie type hat on another's head. He stepped back to view his work and must have noticed Will limping into position. Brad disappeared into the trailer and returned with a walking stick, which he offered to Will. The six-foot hardwood stick towered over his head, but Will accepted it eagerly.

Harry stood next to me. I leaned toward him. "How's Will? Is he okay?"

"He says so, but I'm not sure. Doesn't want to make a fuss. Doesn't want to leave."

I remembered all the scrapes and bruises, and sprains my brothers had survived on their trail to Eagle. After the third Morelli joined Berkeley's troop, the quartermaster resigned himself to stocking the first aid kit with more gauze and ace bandages.

"We're ready, Mr. Bantonini."

The scout leader produced a camera from inside the Explorer. Harry stepped forward and offered to take the photo so he could be included. Edward and Brad stood like bookends on either side of the boys. The shot needed to be redone when Tim flipped bunny ears behind his buddy's head. The second looked fine, but Harry went for a third, this time asking the boys to say, 'treasure'. The joy and excitement of being a new scout popped out on each young face and Harry captured it. Several parents immediately asked for copies.

"Okay, everything in the trailer, guys." Brad sheep-dogged his flock. "Will, you can take that home. Bring it back Thursday night."

Edward Bantonini raised his magic hand and within seconds had the stage. Even we parents shushed when the sign went up.

"Scouts, this is your first community service work. You will receive credit for four hours, which will help toward your rank advancement. More importantly, you have completed a service for your community. Countless people will benefit and enjoy the preserve's natural beauty without tripping over pop bottles."

The red head added, not quite under his breath, "Yeah, they probably left it this year." Snickers and giggles followed his comment.

"That's right, Tim. Some people don't get common courtesy." Bantonini's agreeable comment caught Tim off guard. "Great job, scouts. You're walking the trail to Eagle. Walk tall, walk straight, walk true. See you Thursday."

The boys scattered to find parents. We found ourselves walking alone watching Will make faster progress using the walking stick. He hobbled ahead with Tim, their faces animated and their arms gesturing, no doubt recapping the morning's adventure.

A short woman with a familiar shade of red hair approached us. "Hi. You must be the Marsdens. Tim has told us about the new scout in the troop. I'm Mary Quigley." She inclined her head toward the boys ahead of us. "That one is mine."

I smiled and looked at her hair. "That would have been my guess."

She laughed a genuine sound with a deep timber for such a small person. "Guess I have to claim him. I have four boys; two resemble me and two take after their dad." I shook her hand. "I'm Grace and this is my husband, Harry."

Harry shook hands with her. "Will has mentioned Tim to us as well. Seems they've become mates."

As soon as my husband spoke, the dreamy film slipped across her eyes. A totally predictable response to my six-foot tall, blond haired, blue-eyed husband's fabulous English accent. I know; I fell hard the first time I met him over ten years ago. I turned away to hide the smile that had spread unbidden across my face. Tally one more for the Brits.

Mary Quigley blinked quickly and returned to the here and now. I'm never sure where women go in their minds when they first talk to Harry. I remember my particular flight of fancy. Lucky me, I got to live it.

"Oh, ah, yes. Tim talks about Will all the time. Too bad he didn't bridge with the boys in April, he could have gone to summer camp. This troop doesn't camp as much as it used to when my brother and husband were in it in fact hardly at all. Tim loved camp. Of course, he's known about Camp Owasippe since he was a Tiger Cub. He's the last Quigley to terrorize Troop 265." She laughed at her assessment of her sons. We laughed with her. We'd made a good connection.

"Will never bridged from any pack. His mum's job kept him moving around a bit until this year. He's thrilled to be a scout."

I saw the confusion on Mary's face. "I'm the step-mom," I said.

She recovered in a split second. "Good for you; enjoy the ice cream and the grins then send him packing."

I burst into laughter, never having viewed my role in that manner. I felt our connection grow.

She had parked two spaces from Harry's Jag. Tim and Will leaned against the gleaming black machine. "Mom, cool car, huh?"

Mrs. Quigley laughed. "Very cool. Now get your grimy, gritty self off that beautiful finish." Her son grinned and pushed away from the car. "Tim, this is Mr. and Mrs. Marsden, Wills parents." Tim nodded hello to me and shook hands with Harry.

"Hi, nice to meet you. Roadrunner Patrol is going to win the vote because of Will's picture."

I'd forgotten about the competition. I wondered if Will had taken a picture of the box before it had been opened. He had his mother's genes when it came to photography. Several photos earned ribbons in school contests. Will didn't look pleased with Tim's announcement.

"Tell me about it in the car, Tim. We're picking up Tyler at the skating arena in fifteen minutes. See you at the next meeting," she said turning to us.

Harry unlocked his car and directed his son to the back seat. "All right now. You didn't want me to make a fuss, but everyone has left and I need to see your ankle and foot."

Will sat sideways on the seat with his legs sticking out. He lifted his injured foot and Harry took hold of it. He ran his fingers around the ankle. I watched Will's eyes for an expression of pain, but saw nothing that indicated he was hurting. "Let's remove your trainer and have a look." Harry unlaced Wills shoe and pulled the tongue of the sneaker toward him to ease it off.

Wills knee-jerk reaction caught Harry squarely under his chin and bounced him onto his behind.

Harry rubbed his jaw and grinned at the small boy. "I guess I found the spot that hurts."

Will looked relieved that Harry wasn't mad. "Sorry, dad."

"I'll let *you* remove your trainer. Wiggle it off the heel and gently..." Harry stopped talking when he looked down at the foot. Releasing the laces had allowed the foot to swell. Will followed his dad's eyes and stared at his foot.

"Dad?" The panic in his voice matched the look in his eyes as he searched his fathers face for an answer. "It really hurts now." His voice caught and he clamped his lips together. Tears filled his eyes and slipped down his cheeks. He snuffed up a couple of breaths to keep from bawling.

"Grace, you drive. Take us to the nearest hospital. I think it may be broken." He squatted next to Will. "Hold on there, chap. Slide your legs in proper. That's it. Okay, buckle in." Harry sprinted around the car and slid in next to Will.

I looked in the rearview mirror to check their status. I caught Will's eye. Through the pain and the panic I saw another emotion, one he reserved for me.

$\approx$ 3 $\lessgtr$

Harry carried Will into the examining cubicle. I filled out insurance forms and then went looking for a phone. The plan to bring a change of clothes for Will and arrive on time to Under the Ginkgo Tree for Hannah and Karen's baby shower had changed.

I asked for Tracy when I called, she being the least panic prone of the group.

"Grace, I brought Matthew and Benjamin with me because you assured me you were bringing Will. I don't know how long I can keep them sitting quietly on their doilies, if you get my meaning."

"I get it." I laughed at the visual of trying to keep two active, but totally adorable, boys at bay in a quaint Victorian house set to the nines with 'girlie girl' accoutrements for a baby shower. "What were we thinking?"

"If you remember, we planned that Harry would take the boys to Peterson's for ice cream and then take a 'quick trot', Harry's words I believe, to the Trailside Museum."

I shook with laughter now. "Yes, those would be Harry's words. Sorry, Trace. We'll try to get there. I'll call you when I know more."

"Don't worry, sweetie. I'm kidding about the boys. The ropes are still holding; they'll be fine. You do what you need to do."

"Thanks, Tracy. See you soon, I hope."

I turned left before the waiting room in search of vending machines and returned to the plastic gray green chairs with a coffee and a fresh length of yarn. My quirkiness reveals itself as a compulsiveness that must be followed. My mother channeled my childhood 'jitters' into braiding and knot tying, rerouting the nervous energy that caused me to tap, swing, and bounce into my fingers in all but maybe two percent of the time. I played the game now; ten braids, one sip of coffee, ten braids, one sip of coffee. I was on my third sip when Harry joined me.

"How is he?"

"He's a tough one. Cried with us, but didn't drip a tear with the doctor."

Men! "I'm not talking about his 'special ops' qualities. How is he?"

"Oh, yes well. The top of his foot suffered a stress fracture; his first broken bone, Will tells me. They'll have to cast it, but it will heal beautifully. Tough little bugger, walked on it all that time." Harry's face gleamed with love and pride.

"I'm glad he'll be fine. I told Tracy I'd let them know. Are they casting him now? Do you think he'll want to still go to the party? Maybe we should take him home."

Harry's face shifted from gleaming to scheming in the space of my questions. I knew that look. He already had a plan, but hadn't bothered to clue me in.

"What?"

"Grace, I called Lily." He held up his hand and hurried to finish. "She is still his legal guardian and since this wasn't life threatening, they're waiting for her to arrive to sign the permission form."

"They couldn't get a verbal okay?"

"I suppose so, but when I called she wanted to come. You understand, Grace, don't you?"

Of course I understood. I wasn't an insensitive moron. I understood better each day that Harry and Lily would always have this undeniable and uncriticizable bond.

"Sure, I understand. I'll call Under the Ginkgo Tree and talk to Karen and Hannah. We see them all the time anyway."

"Grace. There's more." The expression on Harry's face clearly looked like trouble.

"More?"

"Well, I thought it wouldn't be fair for you to miss the shower. And tonight is a school night and we were going to drop him at his mum's tonight after the party so, Lily will take me and Will to their house after he's released. You can take my car to the party."

My best-laid plan had a hole the size of Sears Tower in it. Harry and Lily shared custody of Will ever since the little boys' arrival to our lives. Lily spent the week in a rented house in Forest Park, a beautiful home on Dixon Street between Brown and Circle, probably the oldest section, the original German enclave. They weren't that far from Hannah and Karen who lived off Washington in Oak Park. Public transportation into the city was nearby for Lily's weekly trips. Although St. Johns was within walking distance, Lily had enrolled Will at St. Edgar Catholic School at the far end of town. He spent weekends at Pine Marsh where Harry could immerse himself in his newly acquired son. I'd been trying to blend into their routine, trying to be a supportive partner to our new life, but I kept getting dealt out of the hand each time the cards were played.

"Grace, I have to get back in there. Say hello to everyone for me, for us." Harry leaned toward me for a perfunctory kiss.

"Wait. How are you getting home? You don't have to go to the brownstone. Call me when Will's ready to leave and I'll come back and get you. The B&B is only minutes away."

Harry picked up my hand and looked quietly into my eyes. "Gracie, I want to spend some time with Will, you know, in case he's in pain or upset. Please be with me on this?"

How could I not be? I leaned forward and accepted the previously offered kiss.

"I'd like to say good-bye to Will. Can I?"

The answer never came. Lily swept into the ER, turning a few heads in her wake. She beelined for Harry. A moment before she reached us, she thrust out her hands to him. He instinctively lifted his.

"Where is he? How is he?" Her face pleaded, her eyebrows knitted in concern.

"He's fine, going to be fine. I'll take you to him."

I couldn't know if it was an attempt to guide or console her but Harry let go of her hand and put his arm around her shoulders as they walked toward the cubicle. In that instant, I saw years of being on the outside looking in. Harry stopped at the curtain to allow her to precede him. He turned to look at me, his face a study in regret. He kissed two fingers and turned them out toward me. I smiled and nodded. Perhaps our bond could survive.

"Where's my dad?" asked a thin voice. I blinked and Harry disappeared behind the curtain.

ᔟ 4 ᔞ

Pink and blue ribbons festooned the tops of similarly striped poles marking the walkway up to Gloria Oinsuk's Victorian B&B. Originally, Gertrude and Tracy had planned to surprise them with a baby shower in their own home. When Karen called from Bosnia to confirm their flight home, Tracy kicked into high gear and decorated the living room with copious amounts of crepe paper, balloons, flowers, and party favors, all pink. Gertrude and my dad started cooking, and I ordered the cake from Lezza's Bakery, specifying pink rattle and matching rosettes. We were good to go and then Hannah called telling us that the baby's medical records were not in order.

A few days later, the food frozen, the cake cancelled, and the decorations down, Hannah called our house. Harry took the call, learning that baby Connor would join baby Clare!

The agency had explained that Clare had a fraternal male twin who had a medical condition that prohibited his adoption. He would be left behind. In less than a heartbeat Karen and Hannah decided they wanted him too. It was only by the grace of God and a clerical error that they learned of the existence of little Connor.

The news of twins spread like wildfire. Single baby gifts turned into doubles, blue outfits joined the pink ones, and an ASAP order for an additional crib was placed that afternoon. Hannah and Karen flew to England first to let the babies' only living grandparents dote over them. Hannah named Clare for her mother's middle name and Karen named Connor after her mothers' maiden name. They arrived in Chicago to a large contingent of aunts, uncles, and friends. They decided to postpone the shower until Clare and especially Connor could settle into a routine.

Party planner Tracy decided to move the shower to a bigger venue and so here I sat before the lovely B&B excited to see my niece and nephew, but dreading the feeling threatening to overtake me whenever I thought of the child Harry and I were supposed to have adopted, before Harry found out about Will. I lifted the huge brightly wrapped box from the trunk and walked up the path to the porch.

Tracy's sons sat quietly on the glider, their heads bowed over hand-held electronic games. The power of technology at work.

"Hi guys. How's it going?" Their heads snapped up.

"Hi, Aunt Grace," they chorused. Matthew looked behind and beyond me. "Where's Will? Isn't he with you?"

"Sorry guys. He broke his foot and is having a cast put on."

"Cool," Benjamin said.

"Very cool. Can he come after? We can sign his cast."

"Oh, honey he won't be coming. He hates to miss the party, but Uncle Harry and Will's mom are taking him home after the hospital."

"Bummer." They returned their attention to their game.

Bummer, indeed.

"Hi, Grace." Tracy greeted me from the doorway. She looked at her sons. "Matthew, Benjamin. One or both of you could help Aunt Grace with the box." Her voice wasn't stern, just exasperated.

Matthew shot from his seat, arms outstretched.

"Thank you." I smiled and transferred the box to his arms. Nothing breakable, crib linens, not too heavy.

"Benjamin, open the door for your brother and walk in front of him so he doesn't bump into Mrs. Gloria's things." Both boys out of earshot, Tracy said to me. "I heard. Don't let it get to you. Of course she'd come running. Think of it this way. Harry had to tell her that he's had the kid for less than two months and he's already broken him."

Her nurse's dark humor suited me. I burst into laughter at the visual her words conjured. Tracy always could get me to laugh.

"Okay, let's get this party started."

We started and finished strong. The gifts brought top notch 'oohs and aahs,' with the babies the highlight, of course. They slept through most of it, which brought knowing snickers from the moms in the crowd about how little sleep Hanns and Karen would get tonight.

I thought about how I might never know that first hand. Then I thought about how Lily would fit right in. Then I poured more peppermint schnapps into my tea and stopped thinking.

I realized that our hostess had spoken to me. I'd missed most of the sentence, but caught the part about 'herbarium.' Something to do with Harry no doubt. I didn't have the green thumb in the family.

"Sorry, Gloria. Your herbarium?"

"I was saying I'm sorry Harry couldn't make it. I know how much he enjoys the herbarium. I put in some new plants for the winter; wanted to compare notes with him."

Harry's love for gardening placed him high on most women's list. On previous visits to the B&B, Gloria had reveled in Harry's praise and interest in the small attached greenhouse where she grew the herbs, spices, and vegetables she used all year round for her wonderful meals. Even I could appreciate a homegrown tomato in the middle of January.

"He's in the area a lot lately. I'll mention it to him."

"Does Harry have business in Oak Park?"

"Not business. His son lives in Forest Park during the week; attends St. Edgar. Today, we picked him up from Robinson Woods. His scout troop cleaned up the area, community service." I briefly recounted the discovery of the crate and the contents.

Karen walked into the room holding Connor. He slept, cradled in her arms. She looked relieved and tired.

Gloria motioned for her to sit in the rocker. I moved a pillow from the couch to the chair. Karen sat and leaned back into the pillow.

"Oh, that feels great. Did I hear clean up talk at Chee-Chee-Pin-Quay Woods?"

"Where?"

"That's the section of the woods you were probably in. Troop 265 always takes the tenderfoot scouts to those woods for their first clean up. That's where the granite boulder marking the chief's grave is. Legend has it that you can see the ghosts of Indian warriors standing in the trees behind the marker. If you're lucky you might get a picture with an orb or mist."

"What are you, a Boy Scout groupie?"

Gloria picked up the explanation. "They run that story every year. Usually the troop does it in the spring before the trees leaf out, but this spring was too wet with the Des Plaines River spilling over its banks. They waited until the leaves fell and made it a fall adventure. I think it adds to the ambiance to have it in November."

"And, to answer your question," Karen grinned, "I am not a groupie; I grew up with an Eagle Scout. Ric belonged to Troop 265 from sixth grade on."

Suddenly, the connection between Lily and St. Edgar became clear. I had wondered why she chose that school. Now I wondered if Harry knew Ric Kramer had helped decide, or perhaps instigated where Will went to school. Harry and Ric had spent years at odds with each other, over life in general, over me in particular.

I certainly wasn't going to offer this bit of knowledge. I wanted our lives to settle into some kind of amiable routine. I knew if I mentioned this to Harry it would look like I wanted to stir the pot of this tenuous stew.

Gloria continued. "When I was a kid it was safe to be in the woods at night. Sometime in the seventies, people started doing weird things out there. Satanic rituals, animal sacrifices, the whole bit."

Pat Davis, a friend of Gloria's and Karen's, spoke up. "That was happening in the sixties. I've lived here my entire life and attitudes changed in the late fifties. People were scared, started seeing the bogeyman behind every tree." Pat's blue eyes gazed thoughtfully at the window. Her blonde head bobbed up and down. "Yes, the late fifties. After the Schuessler-Peterson boys were found murdered near those woods. People never felt safe after that: loss of innocence for an entire generation. That's when all the stories about the rituals and such started."

The conversation had turned dark and it fed my mood. I let my mind wander to the boys' find in the woods. Seemingly innocent. This time. What if other crates were out there, other sacrifices, other murdered children.

"Grace, calling Grace."

I looked at Tracy. She, actually all of them, wore expectant looks on their faces. "Where do you go when you get that look?"

Karen answered. "She goes inside the 'what if' part of her brain. You know the part of her brain that sees and hears what we do, but spins it in a totally different way. You know, the *artiste* in her," Karen finished in a stage whisper.

Little Connor cooed in her arms as if in agreement. We laughed and the dark mood disappeared in the face of the tiny one's smile.

"Speaking of *artiste*," Karen paused for effect, "I hear you've started a new children's series."

"Hey that's great. The boys will be thrilled. They loved Mick the Monster."

"I don't think they'll warm up to this, it's a picture book, you know, a baby's book." I smiled and explained. "Peter Penguin is an amateur sleuth who lives at the zoo with his sister Priscilla and their baby brother Potter. Peter is the P.I. of the park. He solves all the 'cases' at the zoo. I'm calling them ZOO-Dunnits."

"Peter Penguin sounds perfect. If you collaborated with Lily, her zoo pictures and your writing would be an instant success."

Pat knew Lily was Harry's ex-relationship, but she didn't know our particular history; she didn't know she and Harry had a son; she didn't know Lily wanted Harry back. Karen and Tracy knew the score and went quiet. Pat must have sensed the change.

"Did I say something wrong?"

"No, not at all. Lily's work is excellent. I'm not looking for that much realism. I want the characters to be more whimsical. I need an illustrator not a photographer." I thought I'd explained rather smoothly. No sense in stating the obvious about Lily, that there would be ice sculptures in Hades before I'd collaborate on anything with her.

"Of course, that makes sense."

I didn't know if it made sense, but there it was. The light-hearted mood slipped away and I felt I should too. "I'd best get going." I stood and walked over to Karen and Connor.

"Why? Tomorrow's not a school day for you." Karen giggled at her 'teacher' humor. She'd been on leave from Trinity High School where she taught English and coached the tennis team. Not only was it not a school day for me, it wasn't a work day either. I'd lost my job at the prestigious Naperville PR firm of Schwarze and Kreig. My grandiose fundraiser for the Lisle Heritage Society's Depot Days celebration turned deadly when we discovered a body in one of the trunks my firm arranged to auction. That, along with Harry being accused of a hit and run that turned out to be murder, well, I guess it was too much PR for them. "Not a school day, but I do have an appointment with Janet Henry at Regina tomorrow morning."

"Are you going to take that job after all? They haven't hired anyone for the assistant alumni director. I heard someone else declined at the last minute due to health problems."

"I'm going to talk to her. I don't know if I'm what they're looking for."

"Of course you are. You're great at event planning, marketing, well, except for that trunk fiasco all your parties turn out fabulous. Think in terms of larger parties. Anyway, you helped with reunions when you worked in the library."

Karen's logic held, amazing from the brunette we always suspected had blonde roots. She leaned toward me and the baby stirred. "By the way, Gracie, don't forget Brit Haven for reunion attendees from out of state."

Karen and Hannah were currently rehabbing an old boardinghouse in Oak Park into a roaring twenties themed B&B.

"I'll be sure to send the 'Guys and Dolls' to you. The normal ones we'll send here."

"Oh, sure. Send me the boring, normal ones." Gloria pretended a facial twitch and dragged her foot across the carpet.

Laughter drew the others from the dining room. Hannah came in carrying Clare. Most of Karen's friends from Trinity had left; the core party people remained.

"Miss Hannah, can I hold her?" Benjamin sat down on the loveseat and held his arms open. "I know to hold her head."

"Sure, sweetie. Skooch back all the way against the pillow." She laid Clare in the young, waiting arms. Ben pulled the baby close to his chest and smiled. "She's so little. Hey, mom, was I ever this little?" His raised voice, intended to snag his mom's attention across the room, startled the baby. Clare's thin cry caught everyone's attention.

"Way to go, doofus. You made the baby cry. Matthew smirked from his position at the doorway. Ben's face turned white. "I-I'm sorry."

"Benny boy, not to worry." Hannah sat on the edge of the cushion next to him. "Little ones cry. You've not done a thing wrong." She glanced at Matthew and it was gratifying to see him squirm under her gaze. "Give her a little rocking, move your arms, there you go, back and forth, back and forth."

Clare immediately quieted and settled in. Bens' face lit up with accomplishment. I saw a quick movement of tongue pointed at Matthew and laughed. Matthew turned to me. I think he regretted his 'doofus' comment.

"Aunt Grace, will you show us where Will's Boy Scout troop found the crate?"

"Oh, yes." The adult English accented voice didn't surprise me in the least. My sister-in-law loved anything paranormal, ghostly, or plain weird. She differed drastically from her 'two feet on the ground' brother.

"What do you mean, 'oh yes'?" Karen paused and waved one hand over the gifts piled on the table. "We need to get all this home." She waited for Hannah's response. "Hannah, I have school tomorrow."

"Oh, bother. I thought I told you."

"Told me what?"

That lapse in communication, but conviction that it took place, sounded familiar; a Marsden trait.

"I took a room here for us tonight. Didn't know how late we'd be. Thought it would be less stress, you know, take things home bit by bit tomorrow."

"Bit by bit, Hannah? I asked Tracy to bring her SUV so she could cart everything home for us. Anyway, Gloria doesn't have a crib, cribs. Shall we *pop* them in a drawer for the night?" Karen's imitation of a Brit-ism heightened her sarcasm.

"Well there. You don't know it all. Gloria does have a crib, a rather nice one. I, uh, bought it at that shop out by Grace and Harry, Antique Bazaar. Had it delivered last week. Gloria did up some linens for it. Lovely too." Hannah turned to praise our hostess. We looked at Gloria who probably wanted to be invisible and not in the middle of this particular conversation

"Well, Connor and I are going home to our own beds, our own linens." Karen turned to Tracy. "Can you get all this in one trip?"

"Sure. I'll load up and come back for the boys."

"You can't fit them in too?"

"Not in one trip, kiddo. Clare and Connor made a haul here. You know, two of everything."

I sensed that Karen wanted to go home, but didn't want to inconvenience Tracy. I thought she might be ready to give in, again, to her partner. I didn't know why, but I felt I should be on her side. "I'll take the boys to Robinson Woods, Tracy you take the gifts to the brownstone, Karen and Hannah you take the babies home and I'll drop the boys at home on my way to Pine Marsh."

Karen flashed me a grateful look. "You should take the job with Janet, you're a natural planner."

"*Hmm*, thought your brothers used the term 'meddler.'"

"Hannah!" Karen and Tracy both admonished.

"Oh, posh, I'm only teasing." She grinned at me and the lines of her mouth mimicked another's grin so closely I couldn't be upset. "You know that, Gracie, don't you?"

I shrugged. "I haven't figured out one Marsden let alone another." I hoped my enigmatic answer would save me from further response. I truly wasn't sure how to take her comment.

"Whatever we're doing, let's get moving." Benjamin returned the baby to Hannah. He and Matthew were the first ready to go. Tracy made them help load her vehicle and make the rounds of 'goodbyes' before they could leave.

The boys' excitement grew as we drove into the parking lot at the woods. I parked close to the only lamppost in the lot. The light wasn't on yet.

"Can we get out and walk around, Aunt Grace? Please?"

"Absolutely not. The deal was I would show you the area."

"Please. We won't go in far, just a little so we can tell our friends at school. Please?"

"Guys, I'm sorry. It's getting dark, we don't have a flashlight."

"Uncle Harry does. There." Matthew leaned forward from the back seat and pointed to the glove box. "Uncle Harry always has emergency stuff."

Anyone who knew Harry knew that. My husband, the English Eagle Scout was the quintessential 'be prepared' person. What could it hurt? I leaned over and opened the compartment. *Two* mini-Mag-Lites; back-up no doubt.

"Okay, we'll walk in a little. Here are the rules. No running, and when I say we go, we go with no arguments. Agreed?"

"Sure, Aunt Grace."

"Yeah, okay."

They would have agreed to eating worms at that point. Both back doors flew open and slammed shut.

"Here's a light for each of you. Check that they work." I hadn't needed to add that caution. They'd flicked them on as soon as they grasped them.

"Where's yours?"

"I won't need one because I'll be walking between the two of you who will stay at my side at all times. Right?"

Two quick 'yeps' sounded as one. We moved forward as one unit. The waning light disappeared completely as we stepped into the ring of woods. I wondered briefly if this idea held any merit. Ten feet into the woods, a scant few yards from the outline of the parking lot dumpster that I counted on as a landmark, I knew I'd made a mistake.

"Look, a light!"

"Matthew, wait, no." The right half of my escort bolted ahead. I grabbed Ben by the shoulder before he could follow. "Stay put." I looked toward the bobbing beam that marked Matthew's position. He disappeared into the shadows.

The light Matthew spotted remained fixed in the distance. The lack of movement meant either the person holding it stood still or that it rested on something stationary. I thought about locking Ben in the car before chasing after his brother, but that would take time. I needed to follow the thin light in front of me. I took the flashlight from Ben and held his hand while we moved through the woods. I shared real time between silently chastising myself for this stupid idea and straining to keep up with the beam that marked the location of Tracy's son.

A sense of nervousness overtook me without warning, seeping into my brain with each footstep. The flashlight in my hand became a tool as I fingered the on-off slide. *Off, one thousand, on, one thousand. Off, one thousand, two thousand, on, one thousand, two thousand.*

"Aunt Grace, what are you doing?" Ben squeezed my hand and tried to reach across me to grab the light.

Off, one thousand, two thousand, three thousand. On, one thousand, two thousand, three thousand.

"Aunt Grace, stop. I can't see." Ben stumbled and his panicked voice stopped me.

"Where's Matthew?" Ben turned his head away from me and leaned into the night holding tight to my hand. Concern for my young charge ended my need to calm my 'jitters.' I needed to find Matthew.

"Aunt Grace, the light's gone." He moved closer to me and I put my arm around his shoulders. "I'm scared."

The bright stationery light was indeed out. Turned out, covered, I didn't know, but the woods loomed even darker now and I knew Matthew must be frightened. I couldn't see his beam any longer. *Did I give him the flashlight with old batteries? Did he drop the light? Did he trip and fall?* The thoughts raced through my mind, each scenario worse than the previous.

"Mattie, Mattie, where are you?" Ben's childish voice, using his brother's family nickname, tugged at my heart.

I added my voice. "Matthew, follow my voice. Look for the light, come to my voice." I held the flashlight high over my head pointing down trying to give him the best sight. I didn't know how far the beam would penetrate into the darkness if I didn't point it in his direction. "Matthew, Matthew."

Ben whimpered and clung to me. "It's gonna be fine, Benny. Keep calling."

"Mattie, Mattie, over here."

"Matthew, if you can hear me, turn in a circle until you see the light or my voice sounds the strongest. Matthew, call out if you need help."

Ben and I stopped calling to listen. The silence snapped shut around us like we'd never spoken. Ben slid to the ground transferring his grip from my arm to my leg. "What if bad people take him like those other boys?" His sobs increased and his body trembled against my leg.

"*Shh*, Benny, he's fine. No one will take him." I leaned down to comfort Ben and the beam of light swung with my movement. In the weakly lighted periphery I saw movement.

"Hey, Benny, don't cry. I'm okay." Matthew materialized on the path and crouched next to his brother. Their arms went around each other and Ben's soft cries of 'why'd you do that' turned to a quick shrug-off of his brother's arms as he stood. His relief turned to anger and he jabbed at those same arms. "That was stupid, I'm tellin' mom."

I knew how he felt. I wanted to strangle Matthew, right after I finished hugging him. "We'll sort this out later, Matthew, and we will, but right now let's get back to the parking lot."

"Yes, ma'am."

"Where's your flashlight?"

"It's out." He tapped the metal cylinder against his hand for proof.

"Okay, I want one of you on either side and a little behind me. Hold on to the back of my jacket. Watch the ground in front of my feet and keep your heads down in case of branches. Ready?"

"Uh-huh."

"Yes."

I had walked pretty much a straight line in from the parking lot. After Matthew bolted, we'd walked more to the right, following the angle he'd used. I prayed that my dead reckoning still brought me as close to target as it used to on all those hikes with my two older brothers. I'd carried the pack with the water and sandwiches while they carried forty-pound sandbags. Of course with those two, their food weighed almost as much, or so it felt to me. I smiled in the darkness and knew I still had it when I saw the large outline of the dumpster.

We broke into a run for the car as soon as we cleared the trees. The boys were still holding tight. I felt for the keys in my pocket and stopped cold. Empty!

෨ 5 ෮

My abrupt halt caused both boys to collide with me. The contact resulted in giggles from them and a mumbled apology from me. I turned around and held each of them by their shoulder. I wasn't laughing. Their smiles faded as first Matthew and then Ben caught the worry in my manner. "Boys, we have a problem. The keys to the car were in my jacket pocket." I removed my hands from their shoulders and patted my pockets. "They must have fallen out in there." I motioned toward the woods with my head.

"Cool. Are we going to break in? I saw in this movie how they took a really thin piece of metal and slide-ed it inside and opened the door really fast."

I smiled at Ben's idea and grammar.

"Doofus. Where you gonna get a 'slim jim' out here, genius? That's what that bar is called, isn't it Aunt Grace?" Matt acted more concerned with one-upping his brother than opening the car.

"Ah, yes. Slim jim. I'd settle for a coat hanger. Your mom and I used one on several occasions to open the door on the old Ramble she drove in college. Got to be pretty good."

"That won't work with new cars, Aunt Grace. Better design and safety features." 'Ralph Nader' folded his arms across his chest. "This is the nineties, Aunt Grace, not the Ice Age."

Benjamin exploded into giggles, nodding his head quickly so as to be included in the joke. The darkness couldn't disguise the line of white glowing across Matthew's face.

I reviewed my situation armed with a better sense of humor. "Okay, okay munchkins. Uncle Harry might have a key hidden somewhere under the bumper. He never told me he did, but then I don't usually drive his car." I herded the duo to the front of the car, not willing to take my eyes off them.

"Uncle Harry wouldn't put a key there."

Precocious aside, I was losing patience with Tracy's eldest. "Why not?"

"You know." Matt dipped into a crouch, brought up his hands, and mimicked holding a gun. "The bad guys chasing him would look there first."

A discussion of Harry's former profession had reached Matthew's ears one night when he'd slipped from bed to 'spy' on his parents and their guests. We'd sworn him to secrecy and sent him back to bed. To this day, Benny didn't know.

"Who's a doofus now? Uncle Harry doesn't know bad guys." Benjamin leaned his face up to his brother with a *ha-ha* posture.

"Oh yeah. You don't know everything."

"Whaddaya mean?"

I clapped my hands together. "Boys!" The banter stopped. "We have more important things–" I stopped talking and started worrying. A car pulled in and moved slowly toward us. "Get down." I pushed the boys down in front of the Jag's bumper and crouched next to them. I wasn't sure if the driver had seen us yet. I wasn't sure why I decided to hide instead of wave for help. My heart thumped against my chest and my body's tension transferred to the boys. Matthew wrapped his arm around his brother. The smell of damp leaves and dirt mingled with the scent of shampoo from the boys' heads as I tucked them closer to me.

"Aunt Grace?

"*Shh.* Inside voice. Better yet, no voice. *Shh.*" My whisper muffled against the dull metal. I could see the lights sweeping toward us. *Lights. That's what bothered me. The lamppost wasn't on. It wasn't on earlier; I thought it was too early, hadn't changed the timer. Daylight Savings? Central Time? Who cares? Stop thinking about lights. Concentrate, dammit.*

The car stopped, but the lights stayed trained on the Jag. The pattern looked like a funnel with us at the top ready to topple in.

"Grace?"

I knew that voice. We all did. Three bodies popped up into view like corks on a wave.

"Uncle Ric!" Matthew and Benjamin scampered around the car and raced toward Ric.

"Whoa, fellas. Don't knock me over."

The boys laughed as they reached him. He ruffled each boy's hair and slipped an arm around each pair of shoulders. They walked toward me, the boys providing the explanation in a manner as succinct and yet fantastic as only kids can.

"Well, Mrs. Marsden, seems like you've had quite an evening." His formal tone made the boys giggle. Ric Kramer still ranked as the most handsome man I'd ever known. Years before, during the most difficult time of my life, I had turned to him for comfort when he'd brought me the news that Harry had died overseas. Months later, when the truth of Harry's disappearance and death came out, our budding relationship ceased. That time, that bond, loomed between us. I pushed my fingers through my hair and tucked the heavy strands behind my ears. I immediately regretted the primping.

"How did you know to come here?"

"I helped Tracy and Karen unload the loot from the shower. Tracy told me what you were up to. This isn't a safe place at night. I figured you'd get caught out here in the dark."

Suddenly, as if on cue, the lamppost light flickered on. Matt's voice raised as he pointed to the light. "It's true. The light goes on and off when the Indian ghosts are here."

"Ghosts? Are there really ghosts here, Aunt Grace?" Benny's sweet face verged on tears.

"Absolutely not. Matthew that light went on because it's on a timer that hasn't been changed or because it has a loose wire or some other normal explanation, but it did not come on because of ghosts. Are we clear on that? I used my best 'you're so in trouble now' voice.

"Yes, ma'am."

"Absolutely clear, Matt?"

"Yes, sir."

"Tracy's still with Karen. She may be there awhile, something about the cribs facing the wrong way." Ric grinned and held up his hand. "Don't ask."

"Hannah's idea?" I knew it would be my New Age sister-in-law with some wacky idea about vibes and auras.

He nodded. "I'll bring the boys back there and they can go home with their mom."

"All the more reason for me to bring them home. Who knows how long they'll be; there's certain to be *discussion* about the furniture arrangement." Ric apparently caught my euphemism for argument because he dropped his idea. I continued. "There's a small problem."

His arched eyebrow coaxed me on. "My keys fell out of my pocket somewhere out there."

"Mattie ran after the light and made us chase him, and Aunt Grace lost her keys."

"What light, Ben?"

"I dunno. In there." His arm swept in an arc. Ric looked at me and I didn't like what I saw. His left hand swept at a lock of hair that wasn't long enough to touch his forehead. I recognized the nervous habit of years gone by and longer hair."

"What's wrong?"

The tiny shake of his head warned me not to push. "What's wrong is we have to get this car open. Okay, team, follow me." His upbeat tone belied what I'd seen on his face. The boys fell in line behind him, excited to be helping. Ric looked back over his shoulder toward the tree line. He'd moved too far for me to see his face, but I'd bet he wasn't smiling. The troupe returned with the coveted 'slim jim' in hand.

"Can I do it, Uncle Ric?" Matthew looked up with hope and devotion plastered on his face. Benjamin wiggled next to him. "Me too?"

Ric knew not to choose. "Sorry, fellas. Only police officers or authorized personnel have permission to use one of these."

They looked dejected, but accepted the explanation.

"The trick is to slide this end, see how it's shaped, between the frame and glass." Matthew reached out his hand to touch the metal bar. Ric took hold of his forearm before he could lower his hand. "You're bleeding."

"It's okay. I tripped and cut my hand on something."

Great! I almost lose him and now he's injured. And I want to be a mother. I can't even be a responsible aunt. I felt tiny pinpricks of tears behind my eyes.

"Mattie, let me see." I reached for his arm and my fingers closed over Ric's hand. I stared at him, aware of how close he stood, how warm his skin felt, how the scent of Gray Flannel teased my nose. He didn't move. *What was he thinking?*

Geez, Grace, what are you thinking?

❧ 6 ❧

The sight of Matthew's palm re-focused my thoughts. An inch long gash above his wrist, at the meaty part at the base of his thumb still leaked blood. His jacket cuff reflected dark brown stains on the yellow material. It looked like he'd applied pressure by pulling his cuff over the wound and pressing down. The wound didn't look urgent, but this wasn't my brother or my child; I didn't feel I had the last call.

"It doesn't look bad, my man, but we need to clean it up. Let me pop this open and we'll all be on our way."

"Ric, it won't matter." I put my hand out to forestall his efforts at the window. "I used my keys. Harry has his."

"It would have saved us a lot of time standing out here if you'd remembered that sooner." Ric slapped the bar down against his thigh. The *smack* startled Matt and he jerked his hand from my grip.

"Aunt Grace, can we go where my mom is?"

"Sure can, Matt. Right now." I put my arm around his shoulders and guided him toward the Porsche. *The Porsche. Oh, geez, we won't all fit.* I kept walking, a plan forming in my head. When we reached the car door I looked over Matt's head at Ric. "You guys go ahead and I'll wait for the next bus." I laughed and hoped the boys thought it funny. Ben giggled and I could feel more than see Matt loosen up.

"Grace, I don't like leaving you—"

"They can both squeeze into the front with you for the short trip. I could have but I ate too much cake this afternoon."

The boys joined in. "You shoulda seen the piece of cake Aunt Grace ate." Ben motioned something akin to a house brick.

"Thanks, Benny, I'll remember that." More laughter. "Okay, get in Uncle Ric's car. Scrape your shoes on the ground first. You know how he is about his baby." I nodded toward Ric and made a face for the boys. They settled in the front seat, only Matt secured by the belt. "Guys this is an emergency and the only reason you're not both buckled in." *Tracy isn't going to let me take them into another room alone after this.*

Ric leaned in from the driver's side. "Fellas, I'll be right back. Gonna open the car for Aunt Grace so she can wait inside." Ric straightened and looked across the roof of the car at me. He motioned me toward Harry's car. I leaned in toward the boys for goodnight kisses. "C'mon, big smooches." They giggled and made extra smooch noises with their kisses. "Night, guys. Sorry this got so messed up."

"Are you kidding? This was great." Both heads bobbed so forcibly they looked like they belonged on the rear window dash. Who says kids don't appreciate the simple things anymore?

A soft glow lit up the interior of the Jag. "Madam, your carriage awaits." Ric mimicked a bad English accent and bowed while he held the door open. He kept the mood light for the boys' sake. I heard low chuckles behind me. If not for Ben and Matt's presence, I'm certain 'madam' would have been something else.

"Thank you for helping out." I spoke quietly while I slipped into the front seat.

He nodded his head. "Grace, please be in this car with the door locked when I get back."

This particular tone, patient and slow, we who knew Rick called his 'cop tone.' It annoyed me to no end when he used it on me, especially without reason.

"Where would I go—"

He interrupted my protest with a finger pointed at my face. "I know you, Grace. Stay put." He lowered his voice and finger. "Please. I hate leaving you here." His voice changed and the relationship we'd once shared charged his words with deeper meaning. The car filled with a cloud of heat and noise taking up space in my head until I jumped out and collided with him standing next to the door.

He put his arm out to steady me. "Gracie, what is it?" The concern and deep timbre of his whisper prolonged the confusion in my mind.

I filled my lungs with crisp autumn air and slowly exhaled. He pulled me closer. "It's okay, they're okay." He murmured brushing his lips against my hair.

The realization of what he thought I thought snapped me our of my fugue state. I pushed away from him with one more deep breath. The night gleamed clear and a draft circled my neck where I'd loosened my scarf. I pulled it tighter.

"What the hell was that?"

"Nothing I'm fine. Get the boys to Tracy." I slid into the front seat and pulled the door toward me, shutting out his final admonition. He pantomimed to lock the door before he walked away. I watched them pull out of the parking lot. Twenty minutes round trip. Tops.

Twenty minutes. I could clean out my purse. Try for a nap. Tie twelve bowlines. The obsessive-compulsive disorder that attempts to rule my life, especially when I'm upset, put in its bid for my spare time. I yanked a length of cord from my purse and mentally agreed to twenty bowlines. Most purses, coats, and jackets I own contain a piece of yarn or length of line suitable for braiding or knotting.

Twenty bowlines. Piece of cake. A piece of cake would be great about now. I remembered the cannoli-filled delight I'd tasted at the shower. I salivated for sweets while I contentedly formed knots. Four down, five down.

The rap on the glass and the face at the window shattered my calm. My scream filled the enclosed space and bounced against the windows. I lurched away from the driver's window, but got caught up on the gearshift. I heard another noise from behind me. The faceless hooded figure at the passenger's door tugged the handle. I screamed again and replayed the moment right after Ric walked away. Did I push down the button? I remembered the pressure of my palm against the smooth plastic nub. I was safe. Sort of.

The face at my window glowed and floated in the darkness. It looked plastic, smooth and motionless. The face began to rise past the next window and I saw another hooded figure at the door. It must have been crouching next to the car holding that plastic mask on a stick in the window. I saw this one reach for the door handle. I leaned on the car horn and had the satisfaction of seeing them both jump. Short-lived satisfaction as I felt the draft from the open door.

Survival instinct ruled my brain. I slipped my arms through the steering wheel and hugged it, leaning on the horn with my chin. My jaw clenched each time I hit the horn, the jolt traveling to the base of my skull. I pushed my knees up under the wheel. Whoever these freaks were they weren't going to get me out of the car.

"Crazy bitch!" The voice sounded young and excited.

A calm voice commanded, "Pull her head off that horn."

Slender hands gripped my shoulders and tried to pry me back. I hunched forward, tightening my grip on the wheel. I heard the scraping of shoes on the pavement and felt my attacker pushed away. "Like this." Thick fingers tangling in my hair offered a split second warning of their intent. I grabbed for the hand and realized my mistake as my attacker's left hand found my throat. The strong pressure and upward pull forced me to move with the hands to avoid choking.

"This is how it's done." His voice intoned like some infomercial on removing a stubborn stain.

I clawed at the fingers at my throat; they felt gnarled and pointed like tree branches poking into my skin. I felt myself sliding out of the low-slung car. My feet bumped out over the running board and my heels hit the ground. I backpedaled against the ground to keep from being dragged.

Chee Chee Pin Quay, Chee Chee Pin Quay. The murmuring intensified as my attacker pulled me toward the woods. There were more of them! My brain kicked in with primeval fear. I whimpered and he chuckle at my fear.

"She understands." His voice lifted to carry his message to the woods behind him.

Chee Chee Pin Quay, Chee Chee Pin Quay...

My heart froze with terror and then my body reacted. I stopped struggling and slumped. The weight shift caused him to loosen his grip on my throat to catch me from hitting the ground. I took that moment and rolled away as hard as I could. The jolt in my shoulder where I landed and the slice of pain from the hair torn from my head paled before the fear of what awaited me in the woods. I jumped up and ran parallel to the woods along the edge of the parking lot.

"Get her!" *Chee Chee Pin Quay, Chee Chee Pin Quay.* Excited voices. Loud voices. I knew they'd spot me easily in the glare from the light. A quick glance back scared me more. A line of robes flapped out from the woods, cutting an angle across the pavement toward me. My best chance would be to stay close to the woods and blend in. Dark jeans, brown jacket, dark hair; I had a chance. Ric would be back soon. I had to stay free a few more minutes.

Suddenly, my odds improved. The light went out and the area plunged into darkness. I turned into the woods and ducked behind some bushes. The pounding feet I'd heard in pursuit slowed and stopped.

"Did you see that? It went out."

"So what? Let's find her."

"Davy, he's right. It's like the other time. Maybe we shouldn't do this. Maybe…"

"Maybe what? The Indian ghost is out here 'cause the light went out? You believe that crap? Mr. Big explained it, didn't he?"

"He's right, Davy, I'm going back."

"Me too."

"Go ahead. I'll get her myself and I'll get the trophy."

I couldn't tell how many left. I didn't dare move. I felt at the mercy of the erratic, possible short-circuited light. Another sound filled the night; a low pulsating beat, a muffled drum. Part of their game, if indeed it were some twisted hazing complete with trophy. The sound came from behind me, deeper in the woods. Was the origin of the sound to have been my destination? Is that were they took the trophy? The word kept filling my head with horrible connotations.

"Cripes! Do you hear that?"

The voice sounded so close I almost gasped in surprise. I caught movement several yards ahead of me in the lot. My decision to duck into the woods saved me. There was enough dark night to keep me concealed. Unless the light came on.

"Yeah, I hear it and I don't like it. I'm leaving."

"C'mon, Davy. You can't tell me you don't hear those drums. It's like the last one. Let's get out of here."

The voices moved away, across the parking lot, toward the dumpster. Apparently, the drumming wasn't of their making. It spooked them. I didn't care what scared them, as long as they left. I waited to hear a car engine to let me know they'd gone. Nothing. Were they on foot? Where'd they come from? There were apartments on the other side of the belt of woods. Had they been responsible for the earlier light? I shivered at the thought of what might have happened if Matthew had reached that light and I cursed myself for my rashness.

I wanted to leave the woods. Slowly, I stood up from my crouched position. I made little noise, but the cracking of a twig under my foot popped like a firecracker in the quiet night. The tom-toms stopped and normal night noises came to my ears. Had they been there all along? Had my mind shut out everything to focus on survival or had even the creatures of the night lay silent in the forest, waiting for the danger to pass? Had it passed?

I walked from the woods as the headlights of a car swept into the lot. The parking lot lights came on filling the dark corners and illuminating my position. The spillover of light stopped at the edge of where I'd hidden, forming a jagged circle and then darkness. My voice caught in my throat as I ran toward the car. Tears and sobs that had bided their time during crisis exploded from me.

"I told you to stay in the car." Ric stood next to the Porsche shouting at me, his arms flung out in exasperation. "Dammit, what were you thinking?" He brought one fist down on the metal roof.

Then the light touched my face. The moment registered in his eyes. "Grace!" He held me, not in exasperation but in panic. I sobbed against his chest and locked my arms around his neck. I could feel him straining to look beyond me and around me in case he needed to take on whatever had terrorized me. He pulled me closer to his car.

"What happened? Are you alright?" He tried to pry my arms from around his neck. "Grace, look at me. Tell me what happened." He looked down at me, and then up again. Were they gone?

I gulped the crisp air and held each breath before exhaling, trying to calm myself. His strong arms assured me I could relax. Ric sensed my body's tone and gently pulled my arms down. He rubbed my hands and blew warmth across them.

"They're like ice. Here." He tucked my arms inside his jacket and around his waist. I pressed closer; his body heat flooded me with warmth and security.

"It was horrible. I thought they were going to kill me."

"Are you hurt?"

"I'm not hurt. I want to leave."

Ric's voice softened. "All right, Gracie." He stepped back and walked me around to the passenger side.

"Ric, my purse." He nodded and walked to the still open driver's door, leaned in and retrieved my purse. He straightened, pushed down the button, and closed the door. He tried the door and it opened effortlessly. He glanced from the door to me and then slammed the door. I jumped at the sound. He covered the ground back to me quickly and at some price to himself. Sudden movement or fast walking, running still caused him pain. I noticed the grimace before he turned his head.

He settled into his seat and gripped the wheel. "God, Grace. I must have broken the lock. I didn't even check." He stared straight ahead, his clenched teeth pushed out a muscle at the back of his lower jaw. He pounded the steering wheel with both fists. The emblem in the center of the padded wheel popped up onto his chest.

"Ric, you couldn't know."

"I left you here with no protection." His tone reflected the foul mood he directed at himself. He turned the key and shifted. We drove out of the parking lot and I knew he wasn't going to say more. I reached over to lift my purse from his lap. We'd be at the brownstone soon. I'd have to explain everything to Ric, and whoever was there. Whoever? Where was Harry? Why didn't he come with Ric?

I felt a tinge of guilt that I hadn't asked for Harry. I cleared my throat. "Why didn't Harry come with you? I thought we'd drive home.

Ric's jaw unclenched, but his pursed lips picked up the tension. His hands tightened on the wheel. "I don't know, Grace. He gave me the keys so you could drive yourself home? He wanted to stay and tuck in Will? Because he needed to talk to Lily about Will? Your guess is as good as mine. Probably better. He's your husband."

Ric's harsh tone depressed me. My adrenaline ebbed to precrisis levels, I didn't want to argue. I only meant to think the words but I heard a soft voice say, "He's Will's father and that trumps me."

Ric turned his head to comment. His low tone barely touched my ears. "You're not a game, Gracie. Least not to me."

I gazed out the window and didn't respond. Unless we caught the light I knew we'd be at the brownstone in a few minutes. We drove through the green and turned onto Lathrop. I spotted Tracy's van and Hannah's MG; a mechanical version of David and Goliath. *Davy.*

"One of the boys called another 'Davy'. And someone referred to the man as 'Mr. Big'. I'd forgotten I'd heard that."

We sat with the engine running. "I should take you to the station to file a report while this is fresh in your mind. I had no business bringing you here. I shouldn't have touched the car. Sloppy!"

I heard the frustration in his voice. Before the explosion that caused his injuries, Ric had been a rising star on the police force; youngest to make Inspector, best 'closer' in department history, but forced to take early retirement. Part of him would always be a cop, but the part of him that cared for me had won the coin toss tonight.

"Before you decide, can we go up? I'd like to use the bathroom."

"Sure. Do me a favor? Use my apartment. Maybe I can at least get some notes before everyone else closes in on you."

In spite of my terrifying experience, I smiled at his assessment of what would happen and nodded. His glance beyond me served as a one second warning, but I still screamed when someone rapped on the window. The door opened and Karen stood staring down at me.

"Geez, Grace. What's wrong? I didn't mean to scare you. I came out when I realized you were in the car. Thought Ric brought you Harry's keys. Weren't you going to drive home?"

The questions would go on and on unless something interrupted the flow. Ric talked to his sister. "Grace had some trouble at the woods. Some people came to the car and scared her. I'd like to get her description of everything before it blurs. I'd like to do it here where she'll be comfortable, not at the station. So I need your help. If she goes into your apartment we won't get this done until the wee hours. I'd like you to keep the girls on hold for thirty minutes while Grace goes to my apartment. Will you do that?"

Karen looked at us. I nodded. "Okay, thirty minutes." I knew she'd set a timer. "No wonder you screamed. Sorry, kiddo."

I slid out of the car and steadied myself against the door. The cold air pinched my warm skin and the effect cleared my head.

"You okay?"

"*Mmm*, fine. See you in a bit."

Ric walked around Karen, took me by the arm, and closed the door. We headed for the separate side entrance that led to the back half of the brownstone. After their mother's death, Ric and Karen sold the family home in River Forest and used their trust funds to rehab this building to provide a two-story home for each of them. People who didn't know them wondered how a teacher and a police officer lived so well. Those who knew them knew they'd throw it away in a heartbeat to have their mother alive.

"Thirty minutes and we're at your door." Karen's firm tone surprised me and her parting comment stung. Did she question my resolve to snub any interest from her brother?

≈ 8 ≈

I followed him into his living room. I saw the Gorham clock on the mantel and remembered the night I'd given it to Ric with a card that read, *You found me just in time, Grace.* He must have sensed my thoughts. He snugged his arm around my shoulder and leaned close to my ear. "Like we never missed a beat."

He'd found me just in time tonight. I shuddered as my mind followed the thought to what could have been more horror for me.

"You're shivering. Your jacket is damp." He moved his hands up and down my back. "Come over here." He led me to the chair nearest the fireplace. "Sit and in two minutes I'll have this baby cranked up."

He referred to his gas starter wood burning fireplace. Karen had resisted a gas starter preferring to be a purist. Ric had opted for speed; two minutes and indeed I felt the warmth from the fire.

"Take that off." He held a burgundy colored throw from the back of the couch ready for me. I shrugged out of the jacket and he pulled the wet corduroy from behind me and laid it near the hearth. I let him drape the throw around my shoulders. He bent in front me and pulled it close around my neck.

"Shit! Why didn't you tell me you were hurt?" He straightened, tightening his grip on the edges of the throw and forcing me up with him. When I stood, he threw the light covering off my shoulders and spread the collar of my shirt. "Dammit, Grace. You have bruises the size of walnuts on the side of your neck and there's dried blood. Why didn't you tell me?" He shook me by the shoulders, harder than he meant, too. I winced and magnified the pain I saw in his eyes. He pulled me into his arms and guided my head to his chest. "God, Grace I'm sorry. I left you there and you're hurt. I'm sorry."

I stood still, trying not to respond to his body. I prepared to push away. Ric sensed my intention and moved his hand to the nape of my neck. He recoiled and we pulled apart an instant before Harry burst into the room. Our expressions and close proximity told the tale as much as if we still embraced.

"This is how you take a statement? With the victim in your arms? I know what you're trying to do, Kramer, but I thought *you* were beyond that."

Harry's blue eyes blazed at me like I'd seen only one other time. My voice stalled in my mouth and only a small gasp escaped. He waved his hand toward the wall. "Cozy fire, clothing strewn nearby, a handy blanket." I stood numbly, thinking I would have thought the same and worse. I wanted to speak, but suddenly my mouth went dry and my throat ached with fear, pain, and shame. I lowered my head and swallowed several times to ease the cottonmouth feeling. I suspect Harry took my movement as an admission of guilt. I grabbed onto the length of yarn on my belt-loop and rubbed the scratchy strands back and forth between my thumb and first two fingers. The compulsive behavior that grips me began to fill me with a need to rub the strands clock-wise and then counter clock-wise. I sensed both men looking at me, but I couldn't raise my head until I finished. No one spoke, but I could feel the anger and the tension in the room. When I lifted my head my eyes filled with tears blurring my vision. I looked at Harry; he turned away. I knew in a moment he'd leave. My throat tightened and my head pounded with pain.

"Marsden, she's hurt." Ric held out his hand, smeared with blood, my blood. The room spun away from me.

"Grace!"

"Grace?" A low accented voice called to me from a distance. I opened my eyes hopeful that I hadn't dreamt the voice. Harry looked down at me. He knelt next to the couch holding my left hand between his, lifting my hand to brush his lips across the tips of my fingers. I understood the concern in his eyes, but did he still think me a traitor to our marriage. I had to know. My efforts to sit up brought comments from both men. I hadn't realized that Ric stood at the end of the couch.

"Harry, I didn't–"

"First Matthew and now you. I'm declaring Chee Chee Pin Quay Woods off limits!" Tracy's voice preceded her. I gripped Harry's hand tight, but searched beyond him for Ric. "That's what they were chanting, that name."

"Who was chanting?"

"Hold on, Marsden. This is important. Grace, the hooded figures?"

"Oh, my God. Hooded figures? Not again." Tracy's face lost color and she searched out Ric's face over Harry and me. I saw the connection their eyes made.

"Grace is important, Kramer." Harry squeezed up onto the

couch next to my hips, his body effectively blocking my view of Ric.

"Harry's right. Let me take a look at her. That's why you called me. Good thing I hadn't left."

Tracy motioned Harry out of the way and took his spot and my hand which he released grudgingly. She deftly shifted her hold on my wrist and took my pulse.

"How's Mattie? I'm so sorry, Trace. It was stupid of me to let them out of the car. Is he okay?"

"Oh, honey he's fine. He's done worse than that in the backyard. I know how persuasive, those two can be. Ben gave me the whole story. Matt shouldn't have run. He's been grounded. Now be quiet while I check your eyes."

I looked straight ahead while Tracy looked at my pupils. She helped me to a sitting position and moved around me to assess my head injury. Her gentle probing found the raw spot quickly. I winced and sought comfort in Harry's outstretched hand. He sat down next to me. Tracy looked at him. "Be useful at least. I can't see the wound through all this thick hair. Hold it back on both sides." Harry released my hand and held my hair as Tracy separated chunks to get down to my scalp. She talked as she worked my hair into Harry's waiting fingers. "Let's clean it up and see what we have here. Damn!"

With my head down I could see only Ric's feet walk toward us. I felt Harry trying to lean around me to see. "Is it deep? Does she need stitches?"

The sudden exposure to air and probing caused my scalp to tingle and then pinch with pain. The sharp smell of antiseptic wash filled my nose and I tasted the solution at the back of my throat.

"I thought you said she fell. There's no gash, no cut. Someone yanked a half dollar size clump of hair from her head; tore it out."

Harry turned from me. "Kramer, what the hell went on out there?"

"I told you, I pulled into the lot and she ran toward me from the woods."

Told him? When did they talk? How long had I been out?

"Shut up, both of you. Harry hold still." Tracy adored both these guys, but I was her patient at the moment, and they'd best not interfere. A tiny grin reached my lips seconds before it spread into a grimace.

"Ouch!"

"Sorry, kiddo. Did I forget to say, this is gonna sting a little?" She patted my arm. "Done. Hold on while I re-style your hair. Pigtails are in order, I think." Tracy reached into her tote and pulled out two covered rubber bands. "These will do." She took one side of hair from Harry and twisted the band around it. The tug on my scalp sent renewed pain signals to the raw area.

"Ow!" Tracy quickly caught up the other lank of hair in the same manner. No sense in repeating myself. I bit my lower lip and lifted my head. The bounce of heavy hair felt odd. "Do I look as silly as I feel?" I smiled, hoping to relieve the tension that filled the room since Tracy's pronouncement about my head wound.

"Never mind that. Here, take this." A small blue pill and glass of water materialized in Tracy's hands. "This will dull the pain and trust me, you're going to be in pain."

I sipped the water and sent the tiny med on its way. Tracy took the glass from me and put it on the lamp table next to the couch. She plumped two pillows behind me and motioned for me to sit back. With a nod of her head toward the abandoned blanket on the chair, Ric moved to hand it to her. She expertly tucked it around me. Only then did she turn and address Ric and Harry.

"Harry, go brew some of your English 'chicken soup' and bring another blanket." I could see he didn't want to leave. "Oh for heaven's sake. At least go ask someone to do it." He moved quickly. Tracy swung on Ric. "If I saw this kind of bruising," she pointed to my covered neck, "I'd be calling the cops."

Ric jammed his hands in his pockets. "I thought I could save her the trouble—"

"Trouble?" Harry hasn't seen those marks yet. Oh yeah, there will be trouble."

"I wanted to get her statement on what happened while it was fresh in her mind and before she got bogged down with everything."

"Would that everything include her husband?" Harry walked in with a blanket. Hannah followed close behind with a mug and round teapot on a small tray. She brought it directly to the table and poured the dark liquid into the mug. A strong cinnamon scent fought the lingering odor of antiseptic and won. Hannah guided the mug to my hands before she spoke. "Harry told us you'd been attacked. Had to see for myself that you're all right."

I smiled at my sister-in-law. The illusion of Harry's features, softer yet present, always caused me to linger when I looked at her. "I'm all right. In fact, I'm sure I'll be 'on the mend' with this." I lifted the mug in a mock toast and took a sip. The hot liquid slid down my throat into my stomach, radiating heat on the way. It warmed me like the blanket hadn't. I sipped more. Each watched me carefully. I drank more tea to assure them I was obeying orders. I felt safe and suddenly drowsy. I guessed I was coming down from the high point my body had hit. The tiny blue pill may have helped too. I continued sipping my tea, aware of the droning voices.

"Marsden, I wasn't freezing you out. I wanted her to focus on what happened before I turned her over to all this. She didn't tell me what happened. I didn't know she'd been hurt, didn't see the bruises or blood until now."

"Bruises, what bruises?"

"Around her neck, here and here. No nail gouges, must have worn gloves." Ric motioned on his neck. "Bastard must have dragged her by her neck."

"Dragged her? Who? What the hell happened to her?"

"I don't know. I didn't get a chance to find out."

"You didn't get her statement?" Tracy's voice sounded loud next to me. "I thought you'd already talked to her."

"That's what I've been trying to do."

"Oh, cripes. I gave her a sedative. With her injury I knew she didn't have a concussion. She'll be out soon."

"Oh, dear." Hannah's voice floated across the room. "I didn't know. I put whisky in the tea. You know, to calm her."

$\approx$ 9 $\ll$

I'm floating through a warm fog. Dreams are strange; I'm ice-skating, but the air feels balmy. A fog surrounds my feet, but only when I'm skating. Moguls spring up in my path and my skates flatten, elongating into skis. The air turns frigid and the ground slants away from me. A white cloud hangs over me, blinding me to the treachery under my skis. I try to scream but my lips are frozen tight.

Suddenly, the cloud clears from above me, my descent slows, and I ski off the run into the woods. People stand at a distance around a small fire that draws me like a moth. My skin is warm and covered by a white robe, heavily belted at my waist. The too large hood falls over my face and I move, blinded by white. I can't raise my hands to push off the hood. The skis flop around me, turning into thick ropes that bind my feet and snake up to tie my hands. I snap my head back and jostle the hood back from my face. Black-hooded, faceless creatures stare down at me. *Chee Chee Pin Quay, Chee Chee Pin Quay, Chee Chee Pin Quay*. The desperate scream wakes me and I lay frightened in a strange bed.

The door to the room burst open and Karen and Hannah rushed in. "Gracie, it's okay. Bad dream is all. It's okay."

My heart still pounds against my chest and my throat aches from my recent scream.

Karen sat on the edge of the queen size bed and held my hand. A chill raced along my bare arm and I snatched up the top of the blankets looking down at my body, clad only in underwear.

"You didn't expect us to tuck you in wearing your clothing. They were dirty and damp." Hannah's soft voice calmed me. Looking around the room, I searched for anything that could have prompted those horrible thoughts. I struggled to sit up and Karen placed a pink fleecy bed-jacket around my shoulders.

I watched Hannah pull a cozy off a waiting teapot. "No alcohol in this one, promise." Her dimpled grin brought normalcy closer with each second. I accepted the mug and slipped both hands around it to draw its heat before drinking the contents. "Thanks, Hannah. Where's Harry?" Had he been within earshot he would have been at my side.

"They went to get Harry's car and I think to check out the area where you were attacked." Karen fidgeted with the covers.

"What's wrong?" She flicked an imaginary speck from my shoulder and smoothed a flat spot on the coverlet before meeting my gaze.

"I heard Ric telling Harry about other attacks on three women since Halloween night. There're always problems in the woods that time of year, kids looking for dead Indian warriors who protect Chee Chee Pin Quay's grave, cinema students trying to film haunted woods, and worse, a cult that chooses that holiday for bizarre rituals."

"What kind of rituals?"

"Grace, you need to rest, doesn't she Karen? Isn't that what Tracy said?" Hannah pronounced the words slowly and with an up-swing; a tone she used on children or the neighbor's cat, Arthur.

"Absolutely. Look at me keeping you up. Slide back down and we'll talk in the morning."

"Morning? Isn't Harry coming back for me?" I felt abandoned and the itch of tears at the back of my throat added to the pain when I swallowed. I must have sounded pathetic if the look on their faces reflected my tone.

Hannah replaced Karen at my side. "Gracie, he didn't skip off. Harry wanted to take you to hospital. You put up a tizzy."

"I don't remember."

"No doubt. Ah, Tracy and I, well we inadvertently drugged you. Sorry. Harry wanted to take you home to care for you." My spirit lightened at her words. He wanted to be with me. "By that time, you drifted off and we had to practically fight him to leave you. We prom-ised to make you rest and Ric told him his theory about what hap-pened. After that, both of them went out with a totally mean look in their eyes. I certainly wouldn't want to meet up with them in the woods."

I would sleep now; I knew Harry hadn't 'skipped' off.

Intermittent mewling seeped into my pastoral dream of riding April Showers across meadows of stirrup-high wildflowers at the slow cantor you can achieve in a dream sequence. The morning breeze brushed the tops of my thighs where I gripped April. I reined her in to listen. She tossed her head, setting the ribbons and beads braided throughout her mane in a gentle cacophony of clicking.

The soft mewling noises escalated to demanding cries. I looked down, afraid I may have led April's hooves onto their den; the cries of baby animals in distress. Babies!

I jerked my feet up and in the full second of wakefulness I realized I hadn't trampled any babies in my dream or in this bed. The monitor on the nightstand blared Clare and Connor's voices. I got up and looked for a robe in Karen's closet. She, who sleeps in the room with the monitor, gets up with the babies. I smiled at my simplification of parenting.

The matching cribs filled one end of the small room, each up against one wall leaving a two-foot aisle between them. "Good morning, little darlings. I hear you." I didn't think the voice of one doting aunt would mean much to a wet, hungry infant. I was right. If anything, they cried louder. "Okay, I'm here for you. Who goes first?" It sounded stupid, but I wondered if there was a routine, an order. Their cries formed a pattern. I listened with my obsessive-compulsive mind, deciding I could move after the next complete *waa* pattern. I had to pick them both up before they started again. I scooped up Connor, tucked him close, and leaned toward Clare's crib. I couldn't safely lift her with one arm. I placed Connor next to his sister. "*Shh*, little one while I figure this out." They quieted. I'd take credit for the calming; they needed each other and I serendipitously fulfilled that need. Only minutes before, the tiny faces had puckered and reddened in distress. Now they smoothed, red splotches fading. I stared

"Good job, Gracie. We'll put you on speed dial for babysitting." Hannah and Karen stood inside the room, grinning.

"How long have you been there?" I hoped they hadn't seen my awkward attempt to lift both or how long before I took action.

"Not long, but we heard what a good auntie you are."

"Heard?"

"We heard you handling the situation, so Karen put their bottles in the warmer. Voila!" She flourished her hand as Karen entered the room. "Want to feed one?"

"Maybe another time. I feel a little queasy and headachy. Maybe a hot shower, something to eat?"

"Sure, Gracie. Use whatever you need. Harry said he'd be over around eight with some clothes. That should be enough time to eat some of Hannah's oatmeal. Fortifies you for the day." Under her breath I heard the coda, 'the week, the month.'

Grinning wasn't an option with Hannah standing nearby. I fixed Karen with an 'I told you how they ate' look and murmured, "Thank you." Karen and I thrived on junk food. My husband and his sister shopped organic, steamed or broiled everything, and grew fresh when possible. My saving grace was that Harry was normal, Hannah was vegan. I thought myself well read about vegetarians, but who knew vegan? My family has known Hannah for ten years, and my brothers, still refer to and sometime greet Hannah by separating their fingers in a 'V' sign like Spock; a silly joke early on, but now actually an expression of affection for Hannah. She returns the sign, tells them to prosper and 'sod off' which in English slang isn't prosperous at all.

The shower stream felt wonderful. I maneuvered under the hot jet, positioning my aching neck and shoulders under its soothing touch. I used Karen's organic fructose shampoo that Hannah ordered from England. Finding the crusty patch on my scalp I gently washed the area. I lathered, rinsed, and repeated, filling the room with the scent of apple and raspberry.

Now hunger pangs replaced the aches. Hannah's oatmeal. *How can you mess up oatmeal? No milk, no butter. Yeah, that's how.* After putting Karen's robe on again, I wrapped my shoulder length hair in a smaller towel. Washing my hair had disturbed the wound and the prickle of pain spread to my forehead. I caught my reflection in the mirrored cabinet. I studied my lavender eyes, flecked with gold. My eyes function not only for sight, but as an indicator of my moods. Stress or excitement turns the lavender to a deeper hued purple. *So much for a poker face.*

I opened the cabinet without guilt; Karen had said to use whatever I needed. The top shelf held the Ibuprofen I hoped would bring relief from my growing headache. I swallowed two tablets and replaced the bottle. The aroma of cinnamon toast reached my nose before I heard her outside the door.

"I made toast while Hanns is feeding the babies. Slathered in butter, the way you like it."

She waved the plate under my nose then backed out of the bathroom, pretending to lure me with the food. I followed. We sat on the bed with our legs tucked up. Karen held two plates with four pieces of toast. We munched in happy camaraderie, listening to Hannah *coo* at the children, grateful she couldn't hear our crunching.

Her accented voice, so different from our Midwest twang, soothed the babies. "There we go. What good babies you are for Mummy. Back to sleep little ones. Mummy has to make a good breakfast," here her voice raised, "for two naughty girls."

We stopped in mid-crunch and choked out laughter.

Hannah's sing-song voice continued. "Do they think I haven't a nose? Where's Clare's nose? Here it is. Do they think I can't hear their

45

arteries clogging? Where are Connor's ears? Here they are."

We bolted off the bed like two busted teens. I crammed the last bit into my mouth fearing Hannah might make me hand it over.

"All right my little darlings. Mummy has to go see those naughty girls." We had only seconds to swallow.

"Honestly, you two act like the babies." Hannah spoke from the doorway. "If you didn't want the oatmeal, if you wanted to poison your bodies with lard and toxic bread you could have said so. No need to scurry around sneaking food. Did you think I wouldn't let you eat what you wanted?"

I knew that was a rhetorical question, but I almost nodded.

"Hanns, for heaven's sake. It's butter and balloon bread. We've had this conversation before. We don't need to have it now." Karen shook her head and handed her the crumb-filled plate. "I have to get ready for school." She walked into the bathroom and shut the door.

"I'll take that," I stretched out my hand. Hannah's cool gaze seemed like an overreaction to four pieces of toast. Obviously, other issues loomed in the Kramer-Marsden household and relationship.

The coolness evaporated and Hannah smiled. Her lips turned up at the corners, but not enough to make if official. "I'll take yours. Harry will be here soon. Karen put on some coffee when she warmed the bottles. Why don't you sit and have a cup."

She took my plate. I followed, more for the coffee than conversation. We sat at the butcher-block table. Hannah poured coffee into a mug decorated with finches. She turned on the electric kettle and then sat across from me. I pointed to the monitor on the counter.

"Handy contraption to have. Must be nice to know you can hear them." *Did that sound as stupid to her as it did to me?* The Ibuprofen hadn't worked. The jitters, the cute euphemism my family coined to describe my obsessive-compulsive disorder, took hold of my fingers and I had to braid or burst. I understand the disorder, but can't easily control it. My fingers found the belt on the robe and I sat happily tying two knots, then taking two sips, tying two knots, then taking two sips, until I'd knotted the belt but still had coffee left; like Oreo cookies and milk–you have to come out even–at least, I do. I solved the dilemma. Two untied knots equaled four sips and then the mug was empty. The sateen fabric rubbing against my fingertips calmed the nerve endings and sent the message throughout my body.

"Would you like another cup?"

"No, God no. I don't think Karen's robe could take it." I hadn't meant to be funny, but we both burst into laughter. This time hers sounded real.

"Ow, it hurts when I laugh. I have a headache the size of Rhode Island."

Hannah laughed at my analogy. She held her hand out for mine. "Oh, come on, Grace, I won't hurt you–much," she added as she captured my reluctant right hand. She held the meaty part of my hand between her thumb and pointer finger and squeezed hard.

"This is a pressure point and should give you relief in a bit." I prepared to dispute her explanation based on the pain I felt from her iron digits when a sensation of easing and then freshness settled over me, like a garment passing over my head and shoulders and then skimming my body to my ankles.

"Wow," I murmured with appropriate awe. Hannah grinned easily at what must have been an expression of sheer contentment on mine. "My headache is gone. That's amazing. Thank you."

"My pleasure. There's no end to what the body can do naturally, if we give it a chance."

I sensed a lecture coming. Normally I'd try to deflect the conversation, but I felt indebted. The door buzzer interrupted her. Not a bell, but salvation nonetheless, and in the form of my husband.

"Good morning, darling. How are you feeling?" Harry bent down and kissed me. My arms reached around his neck and he pulled me up into his arms when he straightened.

"Mmm. Good morning to you too." I lowered my arms and smiled. "I feel fine, especially after Hannah's 'prestidigitation'." I pinched my hand to demonstrate.

"Ah, yes, the old let me hurt you here so you forget the pain there, trick."

"Well, there's my thanks. Say, shall I stand here while you two chat each other up or shall I put this in the bedroom?" Hannah pointed to the green and purple paisley duffel bag on the floor.

"I'll take that." I stretched to kiss Harry. "Thanks for bringing my clothes."

"Also shoes, handbag, socks, underwear, hair combs, and anything else that I thought you might need. Oh, and it all matches." Harry puffed out like a Golden Retriever waiting for an 'atta boy'.

"I expected nothing less. I have Hannah to thank for that."

The Marsden twins' identical smiles confirmed my comment. Hannah had taught Harry the do's and don'ts of fashion sense while growing up. She'd even turned his knot tying ability learned in scouts to her advantage by teaching him to braid her hair. I grew up with four Eagle Scouts and not one of them ever offered to braid my hair...cut it, pull it out, maybe, but never braid. I guess you had to grow up with a sister before you were even born.

Not to be left out of the 'twin phenomena,' the babies began crying. I pointed to the monitor when Harry looked around in surprise. We heard Karen's voice float into the kitchen. "I know someone is out there. I could use a hand in here."

"I'm headed that way. You two have your tea."

"Harry, I'm making oatmeal. Care for a bowl?" I turned the corner into the nursery before I heard his answer.

"Chic, extremely chic." Karen looked up from her task at the changing table. She wore a faded denim shirt that hung down to her knees. She'd rolled her sleeves up several times and pinned them halfway between her elbows and wrists. Bleach splotches gave the garment a tie dyed look.

"Protective clothing. It goes with the territory."

"Katie would love that look. According to her mom, if clothing is pressed and new it is 'so not cool'. How do I get one of those?"

"And on your niece, even this would look good." Karen grinned while she snapped Connor's onesie. "Don't even joke about it with Hannah or she'll start her own cottage industry. One down, one to go." She handed off the blue bundle and lifted Claire from the crib. "Okay, princess, your turn."

I inhaled sweet baby scent, realizing I'd missed out on the less desirable odor by a few minutes. Timing really is everything. Connor 'baby gurgled' and wrapped yet another gossamer strand around my heart. I laid him in his crib.

"Would you strip Claire's linens? When Connor joined her this morning he leaked through."

"It's a guy thing." We both giggled.

"What's a guy thing?" Harry asked and walked over to his nephew's crib. "Good morning little chap. Are these hens having a peck at you?" He lifted Connor easily and tucked him up in his left arm. The sight of Harry holding a baby, a baby that I'd hoped would have been ours, tore a hole in my heart. If Harry hadn't waited so long to agree, if he hadn't found out he had a son, we would have traveled to Europe with them and when the discovery of Connor occurred we could have adopted him. If not him, then another baby who needed our love and whose love I needed. I ached with a bittersweet pain each time I saw him with the babies.

"You know, the usual. Can't aim when they pee. Pee where ever they please. Connor leaked in Claire's bed." Karen's flip answer snapped me out of a too familiar funk.

"Sounds like a case of equipment failure not operator error." Harry kissed Connor and laid him down.

"You would take his side." Karen grinned and handed freshly diapered Claire to her uncle. Karen removed her 'armor' and hung it on a peg next to the changing table.

I finished making up the crib. "I'd better get dressed. Can I use your room? I don't want to make you late for school."

"Go right ahead. Use my room I mean, not make me late for school. Although today might be interesting. It's my first day back since I took family leave. Most girls won't even ask, but there will be a few who will want to see pictures and then one or two who will want to know, 'so how does that work, two moms?'" Karen shrugged and smiled. "Are you keeping your appointment with Janet Henry?"

I'd all but forgotten about the job interview. Harry spoke up. "Not if I have anything to say about it. Grace needs to get home and rest. Besides, I didn't bring her interviewing clothes."

I felt ambivalent about the interview, Harry's interference, life in general. The mood swings started when we discovered the existence of Will, and when Harry decided we should welcome him into our lives before we brought home a newborn.

"She could be missing out on a great opportunity."

"They'll be other opportunities. She needs to rest."

"She can come back here after the interview and nap all day. You drop her off and she can take the bus back; it stops at the corner. Come back this afternoon and pick her up."

Harry re-structured the day differently in his head. He nodded slowly. "That might work. I need to be in Chicago later. I'd planned to take Grace home, and then head back. Want to stop and see Will too. He's not going to school today."

"Perfect." Karen and Harry nodded in agreement and something about that entire exchange annoyed me.

"Thank you both for planning, no, more like plotting my day. What about April and Cash? What about not having the proper clothes for an interview? What about maybe I don't want to be stranded here all day?" I pushed passed two surprised faces and re-treated to Karen's room. I flung the duffle on the floor and kicked it toward the bed. The canvas bag bounced across the wooden floor and slid under the bed. I threw myself across the floral spread and *sobbed* into the pillow. My head ached again. Minutes passed and I felt someone sit on the bed. I knew it was Harry. I'd have to face the music about that display of hysteria.

"I brought you some tea."

Bless his soul, no reproach, only tea. I rolled over onto my elbow. He sat at the end of the bed, more leaning than sitting, seemingly poised to move quickly. I let a smile tug at my lips.

"Couldn't decide how to fit an olive branch on the saucer so I used a cinnamon stick as a stand-in." I suppose we did steamroll over you. Sorry, darling."

I sat up and accepted the tea. "It's not that. It's not even you. It's me." I couldn't say more. Small of me to be the sourpuss amid everyone's joy over the new children in the family–all three of them. "I need to settle in on something to do, keep busy, make a difference."

"Then you'd best get dressed for your interview. I didn't bring your power suit, but I'm certain Janet won't hold that against you. This is a preliminary meeting, right?"

"*Mmm*. As far as I know it's me, Janet, and a couple of coffees."

"Tell you what. Let's stop at the Buzz Café to bring lattes. That should stand you in good stead. Janet strikes me as the latte kind."

"A double and I'm in." We laughed the laugh of conspirators. I don't know how he did it, but Harry always found a way to my lighter side.

"Don't worry about April and Cash. Devin jumped at the chance to turn them out and feed them this morning. As for being 'stranded' here all day–"

"I was being a 'Sarah' wasn't I?"

He reached for my hand and stage smooched it. "Ms. Bernhardt never did it better."

"Okay, out. I need to get dressed." I handed him the teacup and leaned over the edge of the bed to retrieve my bag. He didn't move.

"I thought I'd help with the hooks and things." His grin brought a flash of warmth to my stomach. He put the teacup on the nightstand and moved toward me, the duffle between us. I pulled the bag onto my lap and flung my arm out pointing to the door.

"For sure I'll miss this appointment if you help. Go wait for me in the kitchen. Have some oatmeal."

He leaned over the bag and kissed me full on the mouth. The sensation in the pit of my stomach flushed pleasantly and I thought about pushing the bag out of the way. Harry broke off the kiss and pulled back. He tapped the end of my nose with his finger. "Think about that until I pick you up this afternoon."

ꝏ 10 ꝏ

The inside of Janet's office reflected her fastidious personality. Her 'fishbowl' office, as the glass-fronted rooms were called, contained colorful filing cubes and boxes that kept the clutter to non-existent.

We sat on either end of a loveseat crammed onto the opposite wall from her desk.

"*Mmm*. A double latte. Yes, this is a sit on the couch drink."

Janet had fussed over the lattes the moment I presented hers. She'd looked beyond me when she stood up to greet me. No doubt hoping for a 'Harry sighting'. He'd won her over last year by coordinating an idea for a reunion. I'd wondered if a condition to my being her assistant included occasional involvement from my husband.

Janet wore a turquoise colored sweater with navy blue slacks. The simple silver bar pin she always wore gleamed from the lapel.

She'd been explaining the broader points of the job, which I'd missed. I tried to cover my lapse. "I'm sorry, Janet. I should have asked if I could reschedule. I had a late night and don't feel up to speed. Would you repeat the part about the travel? I didn't think there would be travel."

"Only if you want to take the alumni trips we coordinate. There are two each year. The more popular is the one to England. I thought that would be perfect for you and Harry."

"I do like the sound of that and I love the part time hours. The biggest plus is that I feel comfortable with you." I smiled and tipped my cup. "When do I meet with Sister Joan to pass muster?"

"Oh, no need for that formality. Sister told me to offer you the position. So, you're hired; you start after Christmas vacation. Only don't think of me as your boss." She smiled and put out her arms. We maneuvered a careful hug–the usual seal of approval at Regina.

"I'm so happy I didn't cancel."

"Me too. What was your late night about? You do look tired."

I hesitated about saying anything. I still hadn't talked to Ric or the police. She waited. What the heck, it wasn't like I was naming names. "It started out with Will's scout troop in Robinson Woods and their community clean up service project."

"I haven't thought about that in years. I grew up near there and the community clean up project always happened in the spring."

"It still does, but this year was too wet and they moved it to November. Some of the parents told us about the unusual items collected in past campaigns."

"Unusual is right. I remember one of the newspaper stories. The troop found a brass bed; headboard and footboard, with a tuba hooked on one of the posts."

"Oh, yeah, that would take the prize hands down. This year's find wasn't that unusual, in fact, made perfect sense when you put it all together. Some kids' tribute to a dead family pet."

Janet's eyes widened. "What was it?"

"A cat. They'd put in some toys–"

Her speech came faster. "Anything else? I mean, uh, other toys or things?"

I shook my head. What an odd question.

"Those events are always in the early afternoon. This was your late night?"

I explained how I came to be in the woods with the boys and then glossed over the actual attack. I told her about the hooded figures I saw as a warning to avoid the woods. No sense in elaborating on the scary parts.

Janet's reaction stunned me. "Grace, I'm sorry but I have to leave. I forgot about an appointment." She stood abruptly and coffee sloshed over the rim of her cup. Brown liquid stained the pale blue rug. She took no notice. "Here." Janet pushed the coffee into my hand spilling more. She lifted her blazer from the chair and reached around her desk to pull her purse from the bottom drawer. Her abrupt behavior startled me, but when she wiped her wet hand down the side of her pants, I knew something was wrong.

"Janet, what is it? Are you ill?" Her face flushed further and she shook her head.

"No, I'm running late. Yes, I do feel a little ill. I won't be back." She ran a hand through her hair and looked around the room. "Tell the switchboard I won't be back today, would you?"

I'm certain my mouth hung open. I sat back on the couch and thoughtfully sipped at my coffee. Geez Louise, what happened? I'd never seen Janet so discombobulated. Panicked was more like it. Who had she almost missed an appointment with and if it were that important why wouldn't she have been aware of the time? Why schedule me so close? I still had her cup in my hand; mine was empty. I went to the ladies' room down the hall and dumped the coffee and cups. I brought back some wet towels to soak up the coffee stain. On my hands and knees is where Sister Jeanne found me.

"If you'd taken the archivist position with me, you wouldn't be 'on the carpet' your first day." Her quick wit endeared her to students and faculty.

"No, more likely climbing up the side of a bookcase searching for a miss-shelved yearbook." I stood and greeted my favorite nun with a hug.

"You're looking good, Sister."

"I feel good. You look tired."

I wasn't going to risk another explanation. I shrugged and motioned toward the desk. "Janet had an appointment and wasn't feeling well. She left for the day."

"Oh, dear. I hope it's not that flu everyone around here is passing along. I came in to get the preliminary count for the Alumni Mass next Sunday. It's a remembrance mass for deceased friends and family. Dear me, you know that. You coordinated a few of these in your day as a student." Sister shook her head. "I can't keep track."

"You can't keep track? You've the best memory bar none. If it weren't for your recall, we wouldn't have some of the interesting stories from your day as a student."

As students in Dan Carleton's speech class, Karen and I had developed a 'Speak and Save' program that encouraged alumni, faculty, staff, and community members to retell stories from their years either at Regina or as part of the River Forest/Oak Park community. The results astounded us and thrilled the Regina community.

"No one would have known those stories if not for you and Karen."

"Okay, so we're all geniuses, or geni?"

"Grace, don't make me regret the A grade I gave you." She smiled and shook her finger for emphasis. "I guess I'll have to wait until tomorrow. Always good to see you. I've a class in ten minutes."

"'Bye, Sister. You'll be seeing more of me soon." We hugged and I watched her hurry to a lucky classroom. I pulled the door closed behind me and delivered Janet's message to the switchboard. I walked out the front of Power Hall with no particular plan except to find food somewhere.

"Gracie, over here."

Karen stood next to Hannah's MG, parked on the circle drive.

"What are you doing here and how did you get a spot on the circle?"

"Good karma, small car. C'mon. I took a chance that you'd be finished. I don't have class until two. How about lunch?"

"Perfect. How about Russell's? I haven't been there in ages. I don't know what time Harry's coming back, if we're eating out or if he took something out for dinner. A plate of ribs should hold me."

"Sounds great to me and I know what Hannah's planning, some kind of stomach intestine made into a soup of sorts. Ugh."

"Sounds like tripe."

"I'm serious; I'm not making it up."

"I mean it sounds like 'tripe' the food. It's usually Ox intestine and the way my Nonna prepared it, it wasn't half bad."

"Coming from you I'm not surprised. You'd eat shoe leather if you had enough olive oil and garlic to cook it in."

We both laughed at each other's preferences. She turned on Thatcher headed for Russell's.

⇜ 11 ⇝

"Russell's' ribs, side of slaw and coffee. Life is good." I crumpled my paper napkin and placed it on my empty plate.

I bought lunch as a thank you for her hospitality. She dropped me at her house and hurried back to make her two o'clock class. I wished I had somewhere to hurry to or something to do. I would in a few weeks. Gainfully employed. Just what the doctor ordered.

No one was home. I didn't know when anyone would return. Karen had mentioned a brief faculty meeting after school. I still felt achy and tired, but I didn't want to sleep. A hot soak would do wonders for me.

I ran hot water into the tub and searched the cabinets for bath crystals. For the second time today, I rummaged through delicate and private items. I found a basket with several bottles. *Soothing Chamomile, Invigorating Eucalyptus.* Sooth or invigorate. I wondered if I should shake some of each into the running water. Why not? I was a Gemini.

Ten minutes later, the bubbles at the rim, I eased my sore body into the lovely brew. I used Hannah's headband and combs to capture most of my hair and keep it off my shoulders that I intended to soak. Their old-fashioned tub dipped deeper than most and I could stretch out my short frame and get my shoulders under water.

Heaven. Mmm. Good day today. Got a job. Had a great lunch. Helped a friend. Mmm. Only thing to make it better would be some heavy romance tonight. I smiled and began to think of how to set the mood for a successful seduction. I let my eyes close and my mind float from one tantalizing idea to another.

The sensation of floating ceased and the feeling of being watched invaded my mind. *Oh cripes. Hannah's home or Karen. Maybe Harry.* I turned my head prepared to smile at one of them.

"About time you woke up." Ric Kramer smiled from his perch on the hamper.

"Are you crazy? Get out of here." I tried not to flail and move any strategically located bubbles. I kept my arms inside the tub and slid down a little more. My lips were above the water line.

"Hey, I was concerned. I thought you might slide under and drown." His voice matched his grin.

"Please, Ric. Get out before someone comes home."

"So, if you knew no one was coming home you'd let me stay?"

"No, of course not. I meant–Hey, I don't have to explain to you."

"Yes you do. You never gave me your statement and you left this morning when you knew I needed to talk to you. I think this is a perfect time for you to come clean about last night." His grin couldn't get any broader. "Anyway I know you won't jump up and run out on me. Wish you would though." He punctuated his statement with a wink.

"Ric, I will talk to you for hours if necessary, but please get out. Please." My voice trembled. My stomach knotted in the fear that Harry would walk in.

Ric heard the fear. "Okay, Angel. Don't panic. I'll be right outside the door." He lifted his frame from the hamper and stepped toward me with a towel."

"Ric, stop."

"Only trying to help. Here you go."

He tossed the towel the last few feet and I reacted instinctively to keep it from landing in the tub. My shoulders and more came out from the bubbles as I caught the fabric and immediately draped it over the tub and tucked it under my chin. I had seen his eyes widen when I sat up. I glared at him. He continued to stare at me through the towel.

"Out."

He turned slowly and left me to simmer in the cooling water.

∂ 12 ∽

I found Ric seated at the butcher-block table. He'd made coffee and had a mug poured and waiting for me. He sipped his coffee. From over the rim of the blue mug his eyes watched my approach. I fought the urge to glance down at my clothes to make sure they hadn't become see-through like in a bad dream.

I sat down and Ric switched into cop mode. He put down his mug and pulled a small notebook from the inside pocket of his blazer. He flipped open the spiral book looked up at me. "Let's start with when they first approached the car." His lips tightened to a straight line. I think he still blamed himself for the broken lock. "Can you tell me how many of them there were?"

"Three. Two on the driver side, one on the passenger."

"Good. You're doing great. Did you hear names, distinctive speech pattern, anything to identify them?"

"Nothing at first. Later I heard 'Davy' and 'Mr. Big,' I'm sure of that." I sipped my coffee and waited for more questions. Seated at a table in a cheery room protected by a cop made the telling less scary. Ric asked more questions and I answered all that I could. He asked for my impressions of the number of people, sense of their ages. He kept his eyes focused on mine, calming me, and encouraging me as he jotted down my answers. This was how it had been seven years ago when he'd questioned me about Harry's disappearance. Only Ric believed Harry had been kidnapped. Once again, he guided me through a tough recollection, keeping me connected to the story and to him. I looked into his dark eyes, drawn to their depths. I moved my head from side to side to loosen tense muscles. The movement broke the connection. My gaze slid to my cup. "That's all I remember," I mumbled into the bottom of the mug as I drained the coffee.

Ric refilled my mug, placing the steaming coffee in front of me and moved around behind my chair. His hands settled on my shoulders, kneading the tight muscles. I started to protest, but the words came out in a contented moan. I dropped my chin to my chest and let him press his thumbs into base of my neck.

"*Mmm.*" His powerful fingers loosened the knots and I felt a noodle-like ease through my neck and shoulders. I lifted my forearms to the tabletop to keep from collapsing nose first onto the wood. Ric guided my forehead to the tops of my hands and continued his massage down my back. Strong thumbs stroked each side of my backbone finishing at the small of my back and returning to the top.

His hands moved to the side of my ribcage. If I didn't move I knew where they'd be next.

"Oh, gee. Look at the time." We both knew I didn't have to say anything intelligent, just something besides, "*Mmm*." I pushed up from my arms and sat bolt upright. Ric kissed the top of my head and walked to his side of the table. He lifted his mug in a toast.

Voices filled the hallway. Karen and Hannah exchanged 'their days.' They sounded happy to be together, encouraging each other to expand on their events. I wondered how long before Karen begged off dinner because of the huge lunch I'd 'forced' her to eat. I knew I'd been the bad influence.

Young voices chirped in with their school day. I recognized Will's voice. Clumping sounds meant the boys were almost upon us. Karen and Hannah would have taken the babies to the nursery. Will and Tim burst into the kitchen, headed for the plate of cookies Hannah offered. She didn't tell them they were whole grain something. Let them find out on their own.

The table stood tucked in a corner and the boys were even with us when I greeted them. "Hi fellas. How was school?"

"Criminey!" Will's voice sounded as they both jumped.

"Sorry guys. Thought you saw us."

"Saw you? Hidden in the corner?" I didn't like Will's tone. Ric picked up on it too.

"We're not hidden in the corner, Will. We're seated at the table."

"Sorry, Mrs. Marsden, Mr. uh,"

"Kramer," I filled in for Tim. "This is police Inspector Ric Kramer, Karen's bother." I used his old title for effect. It worked, at least on Tim.

"Inspector. Cool." He turned to Will. "You've got the best grown-ups."

Ric and I barely hid our smiles as Will grudgingly accepted the praise. They turned back toward the counter and the cookies, but I heard Will's comment.

"They're not *my* grown-ups."

"Oh bother! Why aren't you hungry?" I grabbed at the monitor on the table and dialed down the volume. No one in the kitchen needed to hear Karen and Hannah's conversation. Before I dialed down I heard, 'Gracie *made* you eat? Oh come on Karen…'

Way to go Hanns. Look at the whole picture. I felt vindicated.

"Cool, what was that?" Tim pointed at the monitor.

"High tech way to keep an ear on the babies."

"Boy, don't tell my mom about these." His concern seemed so real Ric and I both laughed at the redheaded boy.

"Promise, I won't." I crossed my heart and smiled. "Do I have to 'stick a needle in my eye'?"

"Just hope to die," Will taunted.

"Will, that's a stupid thing to say." Tim looked confused.

"That was more than stupid, it was mean. Apologize to your step-mom." Ric's tone left no thought to disobey. "Step over here–"

"Are you bullying my son?" Harry had come down the hall and misinterpreted the situation. "Don't order him around, Kramer."

"If you taught him manners, I wouldn't have to. He disrespected Grace and doesn't care."

Harry landed between the proverbial rock and hard place. Who would he choose? No contest.

"I'm certain he meant no disrespect. If there is cause for concern I'll handle it. I never want to hear you order him around like one of your criminals." Harry moved closer to Ric. Will stood by, looking up at the two faces, a smirk on his own face. "Do I make myself clear?"

"Crystal clear. He's your juvie." Ric wiped his hands in a 'done with this' gesture and walked into the living room. I heard the connecting door close.

"Dad, I didn't." Will's devoted gaze locked with Harry's adoring one. He patted his son on the shoulder. "I know. He's an odd one that Kramer."

Will hugged Harry around the waist. He stepped back and motioned to the counter. "Aunt Hannah said we could have those."

"Then have away. Take them out to the sun room and mind the crumbs." The boys scrambled to pour glasses of milk and grab napkins. Will carried the heaping plate and Tim carried the glasses. The napkins lay on the counter.

"I think Hannah meant a few cookies, not the entire plate."

"They're growing boys. Besides, if I know my sister they're probably stuffed full of vitamins and such."

Harry sat down next to me. "Now what's all this about 'disrespect'? What was Kramer yammering about?"

I could tell by his tone that he didn't believe Will had said anything wrong. I didn't want to argue over Will, again. I shrugged my shoulders. "Came out wrong, I think."

Will stepped into the room to retrieve the napkins. How long he stood out of sight but within earshot I couldn't know. Harry turned as Will mumbled, "Forgot the napkins."

"There's a good lad." Harry turned back to me smiling as if remembering the napkins proved something. I glanced at Will when he turned to leave. His eyes said it all.

How could I tell Harry that his son hated me?

Tim's mom picked up her son, grateful for the afternoon assist. Mary Quigley owned a boutique and studio on Madison Street in Forest Park. Her store, 'One More Time' carried all manners of upscale clothing, artwork, and decorative items on consignment. She had a large bundle come in for a customer and had to get it packed and to UPS. Hannah had volunteered to pick up Will for Lily since his mom would be in the city until evening. Will had asked if Tim could come home with him. Hannah knew the store and called.

Mary and I spent a few minutes chatting, until she realized soccer practice would be over in ten minutes for her junior high son. She corralled Tim and rushed out the door.

Karen invited us to stay for dinner and graciously offered to spring for Chinese from Red Star Inn. Harry and Will agreed to pick up and deliver.

We finished dinner and began the easy clean up. Harry had the paper bags and cartons in one pile. "C'mon, son. Grab a stack and we'll take these out to the rubbish. No sense your aunties waking up to the smell of Mo-Goo-Gai-Yuk." Will reached across the table for my container. I had plates and silverware in my hands. He pushed at the container instead of pulling it toward him. The contents dribbled off the end of the table and onto my lap.

"Will. Careful!" My sharp tone caused Harry to look back. "He pushed it over."

"It was an accident." Will's voice quivered.

"Of course it was. C'mon help me with the rest." Harry stared at me over the top of Will's head. Will didn't need to look at his father's expression. He could see the effect on my face, flushed with embarrassment.

Lily picked up Will soon after. She and Harry shared the 'hand off' ritual as I'd come to call it. Whoever had Will conveyed an encapsulated version of their time together. Heads nodded, smiles exchanged and then the handing off parent moved in for hugs. I'd seen it a dozen times and each time I felt the glass blocks clinking into place. I could watch, but only from the outside. Watch until my heart ached.

"You're quiet. No chatter about your visit with Janet?"

"Guess I'm tired. All chattered out." I hadn't meant to sound bitchy.

Harry turned slightly toward me and shook his head. "What's wrong with you? I know you suffered a shock last night, but you're not yourself."

Of course I'm not myself. I'm not sure where I fit in. How long before Will drives a wedge between us? How long before it's easier to be with Lily?

"Grace?"

I'd zoned out and unconsciously pulled a piece of yarn from my purse. I kept my head down and shrugged. "Tired." I dared not say more; I could feel the pressure on the back of my throat.

The ride home seemed to take twice as long. By the time we turned onto the single lane road to enter Pine Marsh I had started to doze. The change in the pavement woke me. In a few minutes we'd be home. The overhead door closed behind us. Harry turned sideways in his seat and leaned toward me. His hand stroked the side of my face. I closed my eyes and leaned my chin into the palm of his hand. He leaned closer and kissed my forehead.

"Let's get inside. We're grown-ups with a house, you know."

His humor missed the mark. For the first time in years, I felt no stirring at what he hinted. *In pulling away from Harry am I pushing him toward Lily? Am I trying to find a way out?*

"This offer is valid for a limited time only." He opened my door and put out his hand. "No coupon necessary."

This is Harry, the love of my life. What's wrong with me? I grabbed his hand and propelled myself into his arms. The sobs came unbidden. His arms reached around me and held tight. My shoulders shook in his embrace and he held me until the spasms subsided and I could stand quietly encircled by his arms.

"We'll work it out, darling. I promise.

I knew he meant what he said.

"Come out to the barn, see April. I'm betting Devin took her through her paces but she'll be missing your special touch." Harry waited a heartbeat. "I know I do."

He kissed the top of my head and rubbed the spot between my

shoulders with one hand. "Maybe I'll take her in the ring for some dancing." I'd been working with April on *dressage*, a pattern of difficult steps and gaits communicated by slight movements from the rider. "Wish it were light enough to take her out. I hate winter."

"Since when? Who runs out and makes snow angels? Who organized the first annual snowmen building competition at your father's house last Christmas?"

"Snow people," I corrected.

"Who conceived the snowball fight between the students and nuns at Regina as a fundraiser?"

"Man, Sister Candida and her squad kicked our butts. Who knew nuns could throw like demons."

"Who cross-country skis through the woods visiting our 'snow bound' sensible neighbors bringing them cookies in snowmen and snow flake shapes?"

"Okay, so maybe for right now I hate winter."

"You don't hate anything. That's why everyone loves you. And he will too."

Harry knew. I couldn't meet his gaze. He guessed all this anxiety stemmed from my need for Will to love me, to accept me as a step-mom.

"You head for the barn and I'll meet you there after I change. I'll keep Cash occupied while you work April."

"Deal."

"I'll lay a fire for later. Hanns found a marvelous new tea, *Panda Pearls*, excellent for centering the spirit. We can try it."

Harry and I separated toward our different destinations. *New tea. Centering the spirit. Ugh. Maybe I could brew some Mocha Madness and claim amnesia about the tea plan.* Harry and Hannah Marsden sought out new tea like my childhood beagle, Sadie Jane, on a rabbit scent.

April heard me before I turned the latch on the door and *whinnied* her greeting. Cash nodded his head and pawed for attention.

Both horses were stunning Tennessee Walkers. I had purchased April from a snobby socialite who was going to have her destroyed because her gait was imperfect making her useless for show purposes. Cash was a surprise addition this summer. His 'rocking chair' canter was to die for, but I couldn't bring myself to ride him on a regular basis. April was my pal—we'd been through a lot together. I couldn't abandon her because of an imperfection. On that basis I would have been chucked out years before.

"Hello, horsies." My singsong silliness brought snuffles and pawing, laughing and clapping to us Homo-sapiens. I stood midway at the front of the stalls and could scratch each outstretched muzzle. "I'm so sorry I missed you this morning. Did Devin do right by you? Beautiful horsies. Cash, you be patient. Harry will be here soon." I gave him a final pat and unlatched April's stall.

She waited for me to snap on the short lead and bring her out. Her body quivered with anticipation and I shared the same rush of excitement. I loved riding. I loved April. Within minutes, we were in the ring. Three floodlights, mounted at rail height around the arena provided enough illumination without turning our backyard into a landing field. I groomed the ground weekly; we could have practiced safely in the dark.

"Okay, angel girl, here we go." The pattern of steps executed over and over calmed me, releasing the tension, enabling the transition from rider and horse to one unit, moving seamlessly through the night. So immersed in the sensation, I didn't sense Harry until his voice murmured from the darkness beyond the lights.

"Beautiful."

My knees signaled April to turn toward Harry and perform an equine equivalent of a curtsey. I laid the reins in my lap and lifted my arms out away from my sides in a flourish.

Applause and ground pawing greeted our performance. Harry opened the gate from horseback using a special pole he'd installed and led Cash in. He walked Cash around the arena once to stretch his legs and remind him who was on top. Cash pranced across the dirt, tossing his head, obviously anxious to reach April.

"You and April are quite a team." Harry's eyes gleamed in the low light.

Before I could respond, lights glared up the driveway, doors opened and slammed, footsteps thudded across the yard. Four men moved toward us outlined by the dim light but unidentifiable.

Harry lifted the latch from horseback. "Be ready to ride out of here."

∂∘ **13** ∘∂

"My daughter is attacked and you don't tell me?" My dad stood next to Cash shaking his finger at the rider. The Morellis had landed. My brothers and father converged on us from four vehicles. He'd summoned the boys and they must have synchronized their watches.

"Dad, it's not what you think."

"How would I know what to think? I find out from Jeannette, who found out from Gertrude, who overheard it from Hannah who was talking to Tracy." He stopped talking long enough to breathe.

"Who's—"

"Don't talk, I'm not finished."

"Mike, calm down. Let's—"

"You don't tell me to calm down. First, what's she doing in Robinson Woods at night? Second, you don't come back to get her, you send Kramer? Where's your head? Up your—"

"Dad!" I leaped from April and tossed the reins to Marty. He led her away, happy to be out of the fray by the look on his face. "Don't talk that way to Harry."

Harry dismounted and handed Cash to Glen. "Stop, Grace. Your dad has a right to be furious with me." He put his arm around my shoulders. "Mike let's take this inside." Harry walked toward the back door with me in tow. We entered and led the way into the kitchen.

"I'll make some coffee. There're biscotti in the jar." My brother Mike moved in that direction.

"We didn't come here for coffee and—"

"Dad, you didn't have to rush out here. You could have called. If you heard about it through that incredible grapevine, then you knew I was okay. Oh yeah, who's Jeannette?"

My father waved off my comments. "I called the house all day." He ran his hands through his thinning hair and clasped them behind his neck, bringing his elbows forward to touch. I'd seen this move a million times when he was ready to explode. The next gesture would tell if the explosion would hit. If he rubbed both hands over his face he had calmed himself. If he lowered his hands to his side, look out.

Hi hands moved to his face. I heard a deep sigh and realized I'd been holding my breath.

"Coffee."

I hurried to continue my preparations. My other brothers came in, oblivious to the stand off we'd survived. I saw the looks from Marty and Glen; Mike Jr. casually ran one hand over his face to send a signal. My other brothers looked like they wanted to leave.

"If we're having coffee we should have the and." Dad looked at Mike and nodded toward the jar. "Do you have any of the tiramisu from the baby shower?"

"How did…" I stopped. My dad knew everything. Well, almost.

He smiled at my confusion. "Tracy asked me where we ordered the cake for your party last summer."

"Lezza's."

"Bakery to the Morelli family for years. Did they send you home with a plate?"

"Actually, no. I guess I left without it. We were rushing around packing up the gifts so I could take Tracy's boys to the woods."

"You took those boys into the woods?" The timbre of Dad's bellow made a question sound like a statement.

I nodded my head. "It was light when we went. They wanted to see where Will's troop found the crate with the dead cat."

My father's small frame straightened. His eyebrows dipped over dark flares. "Troop 265? What crate? Who was there?"

Surprised by his change of course, I stammered my answers and my hands began to itch. His inquisition tossed my nerves into turmoil.

"Mike, I was there when the boys found the crate. They were doing a service project."

"I know all about the service project. That was my troop. They've been doing clean up as a service project for forty years. Started with my scout leader, Edward Bantonini."

"He's Will's leader. We met him."

"Must be Moochie you met; his youngest son. He made Life in that troop the year I eagled in Troop 813. I was an eleventh hour eagle, two weeks before my eighteenth birthday so that would make him about early fifties." Dad looked to Harry for confirmation.

"That's about right. Must have had his kids later in life to still be so active."

"No, it's a dynasty." My brother spoke up. "Carolyn taught at St. Edgar. That's all you heard about, the Bantonini Era of scouting. The Bantonini family has headed that troop since its charter in 1945. The old man came back from World War II a decorated hero and put it all together. The current reigning Bantonini needs to hang on until he can pass on the mantle of leadership. Only problem is he had daughters."

"Why is that a problem? Scouting accepts female leaders."

"Not then and not Bantonini. Edward Sr. won't have it so they're waiting for the first grandson, Edward III to be old enough. Up until a few years ago, the old man still called the shots, the power behind the throne."

"Didn't anyone else want a go at it? Grace and I met several parents when we picked up Will."

"Probably first time Webelos parents. If their kids go to St. Edgar, it's a given." My brother grinned. "Not like you dad, right?"

We burst into laughter. I explained for Harry's benefit. "We're all about eighteen months apart in birth order. Dad started in scouting with Joe and moved up the ranks until he became the scoutmaster for the St. Domitilla troop. He had his own dynasty going while my brothers were in scouts. He always teased my mom that my being a girl messed up his timetable; I should have been the last born so he could get the boys through faster. He wanted to be scoutmaster when his sons made eagle."

"You," he pointed at me, "threw off my ten year plan. Instead it turned into a fourteen year plan."

"Yeah, but the difference was everyone wanted you to stay on. It's self-serving for this guy, vetting his grandson for the position."

"I only spent a year with 265. I never felt comfortable with those boys; I was an outsider. I was no choir boy, but I didn't like the fireside chats and shenanigans."

"You never mentioned this before." Marty drew closer to the table. Glen and Mike nodded.

"I haven't thought about it in years." Dad tilted his chin up and looked at a spot high on the wall. "Squirrelly bunch of guys. Didn't talk about girls. Talked about Indian ghosts and haunted woods."

"Sounds like great campfire stuff, Mike."

"It wasn't like that. They didn't want a scare; they wanted to contact and direct the spirits to do their bidding. They brought a Ouija board one campout. I didn't want to do it; guess that didn't raise my stock with them. Something went goofy and one scout, little guy with glasses, Specs we called him, got scared and took off into the woods."

"Where were Bantonini and the other leaders?"

"What other leaders? Bantonini handled everything. The senior patrol leader set up camp and assigned the duty roster. Each campout had a junior assistant scoutmaster. Bantonini rolled in, had his JASM set up his tent outside the perimeter of the camp and we never saw him until we struck camp. He took his meals separate from us; his JASM cooked for him. We'd see the glow from his cigar from our campfire ring. He never pitched his tent in a direct line with the trail to the *kybo* like most scoutmasters do to keep track of who's up at night. On one campout Jimmy Armanetti got turned around in the dark going to the john and told us next day he saw light in Bantonini's tent and swore he saw two figures moving around, like wrestling he said."

"Wrestling like with a guy, or wrestling like with a woman?" Marty moved his hands pantomiming a curvy figure eight.

"We were twelve. We didn't know. Just wrestling."

"He sounds like an awful leader."

"Gracie, it was the fifties. The scoutmaster ran the troop, almost like a para-military operation. Bantonini claimed he built men out of boys. He justified his hands off style with that claim. Those weren't the days of nurturing and mentoring. He bullied everyone."

"I see how twelve year olds would knuckle under, but how did he bully the parents?" Harry asked.

"He'd tell them they couldn't go on the campouts because the boys wouldn't behave self-sufficiently with a bunch of dads around. Specs' dad insisted so much that Bantonini had to let him come. The JASM set the dad's equipment on the ground even further away from the camp than Bantonini's tent. I think the old man thought if he couldn't set up his own tent, he could ridicule him and force him out. What the old man didn't count on was that this was the fifties and most men had been in service.

"Specs' dad not only set up his tent, he had some of his equipment from his service days, helmet, mess kit, pots, and field rations. He had a fire going and his dinner cooking before long and then he started playing the harmonica. Talk about the pied piper. One by one we strolled over to hear the music; even the patrol leaders. The only ones who held back were Bantonini, the SPL, and the JASM.

"Pretty soon we had a sing-a-long going. There must have been twenty of us hooting and laughing. It was the best. That's probably what ticked off Bantonini. Must not have been a manly enough for his troop. Funny thing, this dad served in the Marines, damn manly by anyone's standards. Anyway, the old man went berserk, breaking us up and sending us back to our camp. We couldn't hear all the words, but he was angry. He doused his fire, came over to say good-night to Specs then left camp. I think he wanted to go with him, but his dad told him he'd see him in the morning after he talked to Father Briscoe. They lived on the other side of the woods."

"How come you never told us this story? This guy sounds like a creep." Glen and Mike both nodded at Marty's question.

"What happened the next day when the boy's father came back?"

"Nothing happened. He didn't come back. Hit and run. Cops figured some drunk driver coming out of one of the bars on River Road."

"That's awful. Did someone come to tell his son?"

"Someone came, but Specs wasn't there. Remember the little kid with the glasses who ran off? That was Specs."

"Gee, that's bizarre."

"It gets stranger. That's the night of the Ouija board incident. I wasn't playing, but I was close enough to hear the questions. Each boy took a turn asking silly questions about fame and fortune. Only Specs had a selfless question. He asked the board if his dad would be the next scout master. That's when the board went weird."

We leaned toward my dad.

"The damn board spelled, 'D E A D M A N.' He went nuts, pushed the board over and took off through the woods. I called them jerks and started out after him. I ran passed Bantonini's tent and right into him as he came up the trail. I lost my balance. He could have caught me, but I felt his foot push against my leg. I went down hard and hit my head. He said later he'd been off balance too and tangled with my feet. He took me to his tent and made me take off my shirt so I wouldn't get blood on it. The JASM asked if he could help. Bantonini told him I'd be spending the night in his tent so he could observe me in case of concussion. He asked for my sleeping bag."

Harry looked at Dad. "Mike, this isn't going—"

My dad laughed. "No, no way. Not me anyway. He sat me down on his cot and put his hands on either side of my neck and made a show of checking my pupils. His hands moved down to my shoulders and he pressed around the back of my neck checking for anything broken. He put one hand on my stomach and the other in the middle of my back and asked if I felt any pain. I told him no, that it was my forehead that hurt, nothing else. I swear he took great pleasure in cleaning out my cut with alcohol. I wasn't going to cry out, but the bastard rubbed at the wound until tears blurred my vision. He said,

'There's a lot of debris. Close your eyes and hold still. Almost done and then I can bandage it.' He stopped poking at my head and then I felt the gauze cover my skin. I opened my eyes and Bantonini had his shirt off. He saw the confusion on my face and told me he didn't want to get my blood all over his uniform shirt. I didn't buy it. My stomach felt queasy and I wanted to leave. I grabbed my shirt and stood up to leave. Bantonini blocked my way and I stumbled into him. His arms went around me in a flash, his hairy chest pressing up against me. My queasiness turned to nausea and I shouted I had to throw up. He unzipped the tent and I ran out. I found my bag rolled next to the flap. I hooked it with my hand and kept moving toward the camp and people. Barely slept a wink that night; felt sick, scared, and ashamed. Terrible night for a kid. Never went back to the troop."

"Did you tell someone? The police? Your parents?"

"Glen, it wasn't like today; no child abuse hotline. Yeah, I tried to tell grandpa, but we didn't talk about those things. He told me Mr. Bantonini was in charge and he had to take care of the boys. He said I probably was overtired and sick from getting hurt. I knew he wasn't going to say anything to Father Briscoe. He didn't want to make trouble. He didn't say a word when I told them I wanted to quit the troop. I knew he believed me even though he didn't act on it. We never spoke of it again, but when I joined 813, he came to my first meeting and met all the leaders and asked a lot of questions about campouts."

"For God's sake, Will's in that troop!" Harry's angry voice filled the room.

"This happened thirty-five years ago. Different people, different rules. I wouldn't worry about it."

"Of course not, your boys are raised. That's why you got involved and stayed in all those years, isn't it?" We stared at my dad. Had that been the real reason?

"In the beginning, then I saw how it was different. I went for the training and realized scouting had put rules in place to address the possibility. I stayed in because I loved scouting and I wanted to give each boy in my troop the opportunity to grow at his own pace and in his own style."

"I guess that's what I'll do." Now we looked at Harry. "I'll join the troop and go on campouts. I'll be Bantonini's new best friend."

The look on Harry's face left no doubt about his purpose. I couldn't imagine what this new development meant to our already tenuous relationship with Lily and Will.

I hoped our stroll down memory lane had taken Dad's mind off his original reason for swooping down on me.

"Now back to my daughter in those woods." He fixed his stare on Harry. "You're concerned about your son; I'm concerned for my daughter. We speak father to father."

I'd heard Marine to Marine, but never this one. Harry faced my dad.

"Wait, Dad. This is totally my doing. Will broke his foot jumping on some rocks at the woods." I went through the entire story for my father. "Harry had nothing to do with it."

He didn't explode but what he said was worse. He stared at Harry. "I can see that; nothing to do with it." He shook his head.

"Mike, you're not being fair. Kramer told me Grace was fine, locked in my car, waiting for my keys. Will begged me to stay with him. You would have done the same; chosen your child."

Of course he would, anyone would, given that information, but it still stung to hear it put so bluntly. *He chose his child. That's what he's supposed to do.*

Dad's expression hardened. "I would. I guess then I'm lucky to have a back up protector for my daughter." His implication angered Harry; the vein at his temple throbbed with hot blood. To his credit, he stayed quiet. He walked into the living room to avoid further confrontation.

I stood torn between the two men I loved most in the world.

"I'll help you find your keys. Come over Wednesday and I'll bring my metal detector." He was trying to make up for his outburst. His expression turned conciliatory.

"Uh, thanks, dad." I felt like a traitor accepting his help, but I couldn't turn him down. Might as well get it done. "What about tomorrow? I'd like to find them as soon as possible."

"Can't tomorrow, gotta straighten the house; the cleaning lady is coming." He was serious. My brothers and I broke into an uneasy laugh; seemed awkward to laugh after what had been said.

"I don't have any appointments. I'll come with. After all, it is my metal detector." Marty smirked the cock-eyed Morelli grin. He'd chosen the detector as a prize for high sales in popcorn. The boys had already 'won' all of their camping gear and paid for most of summer camp through popcorn sales. The Berkeley/Hillside communities and the Western Electric Company were thrilled and grateful when the last Morelli turned eighteen and left scouting.

My family left around nine o'clock. Seemed a lot later. Sometime during the evening my headache returned full force. I puttered in the kitchen until I had no reason to stay there. I flipped the towel over the drying dishes and turned out the light. I passed the living room and noticed the fireplace set with kindling and logs. I settled on the couch and curled up facing the cold firebox. *Cold. Like me. No use to anyone; no purpose.*

A noise drew my attention. Harry's step on the stairs.

✽ 14 ✿

I didn't face him. I feigned sleep and he let me pretend. He covered me with an afghan and brushed his lips across my forehead.

My plan had been to wait until he slept soundly before I went up to our bed. Instead I'd fallen asleep and spent the night on the couch.

I woke up to the smell of coffee, but not to his morning noises; no humming while he put on his kettle; no chastising the marauding squirrels outside as he sipped his tea seated at the breakfast nook; no hearty baritone as he road his exercise bike. I knew he'd kissed me good-bye, his scent, *Colors,* lingered.

He'd left a note propped against my angel coffee mug, knowing I'd go to coffee before anything else.

Good morning, Sweetheart,
Had to be in the city early. Devin took care of April and
Cash. Won't be home 'til late, don't wait supper. Sleep in,
feel better. I miss you already.
Harry

"Ditto," I murmured, acknowledging our private joke when we were apart. I wondered if he'd be late because he wanted to stop and see Will, maybe take him to dinner. Why shouldn't he? He couldn't take Will without Lily. Could he? Would he?

Yikes! Shoulda, coulda, woulda, I'm going nuts here! I quickly poured Mocha Madness into my mug and walked into the mudroom. Boots, barn jacket, horse treats, all the accoutrements of my life. I sipped my coffee while I sat on the boot bench.

I want purpose in my life. I want a child in my life. Not theirs,
ours. Horses and part-time jobs and writing and travel, isn't enough.

While my mind ranted, my fingers braided. Coffee forgotten and turning cold on the bench next to me, I braided the rough rope I use in the barn until my fingertips bled from the tiny cuts. I jumped up to break the trance. A wave of dizziness hit me full force and I slumped back onto the bench, immediately putting my head between my legs. I braced my fingertips on the tiled floor. The smooth, cool surface felt good on my bruised skin. I stayed that way until the swaying stopped. I lifted my head slowly, fearful of a relapse. So far, so good. Next would be to stand. Pushing up from the bench, I felt no ill effects. I tucked the heavy strands of hair behind my ears and took a tentative step.

Food. I need to eat. Back in the kitchen, I pulled out muffins, cheese, and salami. I made a McMorelli, my version of the McMuffin. Two muffin creations later, I felt much better and retraced my steps through the mudroom, stopping long enough to don boots and jacket.

April and Cash heard me coming. Happy *whinnies* greeted me and lifted my spirits. "Good morning, my darlings. Did we sleep well?" My singsong greeting brought head tossing and snorts in response; my carrot treats brought warm snuffles and licks. I knew Devin had aired and fed them this morning. I would clean out their stalls and sort through the pile of tack I'd meant to get to. The brisk air hung pleasantly in the snug barn. I switched on the radio I kept on the shelf. *WLS* responded with the current traffic and weather report. *I'll be thinking about traffic reports soon, wondering if the Hillside strangler bottleneck will make me late. But today, high forties and sunny is all I need to know.*

I led April out of her stall and clipped her short lead to a post. Working at a steady pace I soon shed the jacket and felt comfortable in the long sleeved pullover. I'd slept on the couch in my clothes, hadn't washed off my make-up, a Mary Kay no-no, smelled akin to the animals I served, but all in all, I felt good. My pace hurried and slowed with whatever tune played. During the traffic and weather breaks, I tickled muzzles and ears. During one of those breaks I heard a strange noise, a desperate mewling. It stopped before I could zero in on the location. The barn wasn't that big. Something was hiding in here. Could it harm the horses? Apparently whatever it was hadn't yet. The cry sounded weak, maybe dying.

I knew it wasn't in the stalls. I pushed the brimming wheelbarrow outside to Harry's compost pile. April and Cash eagerly went into the corral. I turned off the radio and waited.

It came again, weaker but no less desperate. I moved a crate and something furry pulsed behind the wood. The movement surprised me and I jumped. *Get a grip, Gracie. It's not Godzilla.* I dragged the crate out a few more inches. Again the pulsing movement. Why didn't it run? A few more inches and I solved the mystery. A kitten lay tangled in the mess of old broken tack, fish netting, and rope coils that had fallen behind the crate. It couldn't raise its little orange head caught as it was in a bridle. Tiny feet were held somewhere beneath the quivering body. The poor thing could only shiver in fear. I carefully lifted the mass of leather and hemp and carried it into the stall and onto the insulating straw. A tiny hiss from the tangle surprised me and I laughed at this little creature's tenacity. "Okay, baby Rambo, chill." My hands shook a little while I untangled what I thought held the kitten's head down. I slipped my hand under and in through a coil and felt sharp teeth on my thumb. "Ouch!" My knee-jerk reaction to pull away brought a yelp from the baby feline. "Sorry, you bit me. Don't do that, I'm trying to help." *Yeah, right. Like I wouldn't have bitten a big old thumb coming at my face.*

I searched the shelves and found my work gloves. The thin leather gave me some protection and I began feeling my way through the leather, sustaining minor bites. I tried to pull it out of the tangle, but only the front paws came up easily. I didn't want to tug and hurt it more. I peeled away another coil and discovered what held it. Somehow the kitten's back legs had slipped through the same hole in the fish netting twined around the snap hook on a broken bit. I could see where the animal's attempts to pull free had cut into its young flesh, the fur matted with blood. "Poor thing." I had to put it down to get my knife; I couldn't unwind this netting. Two cuts and the back legs were free but the kitten didn't move. I scooped it up, grabbed my jacket, and ran for the house.

I knew there was an emergency vet's office on Ogden Avenue in Lisle. The short run through the house to get the spare keys and my purse left muddy footprints as a trail. The cleaning lady was due tomorrow; give her something to do since I was more like my dad than I wanted to admit and usually picked up and straightened the day before her arrival.

The drive through Pine Marsh out to Route 53 then north to Ogden and the veterinarian's office took fourteen minutes on the dashboard clock, time I feared my kitten couldn't afford. *My kitten. So it's mine now.*

I rushed into the waiting room holding my cargo in the folds of my jacket. The attendant at the desk came out from behind the counter, looked into the jacket, and motioned me toward an examining room. The doctor walked in right behind her and took my bundle. He transferred the kitten to the stainless steel tabletop; I shivered for him when his thin frame touched the cold metal.

"I'm Doctor Chung. Tell me what happened."

I explained the discovery.

"Any idea how long he's been there?"

"None. I'm in the barn every day, but I'd never heard him before."

I watched as the vet gently probed the gaunt belly and lifted the thin orange limbs as he spoke to his assistant. He listened to the kitten's heartbeat and nodded. He pressed into the flesh at the kitten's hip area and the back legs twitched.

"That's good." He gently began massaging the small legs using his thumb and forefinger.

"Can I do that?"

"Sure. We want to increase the circulation in the legs. I don't feel any broken bones. Trapped like that the muscles may have atrophied a bit and we want to rehab them. I'm going to give baby," he hesitated and looked at me for the name.

"Elmo," I blurted. I had meant to say Arlo, after the Marsden's cat. I thought we'd call him A.J., Arlo Jr. Don't know where Elmo came from. I could change it later.

"I'm going to give Elmo his series of shots and start him on a hydration program."

"An I.V.?"

Doctor Chung smiled. "No, nothing like that. More along the lines of this." He reached into the cabinet and brought out a six-pack of short baby bottles. "These are filled with Pedialyte and fitted with a special nipple. I want you to start feeding Baby Elmo right now and continue offering a bottle every hour until all six are consumed. You can sit here and we'll make sure Elmo responds."

He picked up the quiet little fur ball and brought him to me. The attendant who'd first greeted me pulled one bottle from the plastic ring, uncapped it, and handed it to me.

"Hold him here under his belly, let his body rest on your forearm, and don't let his rear dangle. Unlike a human baby, animals shouldn't be fed while on their backs."

I positioned my hand so my fingers could support his chin and gently touched the nipple to his mouth. His eyes stayed closed. I looked up at the doctor.

"Massage his throat a little and tipped the bottle up more."

Geez, I had a Betsey Wetsey. How hard could this be?

My hand holding the bottle felt sweaty and slid over the smooth glass. I wiggled my fingers under Elmo's neck and touched the nipple to his pink mouth. He stirred, opened his eyes, looked up into my face, and began suckling the nipple.

"You're all set 'mom'. Feed him one bottle here and then we'll send him home. I'll prepare some instructions on care and food. Relax and enjoy your new baby."

Doctor Chung smiled and left the room. I leaned back in the chair and crossed my ankle onto my thigh, creating support for my arm. I kept up the gentle stroking under his chin as he tugged at the bottle. It wasn't like feeding Claire or Connor and certainly he wasn't as precious as they, but still, he was a baby too. I knew that if I didn't rein in my emotions I'd be throwing a shower for this little fur ball.

A warm, wet spot on my arm sent me into giggles. *Fluid in, fluid out.* I guessed that was a good sign. Time to go home. The attendant helped me wrap Elmo in my jacket and put the remaining bottles in a plastic bag for me. Ready to go except for the bill. One hundred and sixty two dollars. I handed her the check and received my instructions, Elmo's tag, and my follow-up appointment on a little card in the shape of a paw with his name, *Elmo Marsden*. I felt the itching at the back of my throat and knew I had to bolt before I embarrassed myself by bursting into tears.

In the safety of my car, I gulp and swallowed until the insane urge to cry passed and the more common urge to braid overcame me. I twisted and looped a series of knots until I felt the tingling in my fingers subside.

"C'mon, Elmo. Let's go home." To my delight he mewed and licked at his front paw. I tried again. "Okay little guy, time to go." Again the tiny response. We had bonded. I hurried home to settle him in and take care of April and Cash. I never left them out when I wasn't home. I didn't want to leave Elmo alone so I tucked him into an empty feedbag and slung it over my shoulder. April and Cash trotted to the gate and eyed the bag with interest. "Oops, sorry guys. Definitely not your lunch." I held out the quartered apples and baby carrots I'd brought from the mudroom. April's gentle mouth lifted the treats from my palm. Cash's manners weren't as refined. I made sure I arched my fingers down and kept my thumb out of the way.

Feeding time again. I couldn't believe an hour had passed. I enjoyed my task and Elmo enjoyed his second bottle. Afterwards, I massaged his legs. No thought to the muddy footprints, messy house, or even peed on clothes, I spent the entire day alternately feeding Elmo, watching him sleep, and massaging his legs. I used the ointment from the vet on the torn skin.

We'd always had dogs. I knew I needed to get to a store for a litter box and cat accoutrements. In the meantime, I could jerry-rig something since we used cat litter around the barn area to avoid having the salt get into the horses' hooves or in their feed. I lined a Marshall Field's shirt box with aluminum foil and carried it out to the barn. Two scoops of litter filled it half way to the top. I turned to leave and caught movement from the corner of my eye. Two kittens looked at me from behind the crate that had hidden their littermate. I presumed that since they looked the same size except they were plump and mobile. I stepped toward them and they scampered into tiny places only they knew.

"Oh, dear. You have siblings, Elmo." A mew from the feedbag on my shoulder answered. I knew I shouldn't separate them, but he couldn't survive out here on his own yet. And I didn't want three house cats. I walked back to the mudroom and cleared a corner for the litter box. I could nurse Elmo until he grew strong enough to rejoin his family. *Family. Where was mom? Had she been in the barn, hiding?*

I called Hannah who knew everything about cats.

"Hi, Hannah, it's Grace."

"Hullo, how are you feeling?"

I realized I'd forgotten my headache and hadn't thought about the attack for hours. Elmo's entry into my life spun it in a better direction. I answered quickly.

"Fine, I'm feeling much better. I called because I have a little four-legged friend who isn't feeling as fine." I explained the entire discovery and subsequent treatment. Hannah clucked and *tsked* through the entire story. She loves cats, but Karen is allergic to them.

"Oh, Gracie, he sounds darling. When will you bring him over?"

"He's still pretty zonked out. I'll bring him by soon, but in the meantime, I need to buy stuff for him. I grew up with dogs. What does he need? I mean does he need a coat, he's so thin, or little booties?"

Hannah bubbled with laughter. "He's a cat not a baby." Her squelched laughter and awkward silence told me she realized her gaffe. The silence grew; I knew it was incumbent on me to break the tension. Of course he's not a *baby* baby. The lump in my throat grew along with the silence. I imagined the concern on her face when she heard the soft *click* from my end.

If she called, I didn't want to be here. I scooped up Elmo and tucked him into the feedbag. "C'mon, little guy. Let's go visit Auntie Barb." His amber eyes blinked once and closed. I took another bottle along for his next feeding.

Barb Atwater lived next door. The six homes in Pine Marsh either fronted on woods or field, each house connected at the back end of their property by a groomed walking trail. Barb and I usually walked every morning at six o'clock. I'd been remiss lately, having one excuse or another. I needed to get back on track.

The crushed pecan shells crunched under my boots and the sound reverberated in the brisk air. I held the bag close to keep Elmo from swinging. Barb stood in her yard filling her dozen bird feeders. She was an avid 'birder' and kept a journal of her sightings.

"Ah, the elusive dark winged Gracie bird. Thought extinct except for sightings near barns." She waved and walked toward me. "I heard about your attack. Are you alright?" Barb peered at my face looking for confirmation.

"You heard, from who, when? I haven't…"

"Jan Pauli!" We both shouted the name at the same time and burst into laughter.

The cleaning lady, of course. Jan Pauli had swept down on Pine Marsh in a big way last summer. I hired her and then she marketed herself to the other families in the compound. So far, of the six families, Lily was the only holdout. I totally understood her reluctance to use the same cleaning lady as I did.

Barb's laughter slowed and she pointed to the feedbag on my shoulder. "Coming to borrow a cup of oats?"

"Not hardly. Coming to introduce you to your new neighbor." I held the sides open so she could peek inside.

"Oh, he's adorable. He's so thin, is he okay?"

"He will be." Again, I explained his rescue. "I have to plump him up a little and he'll be dandy. In fact, it's feeding time. Watch this." I sat down on one her many viewing benches located throughout her yard to facilitate bird-spying and pushed the collar of the bag down around Elmo's shoulders. His soft *mew* drew Barb to the bench. I uncapped the bottle and my little orange bundle did the rest. He reached for the bottle with both paws and I felt Barb melt next to me. Elmo sucked heartily at the bottle making short work of the contents. He seemed stronger at each feeding. His attention wandered from the empty nipple and riveted to a point over my shoulder. His little frame tensed in the bag and the amber eyes that had drowsed now grew wide. Both Barb and I noticed the transformation. The reason, a black capped chickadee, feeding eagerly from a swaying Yankee Droll tube, hadn't noticed the tiny predator.

Barb laughed and snapped her fingers to distract Elmo. "Hey

there. You and I are going to tangle if you don't get that 'what's for dinner' look out of your eyes." He glanced at Barb. The chickadee moved on in that moment. I pulled the collar up around his furry head and stood up.

"I need to pick up things for him. Any idea how I get him to use a litter box?"

"We're dog people, but I think mama cat shows them."

"Not if they're barn cats."

"Right. Maybe it's like dogs. After they eat, take them out and wait. In his case, after you feed him, put him in the litter box. I think it's instinct. He'll do that scratching, cover-up thing."

I lifted the bag away from my side. "Oops, too late." We both burst into laughter. "Do you want a rag?'

"No, he already christened the other side this morning. Think I'd best change before I go shopping. See you tomorrow at six?"

"I was hoping you'd say that. See you then."

The phone stopped ringing. I caught the number on the display before it disappeared and pushed the button on my speed dial pad.

"Hello."

"Barb, it's Grace. I was in the shower. You called?"

"I did. I need a favor. I'm expecting a package this afternoon that requires a signature. But I have to run out. Can you hold off on your shopping spree so I can leave a note for UPS to deliver it to you?"

"Sure. I don't know what to buy anyway."

"Why don't you call Hannah? She's crazy about cats. Probably knows the best stores."

"Yeah," I mumbled. "Do you want me to bring it over later?"

"What?"

"The package I'm accepting for you."

"Yes, I mean, no. I'll send Devin over to pick it up."

"Devin's home?"

"No, I mean he might be later. He's meeting with his scoutmaster about his eagle project. Hang on to it. If anything I'll get it in the morning when we walk."

Her comment diverted my thoughts. "I'd almost forgotten he's still a scout. Which troop is he in, it's local right?"

"It's Woodridge Troop 562. Meets at Goodrich Elementary on Hobson Road and Rt. 53."

"And he likes it? No problems?"

"He loves it. Outside of my foot planted on his behind to move on his project, no problems."

I could hear the pride and love in her voice when she spoke of her son. I'd felt something akin to that with my nieces and nephews, but I knew it's different with your own child. My earlier feeling of shaking the moody blues seemed a memory. Everything, anything, people said struck at my core.

"Grace?"

"Sorry, I'm here. Okay, I'll wait for the package. See Devin later or you tomorrow."

"Right. Thanks, I owe you one. Bye."

"Bye." *Owes me one?* Not hardly. This was the woman who'd been shot by a nutcase who'd mistaken her for me. This favor didn't begin to balance the ledger.

I took 'Elmo in a bag,' as I'd started thinking of him, to the mudroom and sat down on the boot bench. I needed to replace the soiled carrier. My tote bag from the mystery readers' group at the Lisle Library, 'Murder Among Friends,' lay empty on the bench. I hadn't made the last two meetings. Hope the group won't mind its new use; certainly not a reflection on the wonderful books we've read. Kathy and Rhonda would understand. That's whom I should call. They must have twelve cats between them. So it seemed from their conversations.

I realized I was excited to have my cat to talk about at the next meeting. It's hard to swap horse stories with the casual acquaintance. Elmo mewed his approval when I transferred him to his roomier carrier. This would be his last bottle of Pedialyte. I tried to cradle him, baby style, for his last feeding. Needle-like claws hooked and twisted to right the little body.

"Ouch! Okay, okay, you're not a baby. I get it."

Do I get it? Of course, I do. He's a cat.

Elmo sucked at the foreign nipple content to feed. I watched his mouth tug repeatedly until the liquid slid quickly from the bottle into his tummy. He never slurped a drop of his nectar; the wet spots on his paws were my tears.

I placed him gently in his litter box and waited. At first he stood still and looked at me. He took a few tentative steps, his back legs moving awkwardly to match the stride of the front two. And then, success. He squatted, peed, and then walked through the damp litter. So much for instinctive clean up. I took the old coffee strainer I had donated to his cause and scooped up the clump into an empty coffee can. He sniffed the damp area and looked up at me.

I felt a mother's pride. "Good boy, good boy."

His tiny mew encouraged some ear scratching. Once in the kitchen, I sat him on the rug by the sink. He quieted and curled up.

Determined to keep an eye on him while I cleaned up, I pulled the rug over so I could reach the faucet. Fresh coffee and a bagel sounded great. I'd missed lunch. While I prepared the coffee I kept glancing down at the fur ball at my feet. I had the overpowering desire to dress him in one of the cute undershirts I'd purchased for Claire and Connor as part of their Thanksgiving gift.

I carefully stepped over him, reached for the phone, and dialed a number.

"Hello, this is Cassidy McCabe."

"Cassidy, this is Grace Marsden. I need to see you."

"All right. My schedule is open Thursday afternoon, 2 o'clock?"

"Great. Thank you."

"Grace, can you tell me the nature of your concern."

"Yeah, unnatural. That's it."

"We'll talk Thursday. Bye, Grace."

I trusted Cassidy. No one need know about a few visits to sort through things. I used to be able to sort through life from the top of April's ample back; joking that her rates were cheaper than a therapist.

I carried Elmo into the living room to teach him about curling up with a good book and a coffee. The lines blurred before my eyes as lost sleep tried to reclaim me. I lowered my book and leaned my head back. *An afternoon snooze is just the ticket. New job starting, have to rest up. Holidays around the corner, decorating, and gifts to buy. Baby Clare and Baby Connor and Baby Elmo. Life is good.*

The doorbell sounded, dragging me back from fuzzy, unremarkable dreams. Elmo had crawled out of his tote and settled himself on the pages of *'A' is for Alibi*. The ringing woke him from perhaps a kitty dream of little plump mice. I carried him like a football tucked under my arm.

I fully expected the UPS man. I opened the door to four smiling faces and two sleeping ones; Karen, Hannah, Tracy, Barb and the twins. They crowded in the door carrying wrapped boxes, piling them on the hall table and rushing to *coo* over Elmo.

"He's adorable. Look at those beautiful eyes."

"He's so tiny. I've never seen a kitten that small." Barb seemed concerned.

"The vet estimates his age at about seven weeks, a little young to be weaned, but totally viable."

"A fair bit, I'd say." Hannah lifted him up so he looked down at her face. She held him with both hands under his belly and used her forefingers to rub behind his ears. I'd have to remember that position, he looked blissful. She laid him up on her shoulder and placed her hand under his feet. "His back legs seem weak; he's not pushing against my hand."

I explained the vet's diagnosis and the treatment. Hannah nodded. I'd forgotten that while growing up in England Hannah seriously considered veterinarian medicine.

"What's going on? I'm a little slow on the uptake, but I'd venture to say there is no UPS man coming."

Barb snickered. "My ploy, pretty good, huh?"

"We wanted to surprise you with a 'kitty shower' before you went out and bought everything."

"So, Hannah will make the tea, Barb will set out the strudel she picked up at Joyful's Café, Karen will mind the kids, who are being angelic and sleeping." Tracy grinned at Barb. "Wait 'til tonight."

The others moved to the kitchen. Hannah reluctantly relinquished Elmo. "I'll be back in a little bit." She kissed his furry face.

"Excuse me. While your minions do your bidding, what will you be doing?"

"I will be checking you out in the living room." She motioned me ahead of her. I moved the book and we sat down. "You're way behind. She's on *'G' is for Gumshoe*."

Tracy stared into my eyes, gently probed the back of my head, and in general looked me over. "Seems fine. Any headaches?"

I nodded. "How's Matt?"

"He's fine. Big man on campus at Bryant Middle School. He wanted a bigger gauze bandage." Her smile faded. "I wanted to ask you something about that night. Matt's been telling his Dad about the light he followed. He said it glowed like our camp lantern. William asked around at Triton and some of the stories he heard are bizarre."

Tracy's husband taught at Triton College in River Grove. Most students and teachers were familiar with Robinson Woods.

"Define bizarre."

"Animal sacrifices, satanic stuff, and witch covens bizarre."

"Oh God, Tracy. I took the boys there. I'm so sorry."

She patted my hand and scratched Elmo behind the ears. "Hey, we didn't know. Now that we do, I can't imagine that scouts should be out there. Doesn't the scout troop know about this?"

"They should. The leader lives less than a mile away on the other side of the woods. They've been in that area for years. I found out my dad was in that troop when he was a kid. Robinson Woods is part of Troop 265's tradition."

"Do the parents know the 'tradition' of those woods?"

Further speculation stopped with a summons from the kitchen. The colorfully wrapped packages covered the butcher-block table. Hannah had set up tea at the breakfast nook. She sat in Harry's spot viewing the visitors to his many feeders.

"This is so lovely. Peaceful. The sort of place to raise children.

Isn't it, Karen?"

"Ugh, I'd go crazy out here with all this, this space," she blurted. "And my allergies would skyrocket. I like concrete and noise. Makes me feel alive, and I don't sneeze as much."

Had Hannah's wistful tone been apparent only to me? I hurried to change the subject. "Should I give Elmo a middle name? My cousin Chris has a cat named Martin Marmalade."

"Absolutely. Mum's cats, Star and Annabelle, do. Can't remember Star's but Annie's is Rose."

"What about Arlo?" I asked about the stray Hannah's dad had taken in.

"That old Tom? Daddy named him. 'Doesn't need a double moniker, he's a cat, not a Peer for heaven's sake,' he told mum."

We laughed at her imitation.

"You need one syllable so it flows like 'Elmo Jake' or Elmo Jay'."

"No, you need a longer name like 'Elmo Alexander' or Elmo Arthur'. Give him a name to live up to."

"Do all Englishmen have this unnatural sense of the universe, or did I get the only one?"

Harry walked in from the garage door before anyone answered Karen. He stopped, surprised at the scene. "My, my, a hen party. What have I stumbled upon?" In Harry's English parlance 'hen' wasn't derogatory. His smile lit up the room and my stomach did a familiar flip.

"Hullo, who's this?" Harry lifted Elmo up into the air in much the same position as Hannah had. Must be an English thing. The kitten's *hiss* startled everyone. "Calm down, little ort. You're lucky to have landed in here. Out there you'd be a quick bite." Harry held him so that his claws couldn't rake his hands. He rubbed the tips of Elmo's ears and then tickled inside the ears. The hissing stopped and I swear a low purr emanated from that orange bundle.

"How'd you do that?"

"Classified information."

Hannah laughed and spilled the beans or in this case potatoes. "He calls that inner ear twirling 'cleaning the potatoes out of their ears'. Animals love it; he's used it on dogs, cats and even my childhood ferret, Charles."

"Charles? Odd name for a ferret isn't it?" Barb asked.

"Not if he's your king in waiting." Hannah's smile set us laughing again.

"Does it work on all animals?"

"If they have ears. Works on Clare and Connor."

We all looked at the sleeping babies. "You do that to them?"

"It's not like I poke a stick in their ears. Relax. They do. Getting back to 'Ort' here, is he ours?"

I recounted the day and ended with a flourish at the packages. Harry's smile touched each face at the table. "Dandy of you to do this. I suppose the boys have to stay and play some ladies' game."

Laughter ripped around the table. It felt good to be silly.

"We do have one game we didn't play at the twins' shower." Tracy held up a sheet of paper. "I was saving it for the next one. This qualifies. Everyone get your purse. Harry you can use your wallet. When I say a letter the first person to show me an object from their purse or wallet with that name gets a ticket. The most tickets wins."

We snickered at Harry's feeble attempt to pit his wallet against our bulging purses. He'd put Elmo down on the kitchen rug near the nook. Hands poised Tracy began. The first letter is 'T'." Hands dipped and dived.

"Ticket," Harry said as he held up a parking stub.

"Beginner's luck."

"The next letter is 'G'."

"Gum." Harry slid out a flattened stick of Juicy Fruit. He shrugged and grinned. "Beginner's luck."

"Okay, settle down ladies. Next letter is 'I'.

"Eyeglasses, no that's 'e'," mumbled Karen.

Harry flipped his wallet on the table. "Identification card."

We stared from the small photo on his driving license to the real McCoy with the devilish grin.

"Oh, give him the prize, Tracy. He's too competitive. Juicy Fruit for heaven's sake." Hannah's grin matched her brother's.

Karen and I both shrugged and nodded. Tracy pulled a colorful paper tube tied at both ends from her bag. "Confetti bubble bath. I'd pay to see you up to your neck in confetti bubbles. Enjoy." Tracy arched an eyebrow and gave Harry her best leer. We laughed so hard the twins finally woke up. Baby holders in attendance each lifted a child onto their laps. Tracy and Barb fussed with their charges while Karen and Hannah handed me gifts.

Karen and Hannah and the babies left first, wanting to beat some of the traffic home. Tracy and Barb helped clean up before they left.

Harry had spent most of the time on the floor with Elmo showing him his new toys and trying out each one. Elmo responded in apparently typical cat-like attitude, alternating between 'bored' and 'pounce' modes. I carried the bed, decorated with pictures of chubby mice, and colorful yarn up to our room. I also set up his new covered litter box.

The evening flew by with a quick dinner and more play time with Elmo. I told Harry about seeing the other kittens. "I'd best check the barn for them, see if I can find their way in. I don't mind his siblings, but now I am concerned about other critters finding their way into a warm barn. I'll settle April and Cash for the night and do a little reconnoitering." He tucked Elmo under his arm and went out.

It was after ten o'clock when the two of them returned. I had washed up the Mary Kay way and slathered lotion on my elbows, knees, and heels. The firm pillow and fluffed goose down elicited a narcotic response and I dozed, barely hearing Harry enter the room.

He set Elmo in the kidney shaped bed and patted his head. "He's a good boy. Used his downstairs box for me, he did."

I laughed at Harry's 'baby talk' tone. "Oh, so you are awake. Excellent." He brought his hand from behind his back holding the confetti tube. "Party, anyone?"

I rarely turned down an invitation from Harry. My hesitation spoke for me.

"Not tonight? Don't tell me you have a headache?" He smiled and then remembered my recent injury. "Stupid of me. Does your head hurt? Tracy told me she checked you out and you seemed fine. How do you feel?"

"I'm fine. Rain check?"

"Absolutely."

Some time later, I felt Harry slide in under the sheet. His arms found me and pulled me close. He hadn't turned out his light yet; he'd probably hold me until I fell asleep and then he'd read into the night.

"Sweet of the girls to bring those gifts," I mumbled into his chest.

"Yes, lovely party. Now quiet down and sleep. You need to rest. Anything else?"

His close proximity and touch made me regret my earlier decision. I struggled to match his calm tone. "Yes, there is. There better not have been a 'C' for condom in your wallet." I reached out and traced my fingers across his abdomen. His breath caught and I noticed multiple responses from his body.

"Course not," he mumbled as he covered my neck and shoulders with kisses. "That would be 'R' for rubber." His heavy mouth crushed my response.

❧ 16 ❦

Elmo cried all night. I never knew a tiny body could make all that noise. Somewhere between two and three in the morning I hauled his little butt into bed, hoping I wouldn't regret it.

I woke up with orange fur in my mouth and his little body curled up between my shoulder and chin. His scratchy tongue scraped the side of my face. Not to be outdone, Harry leaned over and kissed the other side.

"*Mmm,* what a wonderful way to wake up. Can we do this every morning?"

"Depends. Can we do last night every night?"

I turned my face toward Harry. "*Phewt!* Cat hair."

I giggled and brushed at the thin strands, finally ridding them by pursing my lips and blowing, a motion that almost brought Harry back to bed.

He stood next to the bed wearing only his pants. I loved the way he looked in the morning. Men had it easy; rumpled looked charming on them. He slipped into his shirt. "I'll take Ort downstairs and start your coffee. Are you walking this morning?"

"No, not today. Turns out Barb had something early."

"Sleep in a bit. I'll feed April and Cash; want to look for signs of entry. I sprinkled talc around the perimeter last night."

He left with Elmo tucked under one arm.

Talc. You could take the man out of secret service, but... I dozed.

The aroma of cinnamon reached my nose and signaled my eyes to open. I turned my head to the right and spotted my angel mug on the nightstand; steam curled from the liquid. I heard the shower and Harry's baritone come on. His selection this morning was from *The Barber of Seville*. He loved opera. I blame his mother. Dorothy Marsden played opera for her children while they were in her womb.

I sat up and savored my first sip of the day, an almost spiritual experience for me. I took my coffee to the window seat and curled up, resting one side of my face against the frame. The view made the taxes, maintenance fee, and inconvenience of only one entrance to the area worthwhile. I stared across winter bare trees to an open field on the right and part of the groomed eighth fairway to the left.

My serenade stopped. Harry came toward me wrapped in a towel. He leaned down and kissed the top of my head. "Good morning, again. You really conked out. Horses are fed and turned out, Ort's tummy is full, and his bladder is empty."

Harry looked so pleased with himself. I made what I hoped resembled a grumpy old man face and lowered my voice. "How about the perimeter security?" I couldn't hold the pose for long and broke into a grin.

"Perimeter secure." Harry did a snappy salute and pulled me up into his arms. "Yes, ma'am. All secure." He flexed his abdomen muscles and I felt the towel loosen and drop to the floor. His arms tightened around me. "Your own military advises to 'be all that you can be'."

The thin fabric between us didn't mask all that he could be. "You are that."

Twice in a ten-hour span. This is like our honeymoon. Am I dreaming? The phone will ring about now and wake me up. No, it'll ring just before he...

Whether I willed it, dreamt it, or foresaw it, the phone rang and shattered the mood. Neither one of us has ever been able to leave our private line ring. When we consciously plan an interlude we turn off the phone in the bedroom and retrieve messages later.

"Bloody hell." He re-wrapped himself. "Hello." His brusque tone must have put off the caller. "Sorry Hanns, we were..." Harry stumbled and then his ear turned slightly pink, which amounted to a blush for him. Hannah must have guessed at the 'we were'. I heard Harry mumble, "Can't help it, habit." I hoped that referred to our inability to ignore a ringing phone and not his proclivity to making love to me. I'd hate to be a habit.

Getting the straight story while listening to a one-sided conversation is chancy at best, but when the one side you see and hear is a trained agent the pickings are slim. Only because I've lived with him for ten years could I see the slight slip in his poker face. Hannah's call wasn't social.

The babies! Are they okay? SIDS?

Unlike Harry's face, mine must have screamed panic. He tucked the mouthpiece under his chin. "Everyone's fine."

I relaxed and waited for him to hang up.

"Everyone's fine," he repeated. "It's Janet Henry. She's missing. Her mother filed a missing person report. Apparently, you were the last person to see her on Monday at your interview. Ric asked Hannah to call you, give you a heads up as it were. How odd that Kramer wouldn't use this excuse to call you."

"Harry, don't."

"Sorry, darling. I'm certain he's still in love with you, no matter who he's dating."

"You mean Lily?" In a curve that only real life could throw, Ric had moved in with Lily this past summer. For several months, we lived with 'his and hers' ex-lovers three doors down.

"No. They've some bizarre alliance but it's not sexual. I mean Nancy Royal."

"The Lisle police officer who wanted to lock you up and lose the key? When did that happen?" I don't know if I fumed because I didn't know this or because Harry did. "How do you know all this?" In my mind 'all' meant the part about knowing it wasn't sexual with Lily; hardly a chat he'd have with Ric.

"The Red Hat tree of course. Nancy's mother, nee Gruner, belongs to the Hessian Hunnies and told Jan Pauli, who told Gertrude, who'd missed the last luncheon, who in turn told Hannah when she came to clean. The Red Hat tree." Harry pantomimed hanging hats on alternating invisible pegs. "Works faster than the grapevine."

I laughed at his evaluation. Our window of opportunity had slammed shut. I could tell Harry's mind worked to put some facts together. He worried the left corner of his bottom lip with his teeth when he puzzled things out.

Puzzle all right. Where was Janet?

I'd agreed to meet Dad at his house at ten o'clock, but that was before Elmo. I couldn't leave him home alone and Harry had another meeting in the city. I found an old duffel bag and packed it with two bottles, gourmet kitty kibble, a mouse toy, and a makeshift litter box to go. Elmo traveled in my tote bag.

My dad opened the door, took in the scene, and grinned. "You brought Elmo. I hoped you would." He kissed my cheek as I huffed over the threshold.

"Does everyone know everything about my life?"

"You should let the phone ring through to the machine, honey."

I nearly dropped Elmo in my embarrassment. I felt the rush of color to my face. "Dad!"

"Relax, sweetie. Hannah knew we would be in the vicinity today and she wanted to know if we could swing by and pick up the low carb pasta and fenugreek she found at that exotic market near them."

My father's diabetes had begun to swing out of control even with diet and exercise. Hannah had consulted her books and friends and designed a new diet that included foods and herbs that he couldn't get at the IGA or Caputo's Market.

"And she asked first if this was a good time or if I, um was involved, and mentioned how she'd already disturbed you."

It took a second for me to connect the dots and then I know I turned bright red. *My dad, involved? That way? With who, whom? Who cares? I care. Oh, crap.*

"Gracie, it's okay. I was making lasagna when she called. Thought I'd send some home with you."

"Dad, I'm sorry. I'm such a ninny. I mean, I know you, well, you know. Uh, meet Elmo." I thrust the tote at him and turned away to deposit the duffel at the door hoping he wouldn't see the tears. *For heaven's sake, mom's been gone for five years. Why shouldn't he find someone?* I clenched my teeth and swallowed hard. I knew if he looked at my eyes he'd know I was upset. I think he purposely fussed over Elmo, giving me time to recover.

"Hey little guy, you're a cutie. Want some half and half?"

"Dad, that's too rich for him and you shouldn't be having it either. What's wrong with skim milk for your coffee?"

"I might as well use water for all the flavor it has."

The doorbell rang before we rehashed a familiar discussion. Marty stood on the stoop ready for 'bear,' holding his deluxe metal detector in one hand and a bulging backpack slung over his shoulder.

He lowered his pack to the floor next to my duffel and leaned the detector against the doorjamb. We hugged hello and I teased him about his pack.

"We're not going camping. What's in there?"

"Be prepared. Never know what you may need. Right, Dad?" He spotted Elmo. "Hey, Elmo, how's it going?"

"Did Hannah call you too?"

My brother looked confused. "About Elmo? Why would Hannah call me? Dad told me when I called him back about bringing the lightweight stove."

Now I was the one confused.

"Got some Italian Wedding soup that has to be eaten before it goes bad. I thought we'd lunch al fresco."

They were planning on camping. I eyed the pack suspiciously

wondering if it held a pup tent.

"Let's go. I want to find more than Gracie's keys."

My youngest brother looked like a kid about to embark on a treasure hunt. His eyes gleamed in his face and strands of the Morelli mop of thick dark hair stuck out from under his Cubs hat.

Dad wheeled a cooler out from the kitchen. "Gracie put your duffel on top of the cooler. Okay, that's it. Let's roll."

Dad's grin matched Marty's. Two explorers, out for treasure. I started to feel the spirit. "C'mon Elmo we don't want to be left behind. I tucked him into the tote and pulled the door closed behind our little caravan. We loaded up Marty's Explorer and climbed aboard.

"Hey, Marty. Swing by the IGA, I need a tomato for the salad."

"Oh, yeah, the Morellis were on the road again.

"Gee, I haven't been out here in over forty years. Looks a lot smaller than I remember." Dad and Marty walked into the woods. I stopped at the end of the blacktop and peered beyond them.

In the daylight, with other cars and people about, the woods looked inviting. "Grace, is this the line you walked? We need to start out as close as possible to where you where."

"Yes, I remember thinking we'll walk in a few yards and use the dumpster as a point of reference." I felt like Dorothy in Oz entering the forbidden forest. I glanced overhead, thinking of those flying monkeys. Scared the bejeebers out of me. *And her little cat, too.* I heard the wicked cackle in my head and pulled the tote closer to me. *Scarecrow and Tin Man are here. Where's the Cowardly Lion? Hiding...that's why he's cowardly. He's not a coward,* I argued in his defense. "He has a cub to take care of."

"What, Grace?"

I hadn't meant to speak out loud. "Uh, nothing." I shook my head. "I think this is where Matt took off. We kept walking, following his bobbing light. It was dark by then. I can't say for sure where we stopped."

"No problem. I'll start here and fan back and forth about ten feet either way." Marty slipped earphones over his head, flipped on his 'Tracker' deluxe metal detector, and began his sweep. I didn't know if the earphones were part of the detector or connected to a Walkman tucked away in one of the pockets in his camping vest.

"He's happy as a clam." Dad and I followed a few feet behind. The machine emitted a slow steady beep indicating search mode.

"What's that?" I pointed to the contraption Dad had pulled from his small pack.

"It's a 'Spotter'. The flashlight scans the area and the mirror above the lens catches reflections from anything shiny...I hope."

"You made this didn't you?" I grinned at the boyish look on his face.

"Hey, your brother kept going on about his 'tracker,' I thought I'd give him a run for his money with my 'spotter.' I didn't have time to find a 'beeper' so I brought this."

He pulled a whistle out of his pocket. I burst into laughter and startled Elmo who'd been asleep. His tiny head poked up and bleary eyes accused us.

"Wait, Dad. You don't need the whistle." I hooked my arm through his in true 'Dorothy' style and did the change up step to match Dad's pace. "Beep, beep, beep," I began in a slow steady pace.

"We don't need no stinkin' beeper." His voice, a good imitation of Eli Wallach in the *Treasure of the Sierra Madre*, sent me into renewed laughter. Up came the furry head again. I scratched the top of his head. "Get used to this Elmo. Did I tell you my family *e pazzo*?"

After ten minutes, I tired of *beeping* and decided to beep only when we found something.

Marty stopped abruptly and bent to brush away leaves. He grinned and lifted a man's watch from the debris and dropped it into one of his many pockets. "Grace, do you have any recollection of how far in you came or where you turned?"

I shook my head. "Sorry, after I heard Mattie cry out, I lost track. I was so scared something had happened to him." I picked at the button on my jacket and swallowed hard.

"Let's break for lunch. We've been at this for over an hour. Marty you can sweep wider on the way back, maybe catch something else."

"And what is it you plan to catch with that?" He'd noticed the 'spotter'.

"Careful there, sonny. Don't scoff." Dad turned and led the way back. Before Marty replaced his headset I began my slow *beeps* trying not to giggle at the look I imagined on my brother's face.

"Amateurs!"

We pulled the cooler to the designated picnic area and set up camp. I nodded my approval when they set up three chairs but cringed when Marty pulled out a small dining fly and deftly extended the poles that had been lashed to his pack. I sat down with my back to the circus developing behind me. Four ropes landed in my lap. "Bowlines, please."

I took up the ends and quickly tied a bowline in each, the first knot my brothers had taught me. I learned the square knot in Girl Scouts.

He positioned the tarp to cover the table. Dad and I held opposite poles while he attached the ropes to the top and then down to a pegs in the ground. We repeated the steps until all four were in place. I let them adjust the tension on the taut-line. I'd heard a hungry *meow*.

Elmo sucked up his bottle of formula in record time. I lifted his mobile litter box out of my duffel and removed the lid. He sniffed and scratched a bit, but eventually squatted. Claire and Connor wouldn't be able to do this for years. I burst into laughter at my thought. God, I hope they never pee in a cat box.

Marty and dad stopped working. "What's so funny?" Both faces, so similar, one lined and creased, the other smooth, stared at me.

"I was thinking about potty training." I nodded toward Elmo.

"Hey, Sis, so you know, it's housebreaking, not potty training. He's a cat, not a baby."

I know that. Everyone rushes to remind me, inform me, 'it's a cat, not a baby.'

It should be a baby, my baby.

My face must have shown my mood. "Gracie, can you give us a hand here?" Dad spoke the words with exaggeration the way he did when we were kids and he was setting up the joke.

For him, I played along and clapped my hands. The mood lightened a little. At least it broke my train of thought. I turned back to the littler box and put Elmo on my lap. The sun warmed my face and his fur. I heard the hiss of the camp stove in the quiet air. Elmo eagerly drank down another four ounces of formula and curled up for a nap. We snoozed until two sensory stimuli drew my attention: the aroma of campfire coffee and the warm, wet spot spreading in my lap.

"Elmo!" I lifted him from my thighs and placed him firmly in the litter. "You go there." His piddle marks darkened my Army surplus olive drab pants. My father and brother hooted with laughter, dad brushing at his eyes.

"So much for housebreaking." Marty's face contorted with renewed laughter. He could barely speak. "Look on bright side…coulda' been Charley…" He stopped to catch his breath.

I glared at both of them who still rocked with laughter. He had a point. Charley was the German Shepherd puppy Uncle Jim had won in a poker game and brought home. I should be thankful for Elmo's tiny bladder. I shrugged off my chagrin and chuckled; it did look like I'd peed my pants.

Eating around a campfire brought back memories of Boy Scout family campouts with my dad's troop. We fell easily into the 'remember when Joe slid down the embankment...' and 'what about when Glenn used lighter fluid on the fire?'

"That was you, Marty." Dad's stern expression caused more laughter.

"Geez, Dad, that was fourteen years ago." More laughter at Marty's expense, his included.

"Enough reminiscing, we need to get moving if we're going to find your keys." Marty and I packed up the gear and took down the dining fly, carefully coiling the ropes for storage. "Undo the knots before you store those."

"I haven't forgotten." My father insisted on untying knots in the ropes we used before storing them. Dad doused the campfire and stirred the ashes to release the steam and hurry the cooling process. He reached into the ashes and nodded. Camp was officially struck.

We followed our original path, but widened the sweep. I stopped when I thought I found the spot where Matt had rejoined us. I told them how the light Matt had followed went out. Marty started moving in that direction off to explore. My youngest brother had a short attention span. He'd already bored with searching for my keys, now he was on to investigating. I took the metal detector and continued searching with my dad. I left the earphones around my neck so I could keep up a conversation.

"Look at him, practically behind Chee Chee Pin Quay's boulder." Dad shaded his eyes against the sun to follow Marty's progress.

Hearing the name again sent icy shivers down my spine. I remembered the chanting and my sense of dread increased with each step. "I don't need those keys, Dad. There's nothing on them to identify me. Let's go."

"What's wrong? You're pale. Are you feeling all right?"

"No, I mean I don't know. C'mon, let's get Marty and go. I want to leave." The urgency grew so quickly I felt the heightened sensation in my fingertips. I removed the yarn tied to my tote and began a pattern of loops and crossovers. The detector, slung over my shoulder, swayed at my side while I tried to convince my dad to leave.

"Okay, we'll go." Dad drew a deep breath to whistle to Marty who'd gone out of sight. In that instant, the machine at my side emitted fast beeps, the mirror on dad's 'spotter' reflected a glare into my eyes, and Marty's sharp whistle sounded three times, his old troop's signal for help.

"Stay here." He walked toward the sound. A few feet away, he turned and fixed me with 'the look'. "I mean it, Grace. Stay put."

I watched him weave through the bare trees. He stopped at one point, whistled twice, and waited.

Three short whistles sounded again. Dad changed his course slightly and moved again across the carpet of fallen leaves. I lost sight of him and fought the urge to follow. If I stayed put, he could find me. I realized the detector still beeped its incessant discovery signal. I turned it off and dropped to my knees to search the area. My keys lay under a few leaves and we'd almost walked over them. I zipped the keys into the fanny pack. The woods grew quiet without the constant beeping and talking. I crouched, half leaning my butt against a big rock. *Geez, where are they? Is Marty hurt? Maybe he fell.*

I heard them before I saw them. I started to rise and the strangest thing happened. It was as if an occult hand held my shoulder for the briefest of moments. Then the pressure lifted. In those moments, I realized the noise I heard came from the wrong direction. I stayed still, thankful for my woods-colored clothing and dark hair. Thank God I'd silenced the metal detector. I still had a problem; they were on the path behind me coming straight at me.

A single, long whistle with an up note at the end. *All okay signal. Great, they were fine. What about me?* If I signaled for help, would whoever walked behind me leave, or find me sooner. For all I knew they were a family out for a hike. Or not. I worried about the or not.

"A-okay? Who's out there?"

"Dunno, Davy, we're all here."

Davy! Oh my God. My heart pounded against my ribs and I feared the noise would give away my hiding spot. I prayed the noise sounded louder in my head than in the unnaturally quiet woods.

"Q-tip's not here. Neither is…"

Two short whistles and one long note sounded in the stillness.

"What the hell, who's out there." The one called Davy sounded angry, but at least the whistles had stopped their forward movement.

"Maybe Mr. Big got here early. He wants us back." The speaker's voice seemed fainter as though he'd turned his head away. I heard another voice agree.

That's two that want to leave. What about Davy? He seems to run things. C'mon guys don't wait for him. He's not in charge of you.

"Let's go. I don't want to be the last ones in."

Meow.

"Hey, did you hear that? There's a cat around here."

Elmo's soft *mew* sounded louder than a lion's roar in the still air.

"There it is again. Let's get it."

"For what? C'mon, we're going to be late."

"We need it for the winter solstice sacrifice."

I pressed my lips together to keep quiet. *Sacrifice.*

"In about a month. Where you gonna keep it 'til then? When we're ready, cats are easy to snatch."

The voices grew faint, moving away at an angle and I relaxed against a tree, still hesitant to stand up. I knew the whistle meant 'head for camp,' but I wasn't going anywhere in that direction.

Meow, meow. His orange head popped up against my hand and a scratchy tongue lavished my thumb with kitty kisses. I hugged the tote to my chest and kissed the sweet spot between his ears.

I wanted to put as much distance between them and me as possible, so the decision to walk away from 'camp' and toward the last place I'd seen my dad and brother seemed a better one. I stood and listened. All quiet. Even Elmo had settled in the bottom of the tote. I picked up Marty's detector. If anyone came near me, at least I'd go down swinging. The ridged switch on the barrel of the device triggered a compelling urge to insure my safe passage by sliding the plastic back and forth. A soothing rhythm developed within a few steps. *On position, off position step two, three. On position, off position step two, three.*

I moved quickly in that euphoric zone I created when I followed my compulsion to fruition. Great time, except when I finally fulfilled my urge I realized I had no idea where I was or which direction I'd followed. I'd given myself over to that powerful whim and not focused on direction. I closed my eyes to think. *Cripes. I couldn't find camp now if I wanted to. Relax. Breathe. Think. I sat in the chair with Elmo and the sun warmed my face. It was slightly past overhead. Okay, so that was west. When dad and I found my keys the sunlight was on my left so we faced north. Dad took off toward Marty on an angle like two o'clock.*

I opened my eyes and slowly turned until I looked into the sun. *West, gotcha'. A ninety degree turn to the right, hello, north. A smid-*

gen degree to the right again and I'm good to go.

My orienteering prowess seemed wasted when I raised my eyes to the horizon and spotted flashing police lights in the distance.

∂ 17 ∂

The tableau moved in quick flashes like a strobe light over a dance floor. I couldn't be sure if the light bursts were in my head. The *squawk* from their two-ways punctuated the flashes in an odd pattern of light and sound.

I'd been identified as 'with them' when I rushed onto the scene. Marty sat on a log, his left arm lashed against his chest. Scratches and scrapes marred his skin, as though he'd been dragged face down across the vegetation. Bits of leaves tangled in his hair, his cap gone.

Dad stood behind him, a protective hand on his son's shoulder. He motioned me over. They showed no particular interest in me, in all of us apparently. The focus cued on the long black plastic bag strapped atop a gurney.

I watched the gurney being pushed, lifted down the trail to the waiting ambulance. An EMT approached Marty. "You need medical attention. We could call an ambulance for you?"

Marty shook his head. "Thanks, I'll see to it."

"Suit yourself."

I wanted to ask a million questions, but Dad's cautionary forefinger against his lips stopped me. "Sit down next to your brother. Here, give me that."

I still carried the tool from our adventure. Some adventure. Dad put it down next to his spotter. I picked the leaves out of Marty's hair.

"Thanks, Sis."

"What happened?"

A man in a dark suit walked toward us. His long, thin face and high forehead reminded me of Ernie from Sesame Street. Thin lips gave him a 'slash' mouth look. That resemblance couldn't help his tough cop persona with criminals.

"Detective Thomas, this is my daughter, Grace Marsden. Grace, this is Detective Thomas with the Sheriff's Police." Apparently, they'd met earlier.

He nodded his head. "Mrs. Marsden, I asked your father and brother to wait until the body had been removed. I'd like to ask you some questions now if you think you can wait a little longer for medical attention." He looked at Marty. We all looked at Marty.

"I took some Vicodin. I'll be okay for a little longer."

The perks of being a pharmaceutical salesman; Marty had access to pills I'd never heard of.

Thomas opened a small notebook. "I want to get the basics and fresh impressions from you. You'll still need to come into the station for a formal statement. Mr. Morelli, let's begin with you."

Marty brushed his right hand over his face, wincing at the contact. He lowered his head and closed his eyes. When he raised his head he focused on the detective and began speaking.

"I left my sister and dad while they looked for her keys. I've never been in these woods before and had no particular destination. I left the path and walked toward what I thought would be deeper into the woods. I was surprised to find the woods thinning toward this clearing. I noticed the partial stone foundation under the brush and was more intent on looking at that than watching my step. A split second before the wood shifted under my foot I realized what I'd stepped on, but it was too late. I grabbed at anything I could. My arm twisted behind me, caught on the wooden plank, stopping me for a moment, but then gave and I started falling. I pushed my shoulders and feet out to try and wedge myself against the sides. My vest snagged on a root and slowed my fall enough for me to grip the sides. I didn't know how long the root would hold, my legs would last, or how far I had to fall. I couldn't see much, didn't want to wiggle around. I whistled a signal—that movement almost dislodged me—and waited for help."

Marty nodded at my dad to pick up the story. My brother looked exhausted. He brought his elbow up on his knee and rested his chin in his hand. Detective Thomas shifted his stance toward my dad.

"I heard the whistle and followed the sound. I didn't have the direction nailed until he whistled a second time."

Marty's head snapped up. "I didn't whistle again. I told you, I almost lost my grip the first time. Couldn't risk it. I heard you whistle, but I was afraid to move."

"Marty, you're exhausted. You probably whistled by instinct and don't remember." I rubbed my hand up and down his arm and took his hand between mine. "All that 'be prepared' stuff kicked in."

"It wasn't me."

"Right now I'm more concerned with the events after you were rescued." He looked at my dad. He hadn't said it to be rude, but he didn't seem surprised at the disparity between their recollections. Almost as though he believed the instinct theory or maybe something else. His eyes had shifted to sweep the area when Marty had insisted he hadn't signaled twice.

"When I got close, I called out and Marty answered. He couldn't pull himself out because of his shoulder. I had a short rope in my pack and lowered it to him. I tied it to that tree," Dad pointed to an elm; the bark scraped where the rope had bitten. "He was able to get it under his arms and tie a knot. I couldn't raise him, but at least he wouldn't fall. With that security, he started working his way up inch by inch. I used the tree to wind the slack and keep the line taut. I felt as relieved as I did at his birth when he rolled out of that hole."

Marty and I burst into laughter at my father's analogy. My outburst disturbed Elmo and his head stretched out of the tote. I scratched his ears to keep him quiet. Detective Thomas took notice of him, but didn't comment. Marty smiled at the little fur ball and stretched out his fingers.

"When did you notice the body?" The question stopped the grins and tickles.

"Afterwards. I signaled Grace 'all okay.' I immobilized his shoulder as best I could. Marty seemed a little dizzy and I wanted him to rest for a few minutes before we started back to Grace. I wanted to move a few rocks and the remaining pieces of the cover around the path side of the hole to warn other hikers. Thought I'd let the Forest Preserve people know once I got him squared away. Anyway, while I was moving the rocks I wondered about how deep the shaft was and shined my light down the hole."

My father swallowed and cleared his throat. He looked pale, despite his olive skin tone. "That's when I saw the body, the feet at first, then the rest..." He swiped at his forehead with a handkerchief he pulled from his back pocket. "I ran out to the road and flagged down a car and told them to call the police. He had a car phone and pulled over to make the call. I came back to wait with Marty. I guess he directed you guys in. Why the sheriff's guys and not Chicago or the forest preserve?"

"This is unincorporated Norridge, it's Cook County's call."

I left Marty and moved next to my dad. He managed a smile and slipped his arm around my shoulders.

"Mrs. Marsden, you were not in this area, correct?"

"Yes. I waited on the path where they left me. I heard the 'back to camp' whistle, but I couldn't go back to the parking lot the way we'd come."

Detective Thomas's raised eyebrows balanced his broad forehead. I quickly explained the voices and then briefly explained the events of Sunday night.

"My God, Grace, I left you in the middle of all that. I thought you'd be safer there. I didn't know what Marty had gotten into." He tightened his grip around me. "Honey, I'm sorry."

"It's okay. You couldn't know."

"But I did know. I knew there were crazy bastards out here that night. Why'd I think they wouldn't be around during the day? I tore your husband a new one for doing the same thing." He lifted his arm from around me and clenched his hands at his sides.

"Let me get this straight." Detective Thomas closed his note-book and looked at Dad and me, but his sweeping gesture included Marty. "You all came here to find her keys. You," he pointed to Marty, "go exploring, while the two of you searched. Then you," finger back to Marty, "fall in the well and whistle for help." He stopped and considered something. "What's all this whistling? You have your own signals?"

"Scouting. We had a series of whistles when I was the scout-master for my sons' troop. It's easier than shouting. I taught all the boys to whistle. The one's who couldn't learn, carried a whistle."

Thomas accepted the information and continued looking at my dad. "You hear the whistle and take off telling her to stay put. You," pointing at me, "hear voices and the same name as the people who attacked you. The voices leave and you head out looking for them." He swept his hand to include Marty and Dad. "I don't know if one is connected to the other, but I don't believe in coincidence. Did the voices identify anyone else or someplace?"

I nodded excitedly. "Yes, they referred to someone named Q-tip"

"Like the cotton swab?"

"That's what it sounded like. And they mentioned Mr. Big. Said he may have arrived early."

"Sounds like your discovery and our arrival busted up an after school program." Detective Thomas snorted and shook his head.

"Couldn't help notice that big pile of brush." Dad pointed at a teepee type structure fifteen or twenty yards away from the well. "Maybe they were going to have a bonfire as part of their program."

"Nah, too close to the road. The forest preserve clears the dead branches and does a controlled burn. They get some high winds through here, tears up the trees."

"Makes sense, they're probably worried about 'widow makers'."

We all glanced up, looking for the loose dead branches.

"We got more trouble then dead trees in these woods; wish the city would clear cut and blacktop the whole damn thing," he mumbled. "Okay, thanks for your statements. Like I said, we have to do this at the station, but for now let me give you a ride back around to your vehicle." He pointed the way ahead of him. "I'll be right with you." Dad picked up his 'spotter' and Marty's 'tracker'. Our adventure seemed a million miles away. Thomas walked back to the area behind the yellow tape where two technicians still took pictures and measurements. I wondered if one of them would have to go down into the abandoned well to gather evidence. *Ugh. How awful.* I moved closer to my brother, thankful that he hadn't befallen the same fate as the person who'd walked over the well before him. *If that hiker fell in, who replaced the wooden cover? Maybe some other hiker spotted the danger and covered the well. They might not have looked down the well. Damn stupid to have a flimsy, half-rotted wooden cover over a well.* I tumbled the problem inside my head while we walked back, getting angry thinking about the carelessness of the Forest Preserve employees who'd leave a deadly hazard unmarked. I'd have to warn Will's troop. All those kids swarming around this area last week. I shivered when I thought of what might have happened.

"Are you cold, honey?" Dad was halfway out of his jacket.

"No. I was thinking about Will's troop out here. They might have been in this area. They all split up in twos to look for garbage. And then they all went to look at some rock."

"Not 'some rock,' Gracie. Chee Chee Pin Quay's memorial. We're almost on top of it." Within a few steps we rounded a slight turn in the path and I saw a huge boulder through the stark trees. Indeed a memorial. The granite loomed ahead, pushing up to the sky from the dead master it protected.

"Stand here and look straight back into the trees behind it. Legend says you can see the faces of his dead warriors standing guard."

I stared beyond the granite. The fact that those young boys had been this close to danger chilled me and I couldn't separate the wind swirling around me from the thoughts spiraling out of control in my mind. The wind through the trees pushed branch against branch, rubbing, scraping a low melody. *Chee Chee Pin Quay, Chee Chee Pin Quay.* I felt the words in my head; the low tom-tom setting the sequence, *Chee chee pin quay, Chee chee pin quay. Short, short, short, long.* The pulsating music jerked me forward closer to the granite I was compelled to touch. Three faces materialized in the barren branches. Haggard visages burdened with their eternal vow; no anger, no malice, only heavy sadness turning down the muscles at their eyes and mouths. I acknowledged their permission to touch. My hand stretched beyond the cuff and further. It grew longer. My feet rooted to the spot forcing my arm to catapult toward the stone. In a garbled moment, I saw them motion me forward and I knew if I touched the granite I'd be imprisoned with them for eternity. I watched as my hand, no longer following my will, stretched the final few inches. The faces grew animated; I was almost theirs.

"And this damn rock. Wish they'd smash it into a million pieces; sell 'em at the Trailside Museum. 'Get your che che pink eye rock. Watch it glow in the dark.' Only do it in your own damn homes!"

The detective's loud lament startled me. I prepared to explain my movements, only I had none. I realized I hadn't moved an inch since my dad had told me the legend and beyond that if Marty and Dad's calm faces were any indication, only a few seconds must have passed

"Sorry, Mrs. Marsden. Didn't mean to startle you. I get pissed every time I think of all the people that sneak out here after the park closes to have some 'experience' with this jack-ass Indian and his henchmen."

So much for cultural and historical appreciation.

"We can't make a move to relocate the rock that some preserva-tion do-gooder doesn't get an injunction. The forest preserve couldn't even clear away the foundation from this guy's house when it burned in the seventies, some kind of historical marker." He jerked his thumb back the way we'd come. "Every nutcase that starts something in these woods makes a damn pilgrimage to that rubble and this rock." Detective Thomas stopped talking, but his lips still twitched and pushed against each other trying to help their owner keep his own counsel.

The ride to Marty's vehicle took less than five minutes. Detec-tive Thomas gave cards to Dad and Marty asking them to come in tomorrow morning to give their statements. "If you remember any-thing else, call me at that number."

No card for me? What am I, chopped liver? What am I? First I see ghosts, then my arm does a Stretch Armstrong, and then it's all in my head. Of course it's in my head; whose head would it be in? I wondered what other people thought about, if they argued with them-selves. The revelation after my first psychology class in high school that most people weren't wound the way I was, turned to fear at times that I wouldn't be able to keep it together and I would unravel like a frayed rope. Like now.

What happened back there? A fugue state lasting seconds? My head hurt, again. In the last few days I've suffered from more headaches than I have in a year. Dad drove and Marty and I were in the back seat. Marty's eyes were closed, but I noticed his cheek twitch and I wondered if the Vicodin had worn off. I wanted to ask Dad if he was taking Marty to Elmhurst Memorial.

I woke up when the car stopped. I had fallen asleep leaning against Marty with Elmo in the tote bag between us. Like when we were kids on a trip. My other siblings teased us about how quickly we'd conk out. Before we backed out of the driveway was an exaggeration, but before we reached the Eisenhower Expressway was plausible. I found the movement and internal sound mesmerizing. Marty never napped; that was his excuse.

We walked into emergency hoping to find Tracy on duty. She stood next to the idle triage nurse discussing some papers in her hand. The triage nurse looked up first.

"Can I help…"

"Hey good lookin' we need–"

Marty chose that moment to slump against me and interrupt Dad's usual greeting to Tracy. I half held half lowered him to the floor.

The triage nurse swung into action right behind Tracy. I moved back and gently pulled at Dad to do the same. He shook off my touch, but then moved when more personnel came to help.

They lifted Marty to a gurney and started to wheel him away. Tracy motioned and we looked where she pointed. Marty's eyes opened. His weak smile gave us some assurance.

We started forward and Tracy stopped us. "Let me take a look at him and then have Doc tell me I'm right." She smiled and winked. "I'll take the best care of him, Mike."

"I know you will, honey. It's just he's my baby."

I knew if Marty heard that he would have passed out again, from sheer embarrassment. I handed the tote to my dad. "Here, watch your grandson while I find us some coffee. I'd never know that unshakable bond between parent and child. I understood better today that it never lessened; ten years old or twenty-eight. A lifetime.

⤳ 18 ⤳

Tracy sat next to my dad, pointing to some papers on her clip-board. I put the coffees down on the table between us.

"Do you have any idea how to reach Eve?"

"Eve?" The worst case leapt to mind. "What's wrong with Marty?"

Tracy's smile calmed me. "Marty's going to be fine. We re-located his shoulder and treated the deeper cuts on his face. It's his insurance that coded."

"I don't understand. Marty has insurance up the ying-yang. Glenn sold it to him." My younger, but not youngest brother, Glenn, sold insurance. "He wouldn't let Marty be uninsured; heck he won't let any of us be underinsured. We have to sit through a review every spring; he's more reliable than those swallows in Capistrano."

"Marty doesn't have his card with him and seemed vague about his carrier. I thought maybe Eve could give us the information, but your dad said she's out of town with Katie at a cheerleading competition."

"Can I write you a check?" I fumbled through my fanny pack realizing I hadn't packed my checkbook. "How about seventeen dollars and fifty-two cents?" I grinned at Tracy.

"Don't worry, we're not going to dislocate his shoulder and swab up the antiseptic. Services rendered, payment required." She shrugged. "We'll keep him until you pay up."

"Sounds good to me. Make him wear one of those gowns with no back." We burst into laughter at our plans for Marty. Dad didn't laugh or even smile.

"Can I get him?"

"Mike, he's fine. He's getting dressed, he'll be right out."

Dad stood and picked up one of the Styrofoam cups. "Thanks honey." He handed me the tote and walked toward the patient area.

"Is that who I think it is?" She pointed at the lumpy canvas bag.

"What was I supposed to do, leave him in the car?"

"Okay, never mind that. I'll make this fast. When we removed Marty's vest, some packets fell out from one of the torn pockets. I picked them up and looked inside. I could identify six of the eight different pills. They're all heavy hitters, the tamest being Vicodin."

"What are you saying?"

"I'm not saying. I'm wondering. His pupils weren't normal, Grace."

"He said he'd taken Vicodin for the pain."

"Vicodin wouldn't affect him that way."

"This is ridiculous. Marty's not some druggie." I felt the heat flush my face and I knew my eyes gleamed purple.

"Grace, relax. I didn't say that. It's just that sometimes people with access to the candy store don't realize how dependent they've become on modern science. It happens with doctors and nurses more than you'd want to know."

I knew Tracy had my best interest, the entire Morelli family's best interest at heart. I'd met Tracy my freshman year at Regina College and we'd become fast friends. She'd been part of the extended *famiglia* for over almost fifteen years, attending weddings, baby showers, birthday parties, and funerals at my side. What she was suggesting wasn't possible.

Dad and Marty came out from behind the wide metal door. My brother's face had a bit of gauze on his left cheek and his right arm rested at a ninety-degree angle in a low sling. His hair bore no leaf remnants. He looked better than when he walked in.

"Hey, little brother. Why so dramatic?" I soft punched his good arm and stared at his face, especially his eyes. They appeared clear. Tracy over reacted, occupational hazard.

"I needed a big finish to our day." He grinned and winced. "Ow, remind me not to laugh."

"I don't see the humor in that, Martin." Dad only used full names or middle names when upset. "You didn't see that body, all twisted, bent all wrong..." He looked from one child to the other. "You didn't see."

"Sorry, Dad. I wasn't thinking. It's not funny. I guess I'm avoiding thinking about how close...well, you know."

"I know. That's all I've been thinking about. It could have been you down there." Tears filled my father's eyes and he carefully put his arms around his son. Marty stood in his embrace and patted his back with his free hand. Dad's shoulders lifted and fell in silent tears.

Tracy looked at me for an answer. She hadn't heard the entire story, only that Marty had fallen. She didn't know about the abandoned well or the dead hiker. "I'll call you later." I turned my attention to Dad who'd stepped away from Marty. "C'mon, Dad, let's get him home. You drive us to your house and I'll follow you to Marty's house and then I'll drive you back home."

"I'm fine. I can drive myself home. No need for both of you to—"

Dad's hand shot up in a 'halt' position. "I'm taking you home and spending the night. Grace is going home from my house."

"Dad that's not necessary."

"I don't mind following you and bringing you home."

"You two aren't listening. I'm taking him home and spending the night. You're going home and calling me at his house when you get there. *Capisch?*" He also meant business when he did his Italian thing.

I nodded my head. "I understand."

The trip from Elmhurst to Berkeley took ten minutes. I'd traveled this route at least a thousand times during my childhood coming back from the York Theater, the YMCA, or Hamburger Heaven.

Dad left the car running and ducked into the house to get his ditty bag and clean underwear. I followed him in to use the bathroom.

"Call me when you get home, okay." We'd walked out together. I'd been looking straight ahead and noticed Marty putting something in his mouth and swallowing. *I could have brought him some water. Why would he dry swallow pills? Cause he didn't want us to know. Know what?* I shook my head to vacate Tracy's accusation.

"Okay, Grace?" Dad stopped and reached out for my arm.

"Oh, sure, yes. I'll call." I gave him a quick kiss and walked to the passenger side window. In a soft voice I asked, "What did you just take?"

Marty narrowed his eyes and looked away.

"I saw you swallow something."

My dad climbed in and waved me away. "Say goodnight, Gracie." He chuckled at the family joke.

I stepped back, watching Marty's profile. Dad pulled out of the driveway still smiling. His mood had lifted considerably; mine had deteriorated.

"Goodnight, Gracie," I mumbled.

Harry's car was in the garage when I pulled in. I'd sat in Dad's driveway and fed Elmo. While he nursed at the nipple, I thought about my encounter with Marty. *Why wouldn't he answer me? Could Tracy's assessment be right? He was my brother first and deserved the benefit of the doubt. I never would have thought twice about what I saw today in the driveway. Guess that's how things happen. Don't notice, don't want to notice.*

I sat thinking, long after Elmo finished, so long that now I rushed into the house to make that phone call. Harry looked up and smiled. "She just walked in, Mike." He handed the phone to me and took Elmo out of the tote. My conversation was minimal.

"Mm hmm. I know. Sorry. I fed Elmo before I left. Mm hmm. Love you too, bye, Dad."

I rolled my eyes. "I'm thirty-two years old. When won't I feel like a little kid getting yelled at?" The rhetorical question hung between us; the answer was never.

"Your dad and I had quite a chat. He told me what happened. He also apologized."

"Apologized?"

"Apparently, he left you alone to go help your brother. He thought you'd be safer on your own with a metal detector and a kitten for protection rather than accompanying him."

Harry's voice sounded a shade too tense. I sensed trouble.

"At least you're both even." Stupid is as stupid does, and my glib observation, intended to lighten the mood, instead stirred the pot.

"No, we're not even. I had no idea you were in any sort of danger when I gave Kramer the keys and chose to stay with Will who was hurting. Your father damn well knew what could be out there and he left you."

"It wasn't like that. It was daylight; there'd been other hikers, families in the area."

"Wasn't like that? Then why were the same people who attacked you out there yards from you. It's only through God's grace that they left when they did."

"Oh my gosh, it wasn't just God's grace, Harry. The whistle, the signal, they knew it. He said, 'back to camp' when he heard it. I have to call that detective."

"What whistle? You're not making sense."

"Dad taught all the scouts whistles and signals for when they were out camping. Today, those boys recognized the whistles. I'm sure of it. But Dad hasn't been in scouting for years. Where would they have learned them?"

"The same place your dad did." Harry reached for the phone. "What's Marty's number?"

I rattled off the digits and waited as he dialed. "Marty, it's Harry. Can I have a minute with your dad? Thanks." He covered the receiver. "He's making Manicotti, enough for an army Marty says.

Sorry to bother you, Mike. Grace was explaining the whistles, said you started that in scouts during your term as scoutmaster. Had you done that before, in service or before?"

"Why do you ask, thinking of starting your own troop?"

"Not hardly, but I'll be taking Will out of his if what I suspect is correct. When did you first use those whistles?"

"We used whistles in my first scout troop, you know, Bantonini's. That was the only good thing I learned. We had only three whistles then, I added three more when I taught my boys."

"Which three did you start with, Mike?"

My stomach lurched. I knew the answer.

"Help, all okay, and return to camp. What's going on?"

"Give me the number for that detective, would you, Mike? I think Grace needs to talk to him. If he thinks it means anything I'll call you back." Harry waited and then scribbled down a number. He hung up without saying goodbye, a breach of Harry's good manners. He still rankled at my dad's choice.

"Your father learned those whistles from his scout days in Troop 265. Right after you call that detective, I'm calling Lily. Will's not attending another meeting in that troop."

"You think boy scouts attacked me? Harry, think about what you're saying. Those creeps are some kind of a satanic cult or gang. They're not boy scouts."

"They're in the same woods as Bantonini, they know his father's signals, it fits."

"It fits, because you're forcing it. Because Bantonini's troop camps and works in the woods, anyone could hear the whistles and figure it out. Or ask. Or maybe scouts who dropped out or scouts from previous years. I'll bet you Ric knows those whistles." I hadn't meant to throw that out there. When would my brain work faster than my mouth?

"Kramer? Why would he…" I saw the connection snap into place in his eyes. "He persuaded Lily to put Will in that troop. I didn't understand. Thought she wanted a reason to keep him away from me all week. We've proper schools out here, but she insisted on St. Edgar's. Kramer went there didn't he? He keeps after you and now he's zeroing in on Will. He sees him more than I do. He's not pulling Will away. Why can't he be satisfied with Lily or Royal for that matter?"

The ear-splitting smile I wanted to display struggled to remain a feeling. *Harry doesn't care if Ric loves Lily or wants Lily, because Harry doesn't.* The excitement I felt at this backhanded reassurance of my husband's love threatened to bubble out of me. I grabbed the yarn on my belt loop and rolled the rough cord between my thumb and forefinger. I waited to hear more blissful triumph over Lily. I never saw it coming.

"And you knew, all along you knew Kramer finagled this move. Everyone must know, everyone except me. Well, I'm the horse's arse aren't I? Did you think if Will lived in Oak Park during the week I'd stay put each night and wait for the weekend? Do you not understand I want us to be a family? This isn't an either, or. Don't ever force a choice, Gracie."

Harry's words stung. I watched him leave through a blur of tears. I heard the powerful roar of the Jaguar speeding out of the garage and listened until the low whine whispered into the night. Tears streamed down my face. "I want to be a family," I called to the closed door. "I do."

The evening dragged past ten o'clock and Harry hadn't returned. He'd probably spend the night on Lily's couch. I could only hope. I'd fed Elmo his first solid food and snapped a photo of him with bits of mush on his nose. One of my shower gifts had been a small photo album with the pewter outline of a kitty on the front.

I'd called Detective Thomas and left a message that I'd remembered something. I wondered if they'd identified the hiker, contacted the next of kin.

April and Cash fussed over me when I showed up with treats and a curry brush. The time I spent diligently brushing their coats left them gleaming and me sweating. It felt good to work out kinks, both external and internal.

I found Elmo conked out in his litter box. That wasn't good. I lifted him and placed him in his cute bed. Hoped he wasn't confused about his bed and toilet. I pulled myself up the stairs, my steps like lead, but not from fatigue. I'd watched my mother suffer in the clutches of depression. My biggest fear was that it was in my genes. I'd once overhead some relatives talking at an older cousin's baby shower. I was eleven at the time. "She's sweet, nice girl but like her mother, she's not always in the here and now, know what I mean? Like she's sleepwalking or something." My only defense had come from my Aunt Mary. "She's a dreamer, that's all. Nothing wrong with that. You gotta have your dreams, Minnie." To which my oldest aunt had answered, "Dreams don't fill their bellies or wash up dishes." They cackled like chickens as they moved away to fill bellies and wash dishes.

I wondered if the 'sleepwalking' they'd noticed would turn to the same demon my mother struggled with for most of her adult life.

The noise of the overhead door chased away my gloomy thoughts. I'd been going through the motions of getting ready for bed. Suddenly, I was afraid to confront Harry. *What if he's still upset? Maybe he made a decision about where he'll live. Don't think stupid. He lives here.*

I couldn't bear another argument. I slipped into bed and tried to slow my breathing. My heart pounded in my head renewing the nagging headache I'd had since Sunday night.

Think of cotton balls scattered on a counter. Pick them up one at a time and blow the dust off then put them in the box. Pick up, blow, put down. Pick up, blow, put down. Pick up, blow, put down.

My mental pattern worked and I grew drowsy. Harry entered our room. He leaned over me and brushed a kiss across my cheek. "Sweet dreams, Gracie."

I drifted away from his scent and touch. It was safer that way, easier.

It could have been a minute, or an hour later, when the phone rang. I felt the pull of deep slumber loosening its grip as my mind struggled to come to terms with the *jangle* four feet across the bed.

I looked at the clock next to the suddenly still instrument. *10:53. I'd barely slept at all.* Harry must have answered downstairs. I closed my eyes. It hadn't been our private line, so it wasn't family. The rest of the world could wait until morning.

"Gracie, wake up." Harry's gentle tone and touch on my cheek woke me a second time in as many minutes. He leaned over and kissed my forehead. "C'mon, sleepyhead. I have to talk to you."

Hmm. That can't be good. He doesn't sound tense. That's good. But he's waking me up. That's not good.

"Gracie, Detective Thomas returned your call. He wants to talk to you."

I jerked up and glanced at the phone, reaching for it over Harry's pillow.

"Sweetheart, slow down. I told him you were asleep, but I told him why you called. He's driving out to talk with you. Apparently things have come up and he'd like to talk to you as quickly as possible."

Things have come up? Definitely not good.

I swung my legs out of bed and retrieved my Army pants from the floor. I'd planned on wearing them to do barn chores in the morning. I sniff tested the turtleneck and pulled it over my head.

Harry eyed my ensemble. "He won't be here for twenty minutes, no need to rush."

After ten years of marriage, I was still learning 'Harryspeak.' I think this meant, 'Gee, you look a mess and your outfit looks worse.'

"Right. Uh, why don't you make some coffee while I change."

"Capital idea. I'll put on the kettle too; he might prefer tea."

Always searching for the male tea drinkers in this country. A futile mission, but hope springs eternal. I smiled at the thought and suddenly felt guilty for avoiding him earlier. Another item for my discussion with Cassidy.

Within minutes, I luxuriated under hot water pulsating through the number four setting of my *MassageMagic* showerhead. *Hmm, heaven.* I stood under the staccato stream, letting the pressure work out kinks in my muscles. I closed my eyes and let my thoughts scatter. A kaleidoscope of colors drifted across the inside of my lids.

Yeow! I slammed the knob off.

Harry must have flushed the powder room toilet and sent the scalding water up through my tap. A moment later, he opened the shower door and cool air scurried in to mix with the steam. "You've been in here for ten minutes. Thought I'd be a considerate bloke and bring you a coffee."

"You flushed and darn near steamed me."

"Sorry, thought you would have been out by now. Long as I'm here though, can I hang my suit in there, needs a steam."

My husband's dry sense of humor and understatement was one of the things that attracted me to him. The other things were staring me in the face, cornflower blue eyes, great smile, slight cleft in a strong, sexy chin. Taking inventory stirred feelings. I slid the door further on the track. Harry's eyes widened briefly, then narrowed into the sexy slits they did when he became aroused. He moved toward me and I thought he meant to join me. Instead, he pulled me against him and lifted me out of the enclosure. My wet body soaked his shirt and pants. He grabbed a towel and held it against me vertically from my shoulders down. I kept my arms around his neck while he carried me in this fashion into the bedroom.

"Harry, now?"

"Exactly."

"No, I mean what about the detective?"

He lowered his lips over my mouth.

I spoke again when his lips left mine. "What about your suit? You're losing steam."

"Hardly." Harry's husky voice thrilled me.

"What about my coffee? It'll get cold?"

"Too late, it's cold. I'm not." His mouth stopped my response. The doorbell chimes stopped his. "Bloody, hell. A punctual copper? He sighed and kissed the tip of my nose. "All right, I'll go meet him, give you a few minutes to cover up." His eyes toured my body. "Bloody shame."

The chimes sounded again. The usually light five-note tone sounded dirge-like to my ears. A short in the wires, an omen? *Geez, it's a doorbell. Get dressed.*

❧ 19 ❧

I found Detective Thomas and Harry seated in the kitchen. I noticed the teapot on the table between them. I smiled and shook hands with him when he stood.

"Thank you for seeing me so late at night. Things have taken a turn and I felt it necessary to talk with you immediately."

Harry had filled my angel mug and placed it on the table. I sat at that place and slipped both hands around the mug, grounding myself for his news.

"I'm surprised. I mean I didn't think an accident investigation would go on through the night. Not that it's not important," I added.

"An accident wouldn't, but homicide keeps no clock."

"Homicide? This afternoon you called it a terrible accident. Now it's a homicide?" My voice level rose in accordance with the panic I felt.

"Actually, Mrs. Marsden what I said was that your brother had avoided a terrible accident."

"Right, he avoided it, but the hiker didn't. Terrible accident." It made sense to me and Harry had had ten years to sort through my logic, but the detective looked confused.

He sipped at his tea then cleared his throat. "The medical examiner's preliminary report is what we base our call on." He squared his shoulders. "Signs on the body and around the site indicate something other than an accident." In the same precise tone and without missing a beat his asked, "Mrs. Marsden, what was the nature of your meeting with Janet Henry on Monday?"

"My meeting with Janet? What's that got to do…Oh no. Oh, God. Janet?" My hands jerked from around the mug sending coffee over the top. I covered my face pressing my fingertips into my forehead and my thumbs under my cheekbones to short-circuit the tears building behind the shock wave in my head.

Harry stood and slipped his arms around me. I heard his voice over the one crying in my head. "Nice touch, Thomas. Bloody hell, why didn't you just slap her?"

"I'm sorry. I thought it was just an appointment."

"It was an appointment for a job as Janet's assistant. Grace has known Janet since she attended Regina."

"I apologize, Mrs. Marsden, but I still have to get some answers. Can you compose yourself?"

I nodded and took a deep breath. Harry gave me a quick squeeze and moved away. He turned on the faucet and filled a glass for me. Detective Thomas used his napkin to mop up the coffee I'd spilled. Harry replaced my mug with the water glass. "Drink some of this."

I sipped at the water and tried to absorb the enormity of what I'd been told. *Oh, no. Not now.* The sipping triggered a compulsion to perform a pattern. *Sip, sip, grip. Sip, sip, grip.* I *had* to do this until the water was gone. Thank goodness Harry had used a rocks glass and not a tumbler. My hand alternately tightened and loosened around the glass as I worked my way through the liquid.

I'd seen Harry motion Detective Thomas to wait. Running interference for me.

I settled the empty glass on the table and placed my hands palms down on the oak surface. "My appointment was at ten o'clock. We had a great meeting. I got the job. We were making small talk, I'd told her about my bad experience in the woods—"

"With your father and brother? That hadn't happened." He fixed me with a 'what kind of crap is this' look. I hurried to recap Sunday night.

"It was after that she became agitated."

"I checked for anything in the woods and didn't see this on the sheets. Did you file a report?"

The situation became complicated. "Ah, I, well, I did speak to another detective. Well, he's not a detective now, but he was at the woods."

"He saw the attack?"

"No, he picked me up because I lost my keys when Matt chased after the light."

"What light? Who is Matt?"

Oh, Lord. How did this become so embroiled? I looked at Harry for a lifeline.

"Detective, my wife's best friend's brother is Ric Kramer." Thomas's eyes registered recognition. "By an odd coincidence my wife was in the woods showing two young boys where Troop 265 had found the old munitions crate." Harry stopped and waited when Thomas's head snapped up.

"Munitions crate? Don't suppose anyone reported that."

"Maybe Bantonini, the scout master."

Thomas waved his hand, "Go on, I'll sort this out later, but I don't believe in coincidence."

"Yes, well she lost her keys. Kramer went to check on them. His Porsche could only hold the two small boys so he left Grace to wait in the Jag which he'd unlocked using that slide bar you all carry."

Thomas's eyebrows had lifted at the mention of the cars but now narrowed at Harry's last comment.

"We assumed," Harry waved his hand back and forth between us, "that Kramer filed a report. Apparently, we assumed incorrectly." Harry shrugged his shoulders, effectively dumping the mess in Ric's lap.

"Kramer, eh. Yeah, I know Kramer; we worked a few cases from both sides of the street. By the book unless it didn't suit him. But he always landed on his feet, smelling like a rose." Thomas seemed to reflect on his comments. "He's not a cop now, went to the P.I. side I heard. No roses this time."

His smile left no doubt about his feelings. Anger replaced shock. His rush to investigate stalled with the realization that he might be able to take Ric down a peg, or maybe more. I knew Ric was waiting for a medical release to get back on the force. He'd never had the heart of a private investigator. This man in my kitchen could scuttle Ric's shot at returning.

"You were asking about my meeting? There is something odd that happened." *That got his attention.* After I told Janet what happened to me and about the crate, she became visibly upset. I thought she'd become ill, she looked shaken and pale. She jumped up, mumbled something about an appointment she'd forgotten and rushed out of the room asking me to tell the switchboard she wouldn't be back." I choked on the last word realizing its meaning.

"Did she tell you who she had to meet?"

"No, in fact, I think she made that up. The more I thought about it, I don't think there was an appointment. Janet is extremely organized. She wouldn't schedule appointments that close. She's..." I stopped when I realized I'd referred to her in the present. The burn at the back of my eyes wouldn't be denied this time. I jammed the palms of my hands over my eyes, but tears slipped under and around.

"Detective, how did you know my wife had an appointment with Janet?"

"Once we identified her we went to her home and then to Regina. She had your wife's name on her calendar."

"Was there another appointment at ten-thirty?"

"Nothing after that. Only notation was a trustee meeting at seven that night. We're trying to find out if she attended that."

I blew my nose and crumpled the napkin into my pocket. "She wouldn't have been attending, just noting the meeting to follow up the next day to see if there was any noteworthy alumni news."

"If that's the case, Mrs. Marsden, right now you're the last person to see her alive. She lived with her mother, who's in Florida, not due back until Thanksgiving. We checked the house. Can you describe what she was wearing that day?"

I closed my eyes and conjured the vision. I looked at Thomas and rattled off the ensemble. He nodded his head as he wrote. "Yep. We found that outfit in the bedroom. Looks like she came home and changed into jeans and hiking boots."

"Why couldn't it have been an accident? I go riding or walking all the time to work out problems. Maybe that's what Janet did. She could have been preoccupied with her thoughts, not watching where she was walking."

"All I can tell you is that the examination of the body leads us to suspect foul play. I'm sorry I can't say more." His tone and the set of his jaw echoed his words. He flipped back a few pages and changed gears. "I'd like to ask you a few questions about your encounter in the woods. Your husband told me what you remembered. I'd like to hear it in your words."

"It didn't register that they were responding to the same signals as I was. They reacted to both of them immediately. When they left to 'return to camp' they went off in the direction where I found my father and brother. I didn't realize it at the time because I was a little turned around. Could that area be their 'camp'?"

"That area has been a pain in law enforcement's neck since the cops used to shag me and my friends out of there." He smiled for the first time since he'd arrived. "Only then it was drinking parties and a lot of making out. In the last twenty years, it's become a haven for freaks and criminals; drug dealing, rape, satanic shit, and the occasional dumped body." He stopped abruptly and shook his head. "Rips up my stomach when I think of what goes on out there."

"Why in God's name do they let the troop take kids in there?" Harry voice rose in concern.

"It's tradition with that troop. They do it on a Sunday afternoon like that's supposed to be a 'free' day from crime. Troop 16 in Oak Park does a similar clean-up, but they've staked out the woods near the Trailside Museum, much safer." He closed the notebook. "Thank you for the call." He held up the notebook. "This will help."

"I'll show you out, Detective."

I listened to their voices in the hall until I couldn't distinguish the words. When Harry returned, he poured himself more tea. He sipped thoughtfully before he spoke. "Gracie, I want to apologize for my outburst earlier. I know you were in a touchy spot. It was incumbent on Lily to reveal the connection. I'm deeply sorry. You've been through a rough week and I'm the horse's arse that's making it rougher. Forgive me?"

"I wasn't throwing rocks at you upstairs, was I?"

"That was different." He smiled knowing he'd activated the 'gender gap' mode.

"Only for guys. For women, agreeing to sex is agreeing to kiss and make up, or out, in this case."

"Speaking of that case," he exaggerated wiggling his eyebrows, "could we possibly get back to it?"

"Possibly." The phone rang. "But probably not." I checked the caller I.D. It was my brother Marty or maybe Dad checking in on me.

"Hello."

"Hi, sweetie. I knew you'd be up; that detective just called me to verify what you told him. Marty and I are going to the police station tomorrow to go over everything again since they suspect, well you know. He said you knew her from Regina. I'm sorry, Grace."

"Thanks. It was Janet Henry the director of alumni events. She hired me as her assistant."

"Did you say 'Henry'? Was that her married name?"

"No, Janet was single. Why?"

"Her name is the same as the kid in troop 265 when I was in that troop."

"She never talked about a brother. Just her mom. Her dad died when she was a baby."

"Gracie, that's the dad I told you about. He left the campout and got hit crossing the street."

"Bizarre. What a coincidence." Thomas's words, *I don't believe in coincidence* rang in my ears.

"Do you want to come with us? We could meet for breakfast first?"

Everything in the Morelli family revolved around food. Dad had probably already cooked some meals for Marty to enjoy until Eve returned. He should have been a chef. *What the heck, police station, shopping, therapist, typical day.* The scary truth was that in the last year I'd spent too much time at police stations.

"Sure, Dad, where do you want to meet?" Harry heard my question and motioned that he wanted to join us. "The Paddle Wheel at nine? Okay, Harry's coming, too. 'Bye, love you."

"Afraid he'd say no?"

"No, of course not. Just didn't want to keep talking. I'm tired." My head ached again, or maybe it had never stopped and I was just noticing it again. "Oh, we have to go in separate cars. I'm going to do some shopping in Oak Park."

"I'll join you. We can stop in on Hanns and the babies."

Why did the simplest event become complicated? *Because you're attempting to deceive. 'Ah, what tangled webs we weave when first we practice to deceive.' Better close your eyes before you speak.* I knew I was tired and vaguely suspected I was nuts when I quoted poetry to myself.

"I'm meeting a friend, lunch and shopping." I busied myself at the sink, cleaning up the kitchen trying to keep my tone offhand.

"Anyone one I know?" Harry's voice sounded close.

"Uh, no, I mean I don't think so." The angel mug nearly slipped from between my soapy hands.

Harry stood next to me and waited for me to look at him. I hoped my eyes wouldn't expose my lies. I looked up into his face.

"If you didn't want me along, Grace, you only had to tell me." He left the kitchen and went out through the mudroom.

Why couldn't I admit I was seeing a therapist? People did it all the time. Who knows what he's thinking. What would I suspect if he'd lied to me? I should tell him. We vowed for better or worse. Better or worse, not Will.

He'd probably go out to the barn and check on the horses, walk around the house and give me time to get into bed and pretend I slept when he came up.

I lay awake, tormented by a pounding headache and thoughts of inherited mania.

When Harry came up, he undressed in the dark and came quietly to bed.

⮞ 20 ⮜

I begged off walking with Barb. She looked disappointed when I met her at my back door wearing a blanket around my nightgown.

"Whoa, you look beat. What's wrong?"

"Can't shake this awful headache. Didn't sleep well. I should have called you last night; I felt crummy then."

"That's okay. I'll use the time to record my sightings, maybe make a few more."

Barb, an avid birder, filled journals with sightings of her back-yard visitors. She supported as many birds as Harry did with the variety of feeders on her turf. Her disappointment seemed to lift with her new plan. We had agreed to always follow the buddy system and never walk alone.

"All right. I'll just eat those Raspberry bars from Joyful's all by myself." Her smile, so genuine, lifted my mood.

"Sure, then we'll have to walk twice as far tomorrow." Barb had no threat from extra calories. Her lean frame defied her caloric intake.

"Grace, do you want me to ask Devin to stop by the barn; give you a chance to sleep in?"

"No, I'll be fine. Just not up to a power walk."

"Okay, see you tomorrow."

My head didn't hurt that much; I didn't want to be cheery and Barb above all else is cheery. I usually love her company; I certainly wasn't enjoying mine. I watched her walk away then replaced my blanket with an old ski jacket I kept in the mudroom. I filled the pockets with treats and pulled on my wellies. What a sight I made; unruly hair, electric purple jacket patched with duct tape, pink flannel tea length nightgown with ruffle, and olive green rubber boots.

Here she comes, Miss America. Here she comes, your ideal. I hummed the Bert Parks version as I walked toward the barn. April and Cash loved the look, the pockets bulging with baby carrots and yummy pellets. I was a hit with them. Thirty minutes later, I turned them out into the corral. "Bye, beauties. I'll be back later."

Now to find my newest four footed dependant. Elmo walked quite capably now and no longer needed to be toted; a good thing since the baby food and formula had added several pounds to his frame. He looked chunky and healthy now.

I dumped my jacket on the bench and kicked the wellies into a corner. Where was that little scamp? By this time he should have been chewing at the bottom of my nightgown, leaving a rip to match the one from yesterday. I slipped my feet into furry slippers that had they been orange would have looked like Elmo's kin.

"Hey, baby boy, where are you? Mommy's got a treat."

I hadn't thought about how my singsong baby talk sounded until I realized that I wasn't alone when I walked into the kitchen. Harry sat in his usual spot in the nook, with Elmo seated on the newspaper on the table looking out the window at the black capped chickadees eagerly plucking seeds from the Yankee Droll. Harry's hands were on either side of the orange fluff and he leaned near his pointy ears. "Mustn't chase those or the Cardinals I showed you. You can have the Starlings, nasty birds, they're all for you."

What normally would have been a great photo op tore at my heart. Elmo liked him better, I knew it. I saved him, I nursed him, but Elmo seemed to seek out Harry. *Grace, get a grip. The cat's been in a tote bag since you rescued him. Hardly able to choose.* That's right, Harry held him on the table.

I dropped the baby talk but tapped my fingers together like I had a treat. Not even a good morning to my husband I spoke to the cat. "There you are. Come here little guy."

"Good morning. Your coffee's made. I was attempting to teach Ort which birds he should eat. I think he's got it."

Gracie, what's wrong with you? You've a fabulous husband playing Pygmalion with this precious kitty and you're choking inside. Braid, baby, braid. Don't talk 'til you soothe those rough edges.

I ignored his greeting and poured a cup of coffee. Even my favorite aroma, Cinnamon Nut Swirl, did nothing to quell the unease inside me. I couldn't focus on Harry, only the kitten he held. Suddenly, that kitten's acceptance of me meant everything.

"Let him go."

Harry looked at me in surprise. "Say again, darling?"

I hated that expression. Didn't know I did until just then.

"Let...him...go."

"Gracie, what's gotten into you? Last night I knew you were tired, that your head hurt. This morning, you're acting like I don't exist." His voice, pitched low and calm, should have soothed me. It jangled in my head. My fingers twitched with need. I felt an urge to throw the cup in my hand across the room at Harry's head. His eyes never wavered from mine. I closed my eyes and inhaled and exhaled a few deep breaths. I opened my eyes. "Let him go."

He lowered his hands from the furry body, never taking his eyes off mine. His hands lay flat on the table next to newspaper.

"Come here, baby boy." My voice sounded strained. Elmo's amber eyes blinked and his tiny mouth yawned. His front legs curled under him as he lowered himself into curve, nose touching tail tip.

"Elmo, come here. I've got a treat." I heard the panic in my voice. So did Harry. I saw his left hand nudge the contented fur ball. "Elmo, come here, kitty." The amber eyes stayed closed.

"Grace, cats don't come when you call them."

Somewhere I knew that, but I didn't want knowledge, I wanted unconditional love from that tiny creature. I knew the signs of the anger building. I put down the mug and left the kitchen.

"Gracie, Ort's a cat not a dog. Gracie, please." I heard the scrape of the chair and knew he'd come after me. He took my arm at the bottom of the staircase. "Darling, talk to me. Please." His voice caught in his throat. "Please."

I couldn't look at him. "His name's not Ort." I shook off his hand and ran up the stairs to our room. *I hate that nickname, Ort, a tiny bit of food. Dry humor nothing, that's plain dark.* My solace could have been April. A fast ride atop her back almost always cleared the cobwebs and calmed me. I didn't want to bother. I turned the shower on hot, removed my clothes, and stepped under the stream before it had time to heat. The cold shock invigorated my body. I turned the dial to blue when I felt the water begin to warm. I pushed the various bottles off the built in shower seat and positioned the showerhead to spray my head and shoulders. The numbing effect of the cold water pleased me. I idly sat and used my toes to pick out the bottles I'd carelessly dumped, lifting them up to my hands and lining them up next to me. I covered the drain with my feet and waited for the water to rise then I moved my feet and watched the whirlpool. *Swirl away Gracie. Swirl away problems.* My nails looked blue through the clear polish. *Swirl away Gracie. Swirl away problems.* My toes looked larger under the water. *Would I be larger under the water? Larger than life? Larger than death?*

An annoying tapping intruded on my thoughts. *Can't he just leave me alone?* I lifted my head and the tapping grew louder. *Cripes, my teeth. Hold on there, pearly whites.* An ugly braying noise reached my ears above the pelting water. I slapped my hands over my ears but the noise grew louder.

"Gracie!" Harry's voice bellowed over the sound filling my head. *Thunk.* The water stopped and air swooped in from the wide open door to cover me. He lifted me out of the shower and rushed me into the bedroom where he not so gently dropped me on the bed and immediately rolled me into the comforter. He pulled the pillowcase from one of our pillows and wrapped that around my sopping hair.

I felt the shudders racing between my shoulders and knees. The horrible braying had stopped, replaced by quiet sobs and the chatter of enamel on enamel. Harry was all over me, rubbing my body through the heavy material. He rubbed briskly, warming me through his efforts. I felt him remove the wet pillowcase and replace it with a dry one. Would I be a three-pillowcase head? We had only four on the bed. The sobbing stopped when my sense of humor returned. It was difficult for me to wisecrack and cry at the same time…opposite brain functions, I think. Harry must have felt my body relax. He rolled me out of the comforter like a tamale out of its husk and wrapped me in the dry flannel blanket. He continued to rub my back and use his body to warm mine.

My teeth stopped banging against each other and I relaxed in his arms. He pulled me up into a sitting position against the headboard. He plumped our bare pillows behind me and made certain the blanket remained tucked around me mummy fashion. Harry pulled the pillowcase from my hair and carried it into the bathroom. He returned with a hand towel and my hairdryer.

"Lean forward a bit." He sounded concerned, upset, I couldn't tell. Probably both. The hot air from the dryer felt heavenly. He started with the ends to stop the dripping. Firm squeezes with the towel soaked up the wet and then close up drying. The effects of drier hair warmed me immensely. I peeked at his face during his ministrations; a neutral mask. His eyes caught mine. Nothing neutral there. Brooding, maybe a touch of fear. *I did that. My nutcase personality. How could he want to stay? Why would he?*

The hum of the dryer turned to a droning in my head. Encouraged by the warmth, my body floated. *I should keep floating.*

The quiet caught my attention a moment before the *clink* of the cup on saucer or the aroma of spice tea hit my senses.

Harry hovered above me. He placed a tray over my legs. A small pot of tea, steeping perfectly, two slices of toast, light on the butter and heavy on the marmalade, cloth napkin, small juice, and small cat. Elmo sat on the tray, certainly a risky position next to the dainty teapot. He *mewed* and lifted his little foot. The tears burst from me so violently that Harry barely lifted the tray before my movement would have sent it crashing. He set it on the floor and sat next to me. "Say, old girl, you're giving me a bit of a turn. C'mon now settle down." He pulled me against his chest and patted my back.

I sniffed and snuffled and finally stopped crying. Harry handed me his handkerchief. He wet a washcloth and gently wiped at my splotchy skin. I was an ugly crier. I knew my eyes were the size of peas and my cheeks a paisley pattern of red and purple.

"Settle down, sweetheart. It's okay. We'll get through this. I'm not certain what *this* is but I'm here, not going anywhere."

"You should." I spoke quietly not believing I was telling him to leave. *My Prince Charming, my best friend, my soul mate. Had I lost my soul? Was that it?*

"Dammit, Grace, look at me." Harry's hands clamped on my arms. "Look at me Grace. Don't go in there where I can't follow." I opened my eyes and locked looks. You are the best thing that ever happened to me. I couldn't ever do better than to have you in my life. I love you. I love you."

He smiled, but the line never connected to his heart. He knew this wasn't finished, just like I knew my okay was a word with no substance. But for now, we'd moved beyond this crisis. Now was the time to tell him. He filled the silence before I could.

"I called your dad, told him you wouldn't be meeting him and Marty. He's coming to the house this evening under the guise of bringing us the extra lasagna he made at Marty's house. You know your dad; better to let him come see for himself."

I nodded my head. My dad, always protective of his only daughter, never handed off the job to Harry. He may have given my hand in marriage, but he still felt responsible for the rest of the body. Normally, Harry and Dad worked well together in their mutual purpose of keeping me happy and safe.

You are *loved. Stop with the 'woe is me' bullshit and count your blessings. Great, where have you been? Now I get the pep talk.*

"I don't know who you're meeting this afternoon, so I couldn't call them." Harry spoke softly.

Perfect timing. "I'm not shopping with friends. I'm seeing Cassidy McCabe at two o'clock. I've been feeling out of control. Embarrassed to tell you." I revisited the wrinkle in the flannel.

Harry lifted my chin with his thumb and forefinger. "Like I couldn't tell something was amiss when you wanted to chuck that coffee mug at me this morning?" His slow smile made it easier for me to find some humor in this whole mess. "There's nothing to be embarrassed about. You're brave and smart to look for help when you've done all you can."

When he put it that way, I did feel better. I wasn't a loser. I'd quickly suggested a therapist for Karen and her concerns, but felt I should be able to 'cure' myself. The nature of my disorder I supposed.

"Darling, let me drive you. I'll wait outside. I won't ask any questions." His earnest tone begged my agreement as though it were a treat or honor.

I nodded and plopped back against the headboard.

"I think your tea is still hot. Eat something, you'll feel better." He leaned over to retrieve the tray. "Well, not this tea."

"What's wrong?" I leaned forward and looked over the edge. Elmo lay across the tray, his butt against the warm pot and his tongue flicking quickly over the jam on the toast he held with one sticky paw.

We burst into laughter. Elmo sensed the spotlight was on him and stopped licking. He looked up with the quintessential cat expression of *lais sez faire*.

"Where's the camera when you need it?"

I laughed and the melancholy train of thought I'd been tempted to board left without me.

❧ 21 ❧

"Hello, Grace, please come in." Cassidy McCabe welcomed me into her waiting room. Her shoulder length auburn hair suited her petite frame and heart shaped face. Clear blue eyes smiled pleasantly. "Can I bring you tea or water?"

"Water's fine. Thank you."

She opened her office door and motioned me inside. "I'll be right back."

I settled myself amidst the hydrangeas, certain the couch was meant for patients. *Patients? Do I want to be here? Do I want to be one?* I started to stand as Cassidy entered the room. She smiled warmly, not commenting on the awkward half up half down pose I presented. She placed my bottled water and glass on two coasters with Frank Lloyd Wright's Art Glass design.

"Thank you."

Cassidy sat in the chair angled toward the end of the couch I sat at. I wondered if she waited until her client (I'd decided I liked that better) committed to one side of the loveseat. I also wondered if I'd be able to say anything. I glanced at my watch. Two o'clock straight up.

Cassidy addressed that gesture. "It's been several years since you've been here, Grace and it may be difficult for you to start talking to me. Please share as much, or as little, as you're comfortable doing. When you called me, you mentioned something about 'unnatural'. Perhaps you'd like to start with that or is there something else you'd rather start with first?"

Her calm cohesive statement put me at ease. I *can* do this. I can *do* this. I can do *this. Uh, oh. Not now.* My head wanted to play word games. I kept looking at her. It helped to focus on a person's eyes when I felt myself slipping away. Eyes, at least for me, always provided a tether. Cassidy didn't look away. I took a deep breath.

"Okay." I explained Elmo and his circumstances; finding him, freeing him, rushing him to the vet, etc. etc.

"When I realized I wanted to dress him up in baby clothes, well I figured I needed help." I lowered my eyes embarrassed at my admission.

"Grace?" In the pause that followed I looked at her. No shock or recriminations. I wouldn't have expected that anyway. She's supposed to help not judge. Bet she was great at poker. Her smooth brow and folded hands sent a calming message to me. "You looked embarrassed when you told me that. It takes a lot of courage to open up about things that make you uncomfortable."

"I know what I felt was unnatural."

"It's entirely natural to feel a maternal urge toward tiny helpless creatures. Whatever urges and feelings we have, there's always a reason, and once we understand the reason, they don't seem strange or unnatural any more. You've only transferred that feeling to a helpless little creature whose big eyes tugged at your heart."

Sounded logical, almost heroic, when she said it.

Cass swiveled in her chair one way, then the other, in a slow rhythmic movement. "What were you doing just before you found Elmo?"

"I was thinking about Clare and Connor, my niece and nephew."

"I want you to go back to that time in your mind and relive the whole experience; tell me the thoughts as you went through it."

I leaned my head back and stared up at the ceiling fan. I counted the blades checking them off clockwise, counted them counter-clockwise. Same number.

"Grace?"

"He looked so helpless, just like my niece and nephew. I knew only I could rescue him. I wanted to know how he'd feel in my arms, if I'd get that same feeling."

"Have you been thinking about having a baby?"

I lowered my head and stared at her. "Harry and I were supposed to adopt a baby this summer. He found out about Will and never finished the paperwork. Karen and Hannah went through with their adoption, only they got two. They went for one, but she was a twin and they came back with two. Connor should be my baby. If we'd followed our plans Connor would be my son, our son." I'd finally said it out loud to someone else. The enormity of the secret I'd shared embarrassed me. I waited for her response.

"Of course it seems to you that Connor should be yours. Finding little Elmo stirred those feelings. You want to experience motherhood. How do you feel when you hold Connor?"

"How do I feel?"

"Yes. When you hold Connor what are your thoughts?"

I wondered if she were trying to determine if she had a potential kidnapper in her sunroom. "I think about how a child would fill my life, mine and Harry's. I think about how Karen worries about raising a boy. She hardly picks him up, always goes to Clare. I wish they'd give him to me."

"How does Connor's other mom treat him?"

"Hannah? Oh she's great with him. She's a twin, my husband's sister."

I hadn't realized how observant I'd been of Karen and Hannah's interactions with the babies. I suppose I'd watched them, trying to imagine or absorb their feelings and experience.

"Grace, your admiration and affection for Karen and Hannah seems genuine. You said you wished they'd give him to you, not us. Why just you?"

Why indeed? How did we get from babies to Harry?

"Harry has a son from a previous relationship and um, well he uh, just found out about him, so for him it's like a new baby, only Will is ten years old." I thought my Readers Digest version summed it up nicely.

"Have you discussed adoption with Harry lately?"

"No. What's the use? He's so wrapped up with Will why would he want a distraction?"

"Has Harry referred to an adopted child in that manner?"

"No, I guess I just assume he wouldn't want anything or anyone to come between him and Will."

"Do you feel an adopted baby would come between them?"

"Will is his flesh and blood and an adopted baby wouldn't be. I mean people adopt other people's children when they can't have their own, right? So, he has his own. And what if Will told him he didn't want a little sibling, you know, didn't want to share."

"Do you believe that parents' love diminishes as another child comes along?"

"I'm the middle child with four brothers and I remember the joy and excitement in our home when my younger brothers came along. But we were theirs."

"This concern about loving an adopted child as much as his biological child, is it his or yours? In a sense, Will is an adopted child to you."

She made sense but her questions sent me in a new direction, a direction I could possibly control. I didn't feel quite the victim I did almost an hour ago.

"We've come to the end of our time. Do you feel you'd like to schedule another session?"

"Yes, I would. I have to be back in this area on Monday. A friend of mine died and her memorial is Monday at Regina College."

"I'm sorry, Grace. College friend?"

"In a way. We both attended Regina at different times, but she had just hired me as her assistant in alumni events."

Cassidy's eyebrows lifted and her eyes widened in surprise. "Janet Henry? I saw her Monday, I–" Her blue eyes searched my face. "How did she die?"

Now it was my turn to be surprised. "She fell into an uncovered well while hiking in Robinson Woods. Only now the police think it may not have been an accident."

Cassidy stared at me. She rubbed her thumb against the first knuckle of her middle finger. I cleared my throat. "How did you know Janet?"

Her gaze sharpened and she returned from wherever she'd been in her head. "I'm sorry, Grace but I can't talk about that."

Janet must have been seeing her professionally. "Oh, of course, I'd better be going. Would Monday afternoon be okay for you?"

"Not Monday, I'll be busy Monday. May I call you Tuesday and arrange a session?"

I sensed that she struggled with her feelings about Janet's death, but her professional training kept those emotions in check. I nodded my head. I stopped in the doorway. "Thank you, you've helped. I'm sorry I blurted that out about Janet."

Cassidy McCabe stood with one hand on the door. She smiled and shrugged her shoulders. "You didn't know." She stretched out her hand and shook mine. Her light grip connected with me on more than a physical level. I'd found a lifeline.

I hurried down the steps to the car I knew would be waiting at the corner. I wanted to tell Harry about the coincidence. I knew I'd see Cassidy again, not just professionally, but at the funeral. *Could Cassidy be the last person to have seen Janet alive?* The thought stopped me cold. *Should I go back and ask her? Would she tell me?*

Harry pulled up next to me. He lowered the passenger window and leaned toward me. "I asked to chauffeur you, but you could at least meet me at the corner." I heard his light tone, but the words ran together vying for space in my overloaded brain. *Why was Janet seeing her and for how long?* I turned back to the stairs and glanced up at the sunroom; the curtain twitched and covered the glass.

"Grace? What is it?" Harry stood next to me. "You look pale.

Do you feel well?" His eyes followed my sight line. The lemon yellow curtain lay straight. "What is it?"

I shook my head. "I don't know. Something. Maybe nothing. I want to talk to that detective again. Do you know where the station is?"

"Your dad gave me directions. Get in the car and tell me what's on your mind; you look full to capacity."

Harry knew how to read the signs when I reached maximum load. Marty and Glen used to tease me that I should swing my arms around and chant, 'warning, warning, danger approaching,' like the robot in the *Lost in Space* series of our childhood. Harry's tact went more like, 'I'm not a mind reader; tell me when you're upset before you unravel.'

"If you've that much on your mind, let's drive around a bit and hash things out. I'm not a mind reader…"

"Uh, course not. Sorry. Beats waving my arms around," I mumbled.

Harry's smile slipped and he moved me toward the door. "Get in, now." His face hardened and his eyes stole furtive glances in several directions. I moved quickly, spurred by the urgency in his voice. "Lock the door and stay put."

I watched him cross the street and approach a dark blue sedan. Harry stepped onto the sidewalk and stood a few feet from the driver's window. The door swung open and a man in a dark suit got out. I could see him only in profile. He looked average height, shorter than Harry and wore his brown hair trimmed high above his collar. He showed Harry identification and a short conversation ensued. They exchanged business cards and Harry crossed the street. The sedan pulled away from the curb and moved into the sparse residential traffic.

Harry slid in behind the wheel and handed me the card. *Federal Bureau of Investigation.* My immediate thought was that Harry had been asked to get back into harness with the FBI and British Intelligence. "Harry, you said you've finished with–"

His fingertips tapped my lips. "I have, darling. Totally. They don't want me for anything except my version of what happened Sunday with that crate. Seems the numbers on the top are on a list of stolen and, as to date, un-recovered munitions from World War II. There was a factory in Forest Park by the name of Ameritorp that turned out naval ordinance during the forties and fifties. Had an underground section where they tested them. Shut down after the demand ceased;

couldn't retool for peacetime widgets. The box the boys found was part of several crates stolen from that factory. They suspected the night watchman and a foreman but never had enough evidence to arrest them."

"Are they finished with you, I mean satisfied?"

"Why wouldn't they be? I told them what I know. Now what I surmise, or what I can root out, is another matter."

His voice had a crisp business tone, a business I wish he'd never think about. I could imagine him mentally rubbing his hands together in anticipation of an adventure. The retired Dalmatian answering the fire bell.

"Harry, please."

"Don't worry, darling. I'm a desk jockey now; paper trails, follow the money, that sort of thing. No field work for this fellow."

I sensed trouble. I searched for a comment or a caution. I thought of a question. "How'd they know where to find you?"

Harry started the engine and shifted. We moved into traffic and turned left at the light. I thought he hadn't heard me. "Told Walter my schedule; old habit."

Walter Stahl, self-appointed bodyguard, personal trainer, and devoted friend. After almost ten years of marriage I still didn't understand the depth of their commitment to each other, except that there was no truer friend to Harry and to me.

I always suspected that Walter had more to do with Harry's previous line of employment, but of course neither of them talked about it. I didn't understand how the FBI would know to call Walter. That would have been my next question if we hadn't pulled up in front of the police station. My brain shifted and sought to recapture the threads I'd been weaving before the FBI intruded. Harry opened the door. His body partially blocked my view of the building but I didn't miss the petite woman with the curly auburn hair entering.

There had to be a connection, otherwise why would Cassidy McCabe have rushed here? Maybe doctor-patient confidentiality didn't extend after death, especially if something she knew could help solve the case. What had Janet told her?

✿ 22 ✿

The interview with the police moved from bizarre to *bizarro* during the time we spent there, most of which we waited and speculated on the cast of characters that seemed to appear in cameo roles as facts and scenarios presented themselves to Detective Thomas.

Harry had taken a longer route to give me time to relax and we'd missed a chance to see Thomas by a few minutes; the desk clerk told us he had someone with him and would we please wait. I finally had the chance to tell Harry about my time with Cassidy and that I'd seen her scurry into the building ahead of us. Then things got strange.

Edward Bantonini strolled in waving to several policemen as he made his way to the desk clerk who must have told him to take a seat and number if her gesture toward us meant anything. When he turned around and spotted us, he stumbled in his, until then, fluid march across the floor. No sign of recognition. He'd spun back to the desk, mumbled something, and moved off to the side.

Cassidy came out of the office adjacent to the front desk. She stopped and stared at us, and for a moment it seemed unsure if she would acknowledge me. She smiled and started to speak. In the moment it takes for the brain to shift gears she spotted Edward Bantonini striding toward the open office door. Detective Thomas came through the doorway and started to approach us. I know time didn't freeze, but the tableau turned dreamlike as each of us responded to what had been set in motion. Harry stood and moved toward the detective. Cassidy turned from us and focused on Bantonini who moved close to her. He leaned down and whispered in an agitated manner, his hands moving with his speech. I heard her accusatory tone, "You've nerve talking to me. Let alone…you don't own them, not you, not your father." His fists balled at his sides. I thought he was going to hit her. Harry must have thought the same; he changed course and moved in front of Cassidy. Detective Thomas called out, 'Ed, I'll call you later at home.'

No one moved. Bantonini abruptly turned and left. His sharp movement broke the tension and the pace. The background noise of the station increased as everyone released their collectively held breath. Cassidy merely nodded to Harry and left, avoiding the door

Bantonini had used. From that point, our time with Thomas was short, confirming what I'd seen and heard. I asked him if Cassidy came to tell him about seeing Janet the afternoon she left Regina. I detected a tiny lifting of his eyebrow. *Surprised by my question or surprised because Cassidy didn't mention it?*

We sat in Hannah and Karen's kitchen filling them in on the afternoon. The babies were napping and I had tip-toed in for a quick peek.

"I wonder what went on between the scoutmaster and the shrink." Karen's question matched mine exactly.

"She's not a shrink, she's a psychotherapist."

"Whatever. Wonder what she knows about him but can't tell?"

"You, darling, have a very active imagination." It was strange to hear Harry's term of endearment for me spoken by someone else to someone else. Hannah smiled at Karen and shook her head. "No use to speculate. If we want answers, we should go to the source."

"What source?" I had a sinking feeling I knew the answer. I knew about his twin's obsession with the afterlife.

"We should work through a medium and contact this woman. Her death is recent; her spirit might be more receptive."

My stomach lurched as she talked about reaching across the grave to Janet, a woman I'd just had coffee with three days before, who'd been alive and excited about reunion, who actually wasn't even in her grave yet. I turned the cold tap on and ran the water.

"Oh, Gracie, don't drink that horrible water; it's loaded with chemicals. Take a bottle from the fridge."

"Geez, Hannah. Can't anything be easy with you? The water's fine and when people die they don't hang around waiting to talk about it with some *woo woo* person who charges $39.95 a session and validates your parking." I slammed the handle off and instantly regretted my outburst, but stood my ground and sipped at my 'chemical cocktail'.

Hannah's eyes widened and filled with tears. "Um, I think I hear the babies." She hurried out of the room. I shrugged my shoulders. I couldn't think about Janet that way.

"Not your fault, Grace. Hannah spins off all the time and doesn't think about the details. She only sees the big picture. She doesn't mean to diminish the circumstances of Janet's death. Hannah met a woman last spring who claims to be a true medium. She enjoys her company. They meet every now and then for tea." Karen grinned and added, "You're off on the $39.95. Try six times that amount. And parking is free."

"That's incredible. Who'd pay that kind of money?"

"Desperate people who can't let go. She's a Wiccan and that lends her more credibility."

"A Wiccan?"

Harry explained. "Wicca is a belief system and way of life based on pagan traditions. They honor a higher spirit and promote oneness with the elements of our existence."

"And you know all this because…?"

"When Hannah attended University she joined a coven. She was searching for something other than Church of England. Something she felt reflected her inner values and personal views."

"You're parents must have been frantic." I tried to imagine how Dorothy and William Marsden had reacted to that bit of news.

"Hanns has always marched to a different drummer." His tone spoke acceptance.

"Whole damn orchestra," I muttered.

"Say again?"

I was saved from answering, and perhaps an argument, by the doorbell chime.

"I'll get it, I'm up."

Ric stood on the doorstep. He didn't look surprised to see me and barely acknowledged me as he walked past of me into the kitchen.

He nodded to Karen and immediately turned to Harry. "We have to talk." The urgency in his voice made the hairs on the back of my neck stiffen. Something was extremely wrong.

Harry stood and motioned Ric toward the living room. "Hey, what are we, chopped liver?" Karen stood and moved with them. "You come in my house, talk to my guest, and leave me out?"

"Not now, can it." Ric left no room for argument.

"Big shot, tough cop attitude. I hate when he does that."

"Does what?" Hannah walked in from the hallway. Our eyes made contact.

"Hannah, I'm sorry I blew up at you. I'm a little edgy." My sister-in-law waved her hand to stop me.

"I should have been more sensitive to your feelings about your friend. I'm the one who should be apologizing."

We both nodded and then it was over for Hannah. Her face brightened and she turned to Karen. "Hate when who does what?"

I wish I could let go that easily. I suffer from 'residual conversation syndrome,' a made up name for when you continually replay left behind conversations in your head, chastising yourself with *shoulda, woulda, coulda* scenarios. Everyone else has moved on. Like now.

"Ric's in there," Karen thumbed toward the living room, "discussing something urgent with Harry. Pulled him out of the kitchen with that 'clandestine need to know macho guy crap thing' he does.

Hannah's face split into a huge grin. "*Whew*, you are irritated. Maybe I can help." She switched the dial on the baby monitor to another setting. Ric and Harry's voices filled the room. Hannah lowered the volume and we all sat down leaning toward the Fischer Price listening device. "I had the babes in their swings earlier while I made barley soup. We'll give them clandestine."

"How'd they find you so easily?"

"Walter knows my schedule. They know he's my handler."

Handler? What the hell was he talking about? Ric apparently understood the term.

"I did research based on the numbers on the crate. An entire truckload of weapons disappeared from the loading dock of an Army arsenal located in Forest Park on the east side of the Naval ordinance plant. It's now the Forest Park Mall, but during the forties, the factory cranked out thousands of torpedoes for the war in the Pacific. After Japan surrendered, the factory stopped all production. Your FBI cleaned out any classified information or specs and the factory sat empty until the area was developed into the mall. The Army reserve facility is still there. I talked to the chap in charge. The theft has never been solved."

Ric's low whistle barely came through. Does Gracie know how connected you still are? That the intelligence community can still find you through your gatekeeper?"

"Shut up, Kramer. This information is on file in the public library. Anyone can find it if they know how to use a card catalog and a microfilm machine."

He didn't deny the accusation.

"Yeah, well anyone can't find this in the card catalog."

We waited hoping one of them would describe 'this' for our waiting ears.

"Is that what I think it is?"

Still we waited for a visual.

"She went in head first. Her jacket had been pulled down around her torso, effectively pinning her arms to her side. When she hit it was like a bullet, straight in."

Ric's description floated through the speaker's tiny plastic holes burgeoning on our side like a mushroom cloud obliterating the sun.

"When was this taken?"

"At the scene when they removed the body. It wasn't until the autopsy that they found the earpiece of an old pair of glasses caught in the front of her sweatshirt. They sent the lab back to look for more. They took a closer look at the initial photos and one sharp technician spotted the bone."

My hand flew to my mouth in a race to keep a shout of surprise contained.

"Oh my God!" Karen's voice rose in the shock-still kitchen. Almost at a run, Harry came through the door. Ric followed holding the monitor in his hand. He lifted it to his mouth.

"Eavesdroppers never hear good things."

The instant echo from the proximity of the equipment bounced around the small room. He clicked off the switch. "To think the government spends millions on concealable listening devices and our ladies can do it with these. Ingenious."

He didn't sound upset, but the flare in his eyes told me otherwise.

"Ah, but I'm sure Fischer Price spends millions on their R&D. Perhaps law enforcement should take a lesson; the most concealed is out in plain view."

Harry's smooth voice didn't fool me either. "What you heard must go no further. This has developed into a murder investigation with a host of other crimes to be added. Your casual conversation could impede the investigation and possibly put others in jeopardy."

We all nodded our heads in unison. Ric apparently wanted to drive the point home. "Too high brow for me and at least one of them. Keep your mouth shut on this. No *sharing* with anyone–hairdresser, shrink, family, no one." He fixed each of us in turn with a glare from dark eyes.

Eyes as dark as the bottom of a well.

"Grace?"

He stared straight through me, waiting for my signal.

"Yes," I nodded quickly. "Yes."

"Was it a human bone?" Hannah's voice sounded remarkably calm. "Maybe it was some poor animal that had tumbled in years before."

Ric looked at each of us, assessing how much he should tell, or perhaps could tell. He shook his head. "The less you know the less you'll tell." He put the monitor down next to its twin and left.

We swung round to Harry who put his hands up in surrender. "I know what you heard." He nodded his head toward the blue plastic on the table. "Would have been great to have those when we played king's men and colonists, eh, Hanns?"

Hannah grinned at her brother. "Oh la, Stinky Parmeter would have been at sixes and nines."

I never knew when the Katzenjammer Twins were pulling my leg. "Kings men and colonists? And which were you two?"

"Darling, we're crushed." Hannah nodded and Harry continued. "We always chose the colonists, the underdog."

"Hey, we beat your buns royally." Karen's comment caused a ripple of laughter.

"We'd make Stinky wear this God awful bright red sweater that Harry'd got from the church jumble. Then we'd make him count whilst we hid. When he'd come marching through all important and red, holding his broomstick against his shoulder, we'd pounce on him from behind the rocks or down from the trees."

The burst of laughter eased the tension. "What happened to Stinky? Did he grow up insecure and hating 'colonists'?"

"Actually he's in the House of Commons, Lord or something by now. Married a Rhodes Scholar from Connecticut." Harry looked to his twin for confirmation.

She nodded. "Mum keeps track of all the kids. Yes, that's right, a Lord."

Lord Stinky had done fine. Odd thought to have as we left the brownstone. Maybe I didn't want to think about all that hadn't ended well. I assumed we'd be heading to Harlem and the entrance ramp to the Eisenhower. Instead, Harry drove to Chicago and Thatcher and parked on the street. He answered before I could ask. "I made an appointment earlier to pop in and speak with the curator, Miss Moe. She's been here for years, local treasure when it comes to the history of the area."

"And why are you interested?"

"If America weren't such a youngster, you'd know. Can't know a true course forward until you learn the backstory. Once you've seen the truth of that you can set a course that has a greater chance of success."

"What course? Did I miss where you were deputized?" I meant to sound sarcastic—it came out whiney. I hate that.

"I'm certain the police, on both sides of the woods, will do an excellent job of investigation. I'm only concerned with the leadership of Will's troop."

"You're investigating Edward Bantonini?"

"I'm researching the troop's history to see if I want Will involved with them. Even your own father had problems. His story made my skin creep."

"Crawl, your skin crawl." Harry occasionally misused American euphemisms."

"Honestly, Grace what difference does it make? Creep? Crawl? Must you always be pedantic?"

I annoyed people when I picked at insignificant actions or words. I tucked my bottom lip under my front teeth and stayed quiet. Harry got out of the car and walked around to my door. I sat staring straight ahead. *Get over it.*

He opened the door and put out his hand. "Sorry I snapped. I'm twisted up inside over this whole mess. My first chance to log in some dad and son memories and I'm worried about a possible pedophile or a satanic cult."

"I'm sorry. I've been edgy. Not fair to you." I smiled and reached for his hand. "Creep is as good as crawl. We are the *potato, patato* couple."

"And as the suave Fred of this couple, let me lead my Ginger through this labyrinth." He danced a few steps and ended with a flourish.

I walked past him smiling. "Sure, sure. You'll hear my applause when you can do it backwards, in a dress and, in high heels, Fred."

Harry's burst of laughter chased off whatever residual awkward feelings lingered. He reached forward, caught my hand, and pulled me into his arms with an exaggerated twirl. "Ginger, Ginger, Ginger." His lips met mine with a smooth touch that promised more. *Never mind it's Judy, Judy, Judy.*

"Known him since he was a pup. Moody teen, always lagging behind, tweaking an animal's ear then lying if he got caught. He thought he should be able to do what he pleased. The assistant curator at the time took to following the group at the rear, actually Bantonini's rear. Hawked him through the entire tour." She laughed at her recollection.

Miss Moe was one of those people of indeterminate age. Clear, hazel eyes sparkled with acuity as she spoke. Dark hair, streaked with generous amounts of white, lay short and smooth around a full face. We stood eye to eye when introduced. Her figure floated inside a period costume from the early 1900's. She motioned us toward her office and stepped easily over a huge white rabbit that lay directly on the threshold. We followed her in, lifting our feet extra high to avoid the sleeping Lagomorph.

"His son wasn't nearly as defiant, actually minded the rules. But others in his troop took up the slack. One in particular, name of Bigelow or Biggens, seemed the incarnation of Bantonini. Apparent to anyone with eyes that the scoutmaster favored that scout over his own son. I always felt badly for little Edward; probably gave him more help with his Mammal and Nature badges than I did the others."

My mind drifted as Harry encouraged more stories from Miss Moe. I suspected at this point that my husband, the consummate people collector, was enthralled with this woman who connected the fibers of the past to the present. Harry always struck me as an old soul who enjoyed the journey. He would let her choose her pace and direction. In doing so, he'd glean all he needed for his immediate purpose. And the lovely by-product would be a friend.

Miss Moe had offered us tea when we first sat in her tiny office. We'd been startled by a pudgy woodchuck that sauntered out from behind her desk. He'd stopped to stare and then continued on his slow waddle across the office. "Don't mind Chuckles. We think he's trying to find a suitable den for winter; we keep finding him in the strangest places."

"You name your animals?"

"Only the ones that live inside. Same name for each species.

Luisa Buehler

Makes it easier to remember. The white rabbit you stepped over, well, that's John number eight." Her laugh rolled toward you like a wave that crashed over you and pulled you toward her. I felt the need to walk around and excused myself to find the bathroom. A docent, dressed in buckskin shirt and pants, conducted a tour for a group of children who had donned hats, head bands, pinafores and chaps in the period style that they were studying. Great idea for total immersion. I stayed a discreet distance behind the last child and listened to the description of the animals that once populated the adjacent woods. He directed the children's attention to a sign that read:

WORK FOR JUNIOR ASSISTANTS TODAY
- ✓ *Find a small hollow stump for the chipmunk.*
- ✓ *Repair the door on the owl cage don't to startle them.*
- ✓ *Find a garden spider and look for the label in the files.*
- ✓ *Gather dandelion and clover for wild cottontails.*
- ✓ *Shell field corn; be careful not to blister your hands.*
- ✓ *Get fresh sand and bedding for mouse tank.*
- ✓ *Gather dry oak leaves for the red squirrel's cage.*

Great idea to get free labor and engage children in learning to care. I walked past the stone fireplace and read the description of the boa constrictor in the glass cage on top of the stone. I noticed that a heavy chain secured the cover. Probably no need for sand and bedding for the mice if this guy escaped. Or were the mice intended for him eventually? I heard the call of the American Crow from its cage nearby. I couldn't make out his words. I'd ask Miss Moe later.

I stepped into an alcove to read the story of the Potawatomi Indian tribe that once owned, not only this stretch of woods, but land that ran from the northern tip of Wisconsin to Dixon, Illinois and the mounds at Cahokia. Between the Potawatomi and the Chippewa alone they released almost 5,000,000 acres to the United States government. I placed my hand on the glass case that protected a medicine pouch and head band that belonged to Alexander Robinson, Chief Chee Chee Pin Quay.

The room turns chilly and I wish for my jacket warming the back of a chair in Miss Moe's office. Old building, needs better insulation at this end. A soft sound works into my subconscious; thump, thump, thump. A low murmur reaches my inner ear. Chee Chee Pin Quay, Chee Chee Pin Quay. I catch my breath as fingers squeeze my elbow.

"Are you okay ma'am?"

The fingers belonged to a little boy looking up at me with con-

cern in his dark eyes. He must have chosen his outfit first; his cowboy hat and chaps were a perfect fit. He waited for my response, continuing to hold my elbow, prepared to do more if needed.

"Yes, I'm fine. Thank you for asking. I got caught up in the
drums and the chanting..." I stop when his eyes widen to the size of
coasters. The sounds had been in my head. I knew that. I'd probably
scared this sweet little kid. "I'm fine. Thanks."

I would have scampered back to the safety of the group, but he
stayed. His eyes fixed on mine. He still held my elbow and the touch
warmed my arm from my fingertips to my shoulder. With the warmth
came a heavy feeling. I imagined lead trickling into my veins as the
heat permeated my flesh, so strong was the sensation. I looked away
and closed my eyes feeling a profound sense of sorrow in his presence.

"Miss?"

My eyes flew open; the costumed docent stood where the boy
had been. His blue eyes hesitant, his lined face split by a tentative
smile. *Probably coming to ask me to leave before I scared more kids.*

The building seemed warmer, almost stifling. "I'm sorry, I didn't
mean to frighten him."

"Frighten who, ma'am? I didn't notice you until after my group
left. You looked ill standing here with your eyes closed."

Good the children had left. The little boy must not have mentioned the nutcase in the corner. *Whew! Hope I didn't spoil his outing.*

"Would you like a glass of water?"

"Yes, thank you. It's so hot in here."

"We have a cooler in the cloakroom. I'll show you."

I followed the buckskin breeches through the main room past a
cage with soft-shelled turtles with their pointy snouts and olive green
backs shaped like pancakes and another with three baby birds still
fluffy with down. The cages and stuffed exhibits vied for space
against the walls. The aisle narrowed until we reached an alcove
closer to the entrance. Hooks on the wall and a low bench built in
across the width provided storage. I spotted a lunch box and umbrella
under part of the bench and one boot crammed under at another point.
Coming from a family of four boys I knew it was perfectly possible
to lose one boot and not even notice. I smiled to myself and felt the
sadness lifting. A quarter of the wall seemed designated for costumes.
This section had a shelf above the hooks for hats. I didn't see the
cowboy hat amid the tumbled items.

The docent, Andy, by his name badge handed me a glass of water. The cool liquid flushed the lingering malaise from my mouth. "Thank you." I waved my hand toward the wall. "What a great idea to let the kids dress up for the tour. Keeps them focused I bet."

"Yeah, they like it. Miss Moe thought they would. She started bringing in stuff she'd find at house sales, resale stores, places like that."

Andy's lanky frame suited his buckskin duds; an aging John Hart from the TV show *Hawkeye, Last of the Mohicans.*

"Most of us have our own outfit, either bought or made. Found mine in Tucson while visiting my daughter and her family. Miss Moe did some needlework on it for me. Some of the children wear their own outfits for the program. If you noticed the blonde girl with the entire Laura Ingalls Wilder outfit, that was her mothers when she was a little girl in the program. I suppose it'll pass down to the next Laura."

My raised eyebrow coaxed more information.

"Yeah, her name is Laura just like her mom who loved the *Little House on the Prairie* stories. Guess she connected with them as a kid because of her name. She named her daughter Laura and Little Laura most likely will do the same."

I laughed at his story. "Did the cowboy bring his own costume too? I don't see the hat. It looked like the black hat Little Joe wore in Bonanza?"

Andy's eyes flicked away and what had been an open friendly gaze turned suspicious. His lids drooped and effectively prevented me from reading any expression.

"I've got to straighten up before closing. You can put the glass there." He turned quickly in a swirl of leather fringe and moved away from me like I'd pulled a two-headed snake from my purse.

Geez Louise. What was that about? Old fart, probably skipped his Prozac.

I tried to vilify his response because my own state of mind was shaky. In my heart I knew he hadn't been mean; he had become upset when I asked about the little cowboy. Maybe he had a run-in with the kid's, 'my dad's a lawyer you can't tell me what to do' bratty behavior. The little cowboy hadn't seemed the type. *Geez, Grace. You can't explain your own behavior. Leave the guy alone. Long day, bad day. Whatever.*

"There you are, darling. I wondered where you'd got off to. They're getting ready to close. I brought your jacket." Harry held my coat open. I slipped into the wool, grateful for the warmth. The temperature must be lowered at closing. I hadn't realized I was cold again. Harry handed me a thin glass tube with a wildflower and moss tucked inside. The top was sealed with a wax cork. "Native to this area, *Blue Boneset.* Miss Moe is fascinating. Been at her post for over fifty years. She knows everything about this area; the history, the people. Fascinating."

"Wonder if she knows the little cowboy?" I hadn't meant to say that out loud.

"Little cowboy?"

I shook my head and moved toward the door. Harry moved ahead to open the door. He stopped a few feet from the exit and bent down. "Hullo. Almost stepped on this. My foot would have caused a wrinkle for sure." Harry straightened, holding out a hat. "Your little cowboy's?" His smile wavered as he noticed my face. I felt the heat move up my neck and face and what had been cold skin moments before now flamed with anxiety.

"What is it? Are you ill?"

Andy stopped at Harry's side and reached for the hat. "Thanks. I find the costumes all over the place, especially the hats. I tell them to put them back on the hook but you know kids." He walked away flicking a dust particle from the crown of the tan felt hat. His eyes met mine briefly. *No comment eyes.*

Harry guided me out of the building and into the car. When he didn't start the engine I looked at him. "What in the Queen's garters was that all about?" He only mentions the queen's undergarments when frustrated.

I told him about my encounter with the little cowboy and Andy's reaction to my question. "He knows something about that little boy. Why would he become so hostile?"

"He didn't seem at all hostile to me there at the door. Seemed like a pleasant old fellow. Maybe the child in question is famous or wealthy from a local family and Andy is protecting the child's anonymity."

"Maybe. He did look familiar."

"There you have it. He's probably a child star in the cinema trying to lead a normal life with his school pals."

Harry's explanation was as good as any and I liked it better than the one forming in my gut. I put my dark thoughts on hold and embraced his theory.

"Are we headed home? I'm tired."

"Absolutely. With one stop on the way." He put the car in gear and pulled out onto Thatcher.

I waited, knowing there'd be more.

"I promised Will I'd stop by and be his audience for a talk he has to give with his science project. Now he'll have a bigger audience."

Harry's grin tugged at my heart. *Does he really think it's that easy? Will is expecting him, to have him all to himself and Harry trots in with me. No wonder the kid hates me.* "I don't think that's a winning idea. He wants you to be there, not me."

"Nonsense. You have to let go of this idea that Will doesn't want you in his life. He does. He's only now learned about the Morellis. He needs a bit of time to acclimate."

"I'm a Marsden." There it was in a nutshell. He would accept me as Mike's daughter, Karen's friend, Ric's ex, Hannah's sister-in-law, but not his dad's wife. In his heart that title should belong only to his mother. I didn't blame him. I know I would have felt the same way if my parents had divorced and then remarried.

Harry patted my thigh. "He'll come around, darling. You'll see."

We pulled up to the curb in front of Lily's brownstone before I could suggest he drop me at Hannah and Karen's. I wished I could stay in the car. *Buck up, as Harry says, and don't over react or get goofy. Define goofy? Get out of the car, Grace.*

Goofy is as goofy does and suddenly I had to braid something before I could get out of the car. Harry recognized the signs when he opened the door.

"Gracie, now? Come on girl, buck up. You can do this." He offered his hand, but I sat powerless to take it. My fingers tied and untied a series a knots in the yarn I found in my purse. *Over, under, around, down. Over, under, around, down.*

"Come up when you can," Harry's voice, tinged with regret spurred me to hurry, to negotiate a lesser number. No deal; in fact pushing too hard could result in added knots. *Who lives in my head? Feels like Sister Colette from grade four. Tyrant.*

The door closes and I feel a split second of anxiety because I'm in here and Harry's up there and relief for the same reason. My fingers stop their flurry and lay still in my lap. I can go now. It's only been minutes; what has he told them? We should have had a plan. *Why am I late? Had to finish the chapter? Wanted to finish my Dairy Queen? Had to change my muddy boots? What muddy boots? Crap, crap, crap. Why am I late?*

I marched up the steps play acting the role of a normal person.

Ring the bell, set your smile. Door's opening, set your smile.

Lily stood in the doorway, no smile on her face. Her slim body held stiffly against the door. She inclined her head slightly and layers of wheat colored hair swayed in the direction indicated. Lily had styled her one length hair into a series of layers that provided a more fluid frame for her smooth skin and tourmaline eyes. Olivia Newton-John came to mind. "Harry said you'd be up, just finishing a phone call."

A phone call! Why didn't I think of that? A phone call. Perfect. Important, special. Yes, a phone call.

"Yes." *Keep it simple, stupid.* I smiled as Marty's favorite sales phrase popped into my head. I moved into the room. Lily fixed her eyes on the knotted yarn dangling from my purse.

"Yes, indeed," she murmured and her lips moved, but I wouldn't call it a smile.

"We're in here."

Bless his soul and all points in between. My spirit soared and I walked confidently into the living room smack into the baleful glare of the smaller version of Harry. I fought my first reaction; to allow the confidence I felt to manifest itself in a tiny smirk. I told myself I was the adult and reminded myself how I would have felt at ten years of age if this were happening to me. I mustered all the genuineness I had and smiled at the towhead. "Hi, Will. Thanks for the sneak pre-view." It felt as good as it sounded.

His glare lessened. "Yeah." Signatures from friends and family covered Will's walking cast. I'm tempted to ask if I could sign it, but decide not to push my luck.

"Let's get started. Where do you want the audience, son?" Harry beamed and my heart thumped inside my chest as I watched him take joy in Will. The word 'son' reverberates in my head, softly fading after many repetitions.

We take our assigned seats, Harry and Lily to the couch, me to the chair. I am prepared and easily accept the seating. I have a better view of his science project.

He wobbles up to the card table and lifts the cloth with a flour-ish. His excitement is contagious and I lean forward. His project, an ecosystem in an old aquarium complete with fauna: some living slugs, beetles and worms, and a beautifully crafted volcano complete with a village in the foothills, is unveiled. I find his attention to detail amazing compared to the klutzy science projects my brothers created. Will had populated his village with people and animals. He'd added bridges and roads with scale vehicles.

His young voice spewed volcano facts and figures. His real project was to monitor his ecosystem for seven days, notating changes and results. He'd built the volcano for fun and I listened with a growing admiration for him. It was apparent from the couch people that they'd hit that level long ago and were now propelled into the stratosphere with pride for their progeny. Will carefully poured a clear liquid into the top of the volcano and anxiously stared at his creation waiting for it to 'blow.' The vinegar smell filled the room and whatever container was secreted in the center of the clay. Nothing happened and nothing would. I'd seen enough of these volcanoes to know that if they weren't spewing by now it wasn't going to happen.

"I don't understand. I followed the directions." Will's face displayed the same 'thinking mode' that I'd seen on Harry's face a hundred times. He cocked his head slightly to the left and pursed his lips. A slight squint around the eyes indicated he was reviewing events in his head looking for the spot where he'd erred.

"Are you sure, sweetie?" Lily leaned forward from the couch. "Did you follow all the steps?"

The look he gave his mother sent a childish rush of joy to my heart. *He thinks she's dumber than a box of rocks. Alleluia! It's junior high one year early. Or as Marty would say 'déjà vu' all over again'.* I didn't mean to smile, but I knew it was a grin when I felt my lips slide up over my teeth. From my angle I noticed a wet stain at the base of the village.

"Are you laughing at Will?"
Oh, cripes. It looks that way.

I reduced the size of my grin. Somewhere inside me came a calm voice. I felt that this moment in time might define my relationship with my stepson. "Of course not. It's not operator error, merely equipment failure." I pointed toward the base.

Will spotted it. "Oh man, it leaked." His voice relieved and concerned. "This is due tomorrow. The container is glued in there; I can't redo this in time." The panic in his voice pulled at my heart. This was Glennie the night before his volcano project was due. Our dog Tippy chose the box it was set up in to have her puppies. A science project of a different sort. Will has that same look of panic and defeat on his face. Maybe I could be a big sister to him and forget the pseudo mom title.

"What's in there?"

"An old travel mug mom gave me. I wanted a glass jar like it says." He waved a sheet of paper at the room in general. *Ah, yes the 'blame your mom stage';* I loved it. "Dad couldn't get here the other night when I was making it." *Yes, another parent bites the dust.* Harry and Lily looked devastated; they've disappointed the one person that they adore unconditionally.

Poor Harry and Lily; half of a twin and an only child. The first requirement of parenting should be to grow up in a large family, preferably both gender children, to be prepared for the guilt kids can heap on you. *Tsk, tsk.* This was pre-guilt. Not like Glen's insistence that my parents were to blame because they weren't responsible enough to have had Tippy spayed; that Marty let her out those many months before when the neighbor's dog, Bruno, had his way with her; that I should have kept her in my room on my bed where she normally slept, etc. He never mentioned that he'd been told ten times to get the box off the floor and put it on the counter. *Tsk, tsk.*

Big Sis to the rescue. "We can fix this Will. We need a glass sleeve to fit inside. Glass is a better conductor for your baking soda and vinegar." Will's eyebrows raised. I'd seen that exact silent form of inquiry many times before. "I have four brothers, they all did volcanoes." His face lifted with hope. I felt like a million bucks. My feet itched to do the Snoopy dance; I'd save that for later.

"The mug's too small for anything to fit inside." I stood next to him looking down the throat of the clay project. He'd carefully crafted the clay to cover most of the diameter of the mug leaving only a small opening. Would have spewed wonderfully. I'd be on his hit list next if I couldn't fix this as boastfully promised.

"I have to bring this tonight to scouts. Mr. Bantonini said anyone working on an environmental science project at St. Edgar could sign up to work with him on their Environmental Science badge tonight and get credit. I have to bring it." He'd written off his parents and looked to me for salvation. And it came in the form of my newest gift. I rummaged in my purse. I looked up at Harry. He knew.

"We can use this. The diameter should be right."

"It's got stuff in it."

I worked and wiggled the wax to coax it off the bottle, then slid the contents out onto the tabletop. "There." I handed the glass tube to Will. "You'll have to do the math on the new proportions, my job is done." He grinned and for the briefest moment I thought might high five me.

"Thanks. No problem. I'll reduce the amounts by one fourth. That should do it." He looked at the tiny flower on the table. "Is it ruined?"

"Not at all, I can press it and keep it that way. Or," the genius of my thought pleased me, "we could use it on the volcano?"

"Perfect. I didn't think of grass or flowers."

I nodded toward the flower. "It's all yours. You might want to snip pieces to glue down rather than one clump."

He nodded quickly and began to work. I caught Harry's eye. I'd done well. Lily on the other hand, looked liked she wanted to stuff me in the volcano.

"Any chance for a cup of tea? Looks like he'll need a few minutes to prepare."

Harry followed Lily into the kitchen. I knew he wanted to talk to her about the scout troop and what Dad had told us and what I'd told him today. I returned to my seat, happy to bask in Will's approval.

Will called his parents in for the new and improved eruption. I coyly suggested a change with my observation, "I always thought it was too bad my brothers couldn't direct where the lava flowed."

Will's face glowed. "That's easy." He picked up the X-Acto knife he used on the flower and pretended to show me the routes he'd carved while he actually carved them. "You just make grooves like I did here and here and here."

I let him fool me, enjoying the charade like I had with Mike's boys at this age. Maybe I'd be more like an aunt than a big sister.

Will presented his speech again, poured in the vinegar and waited. Only seconds passed before a marvelous sputtering and flow of food coloring red lava followed its preordained course down the mountain missing the tiny village.

His last line was impromptu, but fit beautifully. "So you see living at the base of a volcano is a chancy life. The village was spared…this time." That line would get him extra marks in school. Here, he didn't need to do anything but exist to win approval. The way it should be. The applause lasted through a second bow.

"Wonderful ecosystem, very realistic." Harry ruffled his son's hair. "Thank you for the advance viewing. I haven't seen that many beetles in one spot since your Aunt Hannah came home from Lady Atherton's girl's camp with a duffle full. We'd best be leaving so you can eat your supper and get ready for scouts."

Will hugged his dad and then became preoccupied with rolling up the poster he'd made to show the internal aspects of a volcano when it came my turn for a hug. The rubber snapped and the poster popped open and dropped to the floor. "Bloody!"

"William. I told you not to use that word. It's not appropriate."

"I like the way it sounds. Dad uses it all the time."

Lily fixed Harry with a withering gaze. "Yes, well your dad uses it because he's an adult. You're not and I won't have it."

Will lowered his eyes. "Sorry."

"Your mum's right. I should try harder not to use it myself. Let's agree to use 'blimey' instead. Deal?"

Will looked up at Harry with something akin to hero worship and grinned. "Deal." They sealed with a handshake.

I picked up the poster, re-rolled it, and used my yarn to tie a timber hitch, leaving a length across the middle as a carrying handle. I handed it to Will.

"Cool. Uh, thanks, for everything." Halting, but spoken.

I left the brownstone feeling for the first time in months that this situation might work out. Harry noticed my euphoria.

He opened the door, but before I got in pulled me up in his arms. The passion of his kiss caught me off guard. Someone watched from the window if the flick of the drape meant anything. Lily or Will?

Harry released me and I slipped happily into the car. "You were wonderful with him. Just super."

Hmmm. Please the kid, turn on the father. Makes sense. Guys who were great with kids were attractive to me. What was that saying, 'a man never stands so tall, as when he stoops to help a child?' Didn't think it worked both ways.

I didn't want to dampen the praise or the mood, but I had to know. "What did you tell Lily?"

Harry's face reflected his mood change. "Told her everything. One of us needs to attend every meeting. Asked her to have a chat with Tim's mom. He has older brothers who've been through the troop. Lily's going to make a copy of the troops outings so I can participate in the campouts. Until I know more about Bantonini I'm not letting Will out of my sight when he's with him."

"Miss Moe seemed to like him."

"She knew him as a child. Who knows how he grew up. Sins of the father, Gracie. Can't take any chances."

Neither of us broke the ensuing silence; each with our own thoughts. Mine centered on the horror of betrayal from someone in authority. Someone trusted to care for a child, before his own safety, comfort.

I didn't notice the problem until Harry muttered under his breath and pumped the brake pedal. "Damn car, piece of junk." He maneuvered the Jag to the curb lane and turned on the next side street. The traffic on Harlem Avenue raced past us. We sat with the engine running. Harry slammed his hand on the dashboard.

"What's wrong?"

"Brakes seem wrong; dancing on the floorboards before they catch."

I'd never heard that one before, but I understood it in the context of his actions. "Is it not safe to drive?"

"I'm not sure. Don't want to risk it. I'll call Walter for a pick-up."

"Let's call Karen. She's closer and we can borrow her car until tomorrow."

"I don't want to involve anyone else until I know what's wrong with the car."

"Involve? We're borrowing a car because ours broke down. Didn't it?"

"Gracie, let me handle this." He lifted the phone from the clamp and dialed. Their short conversation left me more confused when I heard my dad mentioned. "Mike's been calling around looking for you. You'd best call him before he sends out the troops." He said it with a smile, but I heard the tinge of exasperation. He knew my family before he proposed. I put my cards on the table; not my fault if his due diligence fell short.

"He can't help himself, I'm his favorite daughter."

"You're his only daughter."

"Exactly my point." I smiled and leaned toward him. He met me over the gearbox. Our lips pressed across the space denied to our bodies.

❧ 24 ❦

We spend Friday being a one-car family, combining errands, accompanying each other to usually solo outings. Will and Lily will be in the compound by Saturday morning. Harry can walk over and spend the day with Will. He plans to bring him to the barn and surprise him with his first riding lesson. I'd already promised Matt and Ben the same experience.

Accompanying Harry to the health food store makes me grateful that he enjoys this chore. We discuss the merits of frozen versus canned, fresh (trucked in from two days away) versus frozen (flashed within hours of being picked) and free range versus cooped up. He pronounces my choices incorrect and my shopping acumen flawed. I get my own cart and proceed to fill it with chips and cookies and ice cream. I finish first, but my victory is hollow; every damn ingredient is *low cal, high fiber* and other healthy combinations. I won't do this again unless I can forearm myself with White Castle sliders or macaroni and cheese.

Walter had dropped us off Thursday night promising he'd be back in the morning to work on Harry. Walter looked like a fireplug with grizzled gray hair and bushy eyebrows but he had the hands of an artist. I don't believe he ever trained in massage therapy. He took over the task from me after Harry had been injured and required daily therapy. I failed miserably wincing and tearing up every time he flinched with pain from the necessary therapy.

He continued the almost daily therapy long after Harry's doctors pronounced him fit. When Walter wasn't pounding vitality into my husband, they discussed projects they had in mind. Walter could do most handyman type jobs and they kept each other busy building a greenhouse, a herbarium and fortress fenced Victory garden. The plans on the board for this spring were for a pond with a waterfall. Walter also ran odd errands for him, no questions asked.

Dad calmed down as soon as he heard my voice. We compared notes about our visits with Detective Thomas and I told him about Bantonini's behavior. I didn't tell him about my visit with Cassidy McCabe. I didn't want him to worry that I possibly inherited a predisposition for depression. He invited us to come over for Sunday dinner.

"Gracie, I'm leaving to collect Will."

My husband's vocabulary still jangled my American verbiage. You *collect* buttons or bells or artwork not people.

Will hadn't met Elmo yet and I hoped I'd win him over a little more. It couldn't hurt, what kid wouldn't love Elmo.

The phone rang. "Hello."

"Hi, Grace, it's Tracy. We have to cancel this afternoon. Matt came down with a flu kind of thing and I'm sure Benny will soon follow. The curse of bunking together. They're disappointed as hell, especially Benny."

"I'm disappointed too. Tell them we'll do it next Saturday after Thanksgiving. In fact, I know you love Oak Brook Mall, drop them off early and you can start your Christmas shopping."

"Start? I'm practically finished. Karen and I logged in more miles at Mall of America last summer than Lewis and Clark's entire Northwest Passage. Now, I'm looking for those finishing touches."

I groaned then brightened. "Great, I'll give you my list and you can relive the joy all over again."

"When I retire and have a pension to rest my butt on, I may very well become *shopper to the slugs.* You're on however about Saturday morning. I can take an inventory of what Santa is bringing the boys and where he hid it then can wrap and store everything in my neighbor's basement–her kids are grown, their presents come in the form of checks and gift cards–easy to hide. This is perfect. Thanks, Gracie."

"My pleasure. Gotta run now. See you next Saturday."

"No, you'll see me Thursday, Thanksgiving. Remember?"

I'd forgotten about the epic Thanksgiving gala that evolved over a few travel plans. Tracy, Bill, and the boys were not spending the day with her sisters because Kathy and Susie were flying to New York to be with their oldest sister, Mary. In my family, this was one of the BIG years when all my brothers' wives were not scheduled for their sides. It didn't happen every other year because someone always had to trade off due to something. Karen and Hannah didn't want to travel to England with the babies. My cousin Nick was home alone because his parents were cruising that week with his two sisters, but he couldn't get leave from his new job. Dad, who always hosted Thanksgiving, has the smallest house. Harry and I always have Christmas Eve and my brother Mike and his wife usually host Easter. Eating out on a holiday just isn't done in my family, but a compromise came to pass. Each family pitched in to rent Under the Gingko Tree for Thanksgiving dinner.

"Oh yeah, The Brady Bunch meets Mariniera Mike and the Pesto Pasta gang."

"Are you calling me Florence Henderson?"

We burst into laughter and say goodbye.

I've been on the phone long enough for Harry to return with Will. I hear them in the mudroom choosing treats for April and Cash. Seems like a perfect time to introduce Elmo. I scoop him up from his favorite spot, the padded bench in the nook, and carry him to the door.

"What's that?" Observant Will points at the little pet bed.

"That would be Elmo's bed," I answer from the door. I move my arm to reveal the little fur ball. "Meet Elmo."

Will's reaction took me by surprise. I never expected what happened next.

Will swung round to hug his dad. "Is this my surprise? Thank you, thank you." He released Harry and rushed toward me. I froze with the realization of Will's conclusion. *No, Elmo's mine.*

He looked up at me with huge expectation in his eyes. His hands reached for Elmo. The moment expanded in slow motion. I tightened my hold on Elmo and stepped back as Will reached for him.

"Let me hold him. I want to hold him."

I looked at Harry across the room. The moment dissolved into real time as I saw the flash of incredulity and then anger in his eyes. I'd lost more than a kitten.

I loosened my gentle grip and Will scooped the mewling puff into his arms. His smiling face drove my new reality into my heart. I'd lost Elmo.

"He's so cute." Will dropped to his knees to cradle the kitten in his lap. Elmo sucked at the little boy's finger bringing laughter from both father and son. Harry ruffled his son's bright hair. *Hero Harry. Loser Grace.*

They didn't see me go. I left before I embarrassed myself with tears or worse a tug of war. I went out the front door and walked slowly around the house to the barn. April would comfort me. She *whinnied* when I entered.

"Hey, girl. Wanna go for a ride?" I had no treat for her; I scratched her nose and the sweet spot on her chin. Her deep brown eyes reflected unconditional love. "I love you, girl." I threw my arms around her neck and sobbed into her mane. She stood quietly, letting me slobber onto her neck until I'd cried out the first round of tears. I could tell there'd be more.

Cash Cow snorted from the next stall. I had no room in my heart for him at the moment. I heard him paw at the floor. Slowly, I released April and acknowledged Cash. "Hi, big boy," I choked out between snuffles. He nodded his head several times. "Can't ride you today, fella. Gotta take April–she's cheaper than a shrink and I need shrinking, big time." *Thank God, no one hears these conversations.*

A noise from the tack wall startled me. I whirled expecting Harry or worse, Will to have heard me. No one. The noise came again. I focused my sight line lower and spotted the source. Elmo's siblings! Two pudgy kittens poked noses out from the tangle of tack and pieces of leather I'd rescued Elmo from last week. *Perfect. Will could have one of them or both of them. Yes, two for one. What little selfish kid wouldn't want more?* Now to catch them. I had no food to offer, but they didn't know that. Squatting on the ground I rubbed my fingers together. "*Here, kitties. Look what I have. Mmm. Here kitties.* One seemed more courageous or curious than his littermate. The little face splotched with orange against a tan background watched my moving fingers with great intent. *Little closer, little more.* I reached for the kitten and felt a sharp slice across the top of my hand. "Ouch!" I hadn't thought this out very well, had nothing to throw over the hissing fur ball to protect my hands. I stood up quickly intending to use a feedbag for a prison. Tiny razor teeth found my thumb. "Cripes, that hurts." My hand jerked and the little creature fell from my grip to the ground and lay still.

"Oh my God, oh my God." I knelt down and pulled off my jacket. My hands shook as I lifted the little body from the straw. "Please be alive." Tears streamed down my face and I tucked the still body into the folds of my jacket. I picked up the bundle and moved slowly toward the door preparing to make another emergency run to the vet.

Harry and Will were on the floor with Elmo taunting him by pulling bits of yarn across the floor. The look on my face announced my feelings. They both stood immediately, Harry careful to pick up Elmo. I lifted the material of my jacket. "I was trying to catch him and he bit me and I dropped him. Drive me to the vet. I think he's hurt. *Patches* stirred and struck in a heartbeat. Again my thumb. "*Owww!*"

This time I lowered the kitten to the ground and pulled away in time to avoid a second gnawing. The panicked animal ran into the sleeve seeking freedom. We followed its progress watching it move through the material like a feeder mouse in a snake's intestine. The little orange head popped out the sleeve and froze at the sound of our laughter. "Gotcha'." I grabbed the jacket one hand at the cuff one behind the little butt that tried to backpedal out of the sleeve. Relieved that I hadn't killed Patches, as I thought of him, I realized I couldn't trade this wild kitten for Elmo. I looked up at little Elmo quietly perched in Harry's hands. My idea seemed a stupid one now.

Suddenly, Elmo didn't agree. He nearly pulled out of Harry's grasp trying to reach Patches. "Dad, he wants to sniff him. Put Ort down. *They'd changed his name to that stupid, Ort. A small bit of food. What kind of name is that for a cat?*

Elmo became a squirming mass of orange fur, leaving Harry no option but to release him before he twisted out of his hands. Elmo moved toward his sibling and the hissy fit from Patches stopped. Both heads stretched forward to touch noses. Then gentle head buts, more nose touching, and finally meowing their salutations and felicitations. I let go of the sleeve and the reunion was complete.

We watched them lick and sniff and tumble for the next quarter hour, laughing at their antics. I learned three things: Patches was female, she took to the litter box concept, and Will wanted them both.

I mentioned a third in the barn and Harry proposed he and Will go corral that one too. I suggested the feedbag as a holding pen.

The phone rang and I took the message for Harry to call the mechanic at Vito and Helmut's garage. Elmo had followed me into the kitchen; Patches held back at the doorway. Little Elmo trotted back to his sister and licked her ear. She followed him to his safe spot under the butcher-block table. *Blow in my ear and I'll follow you anywhere? Such a guy, little man.*

I stopped the natural thought progression that would have Elmo fathering his own litter within the year. *Yuck! With his sister.*

The back door banged and Will hobbled into the room holding a squirming feedbag straight arm in front of him. He spoke in short breaths. "We–got–him. Her. I don't know." Will knelt down and unfolded the opening but didn't get his hands back fast enough. "Ouch! Blood…bugg…blimey," he finished. Harry and I burst into laughter.

"Well done, Will. Well done."

This reunion followed the same pattern. Soon, three little kittens lay under the table in a tangle of legs and tails. I named the third one, a male, Trey. He was the largest. I learned two things, I needed a larger litter box, and Will wanted all three.

Harry drove to Target to buy a multiple cat litter box and more litter. I looked for seldom-used bowls to divvy up the food. My concern was for Elmo; his siblings had sucked up his food. Will stayed behind.

"How did your project go for school?"

"It was good."

The kittens had his attention, but he still seemed distant. I thought we'd come a ways Thursday night.

"Just good? I thought it was very cool." Did kids even say 'cool' anymore?

He arched an eyebrow. Harry's habit. "Yeah, they liked it."

This kid was making me work for it. "How about scouts? Did your counselor sign off on that requirement?"

"Yeah."

Cripes. Fine. Leave him be.

The nearest Target was on Sixty-Third Street in Woodridge. Harry wouldn't get back for thirty minutes, at least.

"Where's your bathroom? I forgot which way."

I directed him. "Oh, there's something wrong with it, runs sometimes. Jiggle the handle, okay?"

I busied myself making coffee, watching the minutes drag around the clock. I'd never felt so uncomfortable around a child. *He's just a kid for crying out loud. What do you do with Matt and Ben? That's different–they love me, think I'm cool.*

"I am cool, no foolin' way coolin', cool I am." I smile at my jingle and push 'on'.

"Excuse me?" Will's in the doorway. I forgot boys pee fast.

Oh crap! He'll tell his mom I talk to myself, in rhyme no less, bad rhyme.

My face burned from embarrassment. I didn't respond.

He took the long way around the kitchen and dropped down next to the sleeping kittens. "I jiggled the handle like you said. Can't you fix that?"

"That's easy to fix. Your dad needs to find some time to replace the float. The bigger problem is the way the water is piped through the house. When you flush that toilet you scald whoever is taking a shower in our bathroom. Figures it's ours, not the guest shower that isn't used that often, hardly ever." I sensed my frantic rambling was making him uncomfortable. I cut to the chase. Anyway, the plumbers routed something wrong when they rebuilt after the explosion…"

Will's eyes grew round and wide.

Oh crap, again! No one told me he didn't know. Why would they tell him, stupid? Does he know about his grandfather?

"What explosion?" He sat with his back against the table leg.

"Ah, a, ah."

"That's a story for another time. For now, help me unload the cat tower and cat hotel from the car."

Will scrambled to his feet. Harry glared at me with a *Can't I leave you alone with him for five minutes?* expression. He followed Will through the door.

God, I was hopeless, useless. I walked out to the barn and watched from atop April as they made a second trip to the car. I turned her toward the field beyond our house. "Giddy up, girl. I need your help." She snorted and nodded, picking her way across the cold ground. I should have worn a heavier jacket; the temperature had dropped. The cold numbed my arms and chest. Now I matched inside and out.

ও **25** ৬

I'd lost track of time as we'd meandered through fields, across the fairways and into the woods. April picked the pace and had no problem negotiating the different terrain in the dark. I cried into her mane feeling frustrated and scared. I leaned my chest on her neck and let her choose the route.

Harry and Cash found us close to home in the woods behind Barb's house at six o'clock. I'd been out there for three hours. He pulled up next to me and guided the reins over April's head. He turned Cash toward home with us in tow. I hadn't bothered to lift myself from her neck. I knew he was angry. I didn't care. I knew I'd been wrong to take off. I still didn't care. Floating atop April stopped and I knew we were in the barn. I didn't move. Harry coaxed me off her back and into his arms. He carried me into the house and placed me on the couch. He piled several throws on me and removed my shoes, tucking the material around my feet. I heard him in the kitchen then he was near my head. "Tea in a few minutes. I'll be back. Need to put up the horses."

He doesn't sound angry. He sounds blurry in my head. I feel blurry and hot. The sound of the kettle begins low and grows in urgency. I hate the high pitch, sounds human to me.

It stops. I hear the clink of china and soon smell cinnamon close by. "Sit up a little, Gracie." Harry puts down the teacup and helps me scoot against the pillow. I close my hands around the cup and the trembling spills liquid over the top. I don't feel the heat, through my riding gloves.

Harry takes it out of my hands. "I'll hold, you sip."

I take tiny sips, the hot liquid tingles and forms a sleeve of warmth within my throat that by the third sip feels like it's expanding. I'm not allergic. My throat is mending, sucking the soothing liquid into bruised pores, raw from crying.

'Un altro zip,' another sip, Nonna Santa would say. *'Graciella, buon fatto,'* she'd praise when I *'zipped'.*

"Another sip." Harry nudged the cup against my lips. My lips reached over the top. "Well done, Gracie." He put the cup down and felt my forehead. "Fever," he pronounced with certainty. "You're going to bed."

I didn't argue. He lifted me from the couch and carried me to our room. Within minutes he'd removed my clothes and dressed me in a fleecy sweat suit, heavy socks, and flannel robe. In the past, we'd argued over if you 'fed a fever, starved a cold', but we agreed on sweat a fever.

"Sweet dreams, Gracie, girl. I love you." His lips brush my forehead. The cool spot evaporates before he straightens. "Sweet dreams."

I had no recollection of dreams, sweet or otherwise. At points during the next thirty hours I recalled feeling the singularly pleasant sensation of cold on my forehead and smelling fresh, mountain spring Downey bed sheets.

I stood under the shower spray, fever free and starving. Against Harry's advice I determined to go to Janet Henry's memorial service at ten o'clock. I wouldn't budge. He decided to be part of the solution and agreed to make breakfast while I showered.

I felt more clearheaded than I had in weeks. Nothing like a raging fever to clean out the synapses. I poured shampoo, creating too many suds and fashioning a hairdo with the clouds of soap, like the Breck Girl on the back of my mother's Good Housekeeping magazine.

I realized how Harry must have spent his Sunday when I saw the pile of bed linens in the laundry room–two sets and the throw from the couch. I striped the bed down to the bare mattress and left that to air. My washer could take all three sets but I never trusted that much would get clean. I set the machine on medium load and positioned one set of sheets and the throw in the rising water.

My navy blue business suit hung ready. I pulled out matching pumps and a small shoulder bag. The real challenge would be my pale face and dark circles. I dabbed extra foundation under my eyes and swished on two layers of blush. My lavender eyes reflected a certain calm that hadn't been there two days ago. I must have accepted something during my thirty hours of sleep. Maybe my mind settled my problems and I only had to wait to get the news. *Naïve, Gracie, naïve.*

"It could be." I spoke out loud to the person behind the gold flecked eyes and flipped off the light switch before I got an argument. I found Harry in the kitchen setting two place mats on the table. He wore a full length apron to protect his crisp white shirt and somber gray tie. His suit jacket lay across one side of the butcher-block.

"Good morning, darling." Harry stopped puttering long enough to kiss me. "You still look tired, but much better." He handed me my angel mug, filled to the brim with Mocha Madness and nodded toward the table. "Sit. Eggs are ready."

Harry, who eats only healthy, boring food, slid two over easy eggs onto a plate already loaded with crispy bacon, hash browns, and white bread toast. The only testament to his eating style was the slice of melon and two strawberries tucked near the potatoes. "May the Cuisine god forgive me for preparing this abomination. He placed the steaming plate of food on my mat. The aromas mingled up my nose and into my brain. I ate like the condemned.

Three mouthfuls into my breakfast I felt I could put down my fork and speak. "Delicious. *Mmm.* Thank you."

"My pleasure. I love watching you eat. I still stand by my statement that I'd rather clothe you than feed you."

The first time Harry had made that announcement was after our honeymoon. He'd joked with my dad, who'd nodded vigorously. I'd retaliated by running up a huge bill at Oak Brook Mall under the tutelage of clotheshorse Karen. I'd become bored after the third store, but didn't have the heart to stop her fun until five stores later when we couldn't carry anymore. I pointed my fork at him. "Watch it, Bub. Karen's just a phone call away." I tucked another forkful of hash browns in my mouth. Eating felt better than talking at the moment.

Harry grinned and dipped his spoon into his fancy, Steel-cut oatmeal. Leave it to health nuts to eschew Quaker Oats. He used to call it porridge until he grew tired of explaining it was oatmeal. His salad plate teemed with melon, strawberries, and kiwi. He lifted his mug and motioned a toast. We *clinked* ceramic. "*Célébrez la différence.*"

"We need to leave in fifteen minutes to get to the memorial."

I nodded and scraped the last of my egg against my toast. I loaded my plate and silverware into the dishwasher. The top rack held several empty Pedialyte bottles. We weren't feeding Elmo...*Oh, my, gosh. I hadn't seen Elmo.*

"Where's Elmo?"

"Those three were underfoot. Afraid I was going to squish one with every step. I condemned them to more food and fresh water in the mudroom."

I felt relief and a little guilt. I hadn't thought of Elmo until I saw the bottles. *The bottles...* My thoughts came full circle. "Did you give

Pedialyte to the other kittens?"

Harry smiled. "No. I called Tracy after you'd been asleep for thirteen hours and she said I should get fluids into you. You, my darling, consumed five bottles of that stuff. Trace said it would replenish electrolytes and keep you hydrated. You spit out the mango juice, but I managed to get a few cups of Chamomile in you. A little tricky, but well worth it. Reminds me of all the times I coaxed coffee into some of the chaps that overindulged out on the town. Much more pleasurable with you. Assuredly." He nodded his head to make the point.

Harry put his arms around me and pulled me up against his firm chest. "*Mmm*. Much nicer when you're awake." I lifted my chin and sought out his lips.

"*Mmm*. Absolutely." The phone rang and stopped what we didn't have time to start.

"Hello. Hi, Mike. Yes, she's right here."

"Hi, dad. No, I'm fine. Touch of flu or something. No, Marty didn't stop by." I raised my eyebrows and Harry shook his head. "No, not yet. We're leaving for Janet's memorial service. Okay. Thanks. Love you too."

I repeated the part he hadn't heard when we got in the car. "Dad said Marty is bringing over some pills to stop nausea. Did I vomit?"

"Only a little." Harry kept his eyes on the road.

"Well, he's on his way. I worry a little about Marty and all his little friends." I'd never said it out loud and I felt, childishly, like I was *ratting* him out. He seems to have a pill for everything." Harry stayed quiet. I turned in my seat. "Thank you for taking care of me. I don't know why I do stupid things. I spoiled your day with Will. I know you were stuck inside taking care of me. I'm sorry."

We were crossing the bridge that defined the entrance to Pine Marsh. Harry slipped his hand from the wheel to my knee. "You didn't spoil anything. I'd already brought Will to Lily's before I came looking for you. As for yesterday, Lily had early plans in Forest Park and they left after church."

I felt relieved that I hadn't spoiled his day with Will and resentful that he didn't have to choose. Talk about conflicted. Maybe Marty had a little friend for that.

Cars traveling on 355 to I-88 to the Eisenhower flowed smoothly in the post rush hour traffic. We exited at First Avenue and used Chicago Avenue to come at Regina College from Thatcher Road. The memorial service in the chapel would be followed by luncheon in Lewis Lounge on the first floor of the building. Early as we were, the parking lot looked full. Harry drove back out of the circle drive and parked on the street.

The sense of serenity I always feel in the chapel settled over me, even in the midst of the crowd of people. I prayed Janet's family would find that peace. We took seats halfway back on the left side. I'd sat there the four years I attended Regina and since then when I drove in for mass.

Karen and Hannah were already seated. No babies in tow, so Gertrude must be babysitting. We moved in next to them. Harry nodded hello and then excused himself. I watched him retrace his steps and stop at the entrance off to one side. Ric stood just beyond the tall doors that closed the chapel from the old library. Before I could speculate or follow, Karen grabbed my hand. "How are you feeling? Tracy said you were running a high fever and puking for hours." My best friend stared, waiting for an answer.

"I'm feeling much better. He did a great job as nursemaid."

"He always did." Hannah's voice warmed as she recollected. "When we were tots and came down with flu, Mum didn't always get to us in time, but Harry would hold back my hair with one hand and hold my forehead with the other whilst I threw up in the loo. More the pity he didn't go into medicine."

Harry returned and whispered, "Two rows up on the right." I found the row and saw Cassidy McCabe. I'd be seeing her tomorrow, maybe. I felt more at peace. Calm before the storm?

Sr. Jeanne and Sr. Gerri walked in together. I nodded when they looked in my direction. I selfishly wondered who my new 'boss' would be. One of the deciding factors in accepting the job had been Janet.

The memorial service began with "The Servant's Song" led by three students in the choir ministry and accompanied by other students on piano and flute. There was to be no mass just the service gathering her friends, honoring her memory, remembering her life. The eulogy, spoken eloquently by Sister Jeanne, reminded that the quality of our love and not the length of our days left the most permanent mark. She ended with a challenge to the assembly when she said, "None of us knows when the Lord will call us home, and it is incumbent on us to be prepared for His call."

Be prepared. I can't help but feel that Janet is dead because of the discovery in the woods and because I told her about my attack. *Sure, Grace, take the fall for this too. Can't disaster strike or sadness befall people without Grace Morelli taking credit?* Karen blamed me for her aunt and uncle's deaths. *Only until she came to her senses. Doesn't now…you're her daughter's godmother, aren't you?*

I didn't want to argue. I fingered the single button on my jacket. *Button, unbutton. Button, unbutton. Button, unbutton.* I lost track of the numbers but regained a sense of calm while I half listened to the next speaker. The small chapel trapped the body heat from the crowd of mourners. I wished I'd worn a short-sleeved outfit. I could take off my jacket but then I'd lose my rhythm. *Button, unbutton. Button, unbutton.*

Blessed relief came with the final music, "On Eagles Wings." I sang from memory and my spirits lifted with the eternal promise of the song, *'make you to shine like sun and hold you in the palm of my hand.'* We filed out of the chapel, headed for the first floor and lunch. Several women headed for the lavatory across from the elevator.

"I'll meet you in the lounge. This bathroom is standing room only. I'm going down to the Grill." Harry nodded and continued his conversation with Hannah.

"Great idea, I'll come with you." Karen followed me.

"*Whew*, it was boiling in there, wasn't it?"

"I was freezing. Are you okay? Maybe your fever is back." Karen thrust her hand against my forehead.

"Geez, take it easy." I pushed her hand away. "My jacket is heavy and I'm wearing a turtleneck."

"It's even colder down here." Karen pushed through the door to bathroom. The cold felt good. I heard footsteps on the stairs. *Another alum avoiding lines.* It was Cassidy McCabe. She hadn't seen me yet.

"Looking for this?" I pointed toward the bathroom.

She swung round and her eyes widened. "Hello, Grace. I didn't see you. Yes, that's exactly what I'm looking for. I figured there must be a bathroom on each floor in approximately the same place but…" she shrugged.

Suddenly I didn't want to be around her and I knew I wouldn't make an appointment. I only wanted the use of the bathroom to splash water on my face. I could do that with a water fountain. "See you upstairs," I mumbled and walked past her.

Mrs. Henry stood at the room's entrance receiving condolences as people entered. She was about Janet's height, but much thinner than her daughter. Short gray hair capped a small face, drawn with sorrow, her mouth turned down and her eyes on auto pilot, shaking hands, lifting the corners of her mouth to acknowledge a kind word.

"Mrs. Henry, I'm Grace Marsden. I knew Janet from Regina. I'm so sorry for your loss. She'd just hired me to be her assistant. I was looking forward to working with her, she was such a wonderful woman."

Did her eyes flicker when I introduced myself? Maybe Janet had mentioned the interview. No, Mrs. Henry had been in Florida. I offered my hand and she raised hers to mine. I expected a limp handshake. She slipped her small hand in my grasp and pulled me closer, I thought for a hug. "Janet trusted you. Help her find peace." Her whispered words and fever bright eyes scared the daylights out of me.

I stood inches away from her, my arms stalled at the pre-hug position, sweat beading on my forehead.

"Excuse me?" I prayed I hadn't heard her correctly, maybe even that she hadn't spoken, but that the words were only in my head. She released my hand, leaned away from me, but her eyes bore into my head burning her plea on my brain. *Help Janet find peace.* What the heck was that supposed to mean? I lowered my arms and moved away. I'd expected the entire room to be staring at that exchange, but the seconds it took for my world to start spinning off axis went unnoticed.

I found the table and spot they'd saved for me. Karen leaned toward me. "Where'd you go? I'm talking away to you in the next stall only it's not you."

I couldn't help but smile at what must have been the look on her face when she realized her mistake.

"Funny to you, missy?" I smiled even broader at her pet name. When she was upset with someone, we all became 'missy'. "I'm pouring my heart out about lack of sleep, cranky babies, and…other stuff and it's not you."

I barely contained the belly laugh, letting it squeak out. "She's the therapist I told you about."

"Great, just dandy. Can I wear this over my head when I leave?" She lifted the edge of the tablecloth.

The luncheon fulfilled its purpose of comforting the bereaved with camaraderie and loving stories about the deceased. People at each table 'told a story' on Janet, most touching and sweet. A few, from her classmates in attendance, portrayed a light-hearted girl with a few pranks to her name. The laughter began the healing that I hoped would calm Mrs. Henry's feeling that her daughter needed peace.

Three easels holding picture collages of Janet's life drew my attention. She'd been involved in the college both as a student and then after her Masters from DePaul as staff. Two of the posters depicted those years.

The other poster showed Janet as a child, playing with friends, First Holy Communion, baking with mom, band concert. Other pictures framed her 'life' pasted along the edges; friends, maybe relatives. Halfway down the left side of the board a face under a black cowboy hat stared up at me.

The room lurched and the only thing I could grab collapsed under me as I dropped to floor tangled in the legs of the easel.

The board is wedged between a chair and the floor, tilted at an angle. He stares at me. It's dark.

❧ 26 ❦

I know I'm on the leather couch at the far end of Lewis Lounge. The air feels the same, some of the smells too. I feel my wrist chafing between strong hands.

I breathed deeply. "She's coming around." Harry's voice, concerned, elated. "That's it, Gracie, girl. Open your eyes."

It's that easy. *Blink.*

Harry's hand on my shoulder keeps me from popping up like a cork in water. I'm embarrassed that I've caused a scene at Janet's memorial and struggle to sit up and look normal.

"Grace, easy." He compromised and helped me sit up. The room stayed put. Karen, Hannah, and Sister Jeanne stood behind Harry. The room beyond them seemed a sea of faces on a shoreline of drab color.

"Are you sure you don't want me to call a doctor?" Sister asked.

I tensed then relaxed immediately, realizing that if they hadn't called one by now they wouldn't–unless I didn't respond normally.

"I just got woozy looking at the photographs. Hope I didn't damage them." I tried for a calm, sincere tone.

"Darling, did you hit your head on anything? I saw you wobble, but couldn't reach you."

"I don't think so, no, I'm sure I didn't. My shoulder stings a little and I'm thirsty.

Three outstretched hands appeared, offering water, hot tea, and wine. I scowled at the Merlot in Karen's hand.

Shaking my head I reached for the water glass in Sister Jeanne's hand. "Thank you, Sister." Several sips cleared my brain and eased the cotton dry taste in my mouth. I motioned that I was standing and Harry let me, in fact he helped me up and kept a firm hold on my arm. The floor lay flat under my feet. *Thank goodness.*

The others in the room returned to their conversations and I walked over to Mrs. Henry to apologize. She stood as I approached her and put out both of her hands to clasp mine. "Are you all right?"

My face flamed and for the moment I could only nod. "I've been ill. Probably overdid it. I'm so sorry to cause a scene. I hope I didn't damage the photographs."

She held my hands tighter. "Nonsense, dear. You probably shouldn't have been up yet. It means a lot to know how much you wanted to be here. Thank you."

No mention of peace for Janet. That was good. "Mrs. Henry, about those pictures? Where they friends or relatives?"

She smiled. "It was a poster Janet did in her psychology class at Trinity her senior year. The project was to center yourself inside the influential people and events of your life. I loved the poster so much I kept it even after Janie moved out and told me she didn't want it. I never thought I'd use it for…"

Her eyes filled with tears. I felt like a creep for picking at her grief. She blinked and smiled back in control. "It's wonderful isn't it?"

"It is. She had a lot of smiling people in her life. That's wonderful."

She nodded. I fought to not ask, but the words tumbled from my loose lips before I could react. If she wasn't still holding my hands I think I would have clamped one over my mouth.

"Mrs. Henry, who is the little boy in the cowboy hat?"

She dropped my hands and stared into my eyes, a hot bright beam probing my thoughts.

"That's John, her older brother." Her face flooded with an emotion I couldn't read. "You've seen him, haven't you?" The intensity of her question left me speechless. "Help them both," she demanded and then her eyes rolled back and she collapsed.

Harry whisked me away from the college once we knew Joan Henry was on her way to Oak Park Hospital. This time an ambulance had been called. Mrs. Henry's age and circumstances warranted the extra caution. "Good grief, Grace, what did you say to her?"

I looked at him.

"I'm sorry, that came out wrong. I meant to ask, what were you talking about before she collapsed? Was she upset?"

"You were right the first time. I asked her who the little boy in the picture was and she freaked out." Harry looked blankly at me.

"The little boy, in the black cowboy hat, on the left side of the poster? Anyway, he was Janet's brother. Mrs. Henry got this strange look on her face and asked me if I'd seen him. Then she went down."

"How odd."

"Not really, I did see him last week at the museum, in the same chaps and black cowboy hat."

Harry nearly side swiped the car next to him when he turned to stare at me.

I don't know if he was assessing if I was hallucinating from fever or making a terrible joke. He knew my sense of humor. I guess he decided the fever had returned with a vengeance.

"Grace, we may have erred in not calling a doctor for you. He put on his directional to exit at Wolf Road. "Tracy's on duty today. Let's drop in."

"I don't need a hospital. Please. I need to go home and get out of these clothes, and just relax. I'll tell you all about it, but please no hospital."

The clicking stopped and we stayed left to follow the Aurora signs.

Thirty minutes later, I stood in my underwear waiting for the Jacuzzi to fill. Harry said he'd make tea, check messages, and check on the kittens.

The steamy water melted the weight from my shoulders and filled me with calm. Muscles loosened and the tension seeped from my body. I let my mind loose on the events of the day and the rest of me went limp. My obsessive-compulsive brain sought to organize and sort the snippets and input I shoved in every day. It seemed for me that my most nervous days were those when too many items in my brain didn't fit properly somewhere. I braided to calm those 'jitters.' I was trying to let my mind 'braid' the craziness of the last week. Slowly my brain scurried through the week, picking up an event, a bit of conversation, a sideways glance, and snugging them into place like a new jigsaw puzzle when you push a piece down and the surrounding cardboard resists at first, but then accepts it. My brain rushed through the days, sorting, organizing, discarding, and dropping pieces in until frames formed like linear cartoons. I cringed at these 'funny papers.'

"Here, sweetheart, I've made tea."

His voice startled me and I realized I'd fallen asleep. A crazy thought popped into my head and I spoke before I thought. "Could someone drown in a bathtub if they fell asleep? I mean they'd wake up when their head slipped under the water, right?"

Harry carried a tray with a small teapot, two cups and saucers, sugar, spoons and napkins. He set it down on the wide edge of tile before he answered. "Of course they'd wake up." His faced didn't have that 'silly goose' expression that he used to respond to frivolous questions.

"What?"

"Unless the person was unconscious." He answered quietly.

"You mean knocked out or drugged?"

"Gracie, why are we having this conversation?" Harry leaned toward the steamy mass of bubbles and traced a sweat pattern on my cheek with his thumb then gently wiped beads of water from my lips. I understood immediately he thought the question reflected my feelings. I grabbed his hand and kissed the top of his knuckles.

"You know me, purely a 'what if' question. Really." He relaxed visibly and busied himself with preparing our tea. He handed me the dainty cup and saucer, china that once belonged to my aunt. I'd found it, along with the identity of her killer in an old trunk abandoned decades earlier. The tiny floral pattern cheered me because I knew she was finally at peace. *Give Janet peace.*

I wanted peace for myself. The fear mounting in my heart was that I would have no peace until she did. Some people thought being open to feel, or sense, a restless spirit is a gift. I'd liken it to a curse. At St. Domitilla the nuns would tell us to be good and maybe God would send a saint to us while we slept. My deal with the Almighty was that I'd be extra good if He wouldn't send a glowing form to stand at the end of my bed. Why couldn't they just have left it with 'leave room in your chair for your guardian angel to sit with you?'

"Grace, what is it?"

I focused on Harry's face, creased with concern. "I was thinking about how the nuns scared me when I was a kid." I told my Church of England husband about the 'night visitors.'

"That's awful. I'm surprised more of your classmates didn't misbehave to avoid the saints." He shook his head and smiled, trying to lighten the mood.

"Oh no, they had that covered. If you were bad the devil would show up at your bedside. Much worse."

"Then the saints were the lesser of two evils?" Harry's grin brightened the room. I played along and looked heavenward. "He didn't mean that God." I waved my hand at him in a shooing motion. "If you're going to blaspheme don't sit so close to me; I'm especially vulnerable to lightening bolts."

We *clinked* cups and sipped tea, content in the quiet. I sensed the shift in Harry when he put down his saucer. He deserved an explanation. I placed my saucer next to his. "It's cooling off in here. Hand me my towel please?" His response would make my decision.

Harry reached behind him and brought up the thick folded square of pink towel. No flirting, no innuendo. He seriously wanted to talk. So be it.

"You can't be serious."

I didn't like it when people told me what I was thinking or feeling. I'd dressed quickly, agreeing to meet in the living room to talk. He made coffee for me, laid out some Raspberry Strudel, and brought in the kittens.

"I'm totally serious. I think the bones they found under Janet Henry belong to her brother, John." I'd said it and it felt right. "We should call Detective Thomas and tell him."

"Grace, be sensible. Call him and tell him that based on your seeing a little boy in costume who resembled the picture of another little boy…" Harry stopped and shrugged.

First I'm not serious, now I'm not sensible. What 's' word will be next?

"It fits. Why else would I meet this little boy? I know it sounds wild (I never used the word crazy when referring to myself) but I feel it's him. I'm calling Thomas. I know it's John Henry."

"Now you're being stubborn. You don't know that John Henry is dead. Just because Janet never talked about him doesn't mean he's dead. What if there were other pictures of John as an adult on that board that you didn't realize were of him?"

"Why wouldn't he be at his sister's memorial service? Why wouldn't the obituary name him in the 'survived by' line? Why wouldn't there be flowers from him?"

I wasn't being stubborn, I was right.

Harry nodded his head. "You've got a point, several in fact. Maybe he did die in childhood."

My grin went mega-bright.

"Not so fast with the phone call. Let's not inadvertently cause Janet's mum anymore heartache."

I hadn't thought of that, being focused on Mrs. Henry's plea not her feelings. We didn't even know if she'd been admitted to the hospital.

"Let's talk to your dad and see if he remembers anything more about the boy and see if we can track him before we call in the troops."

"I'll call and make sure he's home. We can freeload dinner." My dad always has something to whip together for whichever of his wayward kids showed up. And that included kids on the baseball team he managed and the soccer team he coached. "I'll bring a bottle of pinot."

Early in our marriage, Harry would have protested the need since my uncle made his own wine and my dad always had home-made and other types on hand. My Nonna had taught all of us never to go empty handed to someone's home. In my family we never say, 'you didn't need to bring anything' to each other because we know it's in our family code. Now Harry was the biggest proponent of the habit.

"Wrap up some of that Gorgonzola. Your dad loves the stuff. And we have to stop at Vito and Helmut's garage to pick up the Jag."

I realized I'd never given Harry the message that they called. "Uh, they called on Saturday. He seemed anxious to talk to you. I forgot to tell you."

"They called back later to discuss the work. There was a mes-sage on the machine today that the car is ready." Harry's voice seemed a shade tight. Must be an astronomical amount to fix his pride and joy.

We left my car in the mechanics' lot, figuring we'd pick it up on the way home. I think Harry wanted to check out his car. He drove east on Ogden to Highland Avenue and turned north to pick up I-88. I let my head rest against the support and my mind drifted. Neither one of us felt the need to speak. In my mind's eye I replayed the memorial service, who attended, Sister's eulogy and suddenly I remembered Ric had been there, outside the door.

"Why was Ric at the memorial service? What did he want?"

Harry's hands tightened on the wheel. He looked straight ahead.

"It's part of a police report by now, but don't mention it to your dad." He looked at me. I nodded. "The mechanic was anxious to tell me the brake line on the front brakes had been cut. I called Kramer to let him know since it apparently happened in his jurisdiction. Kramer wanted me to stop at the station and sign the report after the memo-rial. I'd wager he's trying to make amends with his brass for not doing it by the book with you."

"No brakes!" My voice squeaked with delayed reaction.

"We weren't in real danger of losing control unless they'd cut both lines. Car brakes are designed to back-up each other in the event one section is damaged. I felt the change in the handling, but knew the back brakes would work."

"In the movies they always cut the brake line and the car ca-reens down the mountain road." I spoke pragmatically to diffuse my shock.

"Before the sixties that would have worked and in the movies, anything goes. I'm more concerned about the nineties, and why someone would do that. Kramer and I can't decide if someone tried to scare me or if they meant real harm but watched too many movies." I knew he'd thrown that in to lighten the mood. "Until we know more, don't tell your dad. No need to cause him more worry."

What Harry really meant was no need to have my dad sound the alarm and gather *his* troops—my brothers, uncles, and cousins.

I remembered how difficult it had been for the casual date to ask me out. The word at high school, 'don't mess with Grace Morelli, her brothers will kick your ass,' didn't encourage the weak of heart. On the other hand, I never had trouble getting a boy to understand 'no'.

We reached my childhood home in no time and parked in the driveway. Good sign, we were the only car. Dad waved from the back yard. He was coiling the garden hose around the 'hose minder' we'd given him for his birthday. He wheeled the holder to the side of the garage. "Hey you made good time." He looked over at the Jag. "So, what was wrong?"

I felt Harry's arm around my shoulder stiffen slightly. A warning to me, or a realization for him that he shouldn't have driven the Jag? This was man-talk, *alleluia* I was off the hook. I did a twirl out from under Harry's arm and gave Dad a hug and kiss. We did our mandatory 'hug rock' *left right left right* and then released each other. "I'm pouring wine in two minutes," I held up the tote bag.

"Is Elmo in there too?"

"No just some Gorgonzola."

"What are we waiting for?" Dad led the way into his house. Harry looked relieved. He didn't know my dad as well as I did. The question would come up again. I hoped Harry had a ready answer.

Dinner was linguine with clam sauce, sautéed lake perch, and the Morelli heart salad—Romaine hearts, artichoke hearts, and hearts of palm—drizzled with a vinaigrette dressing.

"I'll set some cheesecake out to room temp for dessert and get the hot water going. Someone gave me this new tea to try. Harry you can do the honors there. Honey, you get KP."

He opened a drawer next to the sink and handed me rubber gloves. "Nothing but the best for you, sweetie."

"How about getting a dishwasher?" All of us kids had tried to persuade Dad to let us buy him a dishwasher. My mom never wanted one and he didn't see the need either. Now it was a game we played.

"Why? I already have one." He leaned over and smooched my

cheek.

"Yeah, yeah." Truth is, both Harry and Dad are the kind of cooks who wash up as they cook so there isn't a lot to wash. The last dish was set in the drainer and I looked forward to cheesecake.

"Hey, hey, Lady Jayne. Job's not done." Dad tossed a dishtowel at my head. I let it land and drape across my face. My monotone voice came from under the cotton blend. "And why can't we air dry? Less germs. It's a proven fact."

He lifted one corner and smiled. "Morellis don't air dry." The material dropped back in place. By the time I finished, Harry had the tea made and Dad had the cheesecake cut and on plates. We headed for the living room.

"This is one strong tea, *Valhalla*. Where'd you get it?"

"Friend of mine swears by it. I'll get you some if you like it."

We settle in and pass around desert and tea.

"Okay, what's up?"

"Up?" My voice mimics the word.

"As much as I love having you two drop in, I won't flatter myself and think it's just for my company."

"That and the food's good." Harry nodded at my comment.

Dad grinned. "I repeat, what's up?"

"Grace and I went to Janet Henry's memorial service today. A few days earlier we stopped at the Trailside Museum to talk to the curator."

Dad interrupted. "Miss Moe still there?"

"Yes, she is. You knew her?"

"Every kid that went to grammar school in that district knew Miss Moe. She must be in her eighties by now. I should get over there. Anyway, you were saying?"

"I wanted to ask her about the troop and her recollection of any problems. She remembered Bantonini Sr., didn't seem to think much of him. She talked about a scout the old man favored more than his own son."

"That would be Black Bart. I haven't thought of him in years."

"Black Bart?"

"Yep. His name was Bartholomew Guilfoyle. Nasty kid. Always sneaking around, ratting us out to Bantonini."

"Why the nickname? Personality, clothing, what?"

"All of the above and more. He never smiled, always wore a black tee shirt under his uniform shirt or a black sweatshirt and he always wore a black…"

Here it comes, cowboy hat.

…knit watch cap." I was both relieved that my little cowboy wasn't this nasty boy and sad that my theory remained intact.

"He never had to tent with another scout. He was always SPL; we never got to vote for a new one. He'd play us against each other when it came to assigning the camp duties. He was just a mean kid. I'd heard the story about how he broke another scout's nose when the kid teased him about his name."

"Black Bart?"

"No, he liked that. Bantonini gave it to him. His middle name, Ignatius, is what he hated. One kid found out and called him Iggy. The way I heard the story you'd a thought he called him queer. He hauls off and swings on the kid, only he's holding his closed mess kit. Never met that scout, he was gone by the time I joined."

"Any idea what happened to him? Black Bart, not the unfortunate scout."

"Sure. He's on television most nights. 'Black Bart Buick: The Good Guy in the Black Hat'. He started out working for Bantonini in his garage, learned the trade, and then bought the place when the old man retired. I'd heard that he gives discounts to any scout from Troop 265. Wonder if Moochie uses him? Anyway, he parlayed that business into a dealership and now has 'two convenient locations'."

"Okay, here's the sixty four thousand dollar question. What happened to Specs? You said he ran off that night and that you lost track of him because you left the troop. Did you hear anything more?"

"Yeah, I did. In 1955 three boys, two brothers and a friend disappeared from their neighborhood in the city. They found their bodies in the woods near where we used to camp. The murders of the Schuessler-Peterson boys made national headlines and rocked a generation to its foundation. Nothing like that had ever happened and people reacted like the world had started spinning off axis…I guess maybe it had. A related small article talked about a young boy who'd disappeared from the same woods five years earlier. My dad asked me if I'd known him. It could have been Specs. I didn't know his name, we all had nicknames."

He shrugged his shoulders. "Sorry."

"That's okay. What was your nickname?"

He smiled and shrugged again. "That would be 'meatball'."

Harry and I burst into laughter.

"Mister Meatball to you." He pointed at Harry. "Why the interest in Specs?"

The mood crashed and Dad took note. "What?"

"I think I saw him, Specs, at the museum. Only he was still this little kid in chaps and a black cowboy hat. And the clothes looked old."

Dad's face faded a shade. "Specs always wore a cowboy hat, a black one like…"

"Little Joe on Bonanza," I finished. He nodded. "And today at the memorial they had pictures of Janet's family and there was that same little boy, same hat, chaps, everything. He was Janet's brother. Her mother passed out when I asked about him. She asked me if I'd seen him. Like she knew. Like he's there, reaching out to people."

"Gracie, stop." My father's voice was firm. "This isn't happening to you. This kid you saw could be a grandson who found his grandpa's things in a trunk. He could just resemble the boy in the photo. I've got a picture of you on a pony wearing chaps and a black hat. Doesn't mean anything."

My father's voice wound down. I knew his fear was that I might follow my mother's footsteps.

"Dad, I'm fine. I don't know why I get these feelings, but I can't ignore them. We wanted to see if we could find out more about John Henry before I called Detective Thomas. Is there anyone in the troop you've kept in touch with who might know about him?"

"There's Mountain Man. You know him as Don Craig. He's about the only one I've seen. We hooked up again when he had his troop in Villa Park. Ran into each other at a training camp. Even though we were in different councils we ran some campouts together, traded off going to each others council summer camps, that kind of stuff. As an adult he was involved with a Cub Scout pack in Forest Park before he moved and joined Troop 222. He'd be your best bet."

"Was he a big kid? Why Mountain Man?"

"You gotta remember the old man wasn't subtle. Yeah, Don was a big kid, tall and wide across the shoulders. But his name, 'Craig' did it. Bantonini said, 'kid you're not just a crag, you're the whole damn mountain' and it stuck."

"I remember Mr. Craig. He's the scoutmaster that always wore a Smokey Bear hat to outings. And those red suspenders with all the pins and patches from different events and camps he'd been to. You know, he did kind of look like a mountain man as I recall–big guy with gear dangling from his belt–lots of gadgets. I thought he was the coolest scoutmaster…next to you, Dad, of course."

"Of course." He smiled. "I'm still involved in council. There's a

Super Roundtable first Wednesday in December. Don still keeps his hand in even though his son has been out for about as long as Marty. I guess it's true what they say, 'old scoutmasters don't die, they join council'."

"That's over two weeks. I don't think I can wait that long." I took a deep breath. "They found bones under Janet's body. I think they belong to her brother John. I think that's why I saw the little boy in the museum. And I think other people have seen him too. The docent at the museum was as sweet as pie to me until I asked him about the little boy in the cowboy hat and then he got weird, actually rude. I think other people have seen him, but didn't know what he wanted."

My father's voice exploded in the small room. "And you do? What are you some kind of ghost hunter? Why do you let these thoughts get inside your head? You've got enough trouble with what's already there."

There it is. All the years of cute labels for my OCD, 'jitters' 'thinking outside the box' 'marching to a different drummer' phony. He thinks I'm a nutcase.

His voice lowers. "Gracie, I'm sorry. That just came out. What I mean is don't go looking for trouble. You're wired in a way, honey that you've your hands full already."

I hadn't realized that I'd sought comfort in the length of yarn tied to my belt loop. When he said 'hands' we inadvertently looked at mine, full of half-formed yarn. I started to laugh, a little edgy at first but then genuinely seeing the humor. The laughter lightened the mood and we finished our visit on a high note.

Dad promised to call Don Craig after Thanksgiving to set up a meeting with him if that's what I wanted. His parting hug was especially close. The pain, I understood, was more his than mine.

"I love you, honey."

"I know. Love you too."

Harry extended his hand. "Goodnight, Meatball." His voice was three parts joking and one part pissed. My dad shook his hand. "Yeah, that's me."

We're on I-88 before we break the silence. "Don't bring up your idea at Thanksgiving, it's too volatile. For all you know, Gloria might know the family. It's a small world."

"I never thought of that. Gloria's lived there her whole life." The enthusiasm in my voice hit what my family called the 'pit bull' level.

"Bloody hell," Harry muttered under his breath. "Now who's the meatball?"

We drove in silence quickly reaching Vito and Helmut's parking lot. Harry waited until I was nearly to my car when he lowered his window.

"I've a quick stop to make. See you in a fair bit." He pulled away before I could question his destination. I followed him west on Ogden Avenue toward Pine Marsh, but he continued west while I veered onto 355 south to exit at Maple.

My thoughts bring me to the cutoff for Pine Marsh and within minutes to my garage. Harry always tucks the door opener in the side pocket of the car; I like it in the overhead bin. I'm distracted searching for it and don't think about the parked car I pass until it's too late. The hairs on my neck stiffen an instant before the glass shatters on the driver's side. Pain shoots through my right hand and I cradle it against my body while I accelerate up the drive and across the lawn aiming to bump over the curb and take off toward the main road. I catch a glimpse of a hooded figure running toward me as I come off the lawn. We reach the curb in a dead heat. He tosses something through the open window; it's alive and scurries up over the seat into the back.

"Oh, God. Oh, God." I push the pedal to the floor and shoot over the curb and toward the exit. "Oh, God. Oh, God." I repeat my frantic mantra, shooting out of Pine Marsh, swerving down Maple to Main Street, blowing the light a block from the Lisle Police station, and screeching into a diagonal spot from the opposite side. I can't use my right hand to shift to park. I push down on the parking brake with my left foot, and jump out leaving the door wide open. Like I care!

ô 27 ô

Nobody does hysteria better than Italians. The efforts of the duty officer and two detectives rushing from the back calmed me enough for them to lead me to their office to wait for the paramedics.

Detective Garza brought me a glass of water. I'd met him months earlier when the PR firm I'd worked for inadvertently stumbled upon a decades old murder during Depot Days.

"Mrs. Marsden, tell us what happened." I gulped the cool water and took a deep breath. The detective took the glass from my trembling hand. I nodded and leaned back against the chair.

"Someone threw a rock at my window and then they threw in something, something…" My teeth clashed against each other as my body spasmed.

"Take it easy, Mrs. Marsden. You're safe."

A young woman knocked on the doorframe. "Medics are here."

Garza motioned for her to send them in. "Mrs. Marsden, we're going to let the paramedics take a look at you and we'll continue afterwards. In the meantime, is there anyone I can call for you?"

"My husband, please. He should be home by now."

Detective Garza addressed the other person. "Her home number is on file. Let her husband know she's here."

On file. His voice sounded more like they were calling the parents of a truant child. My brothers were never *on file* with the police– my father would have killed them. Leave it to me to end up *on file.*

The petite woman with the EMT patch on her uniform checked my eyes and gently probed a cut on my cheek for embedded glass. "Eyes clear, wound clean," she passed on to her partner. I wondered if she is the teacher or the student. No matter, I liked her easy smile and light hands. And then she lifted my wrist.

"*Oww!*" *Light hands, my butt. "Oww." Which part of 'oww' doesn't she get?*

She glances up at her partner. "Broken."

I stop whining. *Broken? Oh, geez. No wonder it's on fire. At least I'm not a wimp. It's broken for God's sake.*

"Mrs. Marsden, we're going to transport you to the emergency room for treatment."

"That won't be necessary, I'll take her," Harry said from the doorway. The desk officer explained, "I told him to wait."

"I knew the way." He nodded toward Garza and dropped on one knee next to my chair. I saw the wince in his eyes as he looked at my face. I didn't feel any particular pain from the cut. Maybe it severed a facial nerve. Maybe my left side drooped. I touched my face next to my mouth checking for a sag or drool.

"Detective Garza. Do you need Grace to come back?"

"I'll stop in at the ER in thirty minutes, see how she's doing. I've a few more questions

"Gracie, can you walk? My car's outside." I nodded and started to stand assisted by Harry's hand under my left arm. I cradled my injured wrist against my body to minimize movement. We walked slowly down the hallway.

The front door loomed in the distance. This hallway hadn't seemed that long on the way in. My adrenaline levels must be on fumes. My feet felt stiff like trying to walk in the shoeboxes instead of the shoes and I shuffled the last few steps to the door.

"Her vehicle is back in our lot. We're processing the contents."

Harry nodded. "Fine."

My vehicle. I wasn't going to drive that ever again until I knew whatever I thought was in there, wasn't. I turned and looked over Harry's shoulder. "Did you find, I mean, was there anything…"

Garza understood my question. He nodded his head. "Your warning alerted our technician. He removed a rat from the vehicle."

My slump against Harry signaled the end of the conversation. He pushed open the door and propelled us out into the cold air. "Later," he called to Garza.

The crisp air against my face encouraged me to breathe deeply and only by a few saving breaths did I manage to stay conscious. The short ride to Good Samaritan Hospital gave me scant time to explain. I finished and leaned back against the headrest. "I don't understand why those people did this or how they knew where I lived."

"They took down the plate number on the Jag, that's how. But why? Kramer said the other attacks in those woods followed the same M.O. as yours, but he didn't mention any reports of second contacts. I'd better ring him from hospital, see if he can check on that."

Harry turned me over to the ER nurse who took me behind the curtain while he filled out the paperwork and called Ric.

I answered questions, went to X-ray, and waited for the diagnosis. Broken. Then on to casting and a choice of colors. Efficient, fast, no muss, no fuss.

"Gee, you do this like a well-oiled machine." I wondered for a moment if I had offended them by my simplistic observation. After all, they were supposed to work that way.

The technician grinned at me. "This close to Seven Bridges Ice Arena and Downers Grove Ice we get broken wrists all the time. Sort of goes with the territory." Her freckled face split into a wider grin at her own joke.

Final step, a tiny box with pain meds, and the curtain parted. Harry waited on the other side with a coffee on the table next to him. Detective Garza sat next to him sipping at his own cup of something. They both stood when I walked toward them. Harry guided me to the seat next to him on the other side of the table. His eyes clouded and I knew he blamed himself for not being with me earlier.

I held up my short lavender cast. "To match my eyes."

My attempt at humor didn't work. The muscles at his jaw tightened and flexed.

"Mrs. Marsden, if you're up to it now I'd like to finish getting your statement. We pretty much know what you told us." He looked down at his notes. "It was a brick that smashed your window. There was a note wrapped around it."

My tiny gasp turned into a nervous laugh. "That's melodramatic isn't it? And kind of an old fashioned juvenile delinquent prank."

Garza nodded. "Nothing juvenile about the results. The note is strange, just one word, 'Chee Chee Pin Quay'. What's a dead Indian chief got to do with this?"

"You know the story of Chee Chee Pin Quay?"

Garza smiled. "I grew up in Forest Park. My parents still live there."

"You weren't a boy scout at St. Edgar by any chance?"

"Boy Scout? Not me. I went out for every sport in grammar school and high school; the jock for all seasons route."

Looking at his solid build that carried past prime weight I could picture a younger, lighter version.

"Why do you ask? Any connection?"

Harry answered. "We're not certain at this point, but there seems to be." He went on to present the week in review; succinct, factual, and thirty minutes shorter than if I'd done it.

Garza sat back and crumpled the empty cup in his hand. I'd drained mine also. "Can you give me any description other than 'hooded'?"

I shook my head. "Sorry."

"Who's the detective handling this case?"

"Detective Thomas." Garza's face reacted. "You know him."

"Yeah. Another jock from Oak Park River Forest High School. We were at the police academy together, after we each did a tour in Korea. 'Bout the only thing we were good for after eighteen months over there."

"I'll call Thomas, see what he's got. Anything else?" He looked from me to Harry and back to me where his gaze stayed. "Feelings, thoughts?" His eyes never left mine and I knew he would gauge the sincerity of my answer by the color of my eyes. Harry knew it too.

"Garza, I need to get Grace home. If we think of anything else, we'll call you." Harry ended the interview. Garza closed his notebook.

We drove in silence, seemingly calm and collected, but his mind tugged and twisted at the situation; the slow gnawing at his bottom lip revealing his true state of mind. I tried to go blank, especially when we reached the base of the driveway. I closed my eyes and waited until we'd parked inside the garage, sealed in by the enormous overhead door.

"Darling?" Harry's soft voice woke me. I'd drifted off. I lifted my eyebrows in an effort to open my eyes, but the lids stayed put. Harry opened the door and leaned in. "C'mon old girl. Upsey daisy." He gently pulled me out of the car and walked me into the house.

Upsey daisy. Did they know at British Intelligence that their ex-spy said upsey daisy? Maybe a code-name? I giggled.

Harry kissed the top of my head. "What makes you tick, Gracie girl?"

I slipped my good arm around his neck and lay my head with my ear against his chest. "*Tick tock, tick tock*," I mimicked. "One of those." I felt silly and lightheaded and wondered which drugs were responsible.

Harry lifted me into his arms and carried me upstairs to our bedroom. For the second time in less than a week my body succumbed to its overwhelming need for sleep. I dreamed through Tuesday and into Wednesday.

❧ 28 ❧

My tirade had started when my nose detected the delicious aroma of Cinnamon Nut Swirl and I opened my eyes to find my angel mug on the nightstand. Harry leaned down and kissed the top of my head. "Good morning, darling. *Hmm*. You look rested."

Harry laid his paper on the nightstand and sat down on the bed. "Sorry I couldn't get that off short of using scissors." He referred to my polo shirt with *RC* embroidered above the pocket.

"That would be sacrilege to desecrate Regina College active wear." I grinned until my glance at the paper hit the masthead. Wednesday!

"Why did you let me sleep for twenty-four hours? I have things to do before tomorrow. We're supposed to bring appetizers and things I haven't even told you. What were you thinking letting me zonk out?"

"About you." His quiet declaration stopped me. "And don't worry about the appetizers. I called Carolyn and asked her what you were slotted for and shopped for everything. Chinese Popovers. It's under control."

"Yeah, what about the centerpieces? We were going to make several for the different tables."

"Handled. You, Tracy, Karen, and Carolyn, possibly Jolene and her roommate are meeting at Gloria's tonight to set up. At that time, people with two good hands will assemble the centerpieces. You can supervise." He grinned and kissed the tip of my nose. "Now, after you've had your coffee, I'm certain you'll want a shower, so I brought a dry cleaner's sleeve and duct tape."

I still had to translate my husband's English at times. He placed a plastic bag on the bed. "Call me when you're ready." He left with his paper.

Call me when you're ready. I don't know why that bothered me but it did. I sipped at my coffee and tried to analyze why I was so upset. I'd lost an entire day and no one thought to ask me if that was okay. I'm sure Harry called my dad to fill him in, and then Tracy and his sister who told Karen who told Ric. *She's all done in, poor thing, needs her rest.* I could hear Harry's voice explaining. I grew angrier by the minute, the usually calming flavor turning bitter in my mouth.

Through great effort I managed to undress and tape plastic over my cast. *I didn't grow up with four Eagle scouts for nothing.* The warm water felt great over my shoulders. I faced the showerhead holding the pipe with my right fingers to keep the cast out of the stream and to help me hold up the extra weight. The soap slipped from my left hand a second time. Maybe Harry's plan included washing. Thoughts of my husband's hands running over my body stall my efforts as I enjoyed my daydream.

"*Yeow*!" I pushed the handle to the off position and pant through the pain of scalding water. Harry must have flushed.

By the time I'm out of the shower and into a robe, Harry was knocking at the door. "Sorry, love. Didn't realize you'd gone in."

I flung the door open. "We need a plumber." I wore only my robe and walked to the dresser to choose my underwear and socks. Harry followed. "I'll ask your family tomorrow, they know everyone."

Harry offered to make breakfast or buy breakfast. No contest. We were seated in Granny's Restaurant on Route 53 within the hour. Our meal arrived quickly, the check discreetly tucked under the jelly holder. He reached across and cut half of my dinner plate size waffle into bite size pieces. Within a few minutes, he needed to cut up the other half.

I grinned, but noticed Harry's smile was slow to reach his eyes, barely touching them then sliding away.

"What's wrong?"

"Talk about an open book. I must be losing my poker face."

"Not really, I've just looked into your eyes about a million times, I have their moods memorized. Don't change the subject, what's wrong?"

"Detective Garza contacted the Sheriff's police. After what happened to you I decided to tell them your theory. With a specific identity to check it didn't take long. The remains were positively identified through dental records as belonging to John Henry."

I knew they would be, but had hoped that the little boy in the cowboy hat had grown up to enjoy life, live life. My eyes filled with tears and I swallowed to keep from crying. Harry touched my hand.

"I'm sorry. Should have waited to tell you."

I shook my head and sniffed, widening my eyes to clear the tears. "I knew it would be him. I think that's what he wanted." Harry squeezed my hand.

"Grace you don't know that who you saw in the museum wasn't a real little boy who reminded you of the photo or vice versa. You saw the photo and superimposed that face on the boy at the Trailside."

"Are you a shrink now?" I pulled my hand out from under his and used a paper napkin to blow my nose. I heard the cold note in my voice and regretted the tone, but kept my hands in my lap. *It's not like I looked for this, but sometimes feelings, figures came unbidden into my life.* I kept my thoughts to myself and willed my eyes to look at Harry. His face reflected his confusion at my remark.

Neither one of us picked up our silverware to finish our meals. The half waffle I'd eaten lay in my stomach like a rock garden. We left the restaurant not speaking to each other and spent the short ride home with our own thoughts.

Having a cast on my dominant arm slows my routine. I struggled to lift April's saddle to her back and decided to ride bareback. Cash Cow *whinnied* his displeasure at being left behind. April shivered in anticipation of what I can only imagine is release and pleasure for her. We ran through our patterns. My mind settled into the pattern and the planning layer in my brain peeled off like an onion. My eyes were open but I saw my surroundings through an opaque film. My thoughts were crystal clear as they played on the screen behind my eyes. By the time April finished her patterns I had a list of five people to call.

I brushed April quickly. "Sorry girl, I'll give you a superb brush down tomorrow." She accepted the baby carrots and my promise.

I rushed toward the back door and nearly collided with Harry on his way out. "I was coming to find you. Cassidy McCabe is on the phone for you."

That saved me one phone call. I kicked off my boots in the mudroom and aimed my jacket at the peg on the wall. Elmo rushed to climb around my feet and I scooped him up rather than slow down.

"Hello?"

"Grace, this is Cassidy McCabe. I apologize for not calling you yesterday as we agreed."

"That's okay. I was a little under the weather–slept most of the day. I want to talk to you, it's important."

"Of course. I could see you Friday at two o'clock?"

"No, not to talk to you about that. I wanted to do this in person because it sounds weird, but there may not be time."

"Grace, are you experiencing unusual thoughts?"

"It's not about me, it's about you. I wanted to warn you that someone may come around wanting to talk to you about Janet or looking for notes from your sessions."

She stayed silent.

"I don't know for sure, but I think it could be a possibility. Anyway, you need to be careful, maybe go to the police."

"They've already been here." Her voice sounded flat. "Someone broke into my office yesterday morning and tore through my files. Not very subtle, used a crowbar to force the door and the drawer. The police kept asking me if I had any idea what the thief was after and if any files were missing. Three files are gone: Joan Henry's, Janet Henry's, and yours."

My gasp must have sliced through Cassidy, whose first concern would be for her client. Absolute trust is key to her success.

"Grace, I'm so sorry."

I mumbled an absolution and a warning. "It could have been worse and it still might be." I told her what happened to me Monday night. It was her turn to gasp.

"Cassidy, I'm going to be in Oak Park tonight at Under the Ginkgo Tree. Do you know the place?"

"Yes."

"Would you meet me there at seven? Some other people will be there, but we can talk this through."

She agreed and I hung up. Harry had heard only my side of the conversation so I filled him in.

"So someone wants to know what Janet was telling Cassidy and why you were there. Arriving as you did so soon after Janet's death it must have appeared that you might be connected. Timing is everything." His wry comment made sense. "Speaking of timing," he continued smoothly, "I'm headed into Oak Park to St. Edgar for the Thanksgiving assembly and then a meeting for all the scout parents. There's some talk that the school doesn't want to continue the charter."

Is Harry inviting me to accompany him to Will's assembly? Won't Lily be there?

"I've asked Walter to drive you in later. Gertrude is minding the twins and Walter is going to the boardinghouse." I can pick you up at Gloria's afterwards, probably over by nine-thirty."

Gertrude Klops, Walter's lady friend, had sold her once elegant, now run-down, three story Victorian to Hannah and Karen whose plans were to renovate and open as a B&B. Brit Haven would cater to travelers from the UK who wanted a *1930's American Experience.*

Hannah and Karen wisely hired Walter to oversee the project and more importantly discovered a marvelous baby-sitter in the deal.

Part of me was disappointed that there wasn't an invitation, but more of me was relieved.

"Sounds like you've tied up the loose ends." I poured a fresh cup of coffee and sat down in the breakfast nook.

"Not exactly all of them." Harry looked at his watch and at the clock checking one against the other.

"When are you leaving?"

"Soon. Actually by now, I thought." He looked at his watch again.

Then I understood. "You're waiting for someone to show up and baby-sit me aren't you?" My voice raised in question and volume.

"Grace, calm down. I promised."

Then I understood more. Of course Harry would have told my father what happened. How could I show up to Thanksgiving dinner with an unexplained cast on my arm and gash on my cheek? I felt sorry for my husband as I imagined how that conversation must have gone.

"How many?"

"Only your father and Marty. Joseph doesn't arrive until tonight and Mike and Glen are at work.

I nodded. Not bad. I walked back to the coffee maker and filled it for another round of coffee. I saw Harry peek at his watch. "Go ahead. You know Dad, he's on his way–would have called if something came up."

The dichotomy of expression on Harry's face delineated *don't be late for Will* and *don't leave Grace alone* until the door chimes released him.

A quick hug and kiss. "Love you, see you later," as he bounded out the door to the garage. The door chimes, again.

"Okay, okay, I'm coming." *Hold your braciole.* I grinned and then felt the rush of heat as my face reddened thinking about the term my brothers had used and that had been banned in our home. I flung open the front door and greeted my dad and brother.

My father hugged me and then held me at arm's length to inspect me. "Hey, why so red? Did I interrupt something?" He smiled and looked beyond me.

"Not unless they were doing it in the Jag," Marty noted and pointed through the open door at the Jaguar backing onto the street and driving away.

"Martin, don't talk like that about your sister." My brother's smug smile disappeared. I wanted to stick out my tongue in my best *na na na na boo boo* smirk, but I knew I'd catch a reprimand too. I took the high road.

"Harry had to be in Oak Park. He scooted when he heard the doorbell."

"And he knew it was us because he's psychic?"

"Whoever did this," I held up my arm, "most likely wouldn't ring the bell."

"Good point." That was Dad's grudging acceptance. "I smell coffee; I brought *pizelles* from Edna."

Marty and I followed him into the kitchen reaching the arch side by side at the same time. Normally we would have 'play' shoved each other for position. Today we each were aware of the others' bum wing and uncharacteristically slowed to allow the other to pass. We laughed as we both stopped. "After you," I flourished with my good arm.

"Oh no, after you," Marty responded in kind.

"I insist, after you." We grinned at each other.

"No, I insist, after you."

"The both of you get in here before I knock your heads together." My father's tough guy voice sent us into laughter. Dad already had plates and cups out. We sat down with our coffees and *pizelles* and munched in silence. Edna baked like an angel. The family had encouraged her to open an Italian bakery, but she'd insisted that if she did that, it wouldn't be fun it would be work. She baked for everyone. All the wedding cakes in our family came from Edna. Communion, confirmation, graduation, wedding, all of them. That was her gift, a labor of love.

"Mmm." I stopped after three and crumpled my napkin on my plate. Now that we had snacked we could talk.

"Harry called me to tell me what happened. This is getting crazy." He nodded at my brother. "Tell her what you found."

"Eve found it when she got home and did some laundry. It must have caught up in my vest when dad pulled me up. It's a Boy Scout uniform button."

The hair on my neck stiffened and I shivered.

"I know, bizarre isn't it? It's gets stranger. The button is real brass; it's an old one but," he held up his hand to stop my question, "it hadn't been out there that long, no tarnish. I called that detective and turned it in. They think it might belong to whoever pushed your friend into that well."

"Harry's smart to get Will out of that troop. Too many coincidences." My father spoke over the top of his mug. He sipped and spoke again. "I don't trust the Bantoninis, not even Moochie."

"It may happen sooner than later." I explained about the meeting Harry was attending at the school.

"St. Edgar has had a pack and troop chartered since there's been a St. Edgar's. Father Gebhardt's predecessor started the charter and Gebhardt supported it wholeheartedly. Gave the kids extra holy cards if they joined cub scouts."

Marty and I nodded, both aware of the incentive of holy cards in a parochial school. There were like trading cards for Catholic kids.

"Dad, do you think Father Gebhardt knew something hinky went on with Bantonini back then? Would he have done anything?"

"Hard to tell, honey. Who would he have told? It was different then."

"What about Mr. Henry. He told his son he was going to talk to the youth minister, Father Briscoe? Did they ever find the driver who ran him down?"

"What are you saying? Someone killed him because he was going to talk to a priest? I think you're out in no man's land with that one."

"Seems like if Mr. Henry were going to talk to the priest it would be about what an ass this Bantonini was, not that he thought he was a pedophile. I don't think he would have left his son and the other boys at risk."

"Then what was so important that he left so quickly. Can't believe his feelings were hurt by Bantonini and he wasn't even camped close to the boys; he could have stayed put."

"Dad, do you know if the priest is still alive?"

"He would be in his late sixties, maybe early seventies. Father Briscoe came to the parish to fill a new position the Archdiocese had created—youth minister. St. Edgar was the first parish to have a youth mass, the school choir sang the mass and Father Briscoe said the mass with his sermons geared toward the youth."

"How do we find him?"

"I'll call St. Ed's, tell them I was a student there who wants to contact his favorite priest."

Spoken so matter-of-factly, I couldn't see how it wouldn't work.

"With the holiday you can't reach the school until Monday." I tapped my fingers on the table.

"Slow down."

I nodded. "I know. Look, you guys relax. I have laundry waiting and an iron with my name on it."

"So would that be 'Procter Silex'?"

"Lame, Marty, lame."

"I thought it was funny." Dad turned to Mary. "Maybe she just uses her initials, 'G.E.'"

"Okay, merry men of mirth, entertain each other while I get some cleaning done.'

"Leave it for Jeannette. She still cleans for you, doesn't she?"

Jeannette. Jan is Jeannette. Oh my God. My father is bringing the cleaning lady to Thanksgiving dinner! To meet the family? Oh crap.

I mumbled, "She doesn't do laundry," and shot out of the room before my face could turn red and my eyes turn purple. I heard Dad's perplexed tone, "She does my laundry."

Ooh. Too much information. I don't want to picture my cleaning lady folding my dad's boxers. Too late. Does she fold them lengthwise or across the middle? Does she leave them long or roll them up? Does she think about who wears them?

"Stop right now," I scolded myself. Fortunately I was halfway up the stairs when I spoke. I went straight to my room and picked up the phone.

Mike picked up his phone at the office on the second ring. "Mike Morelli, can I help you?"

"Did you know dad's dating his cleaning lady? Bringing her to dinner tomorrow? Did you?"

"Whoa, slow down. Yes, yes, and yes."

My adrenaline dropped and I slumped onto the bed. "You did? When? Why didn't anyone tell me?"

"I thought Harry–" My brother stopped and began in another direction. "Dad told us he'd be bringing a friend to dinner. Said he's known her a short time and enjoys her company. I think it's great he found someone to socialize with."

Socialize my butt, she's already in his underwear. Pictures, unbidden, flashed into my mind. I shook my head to oust them before my obsessive brain gathered and glued them to my subconscious for all time.

"Don't you?" my brother asked. An obvious 'of course I am' answer, but I couldn't speak the words. "Gracie, don't do this to dad. He deserves to be happy."

"He's happy. Did he tell you he's not happy?"

"You damn well know what I mean. Each of us has someone. Someone we can turn to, trust, laugh with. Dad had that with mom. He wants that again. Anyone would. And anyone who loves him would want it for him."

There it is, the gauntlet thrown down. If you love him, be happy that he's happy. My older brother never used cuss words unless he was taking a stand. I knew I'd have no allies in this tug of war.

"Grace? Don't be like this. We all miss mom, but even Mom would–"

"Stop." I interrupted. I didn't want to hear that my mother would want her husband to love another woman. "I gotta go." I hung up on my brother's words.

∂⌐ **29** ↩

I didn't return to the kitchen until five o'clock, an hour before Walter and Gertrude were to pick me up. Dad called me down for dinner. He had spent his afternoon cooking dinner and preparing sweet potatoes, mozzarella, onion, and tomato salad, and an Italian green bean casserole for tomorrow.

He tried to engage me in conversation about tomorrow, I think, because he realized I hadn't known about Jeannette and he wanted to tell me. I feigned a bad headache and kept my eyes on my food.

Marty, who never scored high marks in sensitivity, waved a matchbox size packet in my face. "This'll cure whatever ails you. He slid the box open to reveal tiny yellow pills. "Take one, guaranteed to stop a headache in its tracks. Perfect timing, best taken with food, fewer side effects."

"Geez, Marty, can't you take a crap without drugs?" I hadn't meant to sound so shrill, and certainly hadn't meant to say 'crap' in front of my father. Marty's jocular smile dropped from his face and my father's palm slapped the tabletop.

"Grace! Nice talk from my daughter the truck driver." He turned to my brother. "Stop offering pills every time somebody hiccups, your sister's got a point." He swung back toward me. "And you, young lady, were not raised to talk to your brother that way."

Guilt. Why do I feel guilt? I'm thirty-two years old for heaven's sake. He's the one skulking off with some harpy. I chastised myself before those thoughts went further. My father didn't skulk and Jan Pauli is not a harpy. She's an intelligent, interesting woman with a terrific sense of humor and a warm genuineness. He could do worse, much worse. *But I'll never call her mom. Cripes, now you've got them tying the knot!*

Knots, something about knots. The doorbell rang before I could catch the memory. I hugged Dad in a way that I hoped told him I was fine. I still couldn't say the words. "Thanks for coming out, both of you." I nodded toward my brother, we stepped toward each other. Our mother had taught us never to stay angry with each other and on her deathbed she'd extracted that promise from each of her children. "Sorry," I whispered.

"Me too."

"See you tomorrow."

Walter closed the door behind us and we walked to his car in the driveway.

"How is you feeling, Missus Grace?" Walter's sign of respect for me as Harry's wife has always been the title 'missus'. Gertrude uses it too and it drives me nuts to have people older than my dad calling me missus. I call them Walter and Gertrude and feel like a little kid disrespecting my elders. I try not to use their names just make eye contact and start talking.

"I feel fine. Thank you for driving me to Oak Park."

"Is nothing, we was going there, too, and Mr. Harry say you must not be alone."

Walter had acted as my guardian angel almost a year ago. I knew he'd protect me like he would Harry, and he would die for Harry. I shook the thought and prepared to smile at Gertrude who turned in her seat. "Oh, Missus Grace I am sorry you are hurting." Her thin high voice chirped at me from the front seat. Tiny hands guided fallen wisps of light brown hair back into the grip of bobby pins.

"Thank you. I'm fine. I have no pain."

"No pain, *das ist gut*."

"*Ja, gut*," Walter echoed. We backed out of the driveway and I settled in for some quiet time to decide how to approach Cassidy. Three of the people I wanted to talk to would be there tonight. That left only two names on my list who I'd try to reach after the holiday.

Soft lights glowed through the darkness from the lower windows of Gloria's home. Under the Gingko Tree looked lovely and unaware of its fate tomorrow. The Morelli and friends' dog and pony show would arrive to squeeze their laughter, non-stop chatter and love into this sedate icon from the bygone era when children should be seen but not heard and barely seen if possible.

Mainly Morellis tomorrow except for the friends and one cousin each from the Anderson, Scala, and Fragasso families. I'd found out after my intake of *pizelles* that Edna was bringing the dessert and her family. She'd never been to a B&B.

I stood on the sidewalk looking up at the painted lady, wishing again I'd been more honest with Harry about what kind of a house I wanted. He'd swept me off my feet and liberated me from a 9x12 bedroom with a strict bathroom schedule to the luxury of a twelve room home, three of which were bathrooms. My only real input had been that I didn't want a basement–as a kid I'd always been afraid of going down into our basement.

I realized Walter waited for me to go in. I reluctantly walked up the stairs and rang the bell, preparing myself for the onslaught of questions and comments. But then, I was there to ask questions, too. Tracy opened the door and I turned, releasing Walter from his vigil. I walked into a Victorian Christmas. The banister, draped with gold satin garland, welcomed me. Each stately column bore an old-fashioned wreath with a cut-out card and festive bow.

I knew Hannah and Karen wouldn't arrive until Gertrude got to their place. Tracy and I exchanged quick hugs.

"How's the wrist?"

"Good. It doesn't hurt, just awkward."

"Sounds like a clean break, easy mend. Gloria has coffee and tea in the kitchen. Grab a cup. I want to finish attaching the turkeys."

Perfect. Gloria was one of the people I wanted to talk to. I stepped into the kitchen where she stood chopping celery and carrots at a long white table. She wore a full apron over her navy short-sleeved shirt and matching slacks. Something baking in the oven smelled wonderful and the heat from the blue AGA filled the small room. I slipped off my sweater. She nodded toward the counter. "New coffee, Crazy Eights, a blend of eight beans two of which are cocoa."

"*Mmm*. Caffeine and chocolate. I like that. Saves eating the Snickers." I poured a cup. "The house looks beautiful. I love the garland. Can I help with that?"

She raised her eyebrows. "Thanks for offering but unless you're left-handed I think it's safer you don't use knives. But I never turn down company. I like the way the garland worked, too. Thanks."

"Gloria, you've lived around here most of your life haven't you? I mean did you grow up here, go to school here?"

"I said I liked company, not the third degree." She smiled and pushed a pile of cubed celery into a glass bowl. "What's on your mind and maybe we can get there before everyone else arrives."

I smiled, grateful that she was as intuitive as I was clumsy. I gave her the Readers' Digest version of the events to date. "I wondered if you knew the boys, men now, that were in that early troop."

Her nod sent tingles along my spine. "I knew most of the scouts in that troop. We were at St. Ed's together. The scouts all had nicknames that they used on campouts and at scout meetings. I knew them by the names the nuns used. Edward, Bartholomew, John,

Timothy. The school was small and the sixth, seventh and eighth grades did art and music classes together." She didn't miss a beat, chopping lengths of carrots into small bits the entire time she spoke.

"You knew John Henry?"

Gloria's eyes looked beyond me and beyond the soft yellow kitchen wall, her knife motionless above an orange strip, her voice softer, less matter of fact, she spoke, "I know John, grew up with him in a way. My aunt lived on the same block as his family, still does. We visited her every Sunday. Her kids were older; nice to a younger cousin but not really interested. I'd take their dog, Al, for a walk for something to do. That's how I met John Jacob. I always called him by his two names. He wanted me to call him J.J. I never could. Anyway, once we connected we'd always meet on Sundays, and walk and talk for hours. My family was thrilled that I didn't mope around the house or hole up in a corner with my nose in my latest Nancy Drew book."

Her voice slowed down and she lowered the knife to the table and wiped her hands down the front of her apron. Beads of sweat moistened her upper lip. She lifted the corner of her apron and patted her lip. I thought the corner would travel higher to her eyes, they glistened with tears. She dropped the material and drew a deep breath. "One Sunday he never showed up at our meeting place. I knew he'd been camping the night before and thought maybe he was late because of that."

Gloria continued. "We'd meet at Chee Chee Pin Quay's grave. On Monday I looked for him, but he didn't come to school. Same thing on Tuesday. I thought he was sick. I asked Sister Barbara if she knew if he was sick. She had that expression on her face that adults would get when they didn't want to tell you something bad. I thought he was really sick. At home I heard my mother talking about the accident that killed Mr. Henry. My heart just broke for John Jacob; he adored his father. Now I thought I knew why he hadn't been in school. The following week he still hadn't returned and then my mother told me he had disappeared in the woods during the camp-out."

"I'm sorry, I had no idea. Forgive me for dredging up those memories."

Gloria took a deep breath and blinked several times. She picked up her knife and continued chopping the carrots. "It's all right. I had-n't thought about John Jacob in years. Just every now and then I'll see this kid in a–"

"Black cowboy hat," I finished for her.

"*Ouch!*" Gloria stared at the blood spreading from the slice in her forefinger. She hurried to the sink and ran cold water over the finger diluting the deep red to pink. I ripped off several paper towel sheets to hand her for a compress. She turned from the sink, her finger wrapped and held up close to her face; her pallor matched the paper towel.

"How did you know? He wore that every Sunday. And chaps.not kid kind of chaps. His dad had taken him to a rodeo on one of their vacations. John Jacob had made friends with a boy named Rusty who was a junior rodeo rider. He begged his dad to take him to where this friend wrote to him that the rodeo would be. They did that a couple of times. One Sunday he showed up wearing chaps and the hat. He'd traded his new school pants and shirt for the cowboy clothes. John Jacob didn't want to be a cowboy, he wanted to be a rancher; read everything about it. Talked about it all the time, at least with me."

She lowered her hand and gently un-wrapped her finger. "I think a Band-aid now and I can get back to work. They're in the cabinet behind you, top left."

I found the box and removed one plastic strip, peeled it back and handed it to Gloria.

"Thanks. Look I'm on a schedule here and really not up to talking about him, but how did you know about the hat?" Her eyes pleaded with me for a different answer. I couldn't lie.

"I saw him in the Trailside Museum. My family thinks I'm mistaken, confused, but I know I saw him."

Gloria slumped against the sink and nodded her head slowly. "One of his favorite places."

I poured her a glass of water and placed it in her hand.

"After I found out he'd disappeared, I told my parents I thought he might have gone to find his rodeo friend. I wanted to tell his mother, but my parents felt she had too much grief to handle and that they would tell Father Briscoe. He would know what to do. I don't know if they did. Adults didn't listen to kids much in those days. As it turned out, my aunt went on vacation for two weeks and then my dad had pneumonia so we didn't visit my aunt and uncle for over a month. When we did, I followed my pattern and went to the rock. I think I wanted to say my own good-bye. I hoped he'd found Rusty. I thought he might have left me a note near the rock. There was no note. After a few minutes, I felt someone watching me from the bushes. I leaped from the rock and started across the clearing to the street. I couldn't resist looking back. That's when I saw him standing next to the rock staring at me. I stumbled into the street. A car blew its horn and I jumped back. I looked again, he was gone. I never told my parents and it took me months to build up the courage to go back. I never saw him there again, but each time I went the feeling of being watched overwhelmed me. I haven't been back in thirty years."

"You never saw him there, have you seen him somewhere else?"

Color returned to her face and I felt less guilty probing.

She nodded. "At the Trailside Museum. We'd gone there in high school on a field trip. Miss Moe was explaining what the area looked like a hundred years before and I wandered off toward the display of the Pottawatomie Indians. I thought a grade school group was there too because I saw a young boy near the display case I was headed for. I stopped cold when I realized he was wearing chaps and a black cowboy hat. He started to turn and I could see the side of his glasses. Before he turned full I passed out. Teacher said I'd probably skipped lunch or I was too hot in my school sweater. Only lasted a few seconds. When I looked around I didn't see him. I asked if there was another group, younger kids, in the museum. Miss Moe shook her head, but I remember how she looked at me. Kind of knowing. I wanted to go back to ask her. I never did."

My heart thumped in my chest and a heavy sense of sadness hung around my neck. The warmth of the room dissipated, replaced by a still coolness. I shivered and slipped into my sweater. The light from the ceiling fixture grew brighter, and cast a crystal gleam on the metal surfaces and etched the facets of Gloria's face. She held my gaze, waiting.

"Hey, how big is that cup of coffee? I thought you'd be back to help me hang the turkeys." Tracy's bright voice and effervescent smile shattered the mood. And that was a good thing. "Did you crack the back door? It's freezing in here." She rubbed her hands together. "I started the fireplace. William cut down a tree two summers ago and chopped the wood into small pieces. He's going to drop that off when he picks me up. Should be plenty for tomorrow."

Tracy's mundane chatter chased away the sense of dread. I left Gloria to her thoughts and followed Tracy into the living room. She insisted on making tiny turkeys out of pipe cleaners and attaching them to a long ribbon, which would be strung across the one set of windows. It was their tradition. After dinner and football, everyone would choose a numbered turkey and then a few numbers would be pulled and small prizes awarded. We hung the turkeys, and raised and lowered each side until the gross grain ribbon stretched evenly.

The doorbell rang and the gang arrived within minutes of each other. Karen, Hannah, and someone I'd never met came in first. Before introductions could be made, Jolene and her roommate, Lindy, came in. Jolene stepped up with a hug and kiss. "Hi, Aunt Grace." Then she noticed my arm. "What happened?"

I wasn't about to chill the mood. Besides, I didn't even know the person with Hannah. "Fender bender actually, but my wrist twisted and hit funny. Weird." I had talked looking down at my cast to avoid looking at Jolene. I lifted my arm and waved it around. "I'm going to let the boys sign it tomorrow."

"They'll love that," Tracy said.

"Which bone is broken?" Lindy's interest is purely clinical; she's studying to be a chiropractor. I really wanted off the subject. Tracy sensed my dilemma and interjected in song, "the wrist bone's connected to the hand bone."

Laughter erupted and we moved into the living room for the next introduction. Hannah tipped her hand toward the petite woman standing with her hands tucked in the pockets of her red blazer. She can't be five feet tall, but standing next to Hannah makes anyone seem shorter. "Everyone, I'd like you to meet Marisol, the psychic who has offered to assist the police."

The expected slack jaw expression and murmur of uncertain response made the circuit of the room. So this was the woman Hannah raved about. Her short, streaked hair framed full lips and almond shaped brown eyes. Marisol, perhaps she used one name like Cher or Madonna, looked more like a model than a medium.

Jolene spoke first. "Wow. Do you do readings? Are we doing a reading tonight like a séance?"

Marisol's eyes sparkled. "I thought we were making party favors." Her simple statement bridged the awkwardness and the intros continued. I shook her hand, using my fingertips, and she held mine for half a beat longer than the usual shake and release. She searched my eyes and my face flushed with heat. I broke contact with her and excused myself to refill my coffee.

Jolene and Lindy followed me into the kitchen looking for soda. "How goes school, ladies?"

Lindy, always the A student answered enthusiastically, "great, just great."

I looked at my niece. "Good."

Hannah and Marisol moved past us. Marisol stopped in the

doorway and her body tensed. I saw her shoulders relax and then she stepped into the room.

What the heck is that about? I follow the young women back to the living room. The nine-foot Frazier Fir stands nude in the bow window. One of our tasks tonight is to decorate the fresh tree with the simple, eclectic decorations that Gloria has collected through the years. Tomorrow, each family will bring an ornament to add to Gloria's tree.

Another task, to set up the buffet table for thirty guests was in progress. Karen carefully set up plates, dinner and dessert, at one end. The cherry wood gleamed through the cut out lace runner. I joined Karen. Everyone was either decorating the tree or creating favors made with ribbon, vellum, and dried flowers.

"So had you met Miss 'woo-woo' before tonight?"

Karen shook her head. Her closed expression told me either she didn't want to talk about it or she was so upset she couldn't. "*She* floated in right before Gertrude arrived. I had no idea Hannah invited her. I don't know what's going on in her head anymore."

"I'm sure Hannah just loves talking ghosts and spirits, and hauntings with her. You know how Hanns thinks she's got the gift. I hope this Marisol character doesn't play her for a chump. She hasn't asked for money or anything, has she?"

"I'm sure I wouldn't know." My best friend's face tightened. I hated to see her hurting and rushed on. "Hannah is just eccentric and this spirit stuff is just like, well, a hobby. She'd be attracted to anyone with the 'gift.'

Karen stared at me in disbelief. Something wasn't right. She burst into laughter and now I was really confused. "You think I'm jealous of Marisol?" I followed Karen's nod and watched the young woman talking with my niece. Her hands moved gracefully accentuating her conversation, after a megawatt smile rewarded a comment by Jolene. Slender, young, beautiful and apparently nice; I'd be looking for Harry's reaction. "Well she is incredibly attractive, but that's not my concern." Karen looked ninety percent sure of her feelings.

"What's bothering you then?" She shrugged and gave me the tiny series of headshakes that meant she wasn't ready to spill.

"Fine. When the dam is ready to burst you know where to find the Dutchman." I grinned and held up my pointer finger. "In the meantime, I need a favor that concerns Ric. I don't want to talk to him, but I want to find out when he was in that troop and who his leader was. He seemed so happy to recommend the troop to Lily but everyone else I talk to or hear about thought there was something hinky about it."

"Ric had a great time in scouts–never stopped talking about it. He got promoted to some hotshot position that meant he outranked everybody. He liked that."

"JASM, I mean junior assistant scout master?"

"Yeah, scout master was in there somewhere."

"Do you remember anything strange about the campouts?"

"Grace, that was a million years ago. Okay, maybe twenty. I don't remember. Sorry. Is it important?"

I shook my head. "Not really. Never mind." Dad's words about how the JASM almost seemed an accomplice for the scoutmaster's questionable behavior replayed in my head. *That was Bantonini Sr. Does the acorn fall far from the tree? Ric would never be party to something like that. Not the Ric I know now. Who was Ric then? His dad died when he was young. Maybe Bantonini filled that role. Maybe Ric was compromised.* I stopped thinking.

"Now you look upset, what's wrong?" Karen peered at me through the bottom half of her tortoise-rimmed glasses. My turn for the head movements that signal 'not now'. She smiled and held up her pointer finger. Enough said.

I glanced at my watch and realized that Cassidy was more than an hour late. Maybe she had an emergency client. Maybe she forgot. Forgetting didn't strike me as the answer and if she had an emergency she would have called. Something was wrong.

I found Gloria's phone, an old fashioned ornate replica in the hall and fished out Cassidy's card. Two rings.

"Hello, McCabe residence."

A male voice. I knew she lived with someone, Zach, I think. Maybe he was the reason she was a no show. I smiled prepared to reschedule.

"Is Cassidy available?"

"Who is calling?" The voice seemed familiar. I'd never talked to Zach before. "Hello, who's calling." No question just demand. I knew the voice.

"Detective Thomas?" Two beats of silence. I figured I'd best not leave him hanging. "Detective, it's Grace Marsden. Has something happened to Cassidy?"

"Why do you ask that, Mrs. Marsden?"

"Because you're a homicide detective and you answered her phone. I don't watch much television, but even I know that can't be good. Is she okay?" I thought I heard a slight chuckle.

"Ms. McCabe is fine. Someone heaved a brick through her office window. Since it's a duplicate of your attack I accompanied the uniform that took the call."

"Can I talk to her?"

"Now's not a good time. Call her tomorrow." His voice took on a brusque quality, preparing to shut me down. I'd heard that tone before–must be a required class at the academy.

"Tomorrow is Thanksgiving."

"Then call her Friday. Good-bye–"

"But it's important I ask her…" Suddenly I didn't want to talk to him. Better to keep my own counsel on my theory.

"Ask her what, Mrs. Marsden?"

"Tell her I called and I'll call on Friday. Thank you." I broke the connection before he could tell me I was obstructing or abetting. My hand shook as I lowered the receiver to the cradle.

"You've had quite a shock lately." Marisol stood behind me. I wondered how long she'd been there. She wore low-heeled dress boots but I hadn't heard her footsteps across the wooden floor. Her words were a statement. I assumed Hannah had told her about the attack, the discovery, and the newest attack. *I hate that my life is a series of talking points on an outline.* She held her eyes gently on mine, waiting for me to understand. *She knows about the little cowboy. How?*

"You felt something when you stopped at the kitchen threshold. I saw you stiffen." Two could play at this 'woo-woo' game.

She nodded her head in acquiescence. "He wanted to say thank you and good bye."

Whatever nasty cliché thoughts I harbored dissolved. I knew I'd never see the little boy again. He'd found his way home.

☙ 30 ❧

The zoo that I thought would be Thanksgiving never reared its wild head. There was magic in the combinations of friends and family that gathered. I'd never believe that my cousin Edna could spend twenty minutes in quiet pleasant conversation with Marisol, who'd been a last minute invitee. The buffet set up solved seating issues. Where you sat didn't necessarily make a statement of intent. Will did manage to corner three seats in a row and plant his dad in between himself and his mom. I noticed he greeted the adults he knew with a smile that tightened to a slit when he saw me.

Gloria had welcomed us before she left to join her family at a niece's home. I caught her in the kitchen where she was packing up the dessert she'd made for her own crew and told her about the young body discovered in Robinson Woods. Her eyes filled with tears, but behind the wetness I saw relief. It was always a relief to know, even when it was the worst. My mother died never knowing what happened to her older sister who disappeared while attending Regina College in the 1940's. I'd seen the erosion of spirit and deterioration of health that never knowing brought. Gloria hugged me and hurried off to share her thanks with her family.

Joe said the blessing and the feeding frenzy began. That part rivaled chow time for the monkeys in Tropic World at the zoo. All in all, it was a pleasant time together where everyone blended and enjoyed each other–it could never happen twice. No one suggested we do this again, the feeling being 'don't tempt fate.' The mood could have been in part because of the table wine. Uncle Jim, my dad's youngest brother who had lived with us when we were kids, brought his newest fermentation of red wine. He always named his wine after saints and as kids we'd twist the saint's attribution, like Saint Jude, after drinking it you were a *lost cause* or Saint Blaise, after drinking it your *throat was on fire.* Blasphemous, but funny, and we always knew our saints.

People made seemingly incongruous plans. Marisol would visit Edna and learn how to make *pizelles* and Italian knot cookies. I firmed up invitations to Ben, Matt, Will, and his buddy Tim to come out on Saturday to ride. Since I am one-handed, Lily volunteered to help with the horses. Karen made plans to meet with Mary Quigley, who showed up with Tim and one other son, Tyler, in tow. Her two older boys and their dad were at a basketball tournament. Mary designed and created lead glass objects. Her designs ranged from a pencil holder to a window. Her father taught her the craft as he'd learned it from his father. Karen would be at Mary's studio in Forest Park on Saturday.

We began the movement and noise of saying goodbye; hugs, kisses, promises to meet, confirming ownership of casserole pans, and another round of hugs and kisses. The Morelli family almost always did two rounds of good byes–superstition left over from Nonna Santa.

Harry and I and Ric and Nancy Royal were the last to leave. "Okay the back door is locked." Ric walked in from the kitchen. Grace, make one last sweep to make sure we haven't left anything."

I started in the hallway and worked my way back to the kitchen, checking the floor next to chairs for a glass or a purse, looking for stray scarves and gloves. When I reached the kitchen Harry, Ric, and Nancy were engaged in a low conversation and I wondered if I'd been sent away to give them a chance to talk. Ric spotted me first. He broke from the group shifting his body to block my view. They had something.

"Why don't you make one last sweep," I mimicked Ric. "And don't tell me this is 'police eyes only'. She's the only real cop here." I hadn't meant to say that.

Ric immediately looked away and, amazingly, Harry dropped his glance as well.

It applies to the both of them in a sense. What were you thinking? So much for the magic.

"Look, I'm sorry." My voice barely carried across the room. "You always leave me out."

"Grace, we weren't leaving you out. Well, maybe for the moment. Harry was going to fill you in on the way home. We just wanted to get a few facts down before we split up."

"I suppose it did seem clandestine to you. It wasn't intentional, just sort of evolved. We have a few more items to discuss why don't we at least sit down and spread things out."

Nancy spoke calmly, but with a tone accustomed to acceptance. Her stock went up with me. She'd explained and apologized for the team without saying either in those words.

We pulled out chairs and sat down. Each of them removed sheets of paper from their pockets or purse and set them on the table. I felt odd; I'd come to play, but I had no marker, nothing to contribute. I pulled a length of yarn from my pocket and held it in my lap. The urge to braid grew stronger. I'd been blissfully free from my compulsion all evening, resisting the urge to continue tapping my water glass with my spoon when asking for quiet for grace to be said.

Ric started. "I've been working the police slant. I know enough guys on the force that I've been able to get some details, mainly because of that first attack on Grace."

My fingers began a familiar pattern of loops and crossovers while I tried to concentrate on his words without reliving the emotions.

"Several women have been attacked in a similar pattern during the time period from roughly late October through right before Christmas. This has happened for the last two years running. The attacks involve rape by several participants. During the attack the victim's hair is cut or shaved and taken away. These attackers are not gentle or careful. Several women have been cut severely around the hairline. Others, with short hair have been shaved leaving nicks and gauges on their scalps. The worse treatment is the rape. The stories are similar–several hooded figures drag them into the woods. The rape begins almost immediately and intensifies."

"Do they hear anything? I mean chanting or music?"

Ric stares at me for a moment and I know the answer. He looks down at his notes. "The victims reported hearing their attackers chanting. We couldn't get a fix on the words, but recently one woman remembered the words."

"Chee Chee Pin Quay."

Now Nancy and Harry look to Ric for confirmation. He nods.

"Exactly. Your account of the drums is different."

"Maybe the others couldn't hear them because of the trauma of their attack. There would be the struggle, the outcries, and even if her mouth were covered the internal screaming could block outside noise. There's nothing quiet about rape." Nancy spoke with authority. I hoped from interviews with victims and not experience.

The mood around the table intensified. Ric closed his eyes for a long blink and I wondered if he'd had the same thought.

"That's why your report was important. Apparently there were others in the woods that night; the drummers. We need to find them. The police have identified three groups that may have been there.

These groups are trespassing; the area closes at night. Camping is by permit only to organizations like the scouts. Five women have been attacked to date–three last year, two this year. We're not counting your attack Grace because, thank God, you escaped. I asked a buddy of mine with the FBI about any similar patterns in the Chicago area. He asked a profiler to take a quick look at the pattern. Based on what I gave him, they suspect a cult with a connection to the autumnal equinox. The ritual rape and shearing suggests a weird combination of sowing and harvest.

My sharp gasp stopped him. "I'm sorry. I can't stop thinking of what could have happened." Harry reached for my shoulder and squeezed it. "This is what we were discussing. I know it's painful to hear."

"But it's also necessary. Maybe I'll remember more than the others have been able to. Let's keep going. What else?" Harry squeezed my shoulder again, a signal of 'well done.'

"Wait. You said five so far. Do you think there'll be another attack?"

"We're counting on it to try and catch the bastards. The police have the area under surveillance. According to the FBI they think the window is from October twenty-first to December twenty first. These crazies have over three weeks to complete their threesome."

Nancy picked up the thread. The number three apparently has significance as does the number six and of course 666 in several cults both Pagan and Christian."

"I understand the Trinity for Christians…"

Nancy nodded and looked down at her notes. "Several Pagan religions use the number three to signify elements of worship, 'wind, earth, and fire' or 'sun, moon, and stars' and some cults follow the Satanic numerology assigning incredible value and power to the number six."

"So you think there is a cult of what out in the woods? Satan worshippers?"

"Of the three groups the police have identified and can track for the last two years one is Boy Scout Troop 265; two of their campouts matched two of the three attacks last year, but only one this year unless you count the clean up and Grace's attack. Another group is a Wicca Coven that has held ceremonies within that time frame."

"Wait a minute. Wicca would be women. Worship mother earth or something. You think they'd bring along men to rape a woman as part of a ceremony?"

"I'm just telling you the groups that have been identified in the woods during this timeline. I don't know what their 'religion' tells them to do." Ric shoves his left hand through his thick hair. I know that habit; he's frustrated.

"We'll get information about Wicca culture from Hannah." Harry's voice stayed neutral. "My research has taken me in a different direction. I'm more concerned about the uses that crate has been through since its original purpose. And why try and scare off Grace, and why break into the therapist's records? This isn't the pattern of serial rapists. These attempts seem to be by one hand that perhaps didn't want further investigation into the woods. What's different in the woods? The discovery of the crate and John Henry's body."

"Those discoveries took place before the brick throwing attacks."

Harry smiled at Nancy and nodded. "Exactly. So someone has something else to hide. The key, I believe, is the fact that this person went after the records. Something he thinks Janet may have confided to her therapist. The brick thrown at Grace was because she visited with Cassidy McCabe in this timeframe." Harry paused when he realized he'd let the cat out of the bag. I kept my eyes on his face feeling the other two pairs on me. A slight flush swirled around the base of my neck threatening to rocket to my hairline.

"So he figures Grace is asking the therapist questions about Janet?" Nancy's voice sounds thoughtful. I don't look at her, but my heart decides she is one of the good guys. "How does this guy know Grace's schedule. How many people knew you were going to see her?"

"No one. Harry drove me."

"Those two FBI types saw you come out of her house. Walter knew where I was and he told them."

"FBI? What's their angle?"

"The munitions case for one and a multiple homicide still on the books since 1955. Three boys, John and Anton Schuessler and Robert Peterson, were found dumped on the side of the road near the Indian Chief's grave marker. The two crimes seem to be coming together. The forensics team working on the crate found traces of human blood in the wood and tiny pieces of cloth, like if you caught your shirt on a sharp point. They've exhumed the cat grave hoping to find more trace evidence."

Silence. Each to our own private thoughts about the heinous crime from before I'd been born and when they were toddlers. A crime that resonated with a nation and changed the carefree way parents viewed their children's safety. The monster had never been caught.

"That crate is connected to someone in this area."

"I thought the game was selling guns to the highest bidder. That crate is part of a shipment stolen near the end of the war."

Harry looked at Ric who shrugged. "You're not the only one with FBI connections. My guy didn't say anything about the murders."

"Different task force. Maybe the gunrunner is still alive and masking his involvement because there is no statute of limitations on 'treasonous acts during wartime'. He would be assured of jail time."

"Or maybe he murdered those kids and that's why he's covering his ass, or tying to. Finding that crate kick-started something. I don't think the attack on Grace is connected. I still think we've a cult fulfilling some ritual."

"It's only been these past two years. Has something happened recently, new gang or, hate to ask but, alternative religious group?"

"Good question. They're all good questions." Ric tipped his head back and rolled his shoulders. "We need answers. Quick re-cap and then we call it a night." He stood and stretched his legs.

"Let's take a few minutes before we nail it down." Nancy stood and walked down the hall. Out of habit, I looked for the coffee maker. Ric guessed my intent. "Great idea. I'll even wash up the cups." His smile touched me from across the room. It tugged at my heart and asked for familiarity; it said 'we're doing the coffee together what else can we do...together'. *Did his smile say that or did my brain hear that? It's just coffee for heaven's sake.*

"It's just coffee, not rocket science. Push the button already." Ric's hand brushed mine as he reached over it to push 'on'. He smiled into my eyes. How could he speak the words I'd just thought? It'd happened before. He called us soul mates, I call it dumb luck.

Harry and Nancy foraged for pie and icy cold milk. We brought our nourishment to the large table and began again. I picked at Harry's pie, tasting a bit from his fork. An intimate gesture that said clearly 'we are a couple'. Ric's eyes followed the fork like a hungry urchin staring through a restaurant window. I needn't guess at his hunger.

Nancy Royal's voice pitched a shade higher. Had she seen the hunger in his eyes and realized her place in his heart. "Let's get this nailed down, I've early roll call."

Compulsive personality aside, I was the best note taker in the bunch, cast not withstanding and outside of the mandatory doodles in the margins, my notes were prized for accuracy and completeness. I took Gloria's telephone pad to the table with me.

The list developed under my pen, short statements with mostly question marks at the end:

Who stole munitions?

Where was crate before cat buried?

Was Mr. Henry's death an accident?

Who is leader of hooded people? Is he connected to crate?

Serial rapes same MO.

Does 'Mr. Big' describe a personality, a nickname, a size?

Were the bodies of murdered boys ever in that crate?

Forensics checking blood against boys' records. Long shot.

Who killed John Henry? Did he see something?

Was death accident? Ran off in the dark, well could have been uncovered.

Who killed Janet? Well cover removed then replaced.

What does old priest know?

Was Bantonini involved as a pedophile, murderer, or gun-runner?

Nancy leaned back. "Whew, that's enough to start. Too many questions."

Ric reached across the table and pulled the paper toward him. "We'll take this. He nodded to Harry, "You've got her." Ric referred to my photographic memory. I washed up the cups and plates. We locked up and parted for our cars.

All the way home we kept a silence. Not an uneasy one, but the kind when you're both thinking on the same subject. The list swirled in my brain, moving the order on the page. Did that mean anything that my mind kept trying to re-arrange the order? I knew enough to trust my instincts. I'd let my brain tussle with it while I slept and see what order appeared in the morning.

Harry stepped out of the shower and toweled his blond hair. He walked naked into our bedroom. "How many people are riding to-morrow?" He stepped into a pair of boxers decorated with pictures of cufflinks. I marveled at what ended up on men's underwear. He had one pair with lobsters and another with little bottles of Tabasco. He looked so good naked, lean muscled abdomen, wide shoulders, and not hairy. Some of my dad's relatives had tuffs of hair at their neckline, and those were the women.

I smiled at my Henny Youngman style joke.

"What?" Harry looked down at himself, thinking that perhaps he hadn't tucked in all the way. I smiled even broader and patted the bed. Harry walked toward me and leaned down. He tilted up my chin, brushed my lips with a soft kiss, and whispered, "You are a vixen." Before I could confirm or deny, he whipped the blankets down the bed.

"Hey, it's cold. Gimme those." I scrambled for the blankets, but he pulled them further away. I changed my target and grabbed at his waistband. Aha, that got his attention. Actually, I already had his attention. I tugged and he followed. "You shall be my blankie. I so decree." He loved the Queen scenario.

Warmed by the length of his body I reveled in his tender lovemaking, giving myself up to the pleasure. God save the Queen.

I waited until ten o'clock to start making my calls. Harry left to pick up some odds and ends at his favorite market. He'd extracted a promise from me to stay inside until he returned.

No problem. I had my coffee, my list, and my kitty curled up on my toes. Elmo's sibs had slipped out the door this morning. I thought about installing a doggie door so they could come and go, but I worried about other critters that might follow them inside. I dialed my first number.

"Hello. Cassidy McCabe."

"Hi, Cassidy, it's Grace. Are you all right? I heard what happened."

"Yes, I'm fine. Detective Thomas told me you'd called. I'm just furious with whoever did this. First to ransack my office and then to smash the window. I've been picking glass out of the furniture for two days, not to mention having to reschedule appointments until the window is repaired, which should be today, if the insurance company hasn't messed up my claim." She stopped abruptly and said softly, "physician heal thyself."

"Sometimes you just gotta let go." We laughed at my oversimplification.

"Cassidy, did Janet ever talk about her older brother?"

"You know I can't talk about that. It's confidential. You wouldn't want me discussing our conversation with other people."

I'd been afraid I'd get the 'confessional' argument.

"I would if someone murdered me and it could help nail the bastard." I hadn't meant to be so brutal. She'd probably heard worse. I'm certain she was jotting down, *quick temper, violent outlook,* on my file. Then it hit me. I cut off her measured response. "How much was in my file?" *Why hadn't I thought of that earlier?*

"Not exactly your file. I write up notes after a client leaves while the conversation is fresh. I record comments, impressions, in a shorthand form until I can sit down and type up complete notes. I'd done that with our visit, but hadn't created a file folder for you. The notes were removed but it wouldn't be easy to figure out anything from my shorthand."

Thank goodness for that.

"Grace, I can't tell you anything specific, but I can tell you that Janet was a new client. I didn't know she had a brother until the police told me."

"I saw you at the police station that day. You argued with Edward Bantonini. I thought you knew the story through him."

"Why would I?"

"John Henry disappeared from a campout when he was a scout in Troop 265. Edward's dad was the scoutmaster."

"I didn't know. I met Edward because of a client. We hit it off, I thought. I was wrong. Our ethics didn't match and that was that."

And 'that' explained her reaction to Edward that day. Or did it? Was he trying to compromise her ethics asking for privy information? Maybe he knew Janet was seeing her and he wanted to know the topic of concern.

"Was he asking you about Janet?"

"Seems like everyone is asking about Janet." That's all she said, but it was enough.

"Grace, I'm sorry I can't help you more. Do you want to schedule with me, or in view of everything, would you prefer another therapist? I can recommend someone."

I respected Cassidy for her honesty. I wasn't sure if I wanted to continue with her or with anyone. "Thank you for the offer. I'll think about it and call you next week."

We hung up and I immediately called Detective Thomas and left a message for him to call me. I wanted to give him this piece of the puzzle as soon as possible.

Next, I called Don Craig, a.k.a. Mountain Man. Dad promised to pass along my name and number after the holiday. I'd looked up his name in the Villa Park directory.

A woman answered the phone and I asked for Don Craig. I heard the pleasant exchange muffled only slightly, "Don it's for you. It's a woman and she sounds pretty."

"Darn, I've told them again and again 'if a woman answers hang up'." I smiled as I recognized my dad's sense of humor. I'd heard similar teasing between my parents. I liked Don already and when I heard his booming voice I relaxed. I hadn't realized how nervous I'd been about trying to explain the reason for the call.

"Hello."

"Mr. Craig, you don't know me. I'm Mike Morelli's daughter, Grace–"

"Gracie? The little girl with the purple eyes who knew her knots better than most of my scouts?"

I guess I'd made an impression. "That would be me. Gee, I didn't think you remembered me. It was so long ago."

"Actually, your dad gave me a call couple of days ago. Said you might be contacting me. Just couldn't resist."

I sat stunned. Dad had called after he said he'd talk to him in two weeks. I hated that everyone knew me so well.

"So, what's on your mind? And by the way, I do remember your eyes. Prettiest shade of lavender flecked with gold like a prairie flower."

"Mr. Craig, I'd like to meet with you to discuss the time when you were part of Troop 265. Dad thinks you might be able to answer some questions about the troop at that time. Could you meet me someday next week?"

"I could if you'd stop calling me Mr. Craig and call me Don. How about Tuesday?"

"Tuesday is good, Mr. ah, Don. Where and when?"

"Do you know the Portillo's Restaurant on North Avenue in Villa Park? It's west of Rt. 83 on the south side of the street. How about eleven o'clock? Beat the lunch crowd."

"I know it. I'll see you there. Thank you, Don. I appreciate you meeting with me."

"Don't thank me yet, don't know if I can help you. But I can tell some tales on your dad." His hearty laugh lifted my spirits and I looked forward to Tuesday.

Harry walked in as I hung up the phone. "You're grinning." He arched his eyebrow.

"I called Don Craig. Dad had already called to tell him I'd be calling." I stopped and shrugged. "Am I that predictable?"

Harry nodded. "When you're after something. Most definitely. Back to Don Craig?"

"I'm meeting with him Tuesday in Villa Park."

"Morning or afternoon? I can't make morning but I'm free the afternoon."

"Morning and you don't need to go with me."

"On that point you are mistaken, my darling, and I will brook no argument. Until the police catch the nutcase in the robe you're not going anywhere without an escort. I'll ring Walter to check his schedule."

His eyes bore into me with the look I'd learned to recognize. *Go with the flow, Grace. You've been through this before.*

I nodded and changed the subject. "Did you stock up on all your exotic items?"

"I have indeed replenished our food stores." He rummaged in the paper sack he'd placed on the table. "Couscous, anchovy paste, sun-dried tomatoes, olive oil, extra virgin–"

"Of course," I murmured. "Typical guy." He swatted at me with the French bread.

"Dried beans and split peas, clotted cream and tomato juice."

I couldn't imagine how any of this would become food. Harry's eyes gleamed. He pulled a smaller sack rolled at the top from the larger bag. "And an Italian cheesy beef sandwich."

You would have thought he handed me the keys to Fort Knox. I accepted the bag with both hands, dancing from one foot to the other. "Thank you, thank you. I'm starving." I leaned and air-smooched two inches from his lips. I wasn't taking a chance that a contact kiss would lead somewhere and my Italian cheesy beef would take a back seat. Harry shook his head. "So predictable," he murmured.

I inhaled my beef sandwich while Harry put away his goodies. A jar of pimentos and another of olives materialized from the bag. He hummed while he stacked and sorted to make everything fit at his fingertips, ready for his culinary ministrations. I still didn't see how it would become food.

I pulled out my 'people to contact list' from my pocket. Four down, one to go. The phone rang; Detective Thomas returning my call. I told him about my conversation with Cassidy. He thanked me and admonished me to stop asking anyone else any questions. He told me they'd found out someone in their department had inadvertently leaked information. Pillow talk he'd called it. I hung up the phone and relayed Thomas's comments.

"Does that mean the desk clerk told her boyfriend about her crazy day and he's connected to this mess?"

"Grace, think in the larger scope. Who says a 'she' told a 'he'? There are more men than women in that department."

"So you're saying the hooded figure is a woman?"

"Perhaps, or the brother, father, son of someone who found out through pillow talk."

Now my head spun with the possibilities. "Do you think Thomas is thinking the same?"

"I'm certain he is. You don't get to his level without considering all the angles."

"Can we trust him to be thorough in checking?"

"Unless it's him."

"Oh my God. Do you suspect him?"

"The drill is to suspect everyone. He's the right age, life-long area resident–knows the woods. He has access to police and FBI information making it easy for him to keep one step ahead."

"You think he's this 'Mr. Big' the figures referred to? If they know he's a cop and feel protected they might refer to him that way."

"He could fit for something even bigger."

My heart thumped inside my chest. Could this be possible? Harry rubbed my upper arms. "Hey, these are possibilities, maybe even probabilities, but not proof. We are speculating; the first step in inspecting. Edward Jr. looks good for the satanic group and Black Bart, he's already into the color."

I understood that Harry's attempts at humor were for my benefit. His eyes never lightened and the tiny lines around his mouth deepened as he habitually pursed his lips in thought.

"These people are too young to have been involved in the murders. So, men under the age of sixty but over forty are the target group for the rapes." Harry nodded. "And men over the age of sixty are suspect for the murders?" Another nod. "Is Thomas that old?"

"It's easy to get that information. He was born in 1940. That would make him seventeen when the murders occurred. I'm not saying he's guilty, I'm just saying he is in the timeframe, along with Edward Sr. and Black Bart." Harry saw my question forming. "Black Bart is good for two. He was eighteen that year also. Remember he was the Junior Assistant Scout Master."

"Could he be 'Mr. Big?'"

Harry shrugged. "Any one of a number of people could be 'Mr. Big.' Bantonini, he's the leader that would make him 'big' to boys. I did a check on all the families in the troop. Tim Quigley's uncle, last name Bigelow, was in that troop. He's been in a few scrapes with the law, nothing serious, yet. His name lends itself to that nickname. He worked for a short time as a mechanic for Black Bart, whose entire name is Bart Ignatius Guilfoyle."

"Oh my, there are 'bigs' everywhere.'

Harry nodded. "And finally, you could nickname someone called Mountain Man 'Mr. Big.'"

"Mr. Craig. I can't believe that. Dad wouldn't have befriended and stayed friends with someone capable of rape and Satanism."

"I'm laying out the possibilities. We're talking forty years ago.

People do stupid, sometimes criminal acts in their youth."

"Are you trying to solve the murders or the rapes?"

"I'm trying to stop whoever is coming after you. They may be connected. No one has ever been arrested for the murders. There's been some talk of a Jayne family connection but nothing solid. He or they could still be in the area and not certain what you might have seen or heard. And that is why you are not to go anywhere without me, Walter, or Kramer."

"Ric? You're working with Ric?"

Harry's impassive face remained chiseled and cold. "I need you protected by people who would die for you or kill for you. For the duration we are the three Musketeers, may God smile on this unlikely alliance."

Amen.

ॐ **32** ॐ

Harry and I settled in our separate corners, he to his office and me to the breakfast nook with my notes, thoughts, and current Sharon McCone mystery. I lifted Elmo onto the bench seat and he curled around my tucked up feet. I rubbed his little body with my big toe. "Not a bad way to spend a few hours, eh, buddy?"

I made notes about tomorrow. I knew I'd teach the boys about grooming and caring for the horses first and then give them a chance to ride. Afterwards they could make 'party chow' for April and Cash. I listed the ingredients I'd need: carrots, apples, bran, and starlight mints. The boys would have fun mixing the chow in the wheelbarrow and shoveling it out to the greedy equines. There wasn't anything in the mash that the kids couldn't eat, but the preparation was less than appetizing.

I pulled a sheath of papers toward me. The only name left on my list to contact was Father Briscoe. I wasn't sure how to track down a priest, but I knew who could guide me.

"St. Domitilla Covent, may I help you?"

"Hello, may I speak with Sister Angie, ah Angela?"

A small chuckle from the other end. "Sister Angela is working today. You can reach her at 708-449-8070. She'll be there until five o'clock."

"Thank you." It was after four. I hung up and wondered what my college friend was involved in now. She joined the order of the Blessed Virgin Mary after graduation. I had attended her profession ceremony or 'swearing in' as we teased her. Angie hadn't grown up in my area so I was especially pleased when she joined the convent at St. Domitilla, my old grammar school. Her early education degree made her the perfect candidate to run the pre-school. What St. Dom's didn't know is that she was extremely talented at the other end of the spectrum as well. Angie had organized a neighborhood adult day care originally to give her mom some respite from caring for both of Angie's grandmothers who lived with her family. One Polish grandma, one Italian. Amazingly neither spoke English or the other's language, but became the best of buddies. Polish grandma sewed, Italian grandma crocheted and knitted. Polish grandma baked, Italian grandma cooked. And so forth.

The adult day care became a huge success and eventually Angie lobbied to have the program connected to the Golden Ager program already in place. Angie split her time between bingo with cheerio markers for the toddlers and bingo with cheerio markers for the geriatrics. Her surname, DiBartolomeo, was a mouthful for the young and old alike. We call her 'D' or Angie. Everyone in the community calls her Sister Bingo. I dialed the Hillside number.

"Shapiro Staffing Services. We help you find your best people. May I help you?"

I nearly dropped the receiver. Staffing services? "D? It's Grace. What's going on?"

"Hi, Grace, how are you. I've been thinking about you. I saw your dad's name on the volunteer list for ushers at mass. Hope I don't see him at my bingo table for at least forty years."

"Yeah, from your mouth to God's ear. I guess that's the route for you guys." We both laughed. I don't know why but I blurted out, "He's dating again, my dad. His cleaning lady." I waited for her response.

"Good news. People who have experienced a wonderful relationship once search for another one. And your folks had the best. I'm happy for your dad. How are you doing with it?"

"I'm good. Everybody ought to belong in a special way." I wanted to believe it. "Back to you. What is Shapiro Staffing?"

"Long story short, one of the ladies in the day care has a grandson who finally found a job working here. Orlando, has a moderate learning disability, so it was a blessing that he found this job. He was on his way to work one morning, public transportation, and got hit by a car while crossing in front of the bus. The bus lets off right at Proviso West High School. He crossed the street because a buddy waved him over. He ended up, by the grace of God, with only a broken leg, but he can't come back to work for six weeks. Mrs. Reed is worried that if he loses this job he won't find another one like it and might go back to the rough crowd from high school."

"So you're a temp filling in for Orlando?"

"In a nutshell."

"And your order is okay with this? Who's handling Alpha-Omega?" Our code name for her blended program?

"Mr. Shapiro only needs me part time. It all fits in."

If I knew Angie, it all fit in because she wasn't taking any time for herself. I hoped my request would be a simple five-minute assist.

"Not that I'm not thrilled to hear from you, but what's up? And before I forget, who is in charge of Regina's luncheon this year? I haven't received an invitation yet."

"It may be Karen, but she just adopted twins and the luncheon is not on her priority list. I'll find out." Our little group of college chums got together at least once a year for a holiday luncheon. It was becoming more difficult to schedule a Sunday since most of the women had family holiday activities and commitments.

"Twins? Ambitious. Is she still with your sister-in-law?" Angie's tone reminded me of her difficulty accepting Karen's lifestyle.

"Yes. And the reason I called is to ask the procedure on finding out where a priest is assigned. Do I call up the archdiocese and ask?"

"Not unless you're willing to wait months for an answer. Who is the priest and why are you looking for him? And more to the point, why don't you ask Joe?"

Angie never did beat around the bush–too much going in her life to waste time. I filled her in, stopping for breath twice, ending with, "so I'd like to do this without involving the entire Morelli family."

"Whew, Gracie. How do you manage to find these problems? Never mind. Here's your answer. I'll make some calls to registry and call you back next week. It could take me awhile or I could find him pronto. I've got to run, a courier just came in. Say hello to Harry, your dad, and the boys. Can't wait to see you. Let me know about the luncheon. I've two hours on the seventeenth if you need help." We laughed, but I knew she was serious. I'd never met a more organized energetic person in my life. I hung up the phone in great spirits.

I felt like Chinese and went in search of Harry to see if he wanted to share some Moo Goo Gai Pan from King Choy. He sat behind his desk. The phone receiver scrunched between his ear and shoulder, he wrote quickly on the back of the Com Ed envelope. He must have placed the call between my hanging up with Angie and walking up the stairs. I carried Elmo in the crook of my arm. Harry hung up the phone and rested his forehead against his hand, rubbing his fingers up and down between the bridge of his nose and his hairline. He spotted me and lowered his hand from his head to the top of his desk and over the envelope. Smooth by all means, but I'd stood there long enough to know the envelope meant something. The stress I'd seen on his face meant more.

"Hi, darling." He nodded toward my arm. "What are you and Ort up to?"

I knew Harry's methods. He wanted to engage me in defending Elmo's name. Normally I'd rise to the bait. Not now. I shrugged. "Came up to see what you were up to? Who was on the phone?

I didn't hear it ring?"

Harry shuffled some papers over and under the envelope and tidied them up in the middle of his blotter. "Returning a call, loose end. Client question."

Gotcha! He'd sold it then, bought it back. Harry, whose life at one point necessitated his being an accomplished liar, had explained the psychology of the lie and how if you know someone long enough you will identify the pattern that is the lie. He said we all had one. Through the years I'd come to recognize his pattern; a simple statement with two explanations, *returning a call, loose end,* but then the nail down, *client question,* which he adds only when he is less than truthful. I never told him.

I nodded and smiled. "I'm feeling Chinese. How does Moo Goo Gai Pan sound to you?"

"Excellent. You place the order and I'll run out for it."

Perfect. And I'll run right back in here.

King Choy, best Chinese in Lisle and beyond. I added egg rolls and a small order of shrimp fried rice for good measure.

"Ready in ten minutes," I called up to Harry.

"Be back in a jiffy. Don't go outside."

"Yes, dear."

"If a stranger calls, what's the drill?"

Harry's caution was wearing thin. I'm not a schoolgirl. He wasn't going to leave until I answered.

"I call out pretending there's someone with me like, 'I've got it' but I don't use a name in case someone watched you leave," I recited in my best schoolgirl voice. "Do I get a star?"

"You are my shining star. You think this is silly, but nothing must happen to you." The concern and love in his eyes stopped my scoffing.

"Go on. Moo Goo is waiting." The last thing I wanted was for him to decide I should ride along.

I watched him back down the driveway, counted backwards from twenty, then dashed up the stairs to his office. I sat down behind the desk and studied how the papers were stacked. He had tucked the top left corner under the frame of the blotter. I'd replace it that way. I decided to lift the edges of the papers closest to me and count them until I found the envelope tucked between them. "One, two, three, four, five, six, seven..." The pattern was wrong. I had to start again. "One, two, three–four, five, six–seven...*Still wrong. I hate unevens. Okay, okay I can do this.* "One–two, three. Four–five, six. Seven..." *Gotcha.* My mind allowed my hand to slide the envelope from the sheets. I let the pages fall back in place and read my husband's neat handwriting.

Juvie records. 1957, Fires set, rooster parts (head, feet) Boys remanded to parents, no charges. Self-proclaimed ringleader older (18) probation, Bantonini

The layers of my brain peeled away like an onion. The layer that retains all that I read logged the list into the forever part of my brain. The layer that rules my OCD demanded I divide the names into two groups, Italian and other, and repeat the groups twice, *Bantonini, Morelli, Santori, Tinucci, Guilfoyle, Quigley, Randolph, and Whalen.* The layer closest to reality suggested I lift seven pages and slide the envelope back into the pile. I obeyed. My hands worked on automatic while my mind teetered on the brink of chaos. *My dad connected to rituals. Impossible. Really? Maybe. Definitely not dad.*

The phone rang and my hand twitched sending the papers across Harry's desk. I pushed them back together praying they were in the right order or that Harry hadn't memorized the order, either would work. I raced around the front of the desk and ran for the bedroom. I didn't want to take the call in his office.

"Hello." The word burst from my breathless mouth.

"Whoa, it's not a race. Catch your breath. Your request was a snap. Father Briscoe is pastoral vicar at St. Edger in Oak Park. He was assigned to a parish in Minnesota in the mid 1950's–wonder who he aggravated–and then two more parishes in Michigan and Wisconsin. Finally back to this area in 1989 to St. Edger. He's on part time duty, must be in his seventies."

"Thanks, I owe you one. I'll call him at the rectory."

"Why don't you see him in action first? St. Edger is having an advent kick-off Mass Wednesday night at seven. I'll meet you there and you can see him before you meet him."

I liked the idea. "It's a date. Seven o'clock on the steps." I hung up with Angie and realized Harry stood in the doorway.

"Seven o'clock on the steps?"

"Mass with Angie." I fiddled with the bedcovers, smoothing them where I'd left my indentation, buying time to calm my lying eyes. *Oh cripes! Is that my pattern? I usually explain to the nth degree.*

Harry's eyes widened slightly. "Moo Goo is waiting."

I followed him down the stairs. He knew I lied to him. Did he know I knew he lied to me? *What tangled webs we weave when first we practice to deceive.* Whoever penned that line hit the mark. Why wouldn't Harry tell me about that list? Why won't I tell Harry about Father Briscoe? My thoughts roiled in my head until I felt the beginning of a headache. I gripped the meaty part of my right hand with my thumb and forefinger and squeezed until my eyes blinked back tears.

Harry had thoughtfully set the table with plates, napkins small round cups, and chopsticks. A chipped fat bellied pot sat on a tealight warmer. This was the only pot Harry used for green tea with our Chinese dinners. I spotted the gleam of a fork at my place setting.

We ate in silence, keeping our own council, our own secrets.

❧ 33 ❧

My Nonna Santa used to say, '*il segreti sono brute e vi danno dolori della stomaco'* which loosely translated meant, secrets are ugly and they give you a stomach ache. Secrets or Moo Goo Gai Pan–I had it bad. I tossed and turned, waking several times in the night, resentful that my partner slept the sleep of innocent. *Sonni come un innocent.* Nonna Santa again. When we were kids if we had a sleepless night and weren't sick she attributed the restlessness to misbehaving and not being caught. She would make the sign of the cross and say, *benedicti bambini,* it was God's way to keep us honest.

I'd resolved to come clean with Harry first thing in the morning. I rolled over at three ten with that intent.

Buzzzzzzz. It is now seven thirty. Buzzzzzz.

I lunged across the rumpled bed to slap the plastic derriere of our Betty Boop clock, mainly to stop that awful buzz, but partly because hope sprang eternal that I'd knock her into next Tuesday, and finally be rid of her. The leaded bottom held her fast. This innocuous wedding present annoyed me, but delighted Harry and he wouldn't part with her.

Either fatigue from a restless night or the decision to confess contributed to my oversleeping. I rushed through a shower and pulled on the barn clothes I'd decided on the night before. I smelled the coffee before I reached the halfway point of the staircase. 'Seattle Spice' a new favorite. Elmo and his sibs charged toward me from the kitchen. I bent down to rub ears and tickle chins. "So, Patches and Trey have returned, eh, Elmo? Must have decided kitty chow and tickles are better than mousey burgers."

"Actually, they love kippers." Harry leaned against the doorjamb holding the small skillet in his hand.

"You're joking, right?"

"No, Mum always gave our cats kippers to keep their fur healthy and their skin from drying out."

I burst into laughter at that the thought of Midwestern barn cats dining on kippers. Harry smiled the sheepish grin of one who has admittedly gone over the top. He scraped the skillet into their bowls. The already identifiable scrape turned them away from me and toward the kitchen in a tumble of feet and fur.

We both laughed at their progress. I couldn't stay angry with Harry and I wouldn't spend another night with my secret. I waited until he'd placed the pan in the sink before I hugged him.

"Hullo. What's this?" His arms found their spot right beneath my shoulder blades. He kissed the top of my head.

"I'm sorry–"

"I didn't–"

We stood silent and held on to each other, affirming our regret at the deception we forced on our relationship.

Harry let go first. He motioned toward the table. My angel mug sat next to a plate of *Raspberry Ruin*, my name for the delicious strudel from Joyful's Café. He brought the coffeepot to the table.

Oh-oh, a whole pot conversation. This can't be good.

He refilled his tea mug and made a study of his teaspoon before he spoke. "I would have told you; only I didn't know how. Waiting for some inspiration, I suspect. Should have told you immediately. Sorry, darling."

"I shouldn't have snooped. I never suspected that's what I'd find. It doesn't mean anything. You know Dad. He'd never do something Satanic. I mean it's not like he was an altar boy…actually he was, but you know what I mean. He's an usher and a Knight of Columbus, for God's sake."

"I know all of that. I have the greatest respect and admiration for your father. This list has come to light and will be investigated. We don't know who your dad was as a teenager. He could have mixed in with the wrong crowd. You have to be prepared to accept that he may have been less than an 'altar boy.'"

Be prepared. Everything works back to the Scouts. The answer is somewhere with that scout troop all those years ago. Maybe Father Briscoe will know.

Father Briscoe. Now it was my turn. Before I could fess up Harry asked, "The steps at seven?"

I smiled and took a deep breath. "I'm meeting Angie, who by the way says 'hi,' for Mass Wednesday night at St. Edgar."

"Because?"

"It's a kick off for Advent?"

"More to the point, you've found Father Briscoe."

Cripes. How does he do that? Druids are on his side.

"I hate when you do that–it's spooky."

"Service for Advent. Sounds spiritual. I'm in."

I knew he would be, or Walter or Ric. I resigned myself to his company and ate my strudel in silence.

The phone rang and I continued to eat. I had too much information to process and didn't want more.

"Speaking."

Good, let him deal with whatever or whoever.

"Thank you. I'll be there shortly. Yes, I'll bring her attorney."

My head swung round. Harry hung up and the phone rang again.

"Yes." His terse greeting jumped through the line.

"They just called. I'll call David. I'm coming in, what do you think? She's my sister." He hung up again.

"Is Hannah all right? What's wrong?"

"She's fine, I mean not hurt; she's in jail." He waved his hand at me to stop my questions. "I have to call David and get him out there. She and Ms. 'woo-woo' were picked up by the police for participating in cult rituals in the woods."

Harry slammed his hand down on the table. "What in God's name is she doing, mixed up in all that again?"

For starters it wasn't in *God's* name. I guessed Harry meant the Wicca religion. Why would Hannah be out in the woods with a medium when she could be home with Karen and the kids?

"David? Harry Marsden. My sister has landed in a bit of trouble. Would you represent her?"

"No, she lives in Oak Park. I can pick you up."

"Fine. Thank you, David."

Harry sighed and turned to face me. "You heard. I'm picking up David. Don't know when I'll be back." He looked at his watch and shook his head. I knew he'd been excited about Will's riding lesson. He'd probably miss it now.

"Maybe David could…" I stopped. Harry wouldn't let Hannah go it alone, though if I were her I'd rather try it solo than endure Harry's anger and disappointment. "Sorry, honey. I'll tell Will it was an emergency."

"No need. Hannah made her one call to Karen in the wee hours this morning, she tracked her brother down at Royal's house. He tried to call in some favors from his department; they wouldn't budge because of the rapes. My sister is bloody lucky she didn't become victim number six." His hand slammed the hard surface again.

"Lily arrived as prearranged to take the babies' three month photographs. She and Will walked into chaos. They know the whole story. 'Come here, son and meet your wacky Wicca Aunt Hannah. She'll be out in three to five.'" Harry's condescending tone changed to matter of fact. "Since I'm on my way out, Kramer is on his way here. Not my preference, but I know Walter's not available this morning. Didn't think I'd be collecting my sister from jail."

His voice, his face; I'd opt for jail time. *So Ric is 'it' today. Part of an unlikely tag team.*

Harry glanced at his watch. "He'll be here in ten minutes."

"With or without Nancy?"

"With I hope. Would be difficult for lover boy to sniff at one *bird* while he's brought his own." His sudden grin changed the room from tense to sunny. "He'll behave. We've entered into a gentleman's agreement, tenuous as it is to his being a gentleman, but nonetheless an agreement. He will refrain from making advances until your safety is assured. Or else."

"Or else? Or else what?"

"Or else I won't let him help me protect you the next time you stick your lovely nose where it doesn't belong." His tone mocked me.

My eyes narrowed. A surge of heat moved up my neck. "That's unfair. I didn't do anything." I pressed my lips together to keep my voice from squeaking. Pinpricks behind my eyes forewarned tears. I blinked hard.

Harry pulled me off the stool and into his arms. "Hullo now. What's all this? Developed a sensitivity to the results of your inquisitive mind, have you? You didn't do anything except start asking questions and tracking down old men with maybe a story to tell. You put things in motion, darling and then wonder where the locomotive came from." He stroked my hair and planted a kiss on the top of my head.

When he said it that way, I sounded like an idiot. A meddling idiot. I don't know that his words consoled me, but his arms did.

The doorbell chimed and Harry opened the door to Ric and Nancy. I breathed a sign of relief. Less stress.

"Hi Nancy. Glad you took me up on riding today." I ignored Ric and the reason he was here. I looked approvingly at Nancy's jeans, boots, and lightweight jacket. "Let me introduce you to April and Cash."

Harry leaned toward me and kissed my cheek. "I'll be back as soon as possible. Have fun with the boys."

I had no time to wonder how things were going with Harry, Hannah and the judicial process. Lily, Will, and Tim, his brother Tyler, shortly followed by Tracy, Matt, and Ben arrived. Lily handed me an official looking form. "Mary says if you sign on to be a counselor, the boys can earn their horseback riding merit badge with you."

"I'd love to." *At last, something that Will might value from me. Harry will be pleased.* I knew this wasn't a competition, well maybe a little.

I took the form. "Mary's quick about tapping resources, isn't she?"

"She's got the mayor doing Citizen in the Community."

Talk about resources.

The boys had a ball. Will took to grooming with a deliberate style that showed a desire to really care for the horses. The other blossoming equestrians hurried through the brushing and picking, anxious to ride. Each boy took a long turn on April in the corral.

I suggested Ric take Cash out to give him some exercise before I realized his legs hadn't healed to the flexibility needed to straddle a horse. Nancy stepped into the awkward moment by asking if she could ride first. A classy lady. He'd be foolish to pass her up for a *someday* in his mind. I saw the look of gratitude pass from his eyes to hers. *C'mon Ric, where's that smoldering look you do so well. That's what she wants.*

Nancy saddled Cash and led him out of the barn. I gave her brief directions on the riding areas. Lily, several cameras, lenses, and her trusty tri-pod, set up with the light at the corral, was shooting each boy in different poses. I led the boys around on April, taking them through the feel of the horse. Tim turned out to be a natural. Ramrod straight back, easy movement with the horse, eyes forward, easy hands. After Tim, ranked Matt, Tyler, Ben, and Will. I masked my disappointment that my stepson didn't share my knack for horses— why would he...a step not a natural. He gave up his last turn to take photos of the others.

My heart lightened when he asked to lead April into the barn. He reached up to pat her cheek and talked to her all the way in. His voice and hands were naturals; his enthusiasm grew from respect and awe of the animal. The joy of riding could come later.

Nancy came back after an hour with an expression of sheer bliss. Her long copper-colored hair kept movement with the trot on her approach to the corral. She slowed to a walk and stopped near the corral. Her face lifted to the sun for a final polishing. Lily snapped her as she lowered her face, clear amber eyes, flushed cheeks, and a Mona Lisa smile. Nancy leaped from Cash and threw her arms around his neck. "Good boy, best boy. Let's go find you some treats."

Ric, the designated cook, started the grill. Tracy took charge of the boys. I hooked April's lead to her stall post and worked with Will on the finer points of horse care while Nancy led Cash into the barn.

"Should I groom him now or are we too close." I appreciated her attention to safety.

"These two are fine. It's just that he's such a big guy it gets a little crowded. Hook him to the ring behind the door." I realized my extra brushes were in the mudroom and went to get them. I didn't mean to eavesdrop when I returned.

"You seem to be enjoying April. Pretty nice that your step-mom has horses in her backyard."

"She's not my step-mom. Not to me anyway." His young voice rang out and cut through my heart. They say someone who eavesdrops never hears anything good.

Nancy's voice lowered and I barely caught her words. "Moms are good, any way you can get them."

"Not this one. She messed it up for my mom and dad."

I could imagine what Nancy was thinking–other woman, divorce. To her credit she remained calm and let him continue. Here was an adult listening, what kid could pass that up.

"My dad didn't know, about me I mean. She broke them up." The anger in the word *she* made me shiver. "He would have married my mom if he knew. He's got honor. I hate her. If she would go away I know my mom and dad could be happy together with me."

I couldn't stand on the other side of two inches of wood much longer before either someone saw me or the pain I felt exploded into screams. I backed up a yard or so and stamped my feet as I approached. "Whew. It's getting colder out there. I brought extra treats for your new buddies." Light, cheery on the outside, twisted on the inside. I handed the brushes to Nancy and kept my eyes focused on her hands, not meeting her eyes. "Great job on April, Will. She's practically gleaming." I picked up each hoof and inspected his work. "Excellent. You'll make a first class wrangler."

Was there a tiny bit of acceptance in his eyes? Approval?

"I like taking pictures better," he mumbled loyally. I caught Nancy's glance over the top of the horses. Her smile reached out to me and when she spoke I could have hugged her.

"Imagine the great shots you can get from atop April."

Will's face cleared with the possibility that he could enjoy riding without being disloyal to his mom. Life shouldn't be this complicated for a kid.

April and Cash were in their stalls and munching on treats when Matt appeared at the door. "Hey guys, Uncle Ric says time to eat or he's feeding it to the coyotes." He giggled and then asked me. "Are there coyotes out here, Aunt Grace?"

Before I could answer, Will's voice interrupted. "He's not your uncle and she's not your aunt. What is it with you and your brother? Don't you have enough of your own relatives?"

Will's outburst caught everyone off guard. Matt's face sagged, unsure of how to handle verbal assault. He looked at me and my heart felt the same confusion.

"Will Marsden. That's no way to talk to Matt. He calls us aunt and uncle out of respect for the relationship his mother has with us. A little respect wouldn't kill you."

His chin came up and the same eyes that I'd fallen in love with in his father's face flashed cold at me. "I don't have to respect you; you're nobody to me or my mother."

Matt's intake of breath and rounded eyes mirrored my reaction. Only Nancy remained calm. She spoke as he dashed past her for the door. "You need to slow down and rethink your options, young man." Her firm 'cop voice' stopped him in his tracks. "You're at your dad's and step-mom's home, enjoying their horses and getting ready to enjoy their food. You can't have it both ways, my friend; take the pleasure in what they offer and spit out resentment and rudeness in return. Life does not reward the two-faced…at least not in a pleasant way."

Cripes. If she would have said that to me when I was eleven I would have burst into tears. I purposely didn't look at Will. He turned to look directly at Nancy. The kid had guts.

"Then I'll have it without *her*. I'll see my dad when he comes to our house." He turned and walked past Matt who tried to stop him.

"Hey, c'mon Will. No big deal. We call all the old people my folks know Aunt and Uncle."

Will brushed off Matt's words and hand. He walked to where his mother was packing up her gear and spoke to her. I moved to the barn entrance to console Matt.

"Sorry, Aunt Grace."

"*Shh,* don't be sorry. You did nothing wrong."

I watched Will finish his piece. Lily's head turned toward the barn and our glances fixed across the distance. Her posture similar to mine, one arm around a young boy's shoulder, comforting. Only that boy was her son and Matt was someone else's. Nancy stood next to me as Lily and I continued to stare. She knew this couldn't end pleasantly if we allowed the mood to escalate. Nancy stepped in front of me, forcing me to break eye contact.

"I think he's serious about feeding lunch to the coyotes. Let's go." Her hand on my arm set Matt and me in motion. I fought the impulse to look back.

We met the others on the patio. The heat from the Weber spread warmth to those seated on one side of the wrought iron table. Ric looked past us and caught Nancy's slight headshake. "Will and his mom had to head for home. Something came up."

Tim spoke through a mouthful of hotdog. "How are we supposed to get home?" He didn't sound upset at the prospect just curious.

"I'll take you guys home. I'm headed back to Oak Park. We can drop off Miss Nancy and be on our way. What time is your mom expecting you?"

"Before the cows come home, she always says. But I think before it gets dark. She's funny about the dark."

"Okay my Emperors, time to shift and make room on the warm side." Ben, Tim, and Tyler giggled as they got up with their plates and waddled to the cold side of the table. Tracy never missed an opportunity to teach her kids, any kids. They penguin walked, balancing their plates in their hands instead of eggs on their feet.

My appetite gone, I excused myself to check on Elmo. His sibs made a big hit with the boys as the kittens' appearance coincided with the arrival of the food. I needed to think, get away from everyone, and think. My favorite method of 'clearing the cobwebs' was happily in for the day, munching on sugary rewards.

I grabbed my keys and purse from the counter and headed for the garage door.

"Grace. Where are you going?" Tracy had followed me in.

The back of my throat ached with unshed tears. "I gotta think. I'll be at Dad's. Can you take care of…" I waved my hand around in an effort to complete my sentence.

"Sure. Be careful. Call me here when you get to your dad's. We'll still be here. Mary nailed me as First Aid merit badge counselor. I brought bandages and slings. You'll be missing the return of the mummy."

I smiled and nodded, not certain I wouldn't burst into tears. I'd ruined a great day for myself. At least the kids would have fun. Except one kid, the one that mattered the most. I croaked 'thanks' and left. The road to my father's house melted under my tires. When I closed in on the split to take 290 west for a short drive to St. Charles Rd. east, I stayed left and continued toward the city. My dad would want explanations and then I'd want to ask him about his name on that juvie list. And that could lead to more complications. And maybe Jeannette would be visiting or maybe she hadn't left. More complications.

I turned west on Roosevelt Rd. headed for Queen of Heaven and Mt. Carmel. Cemeteries held no fear for me. During high school at Proviso West, the cemetery was a great place to make out, or just sit behind a crypt and daydream. Now I visit my mom to chat and get life back in line.

I turned right into Mt. Carmel and right again at the first lane. I drove slowly past the overgrown evergreen bush that marked the marble tribute to Capone. There have always been rumors that Big Al isn't buried there, but the flat stones mark the graves of his mother, father, brother, and sister. Seems logical he'd be in there somewhere. As children when my grandmother was alive, we'd always come in this way and my nonna who by all standards was a kind, gentle woman, would curse Big Al's bush with the sign of horns. *Mal occhio.* She resented the shame and stigma that his life brought to the Italian people.

I formed the horns with my fingers and gave three quick shakes of my hand toward Big Al's bush. *That's for you, Nonna.* Her grave was toward the other end, closer to Wolf Road, well away from Big Al, Sam 'Momo' Giancana, the majestic white obelisk marked 'O'Bannion, the Genna boys, and Joey Aiuppa. *Angels and demons all together in the end. Well, together in the ground, but certainly separated for eternity.*

A light rain started. A few degrees lower and we'd have snow. That would be pretty. I stopped my car and took out the old gloves I keep in the trunk. I could wear one and keep my right hand in my pocket.

My mom's grave was on a lane that curved toward the entrance on Harrison Street. The entire section that I drove through showed names with almost more vowels than consonants. *Romanelli, DiCorso, Maida*; two people knelt there. *Fortunato, DiCenzio;* around the curve a lone figure stood head down holding a wreath at his side, *Bantonini.*

My heart hammered against my chest. Why hadn't I noticed that name before? I had no reason...then. I slowed the car and stopped halfway between where the man stood and my mother's grave some thirty feet ahead. I sat in the car and watched him through my driver's side mirror. This had to be Bantonini senior, the old scoutmaster. At a quick glance, it could have been Edward Junior, so close were they in height and build. On closer inspection I could see the white edges under the old-fashioned fedora he held on his head with one hand.

I watched him pull the hat closer around his head to free his hand. He firmly pushed the metal tri-pod stand into the frozen earth and carefully placed the wreath, bow on an angle, against the frame. He tied the wreath to the frame in three spots. The wreath was off to the side of the door to the mini mausoleum. I vaguely wondered which knot he used, square, half hitch, or clove. And with that thought my fingers reached for the length of yarn on my turn signal. *Up, over, pass through and down, up, over, pass through and down.* At ten knots I could look up again. I glanced in my mirror to check on Bantonini. The mirror reflected black.

➴ 34 ➶

I screamed when he tapped the window. The door swung open as I reached for the door lock. I felt a spray of rain on my arm.

"Are you all right? I didn't mean to frighten you. I thought you were lost or ill." His words were good choices to present concern, but his voice screamed insincerity. I couldn't explain it, but I could hear it. The mild tone reminded me of Edward Junior's voice, but the timber was threaded with menace.

"I–I'm fine." My hand slipped down to the handle preparing to pull the door closed. "Thank you for asking."

It looked to me that he tightened his grip on the corner of the door as my fingers slipped around the cold metal. His fingers were deformed or injured–no nails more like smooth, pointy stumps. I pulled the door, felt light resistance, and pulled harder. The door slammed shut and I pushed down the 'all lock' button. *Click*. The sound washed over me and allowed me to exhale the breath I'd been holding. I felt safe in looking out at him. His eyes seemed surprised at my reaction and then they narrowed in suspicion or anger, something I couldn't figure. *Why is he angry with me? He's the one that damn near gave me a heart attack. Mom, I can't get out now. I'll be back tomorrow.*

I started the car and drove away glancing toward the second row where a marble headstone with 'Morelli' etched in the center stood silent, waiting. "Tomorrow, Mom." I made a quick sign of the cross and drove around the curve toward the exit. Left on Harrison and I was on my way home. I hadn't found peace in the cemetery. Dad would give me the third degree. I hadn't accomplished much except to scare myself silly. *What is your problem? Do you hear yourself?*

I slammed my right hand on the steering wheel and winced in pain. "Yes, I hear myself," I shouted to the window. "Who else would I hear?" The rhetorical question calmed me. I waited at the light for the heavy traffic on Roosevelt Road. A little music would help. Strains of the theme song from 'Out of Africa' filled the car. *Hmm. Nice.* Traffic slowed and I turned right, headed for the entrance ramp for York Road south. The music flowed through me and I relaxed. My brain slowed and pieces began moving into place; I could feel the sensation of a puzzle piece that sets in snug. In the next moment, my brain flashed a message that caught me off guard. I lost sight of the shoulder for a moment and my right wheels left the pavement. I gripped at the wheel ineffectively and couldn't turn it enough to get back on the road. The frozen ground reacted like slick pavement and the car slid sideways across the turf stopping inches from the chain link fence that separated the area from the trailer park on the north side of the street.

My hands shook from the adrenaline rush slowly ebbing. I took slow breaths, blowing the air out of my mouth to calm my hysteria. I braced my elbows on the bottom of the wheel and leaned the bridge of my nose against steepled fingertips. More deep breaths, scrunching up my shoulders, and letting them drop. I turned my head from side to side loosening the muscle tension.

The engine had not stalled; I realized I'd had my foot jammed on the brake the whole time. I shifted to the four-wheel mode, straightened my wheels, and slowly let off the brake. My plan was to move forward a few yards before attempting to turn up the embankment. I drove parallel to the fence waiting to feel good contact with the ground when I noticed that if I kept driving straight I could cut over onto the ramp coming down from York Road to enter Roosevelt. I felt better about going straight than uphill. The path took me down a slight gully and then an easy climb and bump onto the ramp. A quick left turn to continue down the ramp put me on Roosevelt and within fifty yards I was on the ramp to York Road.

I passed up the turnoff to I-88 and continued to 22nd Street. I would take side streets home and calmly inspect the conclusion my brain had flung at me earlier…that Bantonini had been the hooded figure that pulled me from Harry's car.

⮞ 35 ⮜

I arrived home to find Harry, Ric, Dad, Mike Jr., and Nick planning a search party. When I didn't call Tracy, she called my dad. When I didn't arrive there he called Harry, who had returned by then. Dad left Jeannette at the house in case I showed up and he drove to Pine Marsh after he called my brother and cousin. They left as soon as I arrived. Three remaining pairs of eyes glared at me from the other side of the table

"I needed to get away, to think. I'm sorry. I didn't mean to worry anyone." I hadn't even had a chance to tell them about Bantonini. Now I wasn't sure if I should. That would only reinforce their opinion of my behavior. I decided to keep it to myself. I told them about the car problem. That story explained the pansy purple eyes that guarded the cemetery secret. I finished with, "I couldn't pull the wheel back. I know I should've waited for a tow, but I knew I could drive out.

I walked Dad out to his car, repeatedly assuring him that I wouldn't make a move without one of the 'four musketeers'; he'd insisted on being added to the duty roster. I stopped walking. The rain had ceased, leaving the air fresh and clean. I took a deep breath to clear my head and build my courage.

"Can I ask you something about when you were a kid?"

"Honey, does this have anything to do with that list of names?" He smiled. "Harry told me about your argument. It's true in one way, but misleading. I was out in the woods that night with those boys. We started out with a pickup game of basketball on the playground at St. Edgar's. When it got too dark to play, Black Bart dared us to visit Chee Chee Pin Quay's grave to look for his ghost warriors. Only Bart, Moochie, and Bigs wanted to go. The rest of us weren't crazy about the idea but didn't want to look like pansies."

I couldn't believe what I'd heard. "Dad, you always taught us to follow our instinct no matter what other people thought."

"Where and when do you think I learned that? That night." He looked at his hands. "We hung around that rock taunting each other to walk behind it, to touch it. The usual kid crap. All of a sudden we heard this chanting. I swear it was his name real soft, over and over again. We scattered. We should have run back out on to East River

Road, but we took off deeper into the woods. Herd mentality, we followed the leader, Black Bart. He took off down a path. It was easier than crashing through the trees. Anyhow, this path ends up in a clearing about a quarter mile from the road. There's all kind of junk out here, boilers, bedsprings, rusted and broken. In the dark they stuck out like shadowy guards. Most of us wanted to leave, but we weren't sure which way was out. Quite honestly it seemed a little safer to be with Black Bart than near that grave. Bart walked over to a fire pit and lit a kerosene lantern. He knew right where it was so he'd been here before. The light drew us like moths and we took seats on cinder blocks and tree stumps that circled the ash filled area. We pulled some wood into the pit and found some smaller pieces for tinder and kindling; had a teepee style fire going in no time. It felt like a campout. At least in the beginning. We speculated on what we'd heard. Wind, street noise, some other kids playing a hoax on us. The only explanation we didn't consider was a supernatural one. Then Black Bart started talking about the curse of Chee Chee Pin Quay and how if you angered him you had to make a sacrifice or something bad would happen. He brought up Specs' disappearance. He told us he didn't want anything like that to happen to us. He pulled a bag from inside a rusting oil barrel next to the pit. I knew then that he'd planned to come out here.

He moved the lantern to the far end of the pit and lit up the ground. A gold colored car door lay face up, scrawled across the top were the words, 'God is dead' and a pentagram took up the middle portion. He placed small candles in each of the five triangles of the symbol. He told us that witches used this to worship Satan. He said we could use it tonight to call the Dark Lord."

My dad stopped talking. He removed a handkerchief from his back pocket and wiped his forehead. The temperature was maybe forty degrees; hardly balmy.

"I'm sorry Dad. If this bothers you…"

"No, I went through this with those two already, the least I can do is let you hear it from me."

That sounded ominous. He swiped at his upper lip and continued. "When he pulled out those shriveled feet and a glass jar with red liquid I made my decision. I tripped trying to get out of there. Got my feet under me and started down the path ready to take my chances with whatever was back at the road. I wasn't the only one. Whalen, Randy, and Tinucci passed me up and Santori kept even with me. We had to sound like a herd of elephants coming down that path, huffing and yelling encouragement to keep going. The three guys in the lead stopped cold. A light appeared in front of them on the path. That's how the Forest Preserve police found us, five kids huddle together ready to pee their pants thinking Chee Chee Pin Quay was coming to make us disappear."

Dad smiled and put his arm around my shoulder. "I was never so happy to see the cops. One officer stayed with us and the other went to round up the guys at the fire pit. We were all charged the same, except Black Bart. He was eighteen. And that is how I learned the hard way what I taught you and your brothers."

The cold on my teeth told me how big a grin I sported. "So that really was one of those 'do as I say, not as I do' events in your life." I kissed and hugged Dad, and waited to watch him drive away. A final wave and I turned to go inside. Harry stood on the front porch.

"Feel better?"

I nodded and smiled. I climbed the steps, suddenly tired from the adventure, revelation, and conflict of the day. *Conflict! Cripes. I have to tell Harry about what happened.* Harry opened the door and let me pass. *Better get it out.*

"I have to tell you what happened—"

"About Will? I heard all about it and he'll be over some time this evening to apologize."

My head snapped so quickly, had I been an owl it would have gone 360. Harry put his arm around me. "I heard everyone's stories: Nancy's, Will's, Matt's, Lily's, as told to her by Will. He said that you grabbed his arm and scolded him rather severely."

I opened my mouth to interrupt. Harry squeezed my shoulder. "This will go faster if you let me do all the talking." His tone was cheery. "Lily came looking for you and loaded with bear as you say."

"For bear, loaded for bear," I corrected automatically.

"Yes, well she was looking to take you on for abusing her cub. Tracy spoke up first about what Will had said as relayed to her by Matt who'd been upset that any one would talk to his Aunt Grace that way. Tracy further debunked any idea that you would grab and shake any child. Nancy confirmed Will's awful behavior toward you. Lily confronted Will on the spot and he admitted he'd exaggerated and behaved badly. She made him apologize to everyone there for spoiling the afternoon and told them he'd be back to apologize to you."

I looked up at Harry aware of the tears slipping from the corners of my eyes. He dabbed at them with his handkerchief that he'd already removed from his pocket in anticipation. He led me to the couch. I sat down and accepted the handkerchief. "Now he really hates me. I'm sorry, I tried to make him like me." I buried my face in the cloth.

"Don't you apologize. He acted like a little hellion and he should be apologizing to you. And he will."

I sniffed and blew my nose. "So, he'll apologize and never set foot here again. You'll always have to go there. We'll never be any kind of family." Fresh tears were centimeters away from falling.

"Gracie, he's eleven. Think back to what your brothers said at that age. We have horses and cats over here. We'll get over this and move forward. You'll see. C'mon, old girl. Show us a smile."

When Harry used his father's term of endearment for his mom I brightened. He'd used 'we' and 'we'll'. I loved that pronoun. I thought about what my brothers had said through the years. Thought about the time Marty and I ran away from home for one afternoon because we weren't allowed the same privileges as the older kids. I pulled Harry down on the couch and put my arms around his neck, our lips inches apart. "I like the way you think."

Ric cleared his throat and Harry and I leaped apart. He'd been on the phone when we walked in.

"I normally tell crazed hormonal couples to 'get a room.' In your case you have several from which to choose."

Harry's rueful grin set the mood. At least they wouldn't be sniping at each other. "Can I get you a drink? Bourbon, right?"

"Sounds good, but I'll help myself. Don't get up." Ric removed the top from a square crystal decanter and poured two inches of the amber colored liquid into a rocks glass. "Can I get you a drink?"

"I'll try some of your poison. We've had the bottle forever; bloody thing even made it through the explosion.'

I leaned back against the soft fabric of the couch.

Ric was acting like the host. It made me uncomfortable. Why was Harry so relaxed, that odd grin on his face? *Oh, Lord, is he thinking about leaving me? Maybe checking out how Ric would fit into this house.* Ridiculous! *Then why isn't he fuming?*

"Grace? Some white wine?" Ric's hand hovered over a bottle of Pinot Grigio.

"No!" exploded from my mouth. "No thanks. I'm making coffee." I left the living room at practically a dead run. Predictably, both men were right behind me.

"What's your rush?"

"It's coffee withdrawal. If we don't administer a cup every hour she gets like this."

Ric laughed. "She needs one of those pumps she can strap to her waist. Direct injection with one squeeze. Better yet, automatic release every hour in case her hands are otherwise occupied." Ric mimed braiding.

Harry burst into laughter.

"If anyone is interested, coffee is ready, Pine Marsh Mellow."

"New cup? A bit rustic isn't it?"

"Looks like something the cat, or the horse, dragged in."

Bouts of laughter from both of them. I looked at the cup on the counter. Where had it come from? I don't own this mug. Speckled blue metal, like camping gear. Where is my angel mug? I opened the cabinet above the counter. All speckled blue. *Someone is playing a stupid joke. Two someones. That's it, I've had it.*

"Where's my mug? Put it back right now." I meant for my voice to crackle with authority and anger. It came out fuzzy and low.

"Gracie, wake up. Gracie." Harry jiggled my shoulders.

"It was so real. You were pouring drinks and talking about me like I wasn't here and then my mug was blue." Harry and Ric stared at me. I felt like Dorothy waking up in Kansas.

I jumped from the couch and rushed into the kitchen, explaining as I went, "I got up to make coffee and my angel mug was metal." Both men followed me. The coffeemaker stood empty and off. "There was coffee, Pine Marsh Mellow." I yanked the cabinet door open, ready to expose the shelf of metal blue cups. My angel mug tipped forward and Harry's hand shot forward and caught it.

"Slow down, darling."

Two pairs of eyes stared with the same mixture of concern and love. I nodded and dipped my chin down to my chest to loosen my neck muscles. I closed my eyes and took two deep breaths, releasing each slowly and fully.

"Just one of those quickie dreams when you doze off." Ric's explanation made as much sense as anything else, except it didn't feel like a dream.

"But why all these mugs?" In a flash of intuition I asked Ric, "Was anything like this recovered in or near the well?"

They stared at me. Ric shook his head. "Bits of things, but no cup."

Harry addressed Ric without turning away from me. "Has there been an extensive search of the area around the well?"

Ric's snort summed up his opinion of Harry's question. "Of

course there's been an extensive search. Do you think the cops just looked in the well? Two teams scoured the perimeter for an entire afternoon. They've got enough stuff collected to keep a forensics team busy for a month." Ric shoved his left hand through his hair pushing back an unruly strand. "It was just a dream, a goofy dream."

Harry turned toward Ric. "And if someone in the police department is leaking information or involved?" He let the question hang in the air.

"This cup is important. We have to find it."

"If what you say is true, it would have been disposed of by now. Our only hope is that it was overlooked in the search."

"We can't suggest another search to the police as long as we think there could be a leak. We'll have to do this on our own."

Ric shook his head. "Whoa, I'm not taking a bunch of civilians into the woods on a wild goose chase."

"Then it's you and me, Kramer."

"How about Stahl? I'd like a third with us."

"No. If we're gone, he's here with Grace."

"Drop me off at Dad's. Only don't tell him what you're up to or he'll want to bring Marty's metal detector and join in the search."

"How about I tell him I'm taking Will on a hike and we want to use it?"

"That would work, just make sure you play up the 'bonding' part or he'll want to come along and bring a lunch."

"Maybe he'll just pack one. I love those salami and provolone sandwiches he makes." Ric smacked his lips for effect.

A faint whirring noise attracted Harry's attention. He pointed a finger toward the upper level. "A fax I've been waiting for. Maybe a little more information, maybe nothing."

"I could use a cup of coffee."

"I thought you had a Bour…" I shook my head. "It seemed so real." I busied myself with coffee preparations while Ric settled into the breakfast nook. He looked so natural, so comfortable, not like a guest but like–

Stop right there. It was a dream. Harry is not sizing up Ric as his replacement.

Harry returned and motioned us to the butcher-block island. He spread four sheets of paper on the surface, using the salt and pepper shaker, sugar bowl, and three pears to hold down the curling edges.

"Confirmation of the stolen weapons, list of people questioned in the theft, list of people questioned in the murders of Robert Peterson and Anton and John Schuessler, and acknowledgement that John Jacob Henry Sr. was FBI."

"Holy crap! Henry was an agent? So was he on a campout with his kids troop or was he tracking a thief? Did he find the thief or a murderer, or both?"

"The hit and run looks more suspicious."

"I've seen the investigation notes. They looked thorough." Ric hesitated.

"What?"

"The rookie detective on the case was Thomas."

"Are there duplicate names on the lists?"

"Absolutely." Harry tapped the side-by-side pages. "Bantonini Sr., Bigelow, Quigley," Harry paused and looked at me, "and Father Briscoe."

"Some of these names were on your list from the woods. Is this Quigley Tim's dad or uncle?"

Without dates of birth it's hard to tell. On the murder investigation it could be a grandfather. Bigelow is Mary Quigley's maiden name. The Bigelow on the juvie list is her brother Thaddeus. Father Briscoe makes another list too." Harry pointed to a handwritten postscript on one list. "Seems when the boys were arrested, the good Father happened to be in the woods–claims he'd been trying to catch those Wicca in the act–to ask them to stop their pagan rituals. He vouched for Black Bart, only him, even though he knew all the boys from school. The cops could have been tougher on Bart, since he was eighteen."

"Maybe that's why he only defended Bart."

"Or maybe Bart was his Wicca hunting partner?"

"Has anyone thought to go back and check records of any attacks in those woods in the fifties?"

Ric's words chilled me. Could a priest have led a vigilante group of boys into those woods doling out retribution for crimes against Christianity? We all seemed to be thinking the same thoughts.

"He would be the biggest 'Mr. Big' of all, wouldn't he?" Harry's soft voice spoke our thoughts. "The list of possible ringleaders is growing and we don't know if these crimes are separate or entwined."

"The only person, or people, desperate enough to want to stop the investigation would be whoever killed Janet."

"There's no statute of limitations on murder–there's John Jacob and his dad. There's the Peterson, Schuessler boys. And there's no statute of limitations on treason."

"Treason?"

Ric nodded. "Those munitions were stolen while this country was at war. That's treason, punishable with life imprisonment, at the least. Doubt they'd ask for the death penalty at this point in time, but had they been caught back then, it's totally possible."

The mood around the table grew darker as we each withdrew to our own thoughts. Mine turned to Hannah and Marisol. I hadn't had the opportunity to ask Harry. At the risk of causing an outburst from him or Ric I asked, "Uh, how did it go with Hannah?"

Ric rolled his eyes and shook his head.

Harry shot him a look and then stared at the tops of his hands. "She's home. Charged with a misdemeanor trespassing charge, like she's a bloody teenager." His even-toned voice tightened, as I'm sure he tried not to explode. "Apparently, Marisol and two other Wicca, including Hannah, were conducting a purification ritual in an attempt to reclaim the area."

"Reclaim the area? Sorry, Marsden, but your sister's choice in friends and causes makes me wonder about her judgment."

"Careful what you say, she's with your sister."

Oh, oh. Here it comes. Which sister started the relationship?

"Is Hannah Wicca again? I mean, did she renew her vows or something?" I purposely used a *gracie*, my family's term for a faux pas, to head off the argument.

They both stared at me. *Mission accomplished!*

"Ah, once a Wicca always a Wicca."

"So she was lapsed, but now she's practicing?"

"Something along those lines. Anyway, she's home and has promised to stay out of the woods and practice her 'religion' in a less dangerous manner."

I thought about the danger she'd been in. "They could have been victims of the rapist."

Ric shook his head. "No, I don't think so. His MO is six and that's all. He's still looking for one more and he's running out of time."

On that chilling note, they called it a night and made plans to meet in the morning after Harry deposited me with my dad. I figured I'd surprise him and we could go to Mass at St. Dom's together.

The phone rang and I motioned that I'd get it.

"Hello."

I heard breathing.

"Hello." I started to hang up when I heard a small sigh.

"Is this Mrs. Mars…"

"Hello, Will." I didn't want to be 'Mrs. Marsden' to him.

"Ah, I wanted to call to apologize for the way I acted today."

"Okay."

"Okay?"

"You're calling to apologize, so apologize." I wasn't going to let him off the hook that easily.

"I'm sorry."

"Sorry for anything in particular?" I remembered this routine from my dad when I was on Will's end of the apology.

"Ah, yeah, I mean I didn't get to play with the cats or eat hot dogs…" his voice trailed off undoubtedly confused by my question.

"Oh, so you're sorry because you messed up your good time? Anything else?"

I looked at Ric who grinned from ear to ear while Harry's smile seemed more tentative. *I won't mear or mar your little boy.* I smiled at my words from childhood when something was scuffed or marked up.

"I'm sorry I didn't get to work on my badge?"

"*Hmm.* Another thing that didn't work for *you*. Anything else?"

Tough little nut. I had years of these conversations to draw from. Actually the key was to keep asking 'anything else'.

"I'm sorry I yelled at Matt. I like him."

"Anything–"

"I'm sorry I yelled at you and lied." His voice shook with his admission.

"I appreciate your apology. We all get wound up sometimes and say things we're sorry for later. I accept your apology. It took courage for you to call."

And his father and mother threatening who knows what. It's a start.

He mumbled something I didn't catch. He cleared his throat. "Can I talk to my dad? Please." The afterthought showed promise.

"Sure. Here he is. Good night."

I handed Harry the phone, refilled my cup, and held up the pot. Ric shook his head. More for me. I cleaned up the kitchen while Harry talked. So much evil information had whirled around this room earlier. I hoped the loving conversation taking place now could vanquish the dark shadows.

≈ 36 ≈

Harry and Ric had arranged to meet Walter at the East River Road entrance to Robinson Woods at ten this morning. They'd also decided against asking my dad for the metal detector. In fact, Harry planned to drop me off and not come in. Harry had asked Walter to find a detector. I don't know where Walter would get one on a Sunday morning, but I had no doubt he'd have one.

"Not even for a minute? He's going to suspect something."

Harry walked around and opened my door. "We've gone over this. Simply smile and tell him we got a late start and I had to dash."

I stood and smoothed my skirt around my knees. "He'll know." I pointed to my eyes.

"Trust me, he'll think you're embarrassed. You know, bit of morning delight."

God help me if I didn't smile at the thought. Harry brushed his lips against my cheek. "There's my girl." He closed the door and hurried around the front of the Jag. "Give him my best."

I rang the bell, anticipating the surprise on his face. I don't know who was more surprised. Jan Pauli opened the door and stared at me for two blinks before her face curved into a smile. She called over her shoulder, "Mike, it's Grace." She looked beyond me.

My face, an open book, must have revealed chapter and verse of my thoughts. Jan moved aside quickly and motioned me in to my childhood home. *Okay, I'm prepared to let Dad date, but why is she here, now, this early? Her car isn't in the drive so that means it's in the garage and that means she spent the night, which means...*

I forced my mind away from the obvious conclusion. "Hi Sweetie, what a nice surprise." Dad hugged me. "Where's Harry?"

I'd never thought to call and ask my dad if he could 'watch' me today. I assumed he'd be home making gravy like he does most Sundays. Who'd have thought he'd be home making whoopee. "Come on in. Don't stand in the doorway. Jeanette and I just finished breakfast, but I can whip up some eggs in a pocket for you."

Sure. Eggs in a pocket, one of my favorite breakfasts. Had he made it for her or is he trying to soften me up?

He kept talking. "I don't have coffee made, but try some of this

Tangerine Zinger tea Jeannette brought. It's a great eye-opener."

Great eye-opener I bet. My eyes are wide open and I'm not liking what I see.

Without thinking I glanced toward the wall leading to the hallway where my parents' wedding picture hangs in the center of all of the kids' wedding photos. Dad's eyes followed my gaze. He moved to interrupt my view. His forehead creased and his eyes filled with concern. "Honey, it's great to see you. How's your wrist?"

Jan had the good sense and decency to leave the room, mumbling some excuse as she left. I noticed she went into the kitchen, the neutral zone, and not the bedroom. Dad took both my hands in his, and guided me to the dark pink sectional I'd grown up hiding behind and jumping on while playing hide and seek with my brothers.

"Honey, you know how much your mom meant to me. We were kids when we met and married. Her Aunt Fiona had a fit, washed her hands of her. Couldn't abide that she would marry an Italian 'gangster'.

Dad sat silent for a moment and then drew a long breath. "We became her family, which was great, but when you don't have your own roots, your own history and memories to bring to a relationship you can start to wonder *why* and *who* you are. It's rough to be someone else's why and who.

"I'm not saying I feel about Jeannette the way I felt about Mom. I'm just saying that for the first time in five years I feel something for another woman. No one is ever going to replace your mom in my heart. I have to tell you, honey, it's nice to be with someone who comes to the table with as much history as the Morellis. We have common interests, hobbies, and we can *share* our experiences. Your mom once told me that she felt that her existence began when she married into the family. At the time, I thought that was a tribute to the family. It wasn't 'til years later and several doctors that I realized it had been a cry for help."

My fingers fidgeted inside my father's grip. This part of the fairy tale I knew intuitively, but had never discussed with my dad. He gave my hands a reassuring squeeze. "I don't want to be everything to someone I just want to be a part of someone's life."

I could only nod while I struggled not to cry. I slipped my hands over his and squeezed. We both let go and hugged at the same instant laughing at our unerring timing.

"We're headed for Mass at Regina. Why don't you join us?"

"Why not St. Dom's?"

244

Dad stayed quiet. Jan had walked in when she heard the laughter. She stood next to him. "It's the Remembrance Mass."

Regina College celebrated a yearly mass for the repose and remembrance of the deceased family members of alumni. I'd totally forgotten; I'd received the card, but never got around to sending it back with my mother's name. Dad didn't forget. I smiled at Jan.

"That would be nice."

We found seats with Sister Jeanne and Sister Clemente and saved two for Mike and Carolyn who were participating in the processional. I introduced my father and Jan to Sister Clemente. He already knew Sister Jeanne.

Afterwards, we met in the dining and social halls for a lovely brunch. I purposely stayed quiet, enjoying the conversation and banter around the table. Mike and Carolyn chatted easily with Jan, laughing at her stories that paralleled dad's. *Someone with as much history as the Morellis.* I recognized the give and take of relationship building. Part of me grew sad, realizing Dad was enjoying that basic element of courting for the first time. My dad caught my look and nodded. I smiled and my mood caught up to theirs.

"We're stopping to see the babies since we're so close. How about you two joining us?"

Stopping to see the babies? News to me.

"Can't make it. We're headed home to pick up Joey, then to drive out to NIU for a visit. He's already checked out Eastern."

We said good-bye on the steps of Lewis Hall. "Mass was a lovely experience. Thank you for inviting me." Jan's eyes gleamed in her heart shaped face. *He could do worse.*

I climbed into the back of Dad's car and listened to their chatter while we drove to the brownstone. Their low voices lulled me and I leaned my head back against the leather. My mind wandered through the events of the last two weeks, trying to sort and pigeonhole and categorize each scene parading across the back of my eyes. The hum of the tires assisted in the process. Sometimes I did my best work in a state of semi-consciousness. A memory waited at the edge of my conscious mind. I couldn't reach it. *Let go, relax. Shiny, small links.*

My eyes flew open and I lurched forward, activating the halting pressure of my seatbelt. Dad and Jan both sensed the movement.

"Grace, what's wrong?"

"I've been a dope. I have evidence, maybe it's evidence."

"Evidence of what?"

"The day the scouts found the crate. When we removed the cat for burial we found two items, a metal tag that Harry turned over to Edward Bantonini and a piece of bracelet that I put in my pocket. I tossed it in my junk box and forgot about it."

"What do you think this bracelet is evidence of?"

"I don't know, maybe the person who put the cat in the crate, or maybe," my throat tightened at my thought, "maybe it was on someone who'd been in the crate."

Jan gasped and it felt like the car wobbled.

"Gracie, that's crazy."

"Dad, maybe not. What if whoever killed John Jacob had to hide his body until he could dump it?"

"Couldn't the little boy have fallen into that well? Mike, you said he'd run off."

Apparently my dad had been discussing the case with Jan. *Odd pillow talk. Cripes, don't go there.*

"That was a working well back then for the house that belonged to Chief Alexander Robinson's granddaughter. Burned down in the seventies. You can still see some of the foundation."

"Chief Robinson? I thought he was an Indian?"

"Confused me, too. Alexander Robinson was his 'white man' name. His Indian name was Chief Chee Chee Pin Quay. He was chief of the Potawatomi, Chippewa, and Ottawa."

"As scouts we always called him Chee Chee Pin Quay, not even Chief. Several of the scout districts in this council use those tribal names."

Dad pulled into a spot at the curb only three houses down from our destination.

"Do they know we're coming over?" I hadn't thought to ask before then.

"Naw. Why should they be any different from when your mom and I used to drop in on the boys with their new babies? That's why they call it a surprise." He started up the stone steps. Jan and I looked at each other, in synch with our thoughts. I guess none of my brothers has ever told him how they, and especially their wives, hated the surprise visits. Oh, boy. Double trouble.

He stopped at the door and looked back. "What are you two waiting for, an engraved invitation?"

Jan and I climbed the steps slowly. I heard her mutter, 'you gotta love the guy.' My throat tightened and I stubbed my foot against the next step. Jan reached out to steady me. She leaned over and whispered, "If we both take a tumble that should distract him before they know we're here." We grinned and climbed the last step as potential co-conspirators. Dad pressed the doorbell. The deed being done, Jan stood by her man and even linked her arm through his. *He could do worse.*

There was no surprise on Hannah's face when she opened the door. "Hello, hello. Come in. What a lovely treat." She stepped aside and we trooped into the foyer. "Come into the kitchen, I have the kettle on. Jan, I found the tea you recommended. Shall I make us some? Gracie I have coffee too, only have to pull it together. I wasn't sure who was coming."

Now we looked surprised. Hannah hurried to explain. "I knew someone would be visiting around now," she glanced at her watch. "Marisol told me."

"You consult a medium?" Jan's voice squeaked her surprise.

Hannah flashed the Marsden dimpled grin. "No, course not. I invited her to come for tea today and she said I'd already have family visiting. And here you are."

We followed her into the kitchen. "Please, sit down." I looked around for signs of Karen and babies. Hannah must have read my thoughts. "Karen's at Trinity, some sort of award ceremony, and the babies are sleeping the sleep of full bellies."

"Marisol told you we were coming over?" Dad sounded skeptical.

"She didn't name names, just that family would be visiting. And here you are."

"Hannah, how often is Marisol correct in her predictions?"

"I'm sure she doesn't keep track and they're not truly predictions, only feelings."

"Couldn't she have 'felt' that the cops were coming when you were in the woods?" Hannah's demeanor shifted from hostess to hostile. Her shoulders tightened and she abruptly placed a mug in front of me. Coffee sloshed over the rim.

"Now you sound like Karen."

"I'm sorry, Hannah. I didn't mean to upset you. It seemed odd to me that she couldn't sense something about the police. I thought maybe she might have wanted the publicity, you know the, 'there's no such thing as bad publicity' angle."

"She's not like that." Hannah's clear voice defended her friend, but in the tone I heard a smidgen of doubt.

Jan leaned forward. "Do you mind telling me about the ceremony? I've always been fascinated by different religions." Dad shifted in his chair to look at his 'squeeze'. I sensed trouble in paradise if she was going where I thought she was going.

"Religion? You call that woo-woo in the woods religion?"

Too bad for you, Jan. Guess you won't be cleaning his house much longer.

She reached across the table and rubbed the top of his hand. "Mike, as long ago as Christianity, actually before, there was Wicca. It's not Satanic, far from it. I would die before I paid homage to the Devil." Her firm voice calmed Dad's concerns. I saw his shoulders relax.

He lowered his chin, cocked his head, and looked up at her. "Do I want to know how you know about this…Wicca?"

Jan grinned and her blue eyes sparkled. "College, Mike. You learn so much away at school, away from parents. You experiment with so many new and different paths."

"That's why her mother and I sent her to the nuns at Regina."

We burst into laughter and after a minute of pretended sternness he joined in.

Hannah could barely get under control. "Oh, yes the nuns kept her on the straight and narrow. That's why she brought home a spy for your son-in-law." Her laughter dissolved into hiccups and giggles.

"I'd hardly refer to my son-in-law as an experiment."

"Men, you all stick together. By the way, where is my brother?"

Three heads turned toward me. I shrugged and looked into my mug. I'd have to raise my lying eyes eventually.

"Are they in the woods, by chance?"

My eyes pinned Hannah's. "How did you…Marisol?"

"Nothing that mystical. I saw Ric leave out this morning. He wore heavy boots and carried a short, folding type spade."

Again they all stared at me. "Honey?"

Cripes!

"Okay, okay. Harry, Ric, and Walter are combing the woods near the well looking for a metal cup. That's why Harry dropped me off at your house." I remembered something and turned to Hannah. "Where were you doing your ceremony? Were you near the rock?"

"No, I don't think so. The altar," Hannah hesitated, "was set up near one of those mounds. We wanted an untouched area. So much of the woods near Chee Chee Pin Quay's grave is filled with junk people have dumped."

"Could this be a type of 'altar'?" I pulled a small Osco picture bag from my purse. "Harry picked these up for Will after the scout outing. Will and his buddy, Tim, were excited about the pictures Will had taken. Here's one of them. You can see why Harry hasn't turned them over yet." I placed the photo toward them. A car door lay on the ground. Across the top scrawled in crooked printing read 'God is Dead' and under that in the center was a pentagram with a circle around it. "Isn't this a Wicca symbol?"

"Absolutely not, but I can see why you'd think so. Look at the figure. It's pointed downward. Wicca uses the pentagram but we point it upward to honor and recognize a Supreme Being. The five sections symbolize, spirit, water, air, fire, and earth. This photo is definitely Satanic in nature. It's these sorts of discoveries that give Wicca a bad name." Hannah's eyes searched our faces for acceptance. I don't know what she found elsewhere, but I couldn't jump on the bandwagon. I suspected she had no takers.

"So, the black hooded people who attacked Grace would not be a renegade Wicca group? This photo looks like the real thing I saw in those woods over forty years ago. History repeats itself?"

"Mike, I assure you Wicca is not about evil. Wicca celebrates the autumnal equinox and the winter solstice as a way of honoring our roots and the earth. It's unfortunate that these attacks fall into the same timeframe, which was a pagan celebration long before Christianity claimed it as All Hallowed Eve.

"Good and evil in the garden of midnight." Jan's quiet voice capped Hannah's comment.

Waa, waa, waaah!

"Battle stations everybody, the babes are afoot."

We laughed at Hannah's assessment. Her humorous acceptance of life with babies lifted our spirits even if she mixed her metaphors.

"Any takers?"

"I've got Connor." I answered first.

"I'll take Clare." Jan's voice aced my dad.

"No fair, I was drinking." Jan and I hurried down the hallway leaving him to sulk.

We turned the corner to the short hallway to the nursery and felt the cold air moving to greet us. "There must be an open window." Jan wrapped her arms around her chest. It wasn't an open window kind of cold, fresh and brisk. More an icy cold emanating from one source. I'd felt it before. I pushed past Jan and rushed into the nursery.

Jan's scream brought Hannah and Dad at a run and started the babies wailing. Dad burst through the doorway ready to fight. He ended up holding a shaken lady friend.

Hannah and I each lifted a baby, rocking and cooing until they quieted.

"I'm sorry. I saw something black, there in between the cribs, swirling. I thought, I don't know. It scared me." Jan gulped back tears and shivered under Dad's arm.

"C'mon. Let's go back to the kitchen and get some of that tea. Too much 'mumbo jumbo' talk." He guided Jan out of the room, but not before he glanced over her head toward me.

Hannah waited a tic then asked, "What happened? We heard this low cooing and then that bloody scream. Scared the devil out of me."

Interesting choice of words.

"Neither one of us spoke. What did you hear?"

"I don't know, Gracie, cooing. But not your voice. I thought it must be Jan. Forget about that. Was there something in this room with them?"

Clare stirred in my arms and I took a few moments to calm her and form my answer. I turned down the dial on the monitor. "It wasn't evil, Hanns. I think he was looking for me, to say goodbye." I couldn't have said that to Karen. Hannah stared at me for a moment.

"The black swirling…"

I smiled. "His cowboy hat."

"Cowboy? Marisol did say an odd thing that I meant to ask her about, but the police arrived. She said she felt the presence of a spirit who'd finally found his way. 'Odd,' she'd said. 'I would have thought he'd be an Indian not a cowboy.'"

Dad spoke from the doorway. "What's the game plan? I think I'd better get Jeannette home. I dosed her tea with some of your whiskey; hope you don't mind."

"That's a grand idea. Fix one for me, please."

"Dad, give me a few minutes, I think someone needs a change."

I whisked through baby wipes and Desitin to clean diaper in no time. Two quick cuddles and a reassuring hug for Hannah and I left.

Jan sat quietly the entire trip home. I felt sorry for her, but I also felt that an explanation now would only make her hysterical. She stayed for a few minutes talking quietly to my dad and then left for home.

"Sorry, Dad. Didn't mean to mess up your Sunday with Jan."

He shrugged. "If she's the person I think she is, it'll be okay. How are you doing?"

"I'm good." I didn't want to get into a deep discussion. "By the way, I'm meeting with one of your scout buddies Tuesday, Mountain Man."

"Haven't seen him in awhile. Make sure you say hello for me. And to his wife, Phyllis. Nice lady. Your mom and I enjoyed the times we'd sit together at a district dinner or end up at the same scout's Eagle Court of Honor."

I nearly asked him to come with me, but stopped seconds short of the invitation. I had specific questions to ask. Hearing their 'war stories' would be fun another time.

The doorbell stopped our conversation.

"Well, if it isn't one of the Mouseketeers," Dad announced.

"That's Musketeers, Mike." Harry shook hands with Dad and leaned over to kiss me. "How was your day in Berkeley?"

Dad and I burst into laughter. He covered the highlights and ended with, "I may have lost a girlfriend and a cleaning lady."

"I wouldn't worry, Mike. I think she's made of sterner stuff."

We moved into the living room. Dad offered to make coffee and tea, but we both declined. "And now for your day in the woods?"

Harry leaned forward in his seat his eyes shinning. "We found the cup, speckled blue, just like you said."

I wasn't sure how I felt. I was right, but why was I right?

"We measured and plotted exactly where we found it. Kramer sketched the area, actually quite a good hand."

"He thought about art school before cop school."

Harry and my dad both looked surprised. "Did you turn it over to the police?"

"Not exactly. That department is a little suspect since we don't know who connects to whom. We talked it over and I will be bringing to the Feds tomorrow. If Kramer did it, he might catch repercussions from his own department."

Suddenly the day's activity pressed down on me and all I wanted was to get home and relax. I stood up abruptly, conversation stopped and both men looked at me.

"I'm really tired. Can we go home?"

Harry and Dad both stood. Dad hurried into the kitchen calling over his shoulder, "I made manicotti. Take some home with you, don't cook tonight."

Dad's manicotti was a treat on any night, but since I didn't feel like cooking it was a double delight. He returned with a soft-sided picnic basket.

Harry immediately took the offered tote and feigned a heavy weight. Dad laughed. "You can't have manicotti without a salad and bread. I put in some Swiss chard and potatoes for color. And sausage; I had two measly pieces of sausage left over. What can you do with that? And Italian Custard. Edna was here yesterday. Um, that's it."

"No *vino*, Mike?" Harry's deadpan humor prompted laughter from Dad and me.

"Geez, guys. Do I gotta think of everything?" We hugged good-bye and I promised to call after I met with Don Craig. Harry and I started down the steps swinging the picnic tote between us.

"Careful with that. Jimmy's newest red, Santa Lucia, is in there." Dad's face wore the Morelli smirk as he closed the door.

I stumbled on the last step and gripped the railing. *Great, Santa Lucia. After drinking it you'll go blind.*

❧ 37 ❧

My eyes opened at exactly 5:45–back on track. I carefully lifted the covers and slipped out of bed. My fast track morning routine, brushing my teeth and splashing water on my face, takes less than three minutes. Down the stairs into the kitchen to make the coffee, another seven minutes. Into the mudroom to change into barn clothes and boots, three minutes, leaving two minutes to stand outside and stretch before the crunch of pecan shells announces Barb on the path.

Patches and Trey bolted past me. I'd have to find a way for them to be together. Either they'd all three be barn cats or all be house cats, but this bouncing in and out took a toll on Elmo. I heard his loud cries from behind the closed door. Once again, he'd hesitated and I'd managed to keep him inside. I wasn't ready to expose him to the dangers of whatever had taken their mom.

I heard the familiar *crunch* and waited to see my bright-jacketed neighbor walk around the slight curve. Devin made the turn instead. He waved when he saw me. "Hi Mrs. Marsden. Mom can't make it, she's not feeling well. Some kind of flu bug. She sent me over to see if you need help with the horses.

My mind switched gears. "Not only help, but how about a quick ride?" Barb didn't enjoy riding, but her son loved it. His face lit up with enthusiasm.

"You bet." He changed his direction and hurried toward the barn not waiting for me. He called out to April and Cash. Their responding *whinnies* sounded high pitched and desperate. The hairs on my neck stiffened.

"Devin, stop!" I shouted. His hand stopped on the latch, his face incredulous at my tone.

"Come here, come away from the door. Hurry." He seemed frozen to the spot, his hand gripping the latch. I ran toward him and guided him away from the door. "Go inside and yell for Harry. Go!" I pushed him toward the house and he sprinted across the distance. A feeling of dread had been mounting and now I heard the panic in my horses' voices. I picked up the ash pole that we used to open the corral from atop the horse and slid it through the double handles before I ran back to the house.

Harry burst through the back door and hustled me inside. "What's wrong? Devin said you wouldn't let him go in the barn."

Inside the safety of my home I wonderd if anything was wrong, but then I remembered the hairs on my neck. I rubbed a hand over the spot to assure myself. "The horses sounded wrong, scared. I think there's someone in the barn."

Harry knew enough about instinct and gut feelings not to question me. He pushed aside the curtain on the window in the door and kept his eyes on the barn. "Call 911. I'll keep an eye on things here. Take Devin with you and put him in the priest hole. You get in there too."

I dialed from the kitchen and told the operator the nature of the emergency then I pulled Devin, who by this time had recovered and grown excited about the events, to the fireplace wall. I turned one of the stones and a panel slid open.

"Cool."

"Get in and stay put."

"Mr. Marsden told you to get in too."

"Devin, don't argue."

I watched him duck his head and step in. "Please stay in there," I repeated and turned the stone clock-wise.

Of course Harry wasn't where I'd left him. I never thought he would be. I knew better than to follow him outside, where ever he was; at least I could watch through...

My heart slammed against my ribs when I looked through the window—one door stood wide open! *Where's Harry? In the barn?* I grabbed a metal scoop that I use for Elmo's chow and rushed out to...I don't know what, but I knew I had to do something. Halfway between the house and the barn I heard scuffles and then sirens. I didn't know which way to respond; guide the police or help Harry.

I rushed around the closed door, going in wide to see the most as quickly as possible. April's welcoming *whinnies* told me she was okay. The scene in the barn stopped me cold. My stomach lurched as I realized that the scraping sounds came from the two hooded figures struggling to escape the leather tack that pinned their arms to their sides and to each other. Harry had 'bundled' the two by using extra reins and training ropes. Harry pulled them along by the free end of the rope. His face clouded as he spotted me in the doorway. I noticed a bruise on his left cheek and blood on his lip. He motioned for me to open the other door and as I did the condition of the barn registered.

A pentagram, point down, glistened, still wet, on the inside of the door. They'd painted several inverted crosses on the walls and one dangled from a cord they had thrown over a beam. Anger rushed through me when I looked at April and Cash. Their faces had been sprayed with the same sign. Their eyes looked red and swollen.

I threw myself at the two swinging my metal scoop and making contact against their heads, wishing it were a sledgehammer instead. I heard Harry shouting at me to stop and felt strong arms pushing my hands to my sides and lifting me off my feet.

Two hours later, the police were gone and my vet was applying an eyewash and salve to April and Cash. They would be fine, no lasting damage, only irritation. We'd forgotten about Devin until he'd finally found the release and let himself out. He emerged in time to explain to the police who he was and what he saw. Harry insisted on walking him home and was back in no time, slightly winded.

Under those hoods we'd found two teenagers, sullen and angry. They carried no identification and wouldn't talk to the police. The two DuPage Sheriff's officers had listened and taken notes while we retold the story of Robinson Woods.

They'd removed the leather and ropes and handcuffed each boy. Under their 'one size fits all' robes they looked so young. Each wore a black skullcap, making their faces appear chalky. Faces that reflected belligerence, but no fear. I stared at one boy, sensing a familiarity. I hadn't met all the boys in Will's troop only the young ones. Had I seen him around Forest Park or Oak Park recently? On a hunch, I'd called out to them as the police led them away. "Davy."

The taller boy's shoulders stiffened and eased immediately, but not so quickly that we didn't notice. My body filled with dread, certain that the boy who so wanted to catch me that night to get his 'trophy' stood in my home. Something else nagged at me; familiar and yet not. *Not knot, not now!* No use. I busied my fingers with loops and crossovers my mind struggling for the illusive connection.

The vet left salve for the horses and a bill that could choke one of them. But they were worth it. I'd used non-toxic thinner to carefully remove much of the black paint; the rest would wear off. I lavished treats upon them and turned them out into the corral while Harry prepared a stronger solution of paint remover for the walls.

His cheek benefited from an ice pack, actually a frozen package of peas, but the bruise seemed darker. The left side of his mouth was swollen around a small split where a splinter had penetrated.

Harry told the police that while he watched from the window he saw the doors moving back and forth against the pole holding them shut. The boys must have realized they were trapped and pushed and pulled harder eventually causing the skinny pole to shift and slide out. Harry explained that he realized what might happen and he hid near the barn to grab whoever came out. When the door banged open one figure ran out, practically into Harry's waiting arms. He grabbed him around his hooded throat and applied enough pressure to stop his thrashing. The voluminous robe tangled around Harry's arm causing a split second delay in blocking the path of the pole the second kid wielded. Harry kept hold of the one and grabbed at the base of the pole twisting the boy's arm and forcing him into his pal. The collision slowed them enough for Harry to push them into the barn and throw a bridle over one head, and loop a set of reins around their arms. He kept adding tack and rope until they could barely move–he'd hobbled them with the last rope in the barn.

I watched him vent his anger on the barn wall. He'd soaked a short stiff brush with the mixture and scrubbed the wall with strong strokes. I cleaned out the stalls, lifting soiled straw into the garden wheelbarrow.

"What do we know that someone wants to scare us? And why did they do this in broad daylight?"

"Five-thirty in the morning isn't daylight. They didn't know you're up at six; thought they had plenty of time to trash the barn."

"Why didn't the horses make noise earlier?"

"This could be our answer." Harry picked up a small empty plastic bag. Looks like bits of sugar. A handful of sweet cubes and those two would have ratted out their mums."

I wanted to believe April knew better, but she was a horse with a sweet tooth. My attention was drawn to a bit of black fabric poking through the once again messed up tack. "Harry, come here. Is that yours?" I lifted a bridle and realized the fabric was a gym bag.

"Don't touch it." Harry moved the last tangle and reached for it. The bag pulsated. We both jumped back startled by the movement. It moved again and then I heard the soft cry.

"Oh my God!" I dropped to my knees and unzipped the bag. Patches and Trey were inside a gunnysack in the bag. My hands shook so much Harry had to untie the rope holding the sack closed. Trey's head appeared first and my heart filled with malice toward those boys. They had taped the kitten's mouth with tape so wide it covered most of his head. Patches too. We lifted them out of the bag each to one of our laps. Harry had his pocketknife out and opened to the sharp small blade. I realized they weren't clawing and thrashing. Could taping their mouths cause them to suffocate? I watched Harry carefully cut a slit through the gray tape.

Harry sniffed and nodded his head toward the bag. "Smell that? A bit of ether I'd wager to knock them out. I wondered why he wasn't trying to tear me to shreds." He completed the second slit and started the third that would remove the part of the tape over Trey's eyes. The pitiful meows from his little body tugged at my heart. Harry worked as quickly as he could.

"Bastards. There's a piece over his eye. I can't cut closer with this. Have you any small scissors?" The pain on his face for this little animal moved me closer to tears.

I gently placed Patches in the bottom of the gym bag and ran into the house and up the stairs to our bathroom. I knew exactly what I needed and for once knew exactly where they were. I pulled an oval padded box from the shelf and flipped off the top. My treasure box– odds and ends that meant something only to me. The tiny baby scissors that my godmother had used to cut my fingernails would save my kittens.

Harry looked skeptically at them.

"They're sharp as a 'tart's tongue'." I'd used one of Harry's expressions. He smiled and went to work. Trey's eye was visible and looked okay. Harry handed me Trey and lifted Patches to his lap. Snip away as much as you can while I do the bigger cuts on her."

And so we worked until we'd removed as much tape and as little fur as possible. Their eyes and mouths were free. We brought them into the mudroom and offered them water. They both drank immediately. The effects of the ether had worn off and they seemed to be moving normally, except when they stopped to paw at pieces still stuck to their skin. Even Elmo tried to help by licking at the gray bits on his siblings.

Harry stayed in the barn to finish the clean up. By the time he came in I'd already fielded three phone calls about the vandalism: Ric, who'd heard from Nancy Royal, Detective Thomas, who'd heard from the Sheriff's police, and my dad, who'd heard from Gertrude as told to her by Gloria.

"Two of them are coming out. Any guesses on which two?"

"Think I'll call Thomas and make it three." Harry held up the gym bag. 'Black Bart Buick' blazed across a cowboy hat screened onto the black fabric.

I made coffee, Harry made sandwiches, and we both made small talk. The doorbell rang, signaling the arrival of the three-ring circus.

~ **38** ~

I'm positive the invitation didn't say 'bring a friend' and yet Ric had Hannah in tow, Detective Thomas brought another detective with him and my father invited, of all people, Marisol to accompany him.

I could almost hear the circus organ playing in the background as people took their seats. We moved the meeting into the living room and Harry waited for everyone to sit. With a cutaway jacket and top hat he'd make a charming ringmaster. *Ladies and gentlemen, direct your attention to the center ring. To thrill you, to captivate you, to astound you, we have gathered from the far corners of the world...*

I uncrossed and re-crossed my legs to focus my mind, realizing I'd missed the intro. No matter, it looked to be a long day. I'd asked Harry why he thought he could trust Thomas. He'd smiled and quipped, 'keep your friends close and your enemies, closer.' He wasn't sure if Thomas was the leak, but he knew if he included him, Thomas would feel he'd have to contribute something. At the least, Harry and Ric could control what information or misinformation they gave.

"With your department investigating the homicide and rapes this belongs in your jurisdiction." Harry handed the gym bag to Thomas. "My concern lies only in discovering why they're after Grace and who is calling the shots. This doesn't follow the MO of the other attacks."

"I believe I can speak to that." The man who Thomas introduced as Detective Mark Hanley identified himself further. "My specialty is violent crime profiling. In the case of these rapes you're absolutely right about the stalking of your wife. This abrupt deviation from the pattern indicates that the leader of this group has obsessed on the 'one that got away' and can't complete his pattern." I swallowed hard and noticed several pairs of eyes glance in my direction. Hanley continued. "The other explanation is that the leader or a faction of the cult wants to scare or silence Mrs. Marsden for a reason not connected to the original attack, but instead propagated because of it."

I didn't like that explanation any better than the first. "You mean they think I saw something or know something?" I realized how inane that sounded and tried to rephrase my question. "I don't know what they want. I didn't see anything that night, can't identify them, well only by the names, Davy and Mr. Big. What good is that?"

"My sense of this is that you're being pursued and punished because you escaped your fate at their hands. They're mandated to complete the attack or punish you sufficiently so that they can move on to the sixth and final rape for this season."

His words stunned me. He hurried to add, "This new wrinkle can go two ways. The cult will either back off, preferring to go underground until the heat from these arrests dies down or they can escalate their campaign against you, blaming you for their comrades' misfortune. In that frame of mind they might want something of yours to perform a ceremony or spell against you."

"Like a curse?" My voice hadn't squeaked like that since the second grade.

"That's enough, Hanley. Why don't you just pull out a voodoo doll, dammit." Ric's voice exploded, surprising the newcomers to my life.

Detective Hanley looked at me with a serious expression on his face. "I wanted you to understand how they might be thinking so you could be forewarned. Sometimes victims don't understand the psychology connected with rituals." His eyes asked for understanding, not forgiveness—he'd done nothing wrong.

I nodded slowly, my mind having skirted away from the *me* of this scenario to somewhere else, in this case, someone else. I heard *psychology* and thought of Cassidy. "Detective Thomas, Cassidy McCabe's office was ransacked and someone tossed a brick through her window. Has anyone checked on her lately? It seems that somehow we're both connected to Janet."

"Good point, Mrs. Marsden. So good in fact that I don't believe this cult crap about chasing you down to fulfill some pattern." Thomas's voice dripped with disdain. "You're being targeted because someone thinks you know more than you do, or maybe know more than you realize. To him, your meeting with Janet, her meeting with McCabe literally minutes later, and your subsequent meeting with McCabe flies in the face of coincidence."

Great! I wasn't the last person to see Janet alive. Great, now everyone in the room knows I consulted a sort of shrink. The silence told me it was my turn to speak. I glanced at Harry and understood his look. "I've racked my brain about what I might know and there's nothing. It really was just a series of unconnected events." I sounded convincing, why shouldn't I? I had no clue as to any connection. Then Marisol spoke.

"They aren't unconnected. Your spirit was accepting a bond with–"

"Bloody hell, Mike. Why'd you bring her?" Harry's turn to explode.

"Not for that." Dad turned toward Marisol. "You told me you found evidence when you were doing your witch–"

"Wicca not witchcraft. There is a huge difference. Wicca does not worship the devil. We do not encourage contact with the dark side. We–"

"Okay, okay," Dad held up his hand. "Just tell them your evidence."

"I'm trying to. Grace–"

Detective Thomas interrupted. "Withholding information or evidence pertinent to an ongoing investigation is a felony. You'd be in big trouble."

Marisol's dark eyes flared. "If all of you would let me finish."

She waited a moment for any dissent. "The coven met at the old burial mounds at the western edge of the preserve. People mistakenly think the ridges and gullies in Robinson Woods are burial mounds. That ground was constructed in that manner to aid in the training of infantry soldiers during the war. We were at the true mounds, consecrated ground. My experience that night convinced me there were young souls in the vicinity not able to find peace. Murders, massacres were committed in those woods."

"You mean the Indians, right?" Hannah's eyes were the size of saucers.

Marisol shook her head. "White boys." The shock of her admission chilled the room.

"What boy? What kind of crap is this? I know the department accepted your offer to 'investigate,' but we don't need more crap about dead Indians." Thomas leaned back in his chair and snorted his comment. "We don't investigate *woo-woo*." His smirk annoyed me, but Marisol stayed calm. She stared at Thomas until his eyes slid away to focus on Detective Hanley. "Did you get that, Hanley? Put that in your report." His tone made it obvious that he ranked Hanley right up there with Marisol.

Hannah rushed to her 'mentor's' defense. "She's brilliant and she does reach beyond the grave. Tell them about the words you–"

"Hannah!" Marisol's voice was sharp and out of character for the little I knew about her. She smiled at Hannah's crumpled expression. "No need to tell hostile souls, Hannah. They won't believe."

"Let me be the judge of that. What words did you hear?"

Hannah shifted uncomfortably. Thomas turned on her. "Did you hear these words too or just the spirit guide here?" He jerked his thumb at Marisol.

Hannah shook her head. Thomas grinned and pinned Marisol with a nasty look. "So the words were in your head? Let them stay there for all I care." He looked at Ric. "Why'd you bring her? Moral support for that one." He grinned again, enjoying himself.

"Knock if off, Thomas. I brought her because she was out there that night and may have seen or heard something that could help us."

"Not unless she could hear inside this one's head." His bark of a laugh jangled my nerves. He stopped abruptly. "You people believe this crap?" He sighed and shook his head. "Hand over the bag and we'll send it through the state lab. They'll add it to the pile they already have from this case."

"What about the button they found?" I wasn't sure anymore if I was supposed to know about that or someone told me in confidence.

"Oh yeah, your brother turned it in. Lot of scouts in that area and since it was found on him not on the victim, he could have picked it up anywhere in the woods. It's either in the evidence room or at the state lab." He shrugged his shoulders. "Not a hot lead. Maybe Ms. *woo woo* would like to touch it, get the vibes." He laughed, alone.

"I'd like that very much," Marisol stated.

Thomas blinked and laughed harder. "Sure thing. Oh, Captain, can this little lady mess up our chain of custody and play with the button?" His demeaning tone rolled right off her shoulders. I wondered if anyone else noticed that before he spoke his face paled ever so slightly.

"You said yourself it wasn't a hot lead. What's the difference?" Marisol's smooth voice rattled him. *She must have ice water in her veins.*

Thomas' ears flamed when he shouted, "The difference is it's in my evidence room and it ain't going nowhere." He stood and grabbed the bag. "Let's go, Hanley. Nothing here for us. We're done."

Mark Hanley closed the notebook he'd been jotting short phrases in during this entire exchange. He stood and thanked us for our time and hospitality. His gaze seemed to linger on Marisol. She was beautiful, but it wasn't that kind of look.

"Whew, glad he's gone." Hannah refilled her teacup. "What a totally disagreeable man. And he's a constable?" She shook her head.

"Well, he'd be sacked in Arundel, that's for certain."

Her understatement eased the tension in the room.

"He didn't start out so nasty, did he, Dad?"

My father took a moment before he answered. "He seemed wound a little too tight from the beginning, but I figured it was the death on his turf. Then again, I was pretty shook up myself."

"All right everyone, now that the constabulary has left the premises can we get down to business?"

I stared at Harry.

"Kramer, lovely as it is to see my sister," Harry smirked, "why did you bring her? And Mike, why her?"

I'd been wondering the same, but somehow I thought he knew and I was the only one out of the loop. Dad spoke first. "She called me and told me she had evidence concerning you," his voice slowed down, "but actually you didn't tell me that until I told you I was coming here." My dad stayed quiet for a moment. "Did you lie to me to get an invitation?"

"Not a lie, Mr. Morelli. I believe I said 'information' not evidence. I do have information for Grace. But I also wanted to interact with Thomas outside of his turf. I've had no cooperation from him at the station; thought maybe he couldn't acknowledge my type of assistance in front of the 'troops'. Now I know he's an ass no matter where you talk to him. An ass with a guilty conscience."

"I agree with the *ass*-sessment." Hannah giggled at Marisol's pronouncement then grew somber. "I'm here because I found this in my wagon." She held up a wad of paper folded and shaped into a triangle. Hannah slowly unfolded it, edge by edge, until the paper lay flat exposing the pentagram, point down, in the center. Under the point was the single word 'believe'.

"Oh my God. When did you find this?"

"Yesterday. I was picking up baby trash from the floor and spotted the corner of this under the seat. Almost threw it out except the shape made me curious."

"Who's been in the wagon with you and the kids?"

"It can only be since the shower because the wagon was in for some minor work that weekend. That's why Karen asked Tracy to bring her SUV. So within that time frame I've had," Hannah closes her eyes and raises a finger for each name. "Karen, Mary Quigley, Tim, Tyler, Will, Marisol, Lily, and Andy." Hannah opened her eyes and looked down at her fingers.

"Who is this Andy fellow?" Harry asked.

"He's the young man from the dealership who brought the wagon to me. Ever so handy not having to go collect it what with the babies and all."

"Which dealership serviced the wagon?"

"The one where we bought it, Black Bart Buick."

"That's the connection. The bag came from there, this Andy works there. Guilfoyle's involved."

"Hold on, Marsden. There are other possibilities you may not want to consider."

"You think the boys are involved? Or Lily? Absurd. They certainly are not devil worshipers." Harry's tone was dismissive but I heard the slight underlying doubt that his training forced on him.

"Grace's attackers were young. Marisol already practices Wicca. Boys are impressionable at their age. What do we know about Mary Quigley?"

"She's a soccer mom and popcorn kernel for the troop for heaven's sake," I blurted.

"Hold on a fair bit. She grew up in Forest Park. Her brother and husband's names were on that list." Harry's training kicked in big time. "She knew we had the crate. Can't connect her to the woods though."

"I think you can." Marisol spoke softly. "She is Wicca. Has been since her days at Madison. She is the Priestess of that coven."

Hannah gasped. "Why didn't she tell me, why didn't you?"

"It wasn't my place to tell you."

"She wasn't there that night."

Marisol nodded her head. "She watched from the woods."

"We would have seen her. We practically glowed in those robes in the moonlight."

"She wore a black robe."

Ric interrupted. "How did you know she was there? Don't tell me you 'felt her presence' either." Ric's eyes were drop dead serious.

Harry had been standing directly behind her, which seemed to make her nervous. He spoke softly to her back. "You conveniently know things and I'm not buying the spirit channel theory. Tell us who you really are and why you're carrying a gun." He grabbed both of her wrists and pushed her chest onto the table. She didn't resist and he removed a small caliber pistol from under her jacket and handed it to Ric.

Dad jumped back from the table like he'd been slapped. "Holy Mother Mary."

Marisol spoke slowly. "Left pocket of my jacket." He held both her wrists with his right hand and reached carefully into her pocket, pulling out a small, black wallet. He flipped it open and released her in the same moment. "Marisol Nunez, Special Agent, FBI"

Special Agent Nunez rubbed her wrists and fixed Harry with a scathing stare.

Harry stared back, daring her to take it up a notch. At least I think that's what the look meant.

"You couldn't tell somebody and not scare the hell out of us?" I know my dad's shaky voice spoke for at least three of us. "I mean he's a cop and he's, well, was sort of like you." If Dad hadn't been so serious, his description of Ric and Harry would have been funny.

She reached for her gun from Ric before she spoke.

"I couldn't tell anyone Mr. Morelli. Undercover doesn't work if everyone knows who you are."

Dad shook his head. "Damn job for a girl." He took his cold coffee and walked to the sink to dump it.

That comment did get a small smile from us, even Marisol.

"How long have you had Quigley under surveillance?"

Marisol seemed to come to a decision. Her body relaxed against the edge of the table.

"We've been interested in the Quigley and Bigelow families for over forty years; theirs is a twisted history, dating back to the grandfathers who immigrated here from Ireland in the 1920's."

"Grandfathers? Are we talking about a Wicca coven or a satanic cult?"

"Neither. You're involved because of the crate, aren't you?" Harry asked.

She nodded. "There's been an open file on these families, those woods since one of our earliest agents, John Henry, was killed investigating the theft of munitions. Mr. Henry had been recruited from the Marine Corps when he left active duty. We're looking at these people for murder and treason. Haven't been able to connect anyone conclusively. The agency has been building its case methodically on what little we get. I'm the thirteenth agent assigned to the file. In the last two years, activity in the targeted area has increased with a rise in violent crime as well as ritual crime."

"Ritual crime? Like rooster and chicken parts used as a sacrifice?

"The cult activity is not our concern; we wanted to piggyback on the dynamics of the woods to minimize suspicion."

"So you *infiltrated* moms and housewives pretending to share our religion." Hannah's eyes glowed with anger and her voice rang with righteous indignation.

Marisol leveled her gaze at Hannah. "I'll do what I must to bring these people to justice and give Agent Henry justice."

"Who'd they sell the guns to?" Dad re-joined the conversation, probably pulled in by his anger at the thought of treason.

"Didn't sell, supplied. The two grandfathers escaped Ireland two jumps ahead of incarceration. They spent the rest of their lives re-cruiting and indoctrinating displaced Irishmen and their descendants in the ways of the *Brennan Infantry Grenadiers*, an IRA splinter group."

"Bloody hell. Those bastards caused more death and chaos in England and Ireland than almost the entire bloody war. That blasted group is one of the reasons I–" Harry stopped.

"I've read your dossier too and yours," she nodded toward Ric. "And even a short note on you, Mr. Morelli."

"Hey lady, you're crazy if you think I'd ever support those bastards."

Dad only swore when hopping mad, and questioning his loyalty was a hopping mad occasion.

Marisol spoke quietly. "Not you, Mr. Morelli, your wife Marga-ret Doyle Morelli."

His hand came down hard and fast on the table. Mugs and sil-verware jumped, teetered, and settled.

Marisol held up her hand to cut off his explosion. "When she was in college, she signed a petition to ease home rule in Northern Ireland. The way it was worded, anyone with a heart would have signed and most college kids wanted to belong to a higher cause. Your wife signed, but she also donated a small amount to the cause and became registered in 'Daughters of Ireland', a group that raised funds ostensibly for those affected by the violence, orphans and homeless. They even used a cute acronym to avoid suspicion from their enrollees, 'Daughters of Ireland League of Youth', *D.O.I.L.Y*"

"Oh my gosh, Mom supported that group all her life. I'd see the envelopes all the time. She really thought she was helping children."

Marisol nodded. "They all did. You'd be surprised how many Oak Park River Forest women signed on the dotted line, how many women from Regina and women's groups in the area supported and still support the group. One of the few organizations that didn't jump on the bandwagon was the 19th Century Club. They kept their fundraising local, supporting social programs in their village."

"My mother's and aunt's names were on that list too, weren't they?"

Marisol looked at Ric. "Your aunt, Sheila Walsh, was a huge supporter. Your mom not as much, but consistent. She left a small amount in her will to them."

"You must have thought you hit the mother lode with our families."

"Actually, I've never considered any of your relatives as suspects. They were cleared two agents before me."

I could tell by his face that the idea of our mothers ever being considered subversive stunned him as much as it did me.

"I'm expecting that none of you will talk about this with anyone. To impede my investigation is a federal crime." Marisol's dark gaze met and held each of ours in turn.

"More importantly, to expose her identity might mean her death." Harry's somber words shocked the room. "Whoever killed John Henry may or may not still be living. I've suspected that the recriminations against Grace are connected to that crate. The timing of her meeting with Janet Henry and then her visit with McCabe has put someone's hairs up."

"Thank you for your concern. It could make things dicey for me. I don't think BIG is after your wife. I think the cult–"

"Oh my God, there's another 'big'."

"Excuse me?"

"The night I was attacked the boys referred to the man who dragged me out of the car as Mr. Big." My voice quivered and I swallowed hard.

"Really. There's nothing in my notes about this. Did you report it?"

I glanced at Ric and felt the warmth creeping up my neck. Marisol followed my look. "I hate loose canons, Mr. Kramer. Anything else I should know?"

Ric's eyes flared at the public rebuke. He didn't make a move to acknowledge or dispute her comment. "Let's go, Hannah." He nodded to Dad and Harry and slowed at the door, waiting for Hannah to finish her hugs and kisses. I heard the door close after them.

"I'll be leaving too." Marisol turned to Harry. "We appreciate what you've tried to do, but you need to back off and stay out of it. You may want to turn that in to the task force working the rapes." She pointed at the paper then spoke to me. "I'm sure there's no connection between your 'big' and my 'big'." I didn't know if that was spy humor. No one smiled.

My dad had driven. He stood up, but she waved him back to his seat. "I have a car waiting for me outside, my partner." She touched her lapel pin.

I walked her to the door. She turned in the doorway. "I'd like to talk with you alone, Grace."

My voice wouldn't activate; I stared at her eyes, losing myself in their darkness, finding more questions about her than answers.

She pressed a card into my hand. "Please call me."

Headlights came on from the dead end beyond the edge of our property. The car drove forward and met her at the bottom of the driveway. I waited for her to open the door to spot her partner, but the interior light never went on. When I first dated Harry, his car's interior lights never worked. Then Ric, same deal. I'm not the sharpest knife in the drawer; one of my brothers clued me in. The dark Buick sedan drove slowly down the lane drawing minimal attention.

Dad and Harry sat across from each other at the table.

"Not exactly Miss Congeniality is she? My big is bigger than your big." Dad's husky voice mimicked her in a falsetto. "Nothing but a bully in high heels." We burst into laughter and I marveled at how the human spirit finds respite at the strangest times.

"Whether we like her or not, her information slants things at a different angle. She may not think your 'big' is connected, but I think it could be. "This paper, look at it closely." Harry turned it and presented it upside down to us. Now the pentagram pointed up. "There's no margin or lines. Who's to say which way the pentagram should be viewed."

"The word 'believe' is backward, that's how you know it's from the bad guys." I agreed with my dad and nodded.

"What if the good guys wanted to leave a message, a warning for someone, a person who would understand, but the message ended up in the wrong place." Harry grabbed the notepad and spelled the word *e v e i l e b*.

"Eve, I *leb*, left, love," I shrugged my shoulders. "Doesn't make sense."

Harry smiled. "What if it read *eveil eb*?"

"A veil? Some kind of veil, a mask. Maybe someone masquerading as a good guy? Black Bart! His commercial says something about good guys in black hats. And those palookas had one of his bags. The note was for you." Dad's hands punctuated his theory with a flourish."

"Would have been a lot easier to say who in the note, don't you think, Dad?" He looked disappointed.

"They did, darling." Harry pointed to the last two letters, *eb*. Think of them as initials and you have the who, E.B."

"Edward Bantonini. I knew that creep was bad news." My father's vehemence didn't surprise me.

"There's another E.B."

"Moochie? Nah, this isn't Moochie."

"Mike, you can't discount anyone."

"You don't like him because he's Will's scout leader. I don't blame you, but my money's on the old man."

"I saw him the other day." My quiet declaration stopped him cold.

"Saw who?"

"Bantonini Sr. At the cemetery. Did you know there's a Bantonini grave not thirty yards from Mom's grave?"

Harry jumped in before Dad could answer. "Back to seeing him. How did you know it was him?"

"He looks like an older version of Moo…of his son. Anyway, I pulled over to watch him in my rear view mirror and well, I got distracted and when I looked back in the mirror he was there, dressed in black. He opened the door and I freaked. It was like it was going to happen again. I yanked the door shut, almost on his fingers and then I saw them. His fingers. But it didn't hit me until I was driving and that's why I went off the road."

Both Harry and my dad interrupted at the same instant.

"Okay, okay. I should have told you the whole story, but it seemed stupid after I thought about it."

"Gracie, what about his fingers?" Dad leaned forward.

"Uh, they were deformed, no nails. And that night, the fingers around my throat felt pointy but smooth." I shivered at the recollection and Harry moved to my side. He put his arm around me and his warmth assured me I was safe. Harry brushed the hair away from my neck. I knew that faint yellow splotches still marked the bruised areas.

"No scratches or gauges. We assumed he wore gloves." Harry let my hair swing back. He squeezed my shoulder. "Now I know who he is." His soft menacing tone left me chilled and I shivered in his arms.

"My money's on him, still, but you should know that finger

thing, it's a birth defect, and Moochie has it, too. On one hand just like his old man, but I don't know which hand."

"I know I clawed at the hand around my throat. Maybe I left marks."

"Kramer should have followed procedure and taken you directly to hospital and had a rape kit done. They would have taken scrapings from under your nails and checked for other evidence he may have left on you or your clothes. By ignoring his training he helped your attacker."

"Let's find a way to look at Bantonini's hands. When's the next scout meeting?" My dad's idea seemed logical.

"And do what if he does have some marks. He was out in the woods that day. Could have happened then. As for the old man, should we stake out the cemetery?"

Harry wasn't normally so condescending. Dad's face reflected Harry's tone.

"Talk about miss congeniality," I muttered.

"Say again?" Harry's eyebrows arched.

"How about this for reality." His eyes clearly didn't believe me, but he nodded for me to continue with a 'get yourself out of this one' smirk. In that split second I grasped at a straw and came up with a handful. "The father is the pedophile who has his gang of young boys who belong to the cult and the son is the rapist who prefers women. The sins of the father kind of thing only twisted."

"With that scenario, both E.B.'s are evil, just in different ways."

"Evil is evil, I don't care how you spell it." Dad's summation sent a chill down my spine. He stood and stretched. "I'm heading home. Who's got Gracie tomorrow?"

"Don't worry, Mike. She'll not be anywhere alone."

My father shook Harry's hand and grasped his shoulder with his left hand. "I'm counting on that."

ࢠ 39 ࢥ

True to his word I didn't go anywhere alone. Tuesday morning Walter drove me to Portillo's for my meeting with Don Craig. Walter and I walked in separately. He waited until he saw where Don was seated and then he took a table where he could watch us. Don Craig was easy to spot, broad shoulders, half-barrel chest striped with red suspenders. He wore forest green twill pants and a sage green shirt. The suspenders added a holiday touch but I knew those red suspenders were year round. I spotted three Dutch Master Cigars in his shirt pocket, pushed aside by the wide red material. I could have picked him out at a Scout-O-Rama. He stood when I approached him. I put out my hand but he engulfed me in a bear hug.

"Sit down, sit down. I'd know you anywhere. Same shiny hair and big smile." I sat down and instantly liked him. He reminded me of all the fun times and wonderful dads I'd met as a tag-along sib at family campouts. He glanced at my purse and spotted the length of black cord tied to the strap. "Still keep up with your knots?"

It was easier to nod than explain.

"Good girl. Always gotta be prepared." His laugh was genuine although I'm sure he'd repeated that phrase a million times. I smiled and he nodded toward my cast. "Hope the other guy got worse." Another laugh. It was infectious. I laughed with him."

Again it was easier to nod and let him move on. And he did.

"I was tickled to hear from your dad. Good man. I'd always hoped our paths would keep crossing. Phyllie and I enjoyed each time we spent with him and your mom. Great lady. We were sorry to hear about her passing. Please accept our condolences."

"Thank you, Mr. Craig. Dad said the same about you and your wife, about the fun outings with the two of you."

He nodded and then turned to glance behind him as though looking for someone. "Thought for a minute my dad came in. It's Don."

"Okay, Don. Thanks for meeting me. Did you already order?"

"Nope, just water and I've drunk enough to float an entire rain-gutter regatta."

I didn't know if I could drag this warm wonderful human being into the sordid morass I'd stumbled into. He displayed that easy grace of my dad's generation; a gentleman who knew his roots, respected his country, and honored his God. He'd gained weight from the robust man I remembered as a child, but then who hadn't.

"Let's get our orders in and then we can relax and talk."

On the way back to the table with our lunches, he leaned toward me and asked, "Would you like to ask your friend to join us?"

I nearly stumbled into the back of another diner. My face flushed and I waited until I'd put down my basket and drink before I spoke. "I, how, my…" What should I tell him?"

His booming laugh caused a few nearby diners to glance our way. "I'm sorry. Didn't mean to make you jump. Phyllie's always telling me not to 'sneak' up on folks that way. Course, she's always telling me to go easy on the onions too."

He held up his steak sandwich smothered, covered, and heaped with onions. Don laughed and continued. "I don't want you to think I don't mind my wife because that would be a lie. My bride has only my best interests at heart, always has, bless her soul. And I do abide by her wishes in most all I do." He jerked a thumb back at his pocket. "Cut back to only two Presidents a day."

"Then why are there three in your pocket?"

"Be prepared, Grace. In case one breaks. Be prepared." I burst into laughter and those same diners glanced our way again.

"I guess then you'll understand that my husband and father want to be prepared in case someone tries to bother me again." I turned and motioned for Walter to join us.

After introductions were made and Walter picked up his food, I put my cards on the table. "Don, do you have any memories of unusual events, uncomfortable things happening in the troop? My dad wasn't in very long but he said you stayed."

"I started out in Troop 602 at a church near 63rd and Loomis. I was there about eight months and it became inactive. About that time we moved to Forest Park and I hooked up with Troop 265. I missed a lot of campouts because of sports. One of the few I went on was the most unusual of my camping career."

"Was that the night with the Ouija board?"

"It was and I hadn't been raised to do that kind of stuff. My tent mate was your dad, that campout. What a screwy night, first Specs runs off and then Meatball lights out after him. Specs never did come back that night and I thought your dad wasn't either when the SPL came and took his sleeping bag from the tent. About an hour later your dad shows up all agitated and with a cut on his forehead. He didn't want to talk about it. Climbed into his bag and laid still staring at the tent flap with one hand curled around his flashlight. He was awake before me; don't know if he slept a wink that night. He rolled his bag and we broke camp. I never saw him in scouts again."

"What about Specs? Did you see him again?"

Don Craig thought about the question. "I didn't go to the same school but at the next meeting we heard his dad been killed and I figured that why he wasn't at the meeting. He missed the next two and then I heard someone say he'd run away. Some girl he knew told some friends she knew that he went to find a rodeo friend. Made sense, he'd have a friend in rodeo he always wore chaps and his cowboy hat."

I'd known the bones in the well were John Henry's but I wanted to hope that maybe everything was wrong and that someone had seen him after that night and that maybe he had run off to find Rusty. My face must have reflected my mood.

"I'm sorry if I upset you but you couldn't have known him."

My lips barely moved. "Not exactly." We were both silent for a moment and then I asked, "Did you ever see anything strange?"

He reached across the table to pat my hand. "Honey, I'm not a mind reader. You're gonna have to tell me what it is you're trying for."

His gentle touch and Harry's phrase crumbled my resolve to try and be cagey with him. I felt relief at dropping the rest of the charade.

"We think Bantonini may have been molesting the boys, especially whoever his SPL was at the time. I hadn't really thought it through before but I think he tried putting the moves on younger boys to find his next SPL and then that scout moved up to JASM. Dad said you didn't have elections that Bantonini picked a scout and he stayed SPL until JASM. This way, Bantonini always prepared a new boy for both of them."

Saying it out loud made me want to vomit. I hadn't realized what my mind conjured until this very moment. I felt my lunch churn in my stomach and I think my words affected Don the same way. He stared at me for a moment and then shook his head.

"The signs were probably there but we were kids. He always played favorites but I never guessed for that reason. Now that I think back there did seem to be an SPL in waiting if you get my drift."

"Who was he? Do you remember?"

"Sure. It was Q-tip. Hard to forget a kid with hair so blond white it practically glowed in the dark."

Q-tip! The name from the woods. A descendant?

"Do you remember his real name?'

Don shook his head. "Sorry. I didn't go to the same school. We always used our scout names; Bantonini wanted it that way. He was just a kid with a mop of white hair."

I asked about Moochie and if he'd ever noticed his fingers.

"Yeah, tough on the little guy. Got teased. Q-tip always wore work gloves on campouts but he took them off to wash up and I noticed he had one of those weird fingers too. Figured it was the same problem or fungus or something?"

My heart pounded in my chest and I swallowed hard to calm myself. Walter sensed my discomfort. "You are feeling well, Missus, yes? He glared at Don blaming him for my state. Don looked dumbfounded but sprang into action.

"Drink this." He pushed a glass of water into my hands. "Now take some deep breaths. In fact, let's get out of here." The noon crowds descended and the tables surrounding us were filled with noisy diners enjoying a break from work and blissfully unaware of our gruesome conversation.

The air felt clean against my clammy skin. I took several deep breaths and we walked toward Walter's Rover. Don and Walter made small talk about the pros and cons of the English-made vehicle until they sensed my recovery. Not even Walter knew about the discussion with Harry and my dad; we'd thought in terms of two suspects. Now I knew there was a third. But who? And how if he wasn't a Bantonini?

"Sorry I wasn't more help. I left scouting the next year. Couldn't make the campouts, couldn't get my rank advancement. Got frustrated. I was the most experienced Tenderfoot that troop ever recruited." He laughed at his own assessment.

"You've been more helpful than you know. Thanks again for your time. Dad said to say hi and that he'd like to get together with you and your wife." I hesitated. "He's seeing someone. First person since my mom died."

Don's face split into a wide grin. "That's great. God gave us both wonderful ladies to be our partners and that's a blessing not to be taken lightly. For whatever reason, God wanted your mom home with Him, but He's sent someone special to your dad. You tell your dad I'll be calling soon; if I know Phyllie, as soon as I tell her." He laughed again and this time I laughed with him.

We hugged good-bye and I climbed into Walter's Rover, feeling happy for my dad that he'd reconnected with this couple. I rolled down the window and waved. "'Bye."

He waved. "Keep the Faith."

I leaned back against the seat. *I like the way he talks about his Phyllie, like she's still his girlfriend. Will Harry and I have all those years as husband and wife? More importantly, will we cherish each other as much?*

It was evening before I called Dad. I'd told Harry about the third person possibility. He'd made a phone call asking a friend to cross-check a database of known sex offenders with white or platinum blond hair, deformed fingers, and the nickname Q-tip. He knew it could take several days but at least he'd started the process.

We'd spent two hours playing truant from our problems…all of them. I'd saddled both horses, while Harry prepared a wine and cheese party to go into a saddlebag. We'd walked the horses through the woods and cantered across the field to the ridge that marked the end of Pine Marsh. The ground was hard and frozen but Harry spread out a vapor barrier and a heavy Hudson Bay blanket. We feasted on Gouda and Edam and crusty slices of sourdough washed down by Uncle Jimmy's *Santa Lucia*. Harry poured Jimmy's wine into two small marmalade glass jars with screw-on lids. 'Individual serving,' he'd explained. I told him there could be something to a single serve bottle with a screw top. He *tut tutted* my suggestion.

"Hi, Dad."

"I wondered when I'd hear from you."

"I meant to call sooner but I took some time off, with Harry."

"I'm not scolding. I just thought you'd be curious about what you set in motion."

"I'm not following you."

"Phyllis Craig called me this afternoon apparently on a tip from you that I was dating someone."

I held my breath not sure if I had overstepped my bounds by revealing my dad's new relationship.

"She invited me and Jeannette to catch dinner and a movie with them this Friday."

His voice wasn't angry, nor was it joyful.

"Are you going?"

"I don't know. It was one thing to bring Jeannette to dinner with the family but this would be like announcing to the world that I've moved on. You know, away from your mom."

His voice pleaded with me for something, absolution, encouragement, something. I couldn't figure out my own relationship, how could I pretend to offer advice to my dad? Then Don's words replayed in my head, 'He's sent someone special to your dad' and I found the words.

"Dad, you're not moving away from Mom you're moving forward on the path God laid out for you." I waited. I heard an intake of breath and then a soft sigh.

"Have I ever told you that you are my favorite daughter?" His voice teased me through the line. I'd heard that question, in that exact tone all my life.

And my stock answer, "Daddy, I'm your only daughter."

"Exactly. I love you Gracie girl."

"I love you too. Good night, Dad."

"Good night, Honey."

I hung up the phone and twirled through the kitchen into the living room singing, "I feel brilliant, oh so brilliant," to the tune of West Side Story's 'I Feel Pretty.'

Harry laughed and caught me in his arms. "You feel curvy and soft in all the right places." He tucked my hair behind my ear and kissed the pulse on my neck then nibbled at my lobe. He pressed against me. "I shan't sing but you can sense how I feel." His husky voice sent tingles through me. I moved against him to send my own message.

❧ 40 ❧

My friend, Angie DiBartolomeo, called Wednesday morning to confirm I was still coming to Mass at St. Edgar. I confirmed Harry and myself. It was after I hung up that I remembered one of her other nicknames–'Bart.'

I pre-heated the oven for our dinner. Harry cooked on Sunday and froze some kind of casserole. I sat down in the nook and stared out the window at the birds that gathered at the feeders. Names floated through my brain while I watched the avian ballet on the Yankee Droll. Up, down, switch, dip. I looked at the newest entry in Harry's notebook–*Common Yellowthroat*. Wondered if there was an uncommon one. I couldn't shake the sense that my brain filed something important I'd heard or seen but I couldn't pull that folder. My fingers skimmed the tips of the out of season daffodils Harry brought home. The clear, glass bowl displayed their sturdy green stems below but didn't compete with the showy yellow heads. Jonquils, Harry called them. *There it is again, names that aren't the same, but are. Think, Grace.*

"Pretty as a picture." Harry held his hands fingers straight thumbs out pantomiming framing a picture. He planted a kiss on top of my head and slid in next to me. "See anyone new?"

The beeper from the oven sounded and Harry swept a hand across his brow in a 'Scarlet O'Hara' fashion. "I swear, as God is my witness, a man's work is never done."

His English-Southern accent cracked me up. He fussed with the casserole and immediately started chopping vegetables to sauté.

I'd been about ready to slide out and help with something when his Southern drawl spoke. "I know tomorrow is another day, but I could use some help with the salad today."

I feigned shock and framed my face with fingers spread and palms out. "I don't know nothing about making no salads." My squeaky impersonation of Prissy was pretty good.

The phone rang and brought down the curtain on our production.

"Hello."

"Hi, Honey. Got a minute?"

I wondered if he'd changed his mind about Friday.

"Sure. What's up?"

"I'm Quartermaster for the troop and we've got a sweet deal from a troop up north to get some gear, tents, couple of patrol boxes and even a canoe. Only problem is we have to pick it up by this weekend. Only one other scouter has a SUV. I called Marty but he's having some bodywork done to his truck. I wondered if I could borrow your Jeep?"

"Of course you can. I can swing by tonight on my way to Forest Park."

"Where are you going and who's going with you?"

"Don't worry. Harry's going with me and we're meeting Angie and going to Mass."

"Sister Bingo?" Dad's voice lifted. "I like her. One of your better choices in friends."

"I'll tell her she's got a fan. We're eating in about thirty minutes and we could be at your house by six-thirty?"

"Hey, that would be great. See you then. Thanks."

"We're going by my dad's house to switch cars. Do you mind?"

"Not at all but let's stop when we get there. So difficult to switch cars if we're 'going by'." Harry grinned at me. He made fun of my word choices almost as much as I teased him about his incorrect use of our colloquiums.

It felt strange riding in Dad's Chevy Impala Super Sport. I'd grown up through a series of sedate blue Chevrolets: Biscayne, Bel-Aire, and Impala. He and mom bought the sportier model after we'd all left home. Who knew our parents were sporty types?

We arranged to switch back on Saturday. The parking lot was crowded when we pulled in close to seven o'clock. Angie waved from the steps only she wasn't alone. Ric stood next to her.

Angie and I hugged and held each other at arm's length then hugged again, basically ignoring Harry and Ric until we finished our greeting.

"Have an extra hug for a Church of England bloke?" Angie and Harry could spend hours involved in eschatological discussions.

She threw her arms around Harry's neck and rewarded him with a peck on the cheek too. Ric shook his head and muttered, "Even nuns."

"It's so good to see you. Too long between hugs."

Harry beamed. "Now that's a proper hello. I just love all you

Italians." Then his smile disappeared. "What brings you to church, Kramer?"

"Just passing through. I wanted to talk to you and I heard you'd be here."

I looked at Angie; she shook her head. Ric explained. "Marty told Jeannette, she's cleaning for Eve now, and Jeannette told Gertrude when they were planning some party they're gearing up for. Gertrude told Karen when she came to watch the twins and my sister spilled to me." He shrugged and smiled. "If we would have had these Red Hat people in WWII we would have stopped the Germans before they got started."

I reminded him, "Ah, Ric, these are the *Hessisan* Hunnies we're talking about. Maybe we'd be goose-stepping."

We burst into laughter and several heads turned toward us, including the one atop the priest's cassock at the top of the steps near the heavy wooden door.

"Oops. We'd better get inside."

"You ladies go. I'll join you in a jiff. Sit near the back if you can. I'll find you." Harry strode down the steps with Ric, leaving me to be tugged up the steps by Angie.

"C'mon, Grace. I get demerits if I'm late to Mass."

We giggled and hurried into church accepting the program sheet from an usher.

Father Briscoe moved down the aisle behind the acolytes then ascended the steps to the altar. "In the name of the Father, the Son, and the Holy Spirit."

"Amen."

I watched the old priest move around the altar, his turf, and wondered what he knew about events in the woods that took place forty years ago. Had those woods been Satan's turf? Had this priest tried to exorcise that evil? Or had he'd been part of it?

Harry arrived right after the gospel. He sat down and slipped his hand over mine. I listened to Father Briscoe speak to us about preparing a place in our lives and hearts for the birth of Christ. I imagined his voice as it might have sounded in his youth, passionate in his vows, urging people, especially the youth of this parish to follow Christ. Had he been in the woods to protect or to prey on that youth? What prompted his quick transfer? To protect the youth or preserve the parish?

I idly glanced at the paper I'd been handed that explained the songs and prayers for this special Mass. *St. Edgar Catholic Church, Associate pastor, Father Emil Briscoe. Eviel e.b.*

I barely followed the rest of Mass; my brain was on overload. I wanted to braid but realized Harry still held my hand; he hadn't let go. Something was wrong. The fingertips of my right hand brushed against the hat snap on the pew. *Oh, no, Grace. Not the hat snap. It'll sound like a twenty-two. Not the hat snap.*

Divine intervention or sweaty palms, Harry released my left hand in the nick of time. I settled into a simple series of knots that required minimal assistance from my bum hand.

When our row went up to communion I carried the yarn in my hand. I stood before Father Briscoe and looked up into his eyes when he said, "The Body of Christ."

"Amen."

Angie knocked at the sacristy door. "Father Briscoe? May we come in? I'm Sister Angela from St. Domitilla in Hillside. This is my friend, Grace Marsden."

He had removed his Mass garments and was in what I referred to as casual wear, black pants, black short-sleeved shirt. The old priest motioned us in and shook hands with each of us. His firm handshake and clear eyes reminded me that age didn't always corre-late to ability or strength.

"Father, would you have a few minutes to talk to us?"

"Now?" He seemed confused at our timing. If he knew the half of it; I'd left Harry in a front pew close enough to keep him happy. I knew my husband's curiosity and he'd be strolling in here after what he thought a reasonable amount of time for Angie and me to be left alone with a suspect.

"Yes, Father." I almost choked on the word but I had not been raised to disrespect a priest without a good reason. "It's important to me and to several of your parishioners."

His expression shifted and looked more guarded. Perhaps he'd thought the issue concerned this nun and her 'friend'. Now he looked at me more closely. "In what way, young lady?"

I decided to start with the subterfuge of Wicca and pretend con-cern for my sister-in-law. "All this must remain confidential Father." I thought that would put his mind at ease. His reaction surprised me.

"This isn't the confessional. If you've something that private maybe you need to take it to someone else."

Angie looked stunned and started to speak. I cut her off not wanting to give him an out. "You're not in the business of listening and comforting anymore, Father?" This time I stressed the word.

His face paled and then he motioned us to sit down. Angie and I sat on the small couch and he sat in a chair opposite us. I hurried before he could change his mind. "My sister-in-law is Wicca." I paused to see his reaction. He stayed still looking at my eyes. "She's involved with these people, as is one of the mothers of my step-son's best friend. I'm concerned about their Pagan ways. You helped my father years ago when he strayed into a cult that met in the same woods."

His face turned animated. His eyebrows lifted and twitched and his glance darted around the room anywhere except my face. "I...I can't help you. Sounds like you need the police."

"I need you to tell me about those woods, those boys and what happened on those campouts." I hadn't meant to lay that out so quickly and I feared I'd pushed him away. He kept his head down moving it from side to side. His lips moved soundlessly and I didn't know if he was praying for guidance or for me to disappear. He slowly lifted his head and stared at me. "Who is your father?"

"Mike Morelli."

His face relaxed and he drew a deep breath. I wondered which name he'd been dreading. He leaned his elbows on his thighs and covered his face with his hands. When he raised his head I knew he'd made a decision.

"Mike was a nice kid, good boy. I knew he'd been coaxed or tricked into going out there. I was more concerned with the ringleader of that group. I knew the police would go easy on the others, their parents would be tougher on them. But this boy, the leader, he was eighteen and vulnerable to prosecution that would have destroyed his chance for a decent life."

"You're talking about Black Bart?"

I hated interrupting but I needed to make sure of whom he meant. He nodded. "You're well informed young lady. I'd known him since I came to the parish in 1945 to be their first youth minister. He'd been an altar boy and his Eagle project benefited the church. He organized and arranged for donated parts and labor to repair and rejuvenate the two station wagons the church owned. He scheduled boys to donate their time working as labor at several of the local dealerships in order to barter for the service. In turn, he asked for Mass cards for all the participants as a spiritual thank you. He was a great kid. I couldn't let him perish."

My mind whirled. How could Black Bart have been such a great kid and turn out so rotten? Or did he? He must have. The bag those two carried came from him. His dealership, maybe not him.

"I tried to intervene at a higher level when certain things became apparent to me."

I couldn't help myself. "Things like the fact that Bantonini molested the scouts in his care?" My voice rose and Angie placed her hand over one of mine. I knew Harry would be in here if I didn't quiet down. "Is that why you were transferred so quickly?"

He nodded and shrugged his shoulders. "I went to Father Gebhardt and shared my suspicions, my fears. He listened and I thought he would do something to protect the boys. Instead, two days later I received a transfer to a parish in Minnesota. I tried to stay in touch with some of the parishioners but after a few letters I felt the connection dissolved. Except with Bart. He kept in touch and after he wrote to me that he'd like to go to college, I arranged for him to go to school in Duluth. He majored in engineering. One of the proudest days of my life was when he graduated. I felt liked I'd saved at least one those boys." His eyes clouded and filled with tears. "Only one," he choked out before the tears overcame him.

Angie shot out of her chair and poured a glass of water for him. She handed him the glass and patted his shoulder. She glanced at me and I felt that she thought I was the bad guy here. I did feel crummy about making a priest cry–how many Hail Marys would absolve me?

"Father, I felt I could call him that now, I have to ask you if you think Father Gebhardt had any involvement..." *I can't believe I'm asking him if his boss had been a pedophile.* I cleared my throat, but he spoke before I continued.

"No, oh dear God, no. If I thought that I would have gone over his head to the Bishop. If Father Gebhardt sinned it was the sin of avoidance. He didn't want to think that could be happening. Possibly thought my account was exaggerated or that the boy lied to me for revenge on his leader for a punishment or reprimand. No, never."

He seemed pretty sure on that account. I believed him. My entire theory about who the bad guys are gaped around a big hole, but I believed him. I stood and extended my hand. "Thank you, Father. I know it was difficult for you to tell me all of this. You're back now and a Bantonini runs the same troop. How do you know the 'sins of the father'..." I let the sentence dangle.

He ran with it. "Nothing like that happens now. The troop has dads and moms involved. I'm the camping chair. I organize all the campouts, get tour permits, make the arrangements, and gather the volunteer for each campout. I know what Edward suffered as a child and I know his resolve to atone for the 'sins of his father'."

"He molested his own son?"

Father Briscoe's eyes widened. His soft voice rose in volume and filled the small room. "I've said too much yet once I didn't say enough. I've lived with that guilt for forty years. Trust me, Mrs. Marsden, Troop 265 is safe. I swear to you in front of God, no child is in danger." His face glistened with perspiration and a bit of spittle flew from his bottom lip with his last words.

His raised voice brought Harry into the room and he rushed to the old priest's side. He loosened his collar below the purplish face struggling to breathe. "Call 911, I think he's having a heart attack."

Angie and I hugged goodbye about two hours after the ambulance carried Father Briscoe to Oak Park Hospital. Parishioners who were still in the area came back into the church to pray and over the next hour more people trickled in getting the word from those already here. Someone led the Rosary and the mumbled responses floated up toward the high ceiling. We sat in the back with our heads together whispering about what we'd heard. When one of the priests came out and announced that Father Briscoe was stable and had not suffered a heart attack the church rocked with applause.

Harry disappeared after the ambulance left, but materialized from the shadows when Angie and I walked out of the church. She hugged Harry and hurried down the steps. At the bottom she turned and waved mumbling something about 'never a dull moment.'

"I heard the applause. He's going to make it?" Harry asked as we walked to our car.

"Yes, he's stable. Apparently not a heart attack."

Harry sensed my mood and put his arm around my shoulders. "Not your fault, darling."

"No? I talk to Mrs. Henry, she keels over. I talk to Father Briscoe, he ends up in an ambulance. I'm not talking to any more old people."

Harry squeezed my shoulders and suppressed a chuckle. He opened the door and waited for me to slide in. The further we drove from St. Edgar and Forest Park the less I dwelled on the priest. By the time we reached the split toward Aurora, I changed my focus. "What did Ric want?" I saw Harry's hands tighten on the wheel.

"Let's get home and settled."

That doesn't sound good. I kept quiet and said a prayer for Father's speedy recovery. I threw in one for me, too. I felt like I might need some divine intervention. The road into Pine Marsh led us home.

"Put the kettle on for me while I check the machine." Harry went up to his office and I headed for the kitchen. Elmo, Patches, and Trey scampered for my feet. *What is it with cats and feet? A dog knows enough to get out of the way.*

I played my newest game with them–kitty hockey. I gently push them along the smooth floor with my foot while they purr like little locomotives on a track. The problem is that I can only push one kitten at a time and the other two flop down in front of the moving one causing confusion and derailment.

"Okay, enough. I have to make coffee and tea. Later." They stopped. They'd spotted Harry in the doorway. They rushed to his feet but he wasn't playing.

"Grace." His voice drew my attention. Something was wrong. "Leave that. It's your dad. He's been in an accident."

My hands went numb and I felt a band tighten across my chest. Harry's voice sounded far away and faded.

"Grace, he's alive. He's at Elmhurst Memorial. We'd best go." He tugged me toward the door. Within minutes we retraced our route.

We'd best go. I knew what that meant. We'd all rushed to my mom's side when that call came. Rushed to say good-bye even though we'd spent the last months of her life saying good-bye and all the other things we'd never said. And still it wasn't enough. One more smile, one more hug, one more 'I love you, Daddy.'

"NO!" I screamed into the windshield. Harry swerved and straightened the car. His hands gripped the wheel until he regained control then he reached over and took my hand. I squeezed it though the pain of my thoughts.

"Gracie, talk to me." He stole a sideways glance. "Tracy's message said serious but stable."

My heart slammed inside my ribcage. The tiny sobs I'd been trying to control seeped through clenched lips.

"Gracie, he's stable. We'll get it all sorted out when we get there, but for now he's alive and he's stable."

Harry's words began to penetrate the wall of mist that swirled inside my head. I took short breaths to steady my body. "What happened? You said an accident?" The voice emanated from my body, flowing into the small space like oil over a pond. I knew I spoke yet wondered with whose voice. I felt disconnected and leaned against the headrest waiting for the pieces to settle.

Harry sensed my struggle and kept hold of my hand, pulling it with his when he needed to shift gears. He drove in silence knowing he needn't answer my question until I was back.

"What happened?" My head felt calm, I could listen now.

"Don't know for certain. Police think another car may have cut him off and your dad swerved. They're still investigating."

"My Jeep handles like a truck, he wasn't used to that. He would have reacted better in his car."

"Darling, your father has driven more types of vehicles than you've heard of. Don't blame your vehicle or yourself in that way you have of connecting the most incongruous facts together."

Harry stopped at the front entrance to let me out. He pulled my hand to his lips and kissed my fingertips. "I'll find you. Go."

I found Carolyn as soon as I entered. She waited at the door to direct the Morellis. We hugged and she took me by the shoulders and stared into my eyes before she spoke. "He's improved already, Grace. He's not conscious yet but he's getting better."

"Okay, okay but I want to see him. Tell me where he is."

"You can't see him yet. The boys are in the surgical waiting room—"

"Surgical? You said he was better." My voice shrieked with fear and Carolyn's eyes widened with apprehension.

"Grace." The firm calm voice belonged to Tracy. She put her arm around my shoulders and her strength flowed into my body. "I'll take her down."

Carolyn looked relieved and turned to wait for the family that would descend on the hospital.

Tracy's professional voice reached through the turmoil. "We did emergency surgery to relieve the pressure from a subdural hematoma. During the surgery Mike developed some respiratory distress. He's on a ventilator right now. I won't lie to you, Grace, he's not out of the woods yet, but he has a great chance at recovery, which he wouldn't have without the surgery. He's a fighter."

I followed Tracy until we stood at the entrance to the small chapel. She opened the door. "Let's stop here first." She glanced at her watch. "He won't be awake for another thirty minutes."

We knelt together and the single prayer we offered bound us even closer. I remembered Sister Colette, who'd taught me in the fifth grade, told us if we didn't have a rosary handy we could use our knuckles. I touched each knuckle in turn as I prayed.

Tracy leaned toward me. "Grace, I have to get back. I promise I will be back for you in fifteen minutes."

Prayers flew from my dry lips lifting to God's ear. "Please, God, let him be okay." I closed my eyes.

I felt a hand on my shoulder. Harry leaned down. "Tracy sent me to collect you."

I left the chapel with a sense of peace that I hoped would get me through whatever happened next.

Mike, Marty, and Glenn greeted me at the door to the waiting room. We hugged each other in silent support. I looked beyond them and realized that except for one couple huddled at the far end of the room everyone else was family. Nick, Uncle Jim, Vito, Edna, Jack, Uncle Pete, Vincent, Jolene sat or stood, filling the room to capacity. Eve and my niece Katie opened their house to all the kids who would need minding, feeding, and anything else until their parents were home. My nephew Joey picked up and delivered the younger ones, and was at his uncle's house entertaining the menagerie of cousins.

Behind the vocal Morellis stood a petite woman whose ashen face told me more than any words could about her feelings for my dad. Her curly hair framed a face distorted by red, swollen eyes. I couldn't reach her through the crowd of brothers all talking at the same time, but I caught her glance and nodded.

"Some bastard drives him off the road and nobody knows anything, sees anything? Bullshit. Somebody had to see something. It was seven-thirty at night for crying out loud." Marty paced and crushed a small paper cup in his hand. I wondered if he'd recently washed down another set of pills. The room grew quiet when Tracy entered. Heads turned in her direction and eyes implored her to have good news.

"Mike came out of recovery beautifully, right on time and with strong vitals. He's in intensive care," she held up her hand to stem the fear and questions, "which is totally normal procedure for the first twenty four hours."

A babble of relief filled the room. "I can take two of you at a time to see him for five minutes. He's on a ventilator and he is still groggy. Don't be alarmed if he doesn't open his eyes. I'm doing this so you have some peace. Okay, how are we going line up, draw straws, birth order, oldest to youngest?" Tracy's prognosis for my dad and now her tone eased the tension.

"Mickey and Gemie first." My cousin Nick, who lapsed into our childhood nicknames, cast his vote.

Marty nodded. "Then me and Uncle Jim."

"Okay, you guys figure it out. We'll be back in a few." Tracy opened the door and we followed her to one of the rooms surrounding the nurses' station.

We weren't prepared, and grabbed for each other's hand as we crossed the threshold and saw our unnaturally still and pale father. His head seemed overwhelmed by the heavy bandages and his face distorted by the tube that led to the machine that breathed life into him.

Tracy urged us forward. "He's doing some breathing on his own. It's not as bad as it looks. You can hold his hand; let him know you're here."

We split at the foot of the bed and carefully reached for his hands. One had an IV taped to a vein and the other fitted with a monitoring clip on a finger. My brother spoke first, his voice husky with emotion. "Hey, Dad, we're here. The whole gang. You know if you wanted a get together we could have just thrown a party." My oldest brother possessed our father's sense of humor.

I cleared my throat and hoped my voice sounded like me. "I'm here too, Daddy." I could only squeeze his hand. I knew another word and I'd lose the modicum of composure I'd struggled to keep.

His eyelids fluttered.

"Talk to him, Gracie," Mike urged from the other side of the bed.

"You're going to be fine, Dad. Tracy says you're her best patient. She'll know you're better when you start flirting with her nurses." Hard to tell but it looked like a smile around the tube. *Keep it light. Don't cry, don't get goofy.* "Can you open your eyes, Dad? Please?"

Tracy's hand touched my shoulder and she used her nurse's voice. "Much too early for that Grace. He's right on schedule doing great." I know her words were intended for her patient as much as for me. "Next shift coming up in one minute."

I leaned around the wires and tube and kissed his cheek. "I love you, Daddy." I straightened and sent a silent prayer. *Please, God, don't let those be our last words.*

I heard Mike mumble the same and we reluctantly left him. Marty and Uncle Jim were in the wings and swooped in behind us.

The family waited to hear our reactions. "His eyelids fluttered when Gracie called him. Tracy says that's all to expect."

"I think he smiled at the flirting comment. Do you think?" Mike nodded.

And so the evening went each person having five minutes with father, brother, uncle, cousin, all the titles, until only Harry and Jeannette were left.

Tracy appeared at the door. "By my calculations, we have one more visit."

Jeannette looked around the room wondering if it was her place to take a turn. Harry took her by the elbow and they followed Tracy for the sixth or seventh trip.

Mike and Glenn were deciding which team would sleep at the hospital and who would relieve them in the morning when Harry and Jeannette returned. She looked shaken and I suggested she splash water on her face in the ladies room. I started to follow her when Harry stepped between us. "No need to smother her. She'll be fine."

What an odd thing for Harry to say. I sidestepped and followed her to the bathroom. The room had one stall and one sink. Jeannette turned on the cold tap and passed her wrists under the stream. I pulled down some paper towels and placed them on the small vanity. She cupped the water in her hands and pushed it up onto her face. When she straightened her color looked better.

"Grace, I don't know if I should tell you this, but when your dad realized Harry was in the room he became very agitated. He seemed to want to tell him something. Harry kept telling him that he was going to be fine, you know, trying to assure him, but he still fidgeted. Then Harry got quiet and leaned close to your dad and in a low tone he said, 'I'll keep her safe, Mike' and then your dad calmed down. Tracy shooed us out of there."

Don't smother her indeed! What was going on? I patted her arm and assured her that she'd been right to tell me. Impulsively I hugged her. "I'm glad you care about Dad." I left before we got mushy.

My shift, it was decided by my brothers, would be tomorrow afternoon. I fretted and fumed all the way home. "I could have stayed. They always pull rank on me; I'm older than two of them."

Harry listened without comment lost in his own thoughts. More likely he knew I'd eventually run down and stop. In a *déja vu* sequence we turned into Pine Marsh and followed the lane to the right to the last house and into the garage.

"Can I make you a snack or are you off to sleep?"

"Are those my choices, food or sleep?" My voice snapped.

He raised his eyebrows. "You look all done in, that's all."

"That's not all. You want me to stuff my face and then toddle off to bed hoping that I forget about Ric meeting you, hoping that I don't ask about what Jan Pauli told me tonight."

"All right, Grace. Let's sit down. I wanted to wait until morning to discuss it but, we can talk now."

"You bet we can. And I don't want any coffee, either."

We sat across the table from each other in an almost combative posture, forearms on the table, upper bodies leaning forward.

"Nancy Royal broke protocol by telling Ric the results of the interrogation before they'd been charged. First of all, they identified them as Andrew Crockett and Thomas Quigley."

Harry paused for the reaction he expected. "Mary's son?"

"Their oldest. Seems he and the Crockett boy have been best

buds since their Boy Scout days in Troop 265." Harry pulled a sheet of paper from his pocket and turned it toward me. He pointed to the names. *'Crockett, Andrew David,' Quigley, Thomas Phillip.'* "If you see the full names printed this way it's easy to get *Davy* and *Q-Tip*.

My finger shook as I traced the names on the paper. "These two were in the woods that night and then again during the day. That's why they knew the whistle signals. Does this mean the troop is involved?"

Harry shook his head. "I don't believe so. Kramer got his hands on their advancement and attendance records. Seems these two washed out of scouts somewhere around their sophomore year of high school."

"This boy can't be the *Q-Tip* Don Craig talked about in his troop; the one with the deformed fingers had platinum blond hair. He said that's why they called him *Q-Tip.*"

"You said Don told you he didn't go to school with those boys. If he didn't know his last name or entire name he could have assumed that was the reason. But this is a nickname passed on from grandfather to father to son. If we meet Mr. Quigley I'd like to wager that he is blond, but more importantly, his nickname in Bantonini Senior's troop was *Q-tip*."

"Something else Kramer found. The older Quigley stayed in scouting after he turned eighteen, enjoying the title and privilege of JASM."

"So why did these two find it so difficult to stay in?"

"I don't give the Queen's garters why, I'm more concerned with why they came after you."

"After me? I thought they meant to scare me and take the kittens." My heart beat faster and my fingertips itched. I rubbed my fingers on the hard surface of the table. Harry caught up both hands and held them.

"They told Royal their mission was to snatch you when you came in to take care of the horses. The duct tape was meant for you." Harry's voice wavered and he squeezed my hands. Crockett carried a gunny sack inside his robe that they were going to use. Their information was that you'd be out before light to feed the horses. They were bored waiting and turned stupid. The spray paint wasn't part of their assignment, they added it for effect. Trey and Patches were in the wrong place at the wrong time. You were always their target."

I wiggled my hands free and pushed my hair back behind my ears. "I don't understand. Why come after me?"

"These two are dupes. They claim it's because you're the one that got away and in order for the ritual to work they needed to complete the sacrifice with you. And they needed to do it Wednesday night because that date represented the mid-point of autumnal equinox and winter solstice. The sacrifice would be most powerful."

I shivered and rubbed my hands up and down my arms. "Stop saying sacrifice."

"I'm sorry, darling. I've been going crazy about this since Kramer told me. And then your dad."

"Tell me the truth about his accident."

"He couldn't tell me anything but his eyes pleaded with me for something. I tried to reassure him that he'd be okay but it wasn't about him. When I finally promised to keep you safe, he relaxed. Whilst you were interrogating Jan I spoke to the police officer who'd been on the scene. By that time a witness had called the station to describe what he'd seen happening between the vehicles and it is obvious from those comments that someone deliberately tailed your dad and then pulled next to him to cut him off. The witness said the aggressor's car swerved toward your dad but then broke off and sped off."

I sat shaken to the core. Dad had almost been killed because of me. It was obvious. When the attacker saw the driver he knew he attacked the wrong person and swerved back in his lane.

"Grace, I know you're blaming yourself. No one suspected anything like this would happen. Grace, do you hear me?"

I'd slipped off to that place in my mind that tries to sort the flotsam and jetsam of my life. Harry's voice pulled me back. I nodded and looked into his eyes. Love, fear, concern, a myriad of expression. "I'm tired. I'm going up."

He moved around the table and hugged me. "We'll sort this out, I promise. Nothing will happen to you." Harry kissed the top of my head and guided me to the base of the staircase. "I'll be up in a few minutes." I started up the stairs on autopilot knowing what I would do before Harry joined me.

I called the number on the card Marisol had handed me. I had my own idea on how to sort this out.

ঌ 42 ঌ

I didn't think I could sleep with all the input from the night before but I slept and slept dreamless until six-thirty. The lack of dreaming disappointed me. I'd learned to pay attention to my dreams and think them through.

Barb and her family were out of town so I needn't rush. Harry slept on. I lay in bed replaying my conversation with Marisol. She'd been surprised at my call until I told her about my dad. Part of me thought she'd turn down civilian interference but when I insisted that the satanic cult and the gunrunners could have common ties and gave her my reasons, she'd agreed to use me as bait. She assured me that a 'sister' in a robe on Friday night would be an agent and that I'd be in no danger. I told her I'd call her today to firm up the plan and to confirm I'd do it. *Are you absolutely, certifiable around the bend crazy? You heard me, crazy. We never use the crazy word.* I shook my head to stop the voices.

My movement joggled the bed and Harry stirred. "Is it morning?" His bleary sleep voice tugged at my heart.

"If you'd open those baby blues you'd see the light from yonder window breaks."

"Ugh, English majors," he mumbled and tucked his pillow closer.

"What time did you come to bed?"

"Hmm. Three, four. It was dark." His pillow muffled part of the answer.

"What were you doing all night?"

Harry rolled onto his back and opened his eyes. He looked up at the ceiling. "I laid out every scrap of information I had and wrote notes until I'd recorded everything I could remember hearing or being told. Then I sat and thought about the entire mess from several angles."

"And?"

"And I came to bed with an excruciating headache that is still with me."

I thought at first he meant me. My comic relief valve opened a skosh and I swallowed a giggle. I spoke in a whisper, "*Ssh*, don't talk.

Go back to sleep, I'll make you some tea."

"I'm awake, Gracie. Thanks to your twenty questions." He rolled onto his elbow and stared at me. "How did you sleep? You were sawing logs when I came up."

I pushed at his elbow. "Was not."

"I'll record you some time. It's a lovely little titter you do; not that droning or snorting type that some chaps do."

"I'm not a 'chap.'"

"Not one bit." Harry's eyes narrowed to slits and he reached for me. "Not one fair bit," he murmured into my ear.

It is now seven o'clock. You requested to be awakened at seven o'clock.

Harry raised his head from my neck. "Not now, Betty dear. Have a heart, can't you see I'm busy."

"She just wants to make sure you're up."

"That I am…and awake too."

We smiled and snuggled closer knowing there were two more gentle reminders until she *buzzed* us.

"I'm there from noon to six and then Glenn comes in until midnight. Nick is taking the third shift."

"This will work out well. I want to stop in and see your dad. I'll drive you and after my visit with Mike I'll leave you with him. Will's Court of Honor is tonight at the school. I could collect you at six and we could stop for dinner before the ceremony at St. Edgar."

"You're inviting me to Will's court of honor? Did you clear that with him?"

Harry wrapped his arms around me. "Don't be silly. Of course he wants you there. You have to stop thinking the worst." He kissed me on the nose. "Let's get going don't want to miss your debriefing from Mike do you?"

We made two quick stops; Vito and Helmut's to check on my Jeep, which had been towed there last night. I stayed in the car while Harry signed the papers. Closer to the hospital, we stopped at Dunkin' Donuts for coffees for my brother and me.

I knew from my brother's call that they'd removed my dad from the ventilator. Mike had spent the night and morning. He'd activated the calling tree twice, as planned; once at eight o'clock to give out dad's vitals and progress and then again at eleven o'clock with the update which included his new room number. A call before eight in the morning would have meant bad news.

I could tell at a glance that Mike's update didn't do Dad justice. He sat at an upright angle in the bed with the table tray in place holding his water pitcher, a pad of paper and one of the two newspapers he reads every day. His reading glasses perched on the tip of his nose. If I could erase the IV leading to his hand and the other hospital paraphernalia, he'd look like he was relaxing on the sectional in the living room on Victoria Street, doing the crossword in the Trib.

Mike dozed in a chair next to the bed. His features a sweet mix of our parents, dark hair with Irish skin and hazel eyes behind those heavy lids. Dad noticed us and motioned us over. I tiptoed past Mike and leaned in for the best hug and kiss we could manage.

"Dad, you look great. How do you feel? Are you in pain?"

"As long as I don't laugh or dance I'm fine." His voice was hoarse and low.

My brother woke up. "Hey, Sis, Harry." He stood and stretched reaching his arms straight above his head then out, narrowly avoiding one of the monitors.

I hugged him and kissed his cheek. "Brought you a little something for the ride home." Harry handed over one large black coffee.

Mike's eyes lit up; he reached for the cup. "You are the best little sister I have."

We laughed at his joke, but then I saw Dad wince. "You weren't kidding about it hurts when you laugh were you?"

He shook his head. "*Oww.* Add shaking my head to that list."

"You look done in. Why don't you debrief your sister in the corridor whilst I make certain this fellow doesn't laugh, dance, or shake." Harry's suggestion didn't fool me. He wanted to talk to my dad alone. I couldn't make a fuss. My brother kissed Dad and took me by the elbow. I longed for those baby monitors now.

My brother's recap assured me that our dad's recovery moved forward at a fast clip. In the block of time he'd been there the staff removed two pieces of equipment the biggest being the ventilator. His vital signs were strong. Tracy would be in at three o'clock and she'd give me the scoop. After that I was to activate the calling tree with the latest update.

"The Bears stand a chance of getting into the playoffs if they stay healthy."

They must have heard me coming. Harry doesn't follow football, wouldn't know a wide receiver from a golden retriever, although a golden might help the Bears.

"Hi, sweetie. Thanks for bringing him coffee, he's been grousing all morning about the crummy coffee."

"Mike, I have to be downtown by one o'clock." Harry stood up and motioned me to the chair. "Here you are. Have a lovely visit with your dad and I'll be back to take you to dinner." He did what I called his 'swoop'; he moved gracefully up and out of the chair, sort of twirled me toward it while kissing me full on the mouth, gently pushed me down into the chair and then swirled out of the room before I could react.

"If the Bears could move like that we'd be champions."

The duty nurse walked in, looking back over her shoulder after her recent encounter with twinkle-toes in the hallway. He must have spoken to her, that filmy kind of look filled her eyes. *Geez Louise, it's only an accent for God's sake.*

She cleared her throat and her head, I hoped. "Mr. Morelli, it's time for your CAT scan. We're going to take you down on a gurney so let's get you ready to roll." She pulled the bed table away. A young man in scrubs pushing a gurney entered the room. They transferred my dad in two shakes and headed for the door. I reached for his shoulder and gave it a squeeze.

"These guys are quick, be back before you know it. He waved toward the table. Finish the crossword…if you can." He winked his challenged.

Two hours didn't seem quick to me. I'd erased holes in the little blocks changing his answers to fit mine. I'm sure there was a word that started with 'dzt' and he still hadn't returned. I'd brought three different colored plastic strips and two key rings with me intending to braid key chains for Matt and Ben. They'd seen mine and admired it. I'd finished one when I heard a gentle knock. Walter and Gertrude stood in the doorway and behind them I spotted Hannah.

"Come in. Dad's down having a CAT scan but he should be back soon." My cousin Nick showed up at the door before we'd finished hugs and kisses. He carried a huge basket of mums and roses.

"Where should I put this, it weighs a ton. I intercepted the nurse's aide bringing it up."

"Put it on the table." I slid dad's papers to the side. "It's beautiful, who's it from?"

Nick shrugged. "I just deliver."

Hannah reached out and lifted the card. '*To Coach Mike, Get better fast, Love, the Vic-Vics*' "They're your dad's ball team, aren't they?"

My dad started a park district baseball team by rounding up all the little squirts, boys and girls, in the neighborhood. Since most of the kids were from the long block of Victoria they picked Victor/Victoria or Vic Vic. Dad told them it stood for victory too. The bouquet came from Luurs Flower Shop in Hillside, Dad's favorite garden center. Through the years they'd sponsored several of my brothers' little league teams.

Jan Pauli hesitated in the doorway. She held a small bouquet in a glass vase. "Looks like it's crowded in there."

I repeated the 'dad's not here' message and then suggested we move to the waiting room at the end of the hall. We'd see him come up and everyone could sit down out there. "I need to make a quick call. I'll be right out." This was my chance to call Marisol and firm up our plan. I'd just hung up with her when Nick popped in.

"I'm making a run to Portillo's. Want anything?"

"Absolutely. A beef with giardinera for me, but then could you go west on North Avenue and get me a Dunkin' Donuts coffee?"

"You got it." Nick took off with the exuberance of youth and goodness.

That's how Tracy found us when she came on duty. We were hunkered down enjoying juicy beef sandwiches and good coffee. She greeted everyone then motioned to me. "I've got to get down to the ER, but I read Mike's chart and he's looking good."

"Why is it taking so long for him to come back from that test? It's been two hours."

"You haven't heard the news. There was a pile up on the 290 and several of the victims were transported here. Your dad's test would have been bumped for theirs."

"When did this happen? Harry left here about twelve-thirty headed downtown."

My heart raced at the thought that fate could be that quirky. Tracy shook her head. "Don't worry, it was on the outbound side. But I will see if I can find out if and when he's scheduled."

"Thanks. I'd best do my update or the Morellis will be descending in droves."

My contact was Edna. I filled her in and found out she'd be out tomorrow with 'contraband' bakery. I confirmed when she'd be there.

I returned to the waiting room to find Dad visiting with everyone. His turn, rescheduled three times, finally cancelled for today, was moved to tomorrow first thing. The nurse pulled over briefly to allow everyone to say hello, but now she wheeled him into the room. We trooped behind her and the aide like a parade. They transferred him back to the bed and left with the admonition to keep it quiet.

I was never alone with my dad. Once I caught his glance and I sensed he was happy for the interference. Harry and Glenn arrived minutes apart and once again I was out of the room filling in Glenn on dad's progress. Harry wasn't alone with him this time. Karen replaced Hannah and Eve and Katie replaced Gertrude and Walter. Only Jan remained from the afternoon visitors. She kept up a flow of conversation that entertained and occupied him. *He could do worse.*

⤳ 43 ⤳

Through four years at Regina and several Oak Park River Forest friends, I'd been to events at St. Giles, St. Edmond and Ascension Catholic churches, but never St. Edgar. The scout troop met in the parish activity room.

A scout stationed at the door handed us a program. We found seats in the second row of folding chairs on the side the scout indicated for parents and friends. Harry invited his sister and Walter to Will's first ever court of honor. We were early but that was by design. We wanted to observe as many people as possible.

Ed Bantonini approached us. I waited until he shook hands with Harry and was looking at him to take a quick glance at his outstretched hand. Could those healed marks be scratches from my nails or brittle branches? Couldn't tell. "You're early, we're barely set up." His statement sounded like small talk, not accusatory.

Harry smiled and shrugged. "You never know on the 290."

Bantonini nodded his head. "True." Small talk. "Well, enjoy the court of honor. Probably our last one. I'm making the announcement tonight after the award ceremony. I think you already know something about the decision made last week by the St. Edgar School Organization. They've decided not to continue their charter of the troop. I'll be giving the parents forms to fill out if they want to transfer their sons to another troop and information about the other troops in the area."

"It sounds like a done deal. No chance to get chartered by the church instead of the school?" I thought my question a reasonable one; one that any parent might ask. I wasn't prepared for his answer.

"No. And don't push for that. It's over for this troop. It's better…" he turned and walked to the front table. He helped Brad set up the final candles on the holder that signified a scout's trail to Eagle.

"Whew, he's touchy."

"More than that, he's out of uniform."

I looked at Bantonini from this distance: shirt, pants, neckerchief, slide, belt. Harry continued, "His back pocket has a button missing." In scouts if your uniform was torn or pieces missing you technically were 'out of uniform'. In this case it meant so much more.

"Should we call the Sheriff's police?"

"He's not going anywhere. Let's see who else shows up."

My head spun with the thought that we were calmly sitting fifty feet from the man who probably pushed Janet to her death. My newest cord twisted in and out of a taut-line as I tried to soothe my jitters. I had a steady pace when I looked up at the doorway and saw the elder Bantonini enter. He wore his full uniform complete with OA sash. He looked directly at me and I shivered under his malevolent gaze. Harry noticed the eye contact and fixed him with his own nasty stare. Bantonini looked away and took his seat up front on the troop side.

Slowly the room began to fill. Hannah, Karen, and Walter came in together. Made sense since Gertrude was babysitting. They'd brought Tim with them. He left their side and hurried to check in. Apparently Mary Quigley needed to attend to other matters.

Hannah sat down next to me and whispered that Mary called at the last minute to ask if Hannah could drop him off and bring him home tonight. "She seemed so preoccupied, distracted actually. You'd think she'd want to see Tim's first court of honor. Course, she's been through several of these with her older boys. He's quite put out that neither of his parents will make it."

Hannah didn't know how distracted Mr. and Mrs. Quigley were. I'd never met the dad. Just for the sake of comparison I'd like to see that blond mop of hair.

I saw Lily and Will come into the room. Will rushed to join his troop while Lily looked for us. Harry waved her over. If she was surprised by all of us being there she didn't act it. Her smile never wavered and she sat down next to Walter after greeting everyone with a generic hello. The only special greeting was directed at me. "Grace, I heard about your father. I hope he's doing better."

Her genuine concern caught me off guard. I felt awkward discussing fathers with her in view of what had happened to hers because of me. "He is, thank you." *Just when you think you know someone.* She settled back against the metal chair and read her program.

Harry watched the troop's side fill up and now he touched my hand and nodded his head toward that group. Bart Guilfoyle greeted Ed Bantonini and took a seat next to Ed Sr. The big surprise was that he was in uniform; I recognized his patch–Chartered Organization Representative. Black Bart was the C.O.R., the liaison between troop and school. I wondered if he'd pushed to keep the troop or felt as Bantonini did that it was better to lose the charter.

A last minute arrival moved casually among the parents not yet seated shaking hands and smiling. His tuxedo seemed extravagant for this gathering so he must have come from somewhere or was going somewhere after this event. The way he worked the crowd reminded me of a politician on the stump. Tim rushed to him and hugged him. I hadn't notice the photographer trailing him but Tuxedo shifted Tim around so the photographer could snap a 'photo op.' Hannah leaned toward me before I could ask. "That's Tim's uncle the Honorable Evan Bigelow. Mary's brother is the mayor of Forest Park."

Another e.b. How many more were there in this tight circle?

"Mary says he's quite the charmer, uses his black Irish good looks with the women voters. Turns on the brogue a bit she says when he's passionate about an issue. He claims the accent happens when he feels the righteous indignation of his ancestors guiding him. Who's *woo woo* now. Looks like a phony to me."

I laughed at Hannah's comments but wondered if this was the same Bigelow on the juvie list. It must be. The records were supposed to be sealed. Kids could straighten out from a rough start. Happened all the time.

The committee chair for the troop stood up and walked to the front. He addressed welcoming comments to the parents, friends, and past leader and Eagles who were in attendance. He returned to his seat and Brad stepped forward facing the audience. He looked to the back of the room. "Troop attention. Audience please rise." Metal scraped against the tiled floor as people stood. "Color guard, attention. Forward, march." Two rows of boys each behind a flag bearer marched toward the front. "Color guard halt. Present the colors." The two flag bearers crossed paths, the American flag crossing to the right side of the table. They turned in place facing the audience. "Hand salute. Please join me in the Pledge of Allegiance." Brad waited a second beat after we finished the pledge. "Post the colors." The flag bearers slid the poles into the metal sleeves in the iron stands. The scouts held their salute until Brad's clear voice commanded, 'Two'. "Scout sign." That signaled the reciting of the Scout Law an Oath. When their young voices stopped they lowered their hands and filed into the rows of chairs. We sat down.

The program went quickly, moved along by Brad's experience. Each boy was called up to the table to receive his merit badge and tell the assembly what he did to earn the badge. Most of the young scouts mumbled through a brief description of their endeavors. The older boys who by now knew the drill said more and hammed it up for the audience. All the scouts who bridged last April received badges they'd earned at summer camp. They were already Tenderfoot.

Lily positioned herself in the back behind the chairs to take photos of the entire court of honor. She snapped shots of all the boys waiting I'm sure for one particular boy. Will stood up quickly when his name was called and hobbled up. Brad explained that Will had just joined but had already worked hard to earn the rank of Tenderfoot. He handed Will his patch with his right hand and shook hands with his left, the Boy Scout way. We stopped short of whistles but the applause was robust. He looked a little embarrassed. He started to turn away and Brad caught him by the arm. "You have to give your mom her pin." Brad lifted a necklace of thin ribbon from the table. "Ask your mom to come up." Lily looked surprised, apparently she hadn't been told. She started up the aisle then stopped even with our row. I realized she wanted a picture taken. She thrust the camera into my hands and pointed to a little red button. "It's focused from back there. Make sure we're in the frame and push the button." She hurried to the front. To pass it off with instructions wouldn't give anyone else enough time to take the photo. I got out of the row and stood where I'd seen her standing. Too late I realized I couldn't hold the camera steady and press the button. I panicked knowing she'd think I'd ruined this photo on purpose. Brad took a moment to explain to Lily that the troop gives a pin to the mother for each rank advancement to acknowledge that both parents support their scout on his trail to Eagle. He handed the ribbon to Will and instructed him to place it around Lily's neck.

"Let me do that." The camera lifted out of my hands and Black Bart easily snapped two photos. "Father Briscoe says you ask a lot of questions, have a lot of crazy notions. You need to stop harassing the old people in this community." My eyes widened in surprise. "Yeah, I heard about Mrs. Henry. You should be more careful."

"Are you t-threatening me?" I hated the stammer and the thin pitch in my voice. I certainly sounded rattled.

"I'm just suggesting you stop bothering these people."

"Or you'll send another pair of goons to my house." I whispered that last piece because I saw Lily approaching. Guilfoyle pushed the camera into my hands and backed away from me like I was a nutcase.

"Grace, I'm sorry. I totally forgot about your hand. I was so excited." She touched the small *fleur de lis* with the etched eagle that signified the second rank on the trail to Eagle.

"No problem. I, that is he," nodding toward Guilfoyle's back, "took the pictures, two of them." I gave her the camera.

"Well, thanks, anyway. I mean it."

I returned to my seat in time to applaud for Tim. His personal cheering section took him by surprise. His face brightened and he stood a little straighter. He, by virtue of being a 'Q' was the last boy.

Brad's voice called the color guard to their final duty to retire the colors. Once done the boys scattered to hand off their badges to their parents before they raced for the refreshment table. My dad's troop's rule was adults first. It was maddening the way adults took forever to get their treats before we kids could line up. Troop 265 allowed the scouts and siblings to go first. Tim came up to Hannah. "Mrs. Hannah, you would hold on to these for me, please?"

"Of course, sweetie. Go on, they're safe with me." He looked relieved and turned to join Will who'd waited.

"Why do you call her 'Mrs.' she's not married?"

Tim shrugged. "She's got kids. In my house if you've got kids you're 'Mrs.'"

Hannah smiled at me. "Now there's a thought, 'Mrs. and Mrs.'. Interesting way to address one's mail."

Harry and Lily were off to the side discussing Will no doubt. They were both grinning. Harry pointed at the camera and Lily released it. He nonchalantly looped the strap around his wrist and aimed the camera around the room clicking here and there and specifically at the back of Bantonini's pants. I saw him wait for Lily to unload the spent cartridge. He slipped it into his pocket.

I migrated toward the refreshments in search of coffee. Karen thoughtfully poured one for me. "Thanks." I held it in my left hand and waved around the room. "Some day this will be you and Hannah."

Karen shrugged. "I'll do Girl Scouts with Clare. Hannah can have Connor and Boy Scouts. She loves that camping, bug stuff. I'll do the shopping badge." We both laughed at her division of duties but I sensed a serious tone under the surface. Karen hadn't made peace yet with raising a boy.

"Just as well," she added, "they probably wouldn't pop for two mother's pins."

We sipped at our coffees and watched as the boys began folding the chairs and stacking them on a frame on wheels. The older boys pulled the filled cart into the closet. I realized then that Bantonini hadn't made the announcement. What happened to change his mind?

Hannah approached with Tim in tow. "We've best be leaving.

Tonight is a school night and I promised Mary I wouldn't let Tim lead us astray." She ruffled his hair. He grinned and lit up. She had a way with kids but especially the boys. "Say *ta* to Harry for me. He looks involved.

He looked infuriated. I don't know what happened to their grins except that they'd been replaced by grimaces. I saw Will headed for his parents and I moved to intercept him.

"Hey, congratulations. Great job making rank so fast. None of your uncles managed that."

"Really?"

"Absolutely. You should be proud of yourself. I know your folks are." I instantly regretted mentioning his parents. He glanced at them and then back to me. My face felt hot and he noticed the blush. "No problem. They do that when they're together; argue about me. I thought they'd be happy to be a family. I guess I'm a problem."

My throat closed with tears and I couldn't speak. I put my hand on his thin shoulder and squeezed. He shrugged and walked toward his parents. Lily spotted him and instantly shifted her demeanor. Harry picked up on her cue. Will stood between them accepting their praise. He looked at me with sad eyes. Had they always been that sad? Had I been too preoccupied with my needs to see his?

Harry helped me with my coat and we hurried through the cold air to his car. I wanted to tell him about the threat from Black Bart but more than that I wanted to tell him about Will. Before I looked into those sad eyes I would have been thrilled that Lily and Harry argued when they were together. I couldn't shake the feeling that his happiness would be determined over the course of the next few weeks.

I waited until we were upstairs getting ready for bed, waited until we were snuggled under the covers. They say timing is everything. Harry pulled me closer and kissed my neck. Now was not the time to interject with, 'gee you and Lily are doing a lousy job of parenting' or 'did I mention one of the bad guys threatened me?'

"What's wrong, you're all tense." He rubbed his hand up and down my arm, stopping to massage my shoulder.

I should tell him everything, even my plan with Marisol.

Instead I let him hold me until I fell asleep in his arms.

I woke up in his arms aware of how heavy they felt around me. I turned to ease my position and his hands clutched at me. I felt the pointy smooth fingers on my arm and I twisted in their grasp. The rough material of his clothing rasped again my skin. His features faded under the black hood until only bones gleamed in a hideous smile.

"Grace, wake up." Harry shook me holding my left hand while he tried to pin my other arm. My wrist felt like it was on fire and I cried out when Harry pushed down on it. "Gracie, wake up."

"I'm awake, thank God I'm awake. It was awful."

Harry pulled me into his arms. "I know, darling. Just a bad dream."

"My wrist throbs like Elmo purrs during an ear scratch. It feels like I broke it again."

"That is a distinct possibility after the crack you gave me in the face."

It took a moment for his words to register.

"You screamed and started twisting and thrashing. Your first swing caught me across the cheek and then you flung the other way and hit the nightstand. I was trying to keep you from hurting yourself, and me," he added.

He turned on the bedside light and got out of bed to bring me a glass of water and two extra strength tablets. "Take these and if you're not hurting less in thirty minutes we'll go to hospital. I'll be right back, going to nip downstairs for an ice pack."

"Do you think that will help through my cast?"

"It's not for you." He touched his left cheek and winced. "What's in there, a horse shoe?"

His trip downstairs took longer and I knew he'd probably brewed some tea to calm my nerves or use on his eye after the cold pack. He carried a small tray with a teapot and two mugs, sugar and honey. The cold pack, a green kitchen towel wrapped around a frozen package of veggies, traveled on his shoulder. He bent at the knees rather than the waist to put the tray on the nightstand.

I pointed to the towel. "Peas or carrots?"

"Black eyed peas."

I patted the bed next to me. "You sit and ice, I'll be mother." I'd always wanted to use the English expression for who pours tea. Harry smiled and winced. "*Oww*. Don't make me laugh."

"Isn't it odd how they say laughter heals but everyone who's hurting says it only hurts when they laugh? I've never heard anyone say 'gee, it only hurts when I frown.'"

"We're not falling back asleep anytime soon, are we?" Harry held the pack against his cheek and sipped awkwardly at his tea.

"When you get philosophical I know something is on your mind. Give it up, Gracie, so we can get some sleep before dawn."

He really did know me. That or he believed what my nonna used to say about not sleeping well because your guilty conscience kept you awake. I sat up straighter in bed and told him about my conversation with Will. "He thinks he's the reason you two argue."

Harry's eyes shifted from disbelief to sadness while he listened. "I thought we were careful not to argue in front of the lad."

"Well, either he was around more than you thought or you and Lily are lousy at acting friendly when you're both hot under the collar. I'd bet the latter."

"I'm making a mess of this fatherhood thing, aren't I? I want him to love me, look up to me."

"Give him a chance. He already loves you; he's been loving you all his life. Every kid wants two parents. He has to adjust to actually having a dad in his life. You're overwhelming, in anyone's life."

"It's Lily. We can't agree on anything. It's as though whatever I suggest she finds the opposite agreeable. We're acting like brats, I see it, but I can't help it."

"It's you. She brought him to you after eleven years. She's been calling the shots, planning for his future, kissing his *owies,* and checking his homework. You can't expect her to relinquish her position as lead. Maybe she moved into Pine Marsh to check out the person you'd become. She approved and decided to reveal Will to you. That doesn't mean she wants to be equal partners in parenting yet."

Harry tossed the cold pack aside. "She knows the person I am. I haven't changed, I would have mar…" Harry's eyes widened and he reached for my hand to either hold it or prevent me from swinging at his head.

I knew it. He would have married her regardless of our relationship. Is that what he wants now, to try and be a family?

"Get that idea out of your head right now." Harry's eyes flared with the onset of anger. "I know how you think and you're thinking with your *arse* right now. I would have married Lily if I'd know she was pregnant but only if I hadn't met and fallen in love with you."

Yeah, sure. Easy to declare in hindsight. I didn't want to have this conversation and I knew how to switch topics.

"That wasn't the only interesting conversation. Black Bart threatened me when I was taking Lily and Will's picture. He told me to stop bothering the old people."

Harry's face tightened. "When did you plan to tell me?"

I felt it was a rhetorical question and sipped at my mug of sweet tea. Normally a coffee would have suited me better but this morning the honey-flavored liquid soothed me.

We sat in silence with our own thoughts. I'd successfully changed the subject; Harry still fumed and the cold pack was back against his cheek. I must have really walloped him. I tried to figure out how to the get the car and no escort for this afternoon. I'd have to lie to Harry and maybe some other people. My plan formed slowly based on real and phony telephone calls.

Harry seemed to have calmed down a bit. "I'm having a shower," was his clipped comment. Maybe he wasn't that calm.

I couldn't call anyone at four in the morning but I could go over my ideas. Only I needed paper, I couldn't keep anything sorted in my head. Once I read it, I owned it. I pulled a sweatshirt from the dresser and struggled to get the sleeve over my cast. I hadn't thought about my wrist until then and it did seem better. No cheerful baritone from the bathroom, guess he was thinking too. I slipped into sweatpants and carried the tray downstairs. My coffeemaker stood ready to serve. I'd filled it last night. A simple push of the brew button and soon Cinnamon Nut Swirl would flood the carafe.

My paper, my purple Sharpie, and my coffee. *Ready, go!* I freed my brain to show me my thoughts. Ideas came to me written on the back of my eyelids or so it seemed. I'd brought my 'mystery box' a name from childhood when I'd collect odds and ends and pretend I was Nancy Drew following the clues and solving the puzzle. To anyone else it was the typical junk box teeming with lost buttons, broken key chains, ticket stubs and the like. I lifted the links of bracelet from the contents and held it up to light to look for markings. Nothing. It looked to me like an old Spiedel I.D. bracelet from the fifties or sixties. We'd each received one for our thirteenth birthday. Mine was a thinner link not like this piece, which was more like the ones the boys received. So this belonged to a boy. One of the Schuessler brothers or the Peterson boy. The crate was too small to have held three bodies but maybe one. Maybe John Henry's small frame. I shuddered and moved on in my mind.

Maybe the bracelet had been worn by a girl but belonged to her boyfriend. I'd worn Steven Gore's I.D. bracelet and class ring in high school. Both were too big but angora fixed the ring and the bracelet hung across the mid-part of my hand just short of slipping off. I could remove it by tucking my thumb under my fingers.

1. Bracelet could have been lost by boy or girl. (Betting on

boy)
2. Bantonini Sr. was the cult leader and my attacker
3. Black Bart was part of the cult
4. Quigley grandfather was gunrunner
5. Quigley grandson was part of cult
6. Crockett part of cult and works at Black Bart and drove Hannah's Roadmaster
7. Bigelow (Mary's dad probably) was gunrunner?
8. Gunrunners killed John Henry (agent). How did they know he was there?
9. John Jacob fell into well rushing through woods? No. Well being used by Robinson's granddaughter and scouts. Was John Jacob in crate for 20 years?
10. Bantonini Jr. pushed Janet into well and lost button. Why kill her? What did she know?
11. Mary Quigley is Wicca but her son is a Satan worshipper. Did he twist what he saw her doing?
12. Detective Thomas is a Satan worshipper. (Looks the type) Probably destroyed evidence.
13. What happened to the rabies tag? Who ended up with it? Bantonini, Thomas?

My brain stopped writing on my lids and I looked at my list. Lucky thirteen. Maybe after tonight some or most of these people would be behind bars and someone else could sort this out. I only wanted to stop the attacks. They'd caught my dad by mistake. Who might they hurt next?

I heard Harry in the living room and slid my list under the pad and busied myself with another cup of coffee.

He put his arm around me. "You have to tell me these things when they happen. I could have confronted him."

"Did you really want to break up the court of honor by calling him out?" I saw the frustration on his face.

"I only want to keep you safe and stop these bastards."

"I know. I'm sorry I didn't tell you." I reached up and gently touched the dark bruise under his left eye. "Does it hurt?"

He pulled back. "Only when you poke it."

"I didn't poke, you're such a baby."

We smiled and non-verbally agreed to stop arguing. Harry pointed to the pad. "Note taking?"

I blushed and gave myself away. Thank God, I hadn't written

anything about tonight. He lifted the pad and looked at my list. "Looks good, although, I think the bracelet was worn by a girl. Do we know for a fact that the well was in use back then? He could have tumbled in; the path out to East River Road leads right past the well. Your dad said he went after Specs but ran into Bantonini. Your dad is his alibi. Who else was out there that night?"

"The gunrunners. Maybe they were moving the crates through the woods. Maybe they started the low campfires and tom-toms to keep people out of the woods."

"That's a good thought. If John Henry spotted lights on his way out of those woods he'd have investigated. He may have stumbled on the very people he'd been searching for. Without back-up he could have been overpowered and killed there then dumped on the road to make it look like a hit and run accident."

"Who has the rabies tag?"

"I gave it to Bantonini." Harry shook his head. "Damn, I gave him a clue to the identity of–"

"No problem," I interrupted. "The number was 55-48236 and the year was 1955."

Harry whooped with excitement as he picked up the phone.

"It's five in the morning. Who are you calling?"

"Kramer and I hope he's sound asleep." His grin lessened as the stretched skin tugged at his tender cheek.

I heard only one side of the conversation but enough to know that Ric knew someone at Cook County Health that could look up old information. Harry read the number and year to him and hung up with a strange smile.

"What's wrong?"

"He thought I might be calling with bad news about Mike. Shook him up. It's not just you, Gracie girl, it's your entire family, isn't it." Harry's voice sounded hurt. I know he could never forget that I had turned to Ric when I thought, when we all thought Harry had been killed. What hurt Harry was that my family never turned their back on Ric even after Harry returned. A Morelli bond didn't break easily.

"How long will it take to find out?" Harry stared at the phone. He looked at me and the pain retreated to wherever he kept it.

"He can call at nine and it shouldn't be much longer if his contact is working today."

"I'm going out to the barn. Hold on to Elmo, he's been trying to escape."

"Gracie, he wants to be outside with his siblings. Let him go."

"No, he's too little. The others are stronger and bigger. He'll get hurt outside."

"You can't keep them apart. He pines for them. Either let him out or keep them in. I don't mind a house full."

I wasn't sure if *I* wanted three cats underfoot. He was right though; Elmo meowed at the back door when his brother and sister were outside. I didn't think that Patches and Trey would ever be housecats unless we kept vigilant whenever the door opened.

"Just a little longer and I promise to consider it. Please?"

Elmo sat on Harry's foot during the discussion of his fate. Harry slowly lifted his foot carrying Elmo with it until he scooped him up in a kitty hacky sack move. "All right by you, Ort? There's a good puss." Harry scratched behind Elmo's ears and I could hear the purring across the room.

April and Cash greeted me in their special equine manner and my spirits rose. The newly scrubbed barn looked and smelled clean, and no marks were left on the horses. Their eyes shone clear none the worse for their ordeal. I spotted Trey and Patches cuddled on an empty feed sack near a bale. They did look comfy and safe.

April always went first. I brushed her and spent extra time on her mane combing out a few burrs. She loved the petting. And the peas, compliments of Harry, pleased her too. I checked her hooves, picked a pebble, and then turned her out into the corral. Cash didn't stand as patiently and his back was too high for me to get, but the treats kept him focused long enough for me to finish. He joined April. I leaned on the fence and talked to them for awhile. When I turned for the house I'd figured out how to give whoever had Gracie watch the slip.

Harry sat at the breakfast nook staring out at the birds on the feeder. He seemed preoccupied but looked up when he heard me.

"Kramer called. Seems the cat belonged to a Randolph family, moved away years ago. Lived in Janet's neighborhood, on her block in fact. Could have been chums. Maybe that's what caused her reaction when you told her."

"I don't think so, it was so erratic. Sounds like a dead end."

"Kramer's trying to track them down through rabies records– once a cat owner…"

I poured myself a coffee and slid in next to him so as not to obstruct his view. I began carefully, knowing the answers to some of the questions I would ask. "I have the afternoon again at the hospital.

Marty is going to be there too. Do you want to meet for dinner afterwards?" I knew he was supposed to develop the film and bring it to Lily who was coming out tonight to spend the weekend in Pine Marsh. Harry promised Will he could help with the horses tomorrow. I watched the conflict on his face and felt crummy about taunting him.

"I've promised to get those photos to Lily tonight. Thought we'd order Chinese. I forgot that you're visiting your dad."

"That's okay. I want to drop off Dad's car anyway. Mine should be ready tomorrow. When Glenn relieves us I'll have Marty follow me to Dad's house and we'll put his car in the garage. Maybe Marty and I will join you for Chinese or maybe I'll take him to dinner. I'll see what he wants to do and call you." The other reason I sat next to my husband was so that staring out the window at the birds would explain why I wasn't looking at him with my lying purple eyes.

"I can follow you and drop off the film at Elmhurst Camera. They do the best work."

Perfect. Okay, Gracie. You sold it, don't buy it back. Get up, get coffee, get out of the kitchen.

"Perfect. I'm going to shower."

࿊ 44 ࿊

I waved goodbye to Harry and stepped over the threshold of Elmhurst Memorial. My plan almost blew up when Harry asked why I was wearing boots with my jeans instead of my usual loafers. 'Are you planning a hike,' he'd asked jokingly, but my guilty conscious over-reacted. I'd stammered about a loose heel. He'd offered to take them in for me. I almost confessed on the spot. At the last moment, he remembered having a pair to bring in as well but didn't want to bother digging them out. 'I'll swing by the cobbler tomorrow,' he'd promised.

I couldn't believe I'd actually managed to stay calm and out of Harry's way until we left. I'd remembered that Dad and Jan were supposed to have dinner at the Craig's so I called Don to tell him what happened. He asked me to pass on his wishes for a speedy recovery. I'd spent a lot of time puttering in the barn and inadvertently strengthening my bond with Patches and Trey.

My brother had left two hours earlier so much improved was our father. He hadn't been alone and he wasn't when I arrive. Jack and Uncle Pete were talking with him remembering old times, laughing at each other's recollections.

They were ready to leave and said their good byes. More kisses and hugs, and promises to get together. Dad sat even more upright today and the bandage on his head was smaller, only covering the area of the small hole drilled to release the build-up. I learned more about subdural hematomas in the last three days than I ever wanted to. It was easier to reach him, something else had been removed–the lead on his finger to measure oxygenation. Our hope was that he'd be going home no later than Sunday.

"Hi, Sweetheart, it's good to see you." His face still wore the pinched looked that pain leaves behind, but his color was normal.

"Ditto, dad. You look so much better. How do you feel?"

"As good as I look." He was never one to dwell on himself.

"Tell me about the court of honor. Sorry I missed it. Did Will make Tenderfoot?"

I spent thirty minutes describing the ceremony and the next fifteen discussing the differences in how he did his courts of honor.

"Dad, I met with Father Briscoe Wednesday night after Mass."

"Yeah, I heard you put him in Oak Park Hospital." Dad's eyes twinkled but the words stung a little.

I didn't take the bait. I shrugged and said, "He was old."

"Cold, Gracie, cold." He still teased.

"Dad, I don't think he did anything wrong except maybe not insist hard enough that something was wrong in the troop."

"Different times, Honey. No one bucked the system."

I nodded and we both grew quiet with our thoughts.

"Somebody named Meatball in here?" Don Craig's cheerful voice preceded him. He grinned and gave me a hug. "Couldn't stay away when I heard a fellow scout was down." He stepped toward the bed and took Dad's outstretched hand. "Phyllie sends her best wishes and her best chocolate chip cookies." Don brought his left hand from behind his back and placed the small brown paper sack on the bed table. "Fresh baked this morning."

"Thanks, Don. It's good to see you. Sorry I messed up the plan for tonight."

"No problem–rain check." He lowered himself into the chair closest to the bed and leaned forward conspiratorially. "I brought you one of these for later." The big man's whisper filled the room. He slipped a Dutch Master into my dad's hand.

I decided to ignore it and let the nurse deal with it. "Anyone want coffee to go with those?"

"Sure, Honey. Good idea." I looked at Don. "Milk for me, icy cold milk."

It took me a little longer to track down Don's milk. When I returned they were involved in a card game using cotton swabs for stakes. I sat in the other chair, content to listen to the two friends malign each other's card playing acumen, like they'd played cards just last week. I guess a good friendship is like that. I pulled my list from my tote bag and mulled over each item. We hadn't heard from Ric before we left. I wanted to call home to check if he'd called but then I'd have to risk a slip up. I did say I'd call about dinner but that could be quick. I wouldn't call from the room cause he might want to say hello to Dad and then he might ask to talk to Marty. I was exhausted from lack of sleep and excessive deception. I felt a hand on my shoulder. It was Don Craig. I sat up and looked at my watch. Four-thirty.

"Your dad says you should go home and get some sleep."

I looked at the empty bed. "Where is he?"

"Some good looking nurse came in for him about thirty minutes ago to take him for another test. If the doc sees what he likes your dad could go home tomorrow afternoon."

Beep, beep, beep. I automatically looked toward the bed but there weren't any monitors in the room anymore. Don laughed. "Oops that's me. I feel like Maxwell Smart when his shoe rang." He un-hooked a pager from his belt.

"I think you're supposed to turn those off in here."

He checked the number on the display and turned it off. "Gotta find a phone, be right back."

Great news about my dad. This would give me the opportunity to slip away without having to explain or lie to him. I nearly bolted from the chair wanting to leave before he returned.

I caught the expression on Don's face a second before he changed it when he entered the room. Odd look from such a cheery guy. Maybe he'd received bad news. "Everything okay?"

"Yes, just my wife, Phyllis checking up on me."

His words seemed stiff. Something wasn't right. What happened to *Phyllie*?

"Listen, young lady, I meant what I said. You go home and get some rest. I'll wait here for your dad."

"Thanks, Don. I didn't sleep well last night. I am beat. Thanks again for staying with him. Don't feel you have to wait for someone to show up, although I'm surprised no one has dropped by."

"No problem I brought my Walkman." He pulled the device from his coat on the back of the chair. "Ever hear of Harry Lauder?" Sweet music, it'll blow you away."

I smiled at the flower child speak from the sixties.

"Tell Dad goodbye, I mean good night," I amended quickly. Had that been a Freudian slip?

"Are you okay? You got a little pale there."

"I'm fine, just tired."

"Okay then, get some rest."

He hugged me and when he released me he whispered in a low tone, "Keep the Faith."

Keep the Faith. Oh, yeah, I was about to go undercover in some Pagan religion to set a trap for some Satan worshippers. Would the Faith keep me?

❧ 45 ❧

Marisol met me at exactly five o'clock where we'd agreed, the ruins of the Robinson homestead. I shivered as we walked near the covered well. It was close to the path–maybe John Jacob had strayed and tragically fallen in.

"Here put this on." Marisol handed me a white robe with a braided rope belt. "My people are in place at the mounds. We'd better hurry."

"I thought these ceremonies were only done at midnight. Isn't this suspicious?"

Marisol shook her head. "Let me worry about timing. I've told two people that you would be visiting with us: Mary Quigley, because she is the Priestess and Detective Thomas, because I think he's the leak. I made those calls an hour ago, enough time for one of them to spread the word but not too much time to verify much."

"How did you explain my involvement to him?"

"I told him we were after the cult and you agreed to be bait. Also told him that I would be flying alone tonight because I couldn't infiltrate new people this quickly."

"Would Mary tell Hannah? That could ruin things."

"I talked to Hannah and explained that I wasn't after Wicca faithful, only the bad guys. I told her I was pretending to bring you to smoke out the creep behind all this. She thinks, like everyone, almost everyone, that you're at the hospital. I planned an early circle call to get you back where you belong ASAP."

"You have to wait until a certain hour, right?"

The petite woman in charge of my wellbeing sighed. "We have gatherings during the day as well. We're not about skulking through the dark hours chanting mumbo jumbo. Wicca celebrates light and goodness. Oh, never mind. All you need to remember is once I guide you to the center as a means of introduction to the others you will be marked. If this creep knows anything about us he'll know you first off." She pointed to the belt around my waist. "The total white cord signifies a guest."

I looked at hers; it had thick strands of gold braided throughout the length.

"Could he see that in the dark?"

"They'll be a small fire burning by the time we arrive. Enough light so we don't trip over anything."

She chuckled. Was the joke for me or to relieve her tension?

Marisol grabbed me by the arm. "If anything happens to me at the ceremony, get to the mound south of the fire. As we face the pentagram south will be directly behind you. There is an agent behind that mound, he'll help you."

"I thought you said your people are in place. Aren't most of those robes going to be covering agents?"

"Grace, don't worry. I can't have that many new people show up. There's one agent in a robe. If anything happens she'll get to you. Hurry now, and from this point put up your hood." She raised her hood and started walking at a faster pace, her white figure glimmering in the twilight.

Marisol moved several feet ahead of me on the path. My fingers fumbled with my hood and then reached for the comfort of the thick braid swaying at my waist. The coiled material rubbed against my fingertips and I tried to calm my mind. My fingers played with the frayed end of the cord, further unraveling the strands. A rhythm played in my head, *one step, two steps, back one, two.*

Suddenly the safe, foolproof plan wasn't. In that moment I realized that she accepted my willingness to be bait for one sting in order to further her own investigation. In her mind the murder of Agent John Henry and the theft of the weapons were connected to the Satan worshippers. The danger factor just went up…and so did the hair on my neck. Marisol's robe glowed further up the path. I'd lost ground with my rhythm. I wanted to shout to her that something was wrong, but I didn't want to alert anyone and ruin the plan. I lifted my robe to run but couldn't hold enough material with my bad hand. I ran toward where I'd seen her last. I pushed back the hood to better see the path.

She must be just around the curve. Can't have gone that far. Wouldn't leave me here.

I heard a soft thud and stopped. Fear twisted my stomach and I bent over to ease the pain. *She told me what to do at the ceremony if something went wrong. What do I do here?*

One thing I knew to do was to get out of the robe that marked me in the dark. I'd stepped off the path and now realized that I'd hooked the hood on a branch. I untied the belt and shimmied out of the material, leaving it hanging like a shed skin.

Snap.

Oh God, oh God. Get me out of this. I knew I had to move away from the path. *Move, Gracie, move.* I crossed the path and took off through the woods hoping that whoever found the robe would think I went in on that side. Further into the woods toward what I hoped would be help from the agent at the fire and the one behind the mound. I strained my eyes through the dark to glimpse a fire—nothing. I stopped and squatted trying to catch my breath and get my bearings. I had no idea which way to go. I felt like slapping myself in the forehead when I realized I should have turned around and run back the way we'd come, back to clearing, Chee Chee Pin Quay's grave and the street. I could attract help easier on a busy street on a Friday night than deep in the woods. *Stupid, stupid.*

Maybe I could still get back there, if I knew where 'back there' was. I could crouch here for an indeterminate amount of time and wait for who ever stalked me to force my hand or I could plan a move.

Suddenly I spotted a faint glimmer through the woods low to the ground. The coven fire! If I could reach that I could get help for both of us. I straightened slowly trying not to attract attention. The fire seemed to be in a different direction from the one we'd started in; I'd crossed the path we'd been on. If I could spot the huge teepee style pile of branches and brush the forest preserve stacked I'd know I was near the old well; unless another teepee was in place somewhere else. It was too early for moonrise and I couldn't be sure which way I was headed. It just felt wrong.

I moved at a slow steady pace keeping the glow on my left. Marisol said the mound hiding the agent was south of the fire. I wanted to avoid the Wicca and get to the agent. If only I could tell which way was South. Someone must have added fuel; the fire flared and crackled for a moment and in that instant my heart hit my throat. The flicker revealed black robes.

Panic gripped me and I ran back the way I'd come. I ran with my right forearm up at my eye level to block branches as I crashed through the woods. My only hope was that the crackling fire and the low chanting emanating from the ground would cover my flight noise.

Chee Chee Pin Quay, Chee Chee Pin Quay. The chanting grew louder until I realized I'd been repeating it in my head. At least it wasn't out loud. Something grabbed and held my left hand. I screamed and tried to pull away. My scream rent the dark still air and I felt as though a spotlight would flick on and expose my position. The belt

I'd carried with me looped around my wrist, tangled in the under-brush. I wanted to laugh in relief but I'd already been too vocal for my own good. I slipped the cord over my hand and let it drop resist-ing the urge to retrieve it as I felt the frayed ends slide across my fin-gertips.

I heard someone moving toward me from the direction I'd been headed. *Cripes! Now which way do I run? Move, Gracie, move. Don't push me, I'm thinking.*

If I could spot the dark outline of the brush teepee I'd know I was near the well. Marisol and I passed it tonight on our way into the woods. I could find my way to the street from there. I turned slowly in my crouched position straining into the dark trying to discern a darker outline. *What if there's more than one teepee? Don't start.*

Halfway through my scan I saw what could be the teepee; the pattern of dark sky seemed unnaturally interrupted. Best shot under the circumstances. I moved slowly toward the dark form trying to feel my next step before I put my weight down. The pile of wood became clear and I hurried toward it. The base of wood looked to be about twelve feet in diameter. I found a nook about three feet high where the vertical branches were further apart. I scrunched in not letting my mind wonder what other critters might be in the woodpile. A different smell lingered on the wood around me. I felt dwarfed by the height of the teepee, but I also felt safe. I heard two sounds both of them prac-tically on top of me that shattered my calm, a moan and a curse.

"Dammit, this isn't no path, it's an obstacle course."

"'Bout time you got here. This place is crawlin' with freaks. Gotch yer witches down by the mounds and Satan's bad boys chantin' by the dump. Getting so it ain't safe to be in the woods." Harsh laugh-ter that slid into a deep loose cough followed his observation.

"Shut up, you crazy bastard. Why'd you want to meet here? I called you to warn you to stay out of the woods tonight. What the hell are you dressed up for?"

I knew that voice. Detective Thomas stood somewhere near the woodpile, probably on the far side, with another man who sounded deranged. We'd been right in our suspicion of him. A small comfort was that Mary wasn't involved. Was the other man Bantonini? Would he refer to his cult as 'Satan's bad boys'? I hadn't heard the older Ban-tonini speak enough to know for sure. But who else could it be?

"Never mind that. I called you out here to take care of loose ends. I got the one we wanted. The other ran off into the night proba-bly knocked herself silly on a tree limb by now. No matter; maybe the boys will find her."

His voice chilled my blood. I tucked further into my haven.

He must have thought I was Marisol.

"The one we wanted? Are you crazy, Bigs? She's a federal agent. What the hell were you thinking?"

Marisol was the target. At least for them.

"She's gettin' too close, askin' questions about these freaks out here, but I know she'd been sniffing around. Now with this Henry girl turning up dead out here, it's too close."

A soft moan broke the silence.

"What was that? You crazy bastard, what'd you do to her."

"Calm down, you was always a jumpy sort. I got her tied up in the woodpile for safe keeping 'til we sort out our next step."

"Our next step is to get the hell out of here. Leave her. Someone will find her or she'll work herself free. She has one agent undercover in the coven thing tonight who'll come looking for her. Let's go."

"I called our third compadre; was gonna wait for him to get here. He wasn't too far away, visiting a friend he said, don't know as I believe him, but I told him to get here."

"He's been out of it for years, why call him?"

"Because we've all blood on our hands and I thought we should end it together. Technically I still outrank you and I call the shots."

"What happened before was forty years ago. We didn't mean to kill him. He tripped and hit his head. I'm not killing anyone for you."

The other voice changed its tonal pattern and mocked Detective Thomas, "We didn't mean to kill him, he tripped." You two make me sick. Of course we meant to kill him. Did ya want to go to jail or worse, hang fer treason? Your brother and dad died fighting fer Ireland. I thought their blood ran through your veins." His voice dissolved into a heavy cough and he spit before he spoke. "He's late, maybe he's not coming. Let's get on with it."

"Get on with what?"

Who were they waiting for and which way would he come from? Would he see me in my cubbyhole? *Visiting a friend. Called him earlier.* My heart froze when the words replayed in my head. It must be Don Craig. *Can't be, he's too nice. He talks about Phyllie. Capone was a hero in the neighborhood. Good guy to his mom and family.* My mind couldn't separate the facts from my fears.

"For God's sake, just leave her. She has nothing on us. She doesn't know who you are. I'm leaving." I heard boots scuff off away from my side. I stopped straining to hear their words and relaxed a little waiting for the one who wasn't Thomas to leave. I shifted slightly and the air current pushed the acrid scent across my face. *Gas!*

"Don't get yer panties in a bunch. I'm coming." I smelled the sulfur strike and heard the tiny *whoosh* dry tinder makes when it catches.

"You son of a bitch. You'll kill her."

"Tommy you was always a choir boy. Let's go."

"No. You can't leave her to burn to death."

"They'll be blaming it on that crazy cult, setting fires to their dark lord. Never find the ropes."

The louder *whoosh,* when the fuel wood catches, sounded deafening in my ears. The dry branches crackled alive with fire as the flames raced from one juicy morsel to the next. The heat moved toward me and I knew I'd have to get out and take my chances with the nutcase. I could barely hear Thomas shouting.

"Jesus, she'll burn. Help me get her out."

They must have moved closer to my side. "You should join her then." The low calm voice reached me in spite of the crackling and spitting of the fire. No emotion. I heard a sharp crack and then crash against the wood. Loose thin branches tumbled onto my head. With all the crackling I couldn't tell if he'd shot him or struck him. I just knew Detective Thomas wouldn't be helping Marisol or himself.

I couldn't tell if the other man left but I couldn't stay inside this inferno. My lungs were filling with smoke and the heat surged toward my back. I crouched walked out of my hiding place and sucked in gulps of fresher air. The light breeze pushed the fire away from me but possibly toward Marisol. I couldn't risk calling for her; I wouldn't hear a moan anyway. I'd have to crawl along the perimeter and look for her. The fire lit up the night. Seeing was not the problem; the heat and smoke made breathing almost impossible. I hadn't crawled more that a quarter of the way around when I spotted the white material. Her body was tucked into another natural cavity. I grabbed the robe and pulled. Some of the branches above her caved in and covered her. I scrambled to pull those out careful not to collapse more of the pile. She was lashed to one of the large branches that traveled across the base. I crawled in the hole on top of her. Her hands were tied in front of her and I quickly broke the back of the knot and untied her. She was conscious now and reached for me to pull herself up. The startled look on her face when she couldn't move changed to fear, as she must have realized her situation. The lashing held her under her chest. I couldn't get under her to the knot. I pulled the tape from her mouth so she could breathe better.

"I've got to get under you to work the knot. I'm going to push some of this brush away from you and see if I can pull you out." I pulled her hood down over her face to give her some protection against the falling debris. She crossed her forearms over her face.

The smoke tore at my eyes and lungs; I could only imagine how she felt under the heavy hood. I pushed several tangled branches over to the burning side of the teepee. Thank God he hadn't been thorough and lit around the base.

I couldn't budge her and crawled back in gasping for air. She lowered her arms and pushed back the hood. Her face was bright red and she drew what air was available through her mouth.

"I can't move it. I'm going to try to drag one end toward me. Can you push in the other direction with your feet?

I felt the sharp pinch on my shoulder. A burning twig landed onto my left shoulder and I couldn't reach it with my cast. The twig was caught on my jacket and burning through to my skin. I feared my hair would be next. Marisol pulled me down on top of her and patted at the burning material, mercifully extinguishing it before it caught my thick hair. I saw her eyes flare with pain. I scrambled off of her. Another twig ignited her robe. I flipped it off the material and patted it out. I half-stood and pushed more brush away from her. I knew I didn't have much time before my instinct for self-preservation would keep me from climbing in again. Pushing the debris away gave her more room but it created a back draft. The fire quickly filled the hole I'd made greedily sucking the fresh oxygen. My cast flamed and I screamed falling backwards on to the ground. I rolled trapping the cast between my body and the damp dirt.

I lurched to my knees, ready to get back to Marisol when I saw a figure running toward us. I couldn't see clearly. Was this salvation or the third man?

He ran toward me, a big man, with gadgets on his belt. Where could I run? I couldn't leave Marisol. She screamed and I turned my back on the man who would probably push me into the inferno and finish the job started by his cohort.

Marisol's arms flailed at the embers she couldn't reach on her legs. I flipped the robe and sent the bits of flame back into the pile. I felt his heavy hand on my shoulder and prepared to push back. Instead he pushed me behind him and knelt over Marisol. His hand rose over her body and I saw the glint of steel in the firelight.

"No!" I screamed and flung myself at his arm. I aimed my cast at his head but he shook off my arm and pushed me back. I hit the ground and felt the air rush out of my lungs. I lay there and watched helplessly while his arm raised and lowered slashing at Marisol. I knew I'd be next and tried to roll, crawl away. My heart sobbed for Marisol. I couldn't save her. I didn't know if I could save myself.

A new sound reached my ears. The low heartbeat throb of tom-toms. *Am I dying? Maybe. Keep moving, die at his grave.* I kept crawling drawn by the sound. Suddenly over the slow beat of the drums I heard sirens and doors slamming. I leaned up against the high stone. Voices shouting directions, lights glaring through the trees brought the woods alive with rescue...for me.

"She's here, behind the rock." A loud voice shouted and roused me. I blinked in the light from his flashlight. "Mrs. Marsden. I'm Officer Jackson, Sheriff's police. Are you okay? Are you injured?"

I stared up into the light letting it pop patterns across my vision. He lowered the beam and knelt on one knee next to me. He stood and shouted, "She's in shock and burned. We need another ambulance."

Harry and Ric arrived before the ambulance. They held me under each arm and gently lifted me from the wet ground. It started raining at some point and the water felt like manna to my skin. I closed my eyes and floated between them.

My eyes stayed closed but I knew only Harry rode in the ambulance with me. I felt the paramedic working on me, checking my signs. He seemed satisfied, adjusted the oxygen mask and backed away to let Harry fill the space near my head.

He picked up my left hand, careful to avoid the saline soaked cool pack wrapped around it. Similar packs covered other burned patches of skin. I opened my eyes and looked into Harry's eyes brimmed with tears as he stared down at my face. I felt the gauze patch on my left cheek and briefly wondered what I'd look like after this. Then I remembered Marisol and swallowed more tears. At least I was alive. *Craig! Did they catch him? Did they find Thomas?* I wanted to tell him but my arms felt like lead and I couldn't lift my hand to move the mask. I squirmed and tried to push the mask off by moving my mouth around.

"*Ssh*, Gracie. I'm here. Don't try to talk." He leaned forward and brushed his lips against my forehead. "You're going to be fine. Ssh, rest. Rest, darling. I won't leave you."

The effort I made to dislodge the mask was too much. I closed my eyes and let Harry's low voice and the hum of the pavement under the wheels lull me to sleep.

I woke up to the smell of clean cotton sheets with a touch of *'oh, oh,'* antiseptic. I noticed a new cast, plain white and I felt clean like I'd been bathed and my hair shampooed. I recognized that I was in the hospital, but I couldn't pin down why and then I remembered in a rolling pattern like clouds moving fast across the sky. I knew I must be safe; I remembered Harry in the ambulance. Where was he? No one was in the room. Well, no visitors. I was in a semi-private hospital room. The curtain between the beds blocked my view of my roommate. I thought I heard movement behind the curtain. I was about to call out when I saw a woman in the doorway. Under five-foot tall, dark hair, big dark brown eyes; she could have been one of mine, but I'd never seen her before. She wore a deep purple wool coat over black slacks. A red scarf dangled from the open coat collar. She pulled off a red wool beret and clutched it in her hands. She looked behind 'curtain number one' and bolted behind the material.

"*Mijà*." One strangled word and then a burst of tears.

I felt awkward eavesdropping on their private moment. Then my gang came through the door and I'd be lucky to hear my own thoughts let alone anyone else's conversation.

Harry entered first, closely followed by my dad, brothers, Mike and Marty, Carolyn, and last through the door, Karen. Hugs and kisses, and well wishes filled the room. I hoped my visitors weren't disturbing my roommate's teary guest, but then I was so happy to see them I shrugged off the concern.

We'd barely settled in when a nurse rushed into the room. "You can't all be in here. Only four visitors at a time. You've six people."

A man's voice from the other side of the curtain surprised me. "We'll take the other two." The curtain slid back and my surprise turned to shock. Black Bart smiled across the room at us. "I don't think my partner will mind."

Marisol. She was alive.

I blinked and felt my jaw drop. Their laughter was good-natured. "I saw, I thought…" The horror of what I'd thought filled my head. I felt the itch at the back of my throat and burst into tears.

Harry looked stricken with guilt when he hurried to my side. "Stupid of us. Grace, she's okay."

I buried my head in his chest embarrassed by my outburst but unable to stop. I sobbed into his shirt until I heard her voice.

"Grace, please. I'm fine."

The woman who'd had her own bout of tears approached my bed. She gently touched my cheek. "Thank you for saving my Mari. She is my life." Her eyes filled with tears, and she stepped back to her daughter's side.

I looked at my roommate. She did look fine. Considering how I'd last seen her, she looked great. I glanced at Black Bart and he nodded. Marisol saw the look. "Grace, this is my partner, Bart Guilfoyle."

"He's an agent, one of the good guys?"

Laughter bubbled from Marisol's lips. "Yeah, one of the good guys."

The nurse made her presence known. Okay I went along with the gag against my better judgment but now I'm in charge. Only two visitors per patient. She pointed her finger around the room. "Dad, Mom, husband, partner stays, the rest of you wait outside and take turns."

I smiled at her brusque manner, knowing her choices would have been ours too. My brother, Mike, led the troops out and called back over his shoulder. "We'll be back to visit."

The room quieted and my father introduced himself. "I'm Mike Morelli, Grace's father. This is her husband, Harry Marsden."

Guilfoyle took his lead. "This is Marisol's mother, Diana Nunez."

My father took her hands in his. "We are lucky today that our daughters were spared."

She nodded and looked at Marisol.

"Apparently everyone except me and Mrs. Nunez know about this surprise."

"It was stupid of us but we got the idea when you both ended up in the same hospital and same room. Sorry, totally asinine. We didn't realize you thought she'd been killed."

"Okay, okay it was stupid. But please tell me how you're not dead when I saw Don Craig stabbing you."

Diana Nunez's eyes widened and Marisol hurried to assure her she hadn't been stabbed. "My mother was at a Red Hat Society convention when Bart tracked her down and told her I'd been hurt. I didn't want him to call and spoil her weekend but he knew he'd have hell to pay and lose his tamale ration if he didn't." She spoke directly to her mom. "Bart said you couldn't get a flight out until this afternoon. How'd you get here so fast?"

"I traded my ticket with a woman waiting at the terminal for the flight I wanted. I explained my situation and got her ticket."

"That was decent of her to wait for your flight," Dad said.

Diana turned toward my father. "*Hmmph*. Forced me to throw in my Red Hat Miss Piggy watch to clinch the deal." Her face broke into a grin for the first time and we laughed at her bargaining chip.

"Back to Don Craig. The other guy said he'd called the third man and that he was in the area visiting a friend. Dad, while you were down for tests, he got beeped. And he looked at me kind of weird after he made that call."

"Honey, he did get a page to call home. His wife wanted to tell him that another friend had been admitted to Good Sam the night before and maybe he'd want to stop and visit."

"Why'd he look at me that way?"

"Grace, he said you gave him a strange look when he returned. Anyway, he was still there when Harry called wanting to know if you and Marty had left yet."

I'd forgotten to call and make my excuse.

"I called to tell you I'd meet you and Marty. Lily forgot about some gala multi-chamber function she promised to attend at the Chaney Mansion. She said she'd drive out afterwards."

Both men stared at me with a 'if we weren't so happy to see you alive we'd strangle you' look.

"Sorry. I knew you wouldn't let me risk it but it wasn't supposed to have any risk." I stared at Marisol. Her cheeks blushed.

"You weren't at risk. I used you as bait, but I ended up being the bait for another predator."

If Harry and Dad's hard stares were any indication they were not absolving Marisol for letting me involve myself in her sting.

"Marisol and I were in radio contact and when I couldn't raise her I knew something was wrong. When I saw the fire in the distance I called for back up and told the other agent to detain all the ladies at the circle. While I was picking my way through the woods to find her I heard the low chanting and figured the cult was out up to no good. I called and requested that the Forest Preserve police pick them up and hold them until I knew about Marisol. By the time I got there Craig had pulled her away from the fire. He kept yelling about finding you, yelling that you'd tried to pull him away from the fire and then you disappeared. God, he was a royal pain in the ass."

"I wasn't trying to save him. I thought he was stabbing Marisol."

"Good thing you got off his back. He cut as much of the rope as he could and then muscled me out of there." Marisol shivered. "Glad he won that tug of war."

"Mrs. Marsden, I'm not just here visiting Marisol. I've been waiting for you to answer questions about Thomas' accomplice."

"Won't he tell you? He fought with him about leaving Marisol to die. He wouldn't do it."

Their silence confirmed what I suspected at the fire.

"They found his remains after the fire burned out. It was apparent from his skull that he'd been shot in the head. Think, Mrs. Marsden did he use a name? And what about the third man he mentioned."

I thought about what I'd heard. I couldn't remember the events that clearly. "I'm sorry, I can't remember everything." I looked at Harry. "What's wrong with me?"

"Nothing. Absolutely nothing. You've suffered a shock and inhaled more smoke than you should have. You'll be right as rain in a few days. Doctor said this is common and not to worry."

I felt better knowing the fog wasn't permanent. "I'm thrilled that you're fine, Marisol, but why is it you're in better shape than me. I mean you were the one trapped in the fire."

"That I was and I'll never forget what you did for me. You kept covering my face, which made it damn hot but prevented a lot of smoke from getting into my lungs. Also, I was closer to the ground. You kept moving higher on the pile to push it away from me. And finally, you blocked a lot of the sparks and cinders with your body. I can never repay you. I thought I…" She stopped talking and clamped her lips together.

Diana Nunez asked the question I'd been thinking. "How did that man, Mr. Craig know where to find you?"

Dad answered. "When Harry called and we determined you'd snookered us, Harry remarked that you were wearing hiking boots. It didn't take us long to figure out where you might be. Don heard what was happening and said he'd go look for you since he knew the area. I told him to head in from the marker. He took off like a bat outta hell."

"Is he okay?"

"He sucked in a lot of smoke himself and cut up his hand pretty bad. He wedged it under the ropes to protect her body. Might have some nerve damage. One hell of a guy." Bart's somber assessment saddened me. He continued on a brighter note. "I'm recommending that they present him with a Certificate of Service to the bureau."

"Is he here?"

"No, honey. They took him over to Loyola for his hand. I'm headed there in a few minutes."

"Dad, don't tell him what I thought. He saved my life too. I don't know if I could have let her…go like that. He pulled me out of there."

Dad's face tensed and I knew he struggled with emotion. "I know. I know."

I squeezed his hand and smooched him loud to make him smile.

"I'll send Marty in to say good-bye. I need him. He's my driver and my golf pro." He winked at my surprise.

"Dad you don't golf."

"Not yet. Jeannette's invited me to play golf tomorrow, and Marty's going to show me a few pointers at the range this afternoon and loan me his clubs." He smiled and strolled out of the room.

Well if he was going to learn, Marty was the son to teach him. He spent more time on the golf course with his customers than he did in their offices. I suspected more deals were made on the 19th hole than made anywhere else.

"So your father is seeing someone?"

"Mom!"

"For your Aunt Rose."

Marisol and I both laughed.

"Mrs. Marsden if you think of anything else, please contact me. Your husband has my number. I'd best get back to the ranch, we're shooting another commercial."

"Wait a minute."

"Did you remember something?"

"No, I want to know which is your real job, the dealership or the FBI."

He waited before answering and looked at Marisol. "Technically, I'm retired from the bureau, but it's not always easy to say no when Uncle Sam dials your number." He paused and glanced at Harry. "And we don't always say no when we see a way to catch the bad guys."

"Why didn't you know that one boy who works for you was one of the bad guys?"

"I know about Crockett's juvie record. Most of the kids I grew up with had one. I had someone in my life who gave a damn; kept me out of jail or worse. I try to help the ones that are poised to slip through the cracks. Some make it, this one didn't. You know he confessed about the attack on you?"

I nodded.

"He wasn't totally forthcoming. Mr. Big, who was questioned, didn't tell him and Quigley to go after you. Davy thought they'd get higher up on the pecking order if they brought you to him. They knew he obsessed over you."

This seemed even scarier that these two boys would try to kidnap me to please their mentor.

"Bantonini is denying he sent them after you, denying he was in the parking lot the night of your attack and denying that he met with Thomas in the woods last night."

Last night. It was only last night?

I shivered and closed my eyes. Harry cut off Guilfoyle's words. "That's enough." The curtain slid on metal bands, *click, click, click.*

I felt a kiss on the cheek. Not Harry's lips. "See you later, gotta teach an old dog new tricks." I smiled but kept my eyes close. I heard Marty whisper to Harry. "If she's in any pain when she wakes up give her two of these. You'd think these nurses were paying for the meds the way they hoard them."

I heard the whispers of Marisol and Diana, finally alone and able to tell each other all the things you don't think of unless there's a close call. Harry asked Marty to tell everyone that I was asleep. I knew he'd stay until they kicked him out. Or so I thought.

"Grace, I'm going to step out and check with your doctor and make a phone call. Be back in a jiff."

I felt a jolt of panic. The feeling passed quickly as I remembered Marisol and her mother sat only feet away from me. I took a quick inventory of my side of the room to pass the time and occupy my mind. Two chairs, one bed table loaded with tissue, water, orange juice, yellow daffodils in a bright blue vase, newspaper, and one Dunkin' Donuts coffee. I thought I'd seen one in Mike's hand. I didn't know if he meant it for me or if he forgot it in the mass exodus. I scooted up in bed and pulled the tip of the table toward me. It wouldn't move. The wheels weren't turned right to let it roll properly. I leaned forward and grabbed the table then pushed and pulled trying to get the wheels aligned. I wiggled the table harder and succeeded in knocking the vase over into the coffee sending both to floor in a blend of Daffs, water, and coffee dregs.

Dregs, something about that. Not dregs, bigs. Bigs, Thomas called him Bigs. Diana ran around the end of the curtain when she heard the crash and was cleaning up the mess when Harry returned. The nurse came in right behind him.

I sat up in bed and reached for Harry. My stretch nearly pulled out the I.V. "Harry you have to–" The nurse stepped between us. "Mrs. Marsden, you have to rest. Lie back. Let me check your line." She matched her actions to her words and gently pushed me back against the pillow, and then lowered the bed. She took a syringe from her pocket and injected the liquid into the I.V. line.

"I have to talk to Harry."

"I'm here, darling. Please relax. I'll sit here and we'll talk. Now what is it? What did you want to tell me?"

"The coffee spilled…and I saw the, the…" My lips slowed and I couldn't go any further.

Harry leaned forward and kissed my cheek. "Poor thing, you're all done in. We'll talk in the morning. Sweet dreams, I love you."

They released both of us on Sunday. Diana lived in Joliet and she took her daughter home with her for safekeeping and recuperation. Marisol and I planned to have lunch next week.

Jan Pauli cleaned on Saturday and the house looked wonderful. I loved the carpet stripes from a thorough vacuuming and the way the house smelled from the wood polish. I wondered if that was 'housecleaning 101'–leave marks and use extra polish for scent.

The doctor gave me no restrictions except to not use my cast as a club, battering ram, or hot pad. My wrist broke inside the cast. I missed my customized purple cast with all the signatures. Marty called to cheer me up with a blow-by-blow description of Dad at the driving range. "There's a reason why you don't see Italian golfers on the PGA tour," he'd said. "Great at baseball, lousy at golf."

I laughed so much my ribs ached. Harry asked me for a recap after I hung up and of course the story grew a centimeter or so. By Christmas the tale would be a classic. Harry told me that Ric was coming over to go over all the odds and ends and try to connect them.

I hadn't seen April and Cash since Friday morning. They whinnied happily when they heard me at the door. "Good morning my beauties. Good girl, good boy." I stood between the two stalls and waited for their noses to touch my outstretched palms. The cast seemed to spook Cash, guess he forgot I had one. He relaxed when my fingers tickled his velvet nose. Harry went out to take care of them this morning before he came to hospital to retrieve me. "Tomorrow will be a normal day. I'll be out early with oodles of treats for my beautiful horsies." My silly tone comforted me more than it did them. "Tomorrow I will clear out that mess and put things up." I waved toward the tangle of leather and rope. They snorted and nodded.

Ric sat at the kitchen table with Harry. He stood when I walked in and then awkwardly sat down. I felt that he might have wanted to hug me and thought better of it. "You look good, better than you looked hunkered down behind that rock."

That wasn't saying much from all accounts that I'd heard. I didn't remember finding my way to the Indian's grave. The burn on my face might require cosmetic surgery, the one on my shoulder should heal nicely and my hair, trimmed by Karen, skimmed my jawbone.

"Thanks. I feel good."

"Darling we were about to put our chips on the table and leave our cards where they fall."

Ric and I both burst into laughter and I suspected this was an intentional malapropism on Harry's part. His innocent smile and query of 'What? What?' confirmed it.

Each opened a folder in front of them. "I'm going to get the bracelet I found." While I was upstairs I stopped in the spare room and picked up my writing box, and brought it down.

I sat next to Harry and put the box on the table. "Pens, paper, markers. Thought you might need them."

Ric opened the top and the trays moved forward on metal hinges. "Are we coloring?" He lifted a package of colored markers. "*Hmm*. Scented."

Harry propped up a large pad against the window. "Keep those out. Let's separate what we've got by color and see who turns up with multi colors." Ric lowered the box to the floor and we began to put our 'chips' on the table.

"We know that Bantonini is the cult leader. One of the boys they detained Friday night implicated him. No one could say for sure when Bantonini arrived at the dumpsite, but they all agree it was after they started the fire. That could have given him time to meet with Thomas and then don his robe for show time."

"Wait. Thomas said something like that." I scrunched up my eyes and tucked my lower lip under my top teeth. I opened my eyes. "He asked him, 'what are you dressed up for?'"

"Could be he was already in his robe."

I nodded my head but Harry hesitated. "Or in a uniform."

A thought came into my mind. "Or in a suit."

The empty pad filled with colors and timelines under Harry's hand. We took a break for refills. I fiddled with the coffee maker while Harry ran fresh water into his kettle.

I studied the pad. "Looks like everyone we put up has two colors. Either they're all connected or this is a big coincidence."

"You mean a conspiracy?"

I shrugged. "I don't know but whoever was with Thomas talked about a third man. I thought it was Don Craig."

"I think we can assume the third man is someone on the juvie list." Harry pulled the list from his folder and placed it on the table. "We're looking for three compadres–"

"Why did you use that word, compadre?"

"I don't know. Must have heard it recently, stuck in my mind."

"Where'd you hear it? From whom?" My voice rose in a panic.

"Grace, easy. From your dad I think. Yes. In the waiting room yesterday he said something about wanting to get his hands on Thomas's compadre, the other man."

Ric stared at me. "What is it, Grace?"

How could I tell them Dad used the same word? Thomas said once he didn't believe in coincidence. This was my father. I knew he couldn't be the third man.

"Grace?"

I shook my head. "Trying to remember" I closed my eyes in a show of gathering my thoughts to give my eye color time to fade.

Harry cleared his throat and continued. "We can eliminate Guilfoyle, Morelli, Santori, and Whalen."

"I understand the first two, why Santori and Whalen?"

"I did a bit of research on this list. Santori died two years ago and Whalen has lived out of the country for over twenty years."

"No chance he was in the country this weekend?"

"No activity on his passport for the last ten years."

"Okay so the fact that these four men couldn't have been nearby, visiting a friend,' clears them. I'd vote for Bantonini, Bigelow, and Quigley."

Harry looked at his list. "Looks good but I'm waiting for information on the other two, Randolph and Tinucci."

"Wait a sec. I thought that name looked familiar." Ric pulled some sheets out from his folder. "Here it is. The family who owned the cat? Randolph. They lived on the same block as the Henrys."

"Is everyone from that generation a suspect? I certainly don't believe in coincidence."

"We're back to conspiracy."

The phone rang. Harry picked it up.

"Hello."

"She's home, yes. She's resting now, asleep actually. I think tomorrow would be better."

"No, hasn't remembered much. Bits and pieces."

"I'll tell her."

"That was Guilfoyle. He wanted to come out and talk with you. He'll call tomorrow see if you're up for his visit."

"I thought he re-retired."

"Probably wants to see this through to the end. You get that way if someone tries taking out your partner."

"We have to track down 'Randolph, Randolph'." Harry shook his head. "Why do people do that to their children?"

Names and initials swirled in my head. B.I.G. e.b. Bigs. My chin snapped up.

"What?"

"In the hospital, I didn't tell you. I was tired, I forgot."

"Relax. Tell me now." Harry touched my arm to calm me.

"When the coffee spilled I remembered thinking nothing but *dregs* and that reminded me that Thomas called the man *bigs*. I can't believe I forgot to tell you."

"It's okay. No harm done. Are you certain?"

"Positive, not Mr. Big it was just *bigs* like you say Hanns."

"And something else. When the other man mocked Thomas his voice changed. He used a high pitch voice but that's not it. It's like he spoke with a sort of accent but then didn't and then used it again."

"You never mentioned an accent? What kind?"

I shook my head. "I don't know. It sounded like an accent, only on certain words like he was pretending. He said *ya* and *yer* and *ta* in place of *you* and *your* and *to*. Things like that."

"Did it sound Irish or uneducated?" Ric smiled and explained. "Perfect grammar and pronunciation was a big bugaboo in my house as a kid. My Irish grandparents, the Connors, insisted that Karen and I speak clearly and correctly to amend the old stigma that the Irish as a whole couldn't speak properly."

"I don't think he was uneducated."

"We're looking for a guy with a nickname of *bigs* and a sketchy Irish accent." Harry looked at the list of names and pointed to one. "And the winner is…the honorable Evan Bigelow."

He pointed to the column next to the names, the one that Dad filled in with their nicknames.

Bantonini, Edward	*Moochie*
Bigelow, Evan	*Bigs*
Guilfoyle, Bartholomew	*Black Bart*
Morelli, Michael	*Meatball*
Quigley, Thomas P.	*Q-tip*
Randolph, Randolph	*Railroad*
Santori, Louis	*St. Louie*
Tinucci, Anthony	*Tin Man*
Whalen, John	*Whale*

"So, we go to the police and tell them based on what I heard and this list we think the mayor of Forest Park is a gun running killer?"

Harry and Ric both smiled at my oversimplification.

"Not exactly. We tell no one and we quietly dig into 'hizzoner's' past and we keep an eye on him. I know a couple of guys we can trust to help us keep tabs on him."

"Is one of those guys, Peterson?" Harry referred to the Sergeant who worked for Pine Marsh Security Police and who joined Ric in a private venture when Ric was released from active duty.

"Yep. He's one of them. Can we count on Walter for some help?"

"Yep," Harry mimicked.

"I don't suppose I can help?"

"Nope," both responded in kind.

"Are we going to tell Marisol?"

Ric shook his head. Harry didn't move. He spoke first. "I don't know, Kramer. We should have some official contact. Always good to let someone know your plan."

I knew Harry wished a million times that someone in his previous organization had known the plan when he and another 'specialist' were kidnapped and incarcerated in a South American prison. It was only through the grace of God and Ric's help that he escaped.

"Okay, but only her. I'm confident she didn't fake her near incineration. We can trust her."

"What about Guilfoyle, he's calling me tomorrow?"

"Gracie, keep your fog intact a little longer. Don't mention the accent or the nickname. I don't like this 'retired, not retired' status. In my experience you're either in or you're out and once you cross that threshold the entire dynamics of your access to people and information changes drastically."

"Maybe you can ask Marisol during your lunch how he came to be involved, who made first contact?" Ric suggested.

"In the meantime, let's track down Randolph and Tinucci."

"What about the button? We know Bantonini lost that button. Are you forgetting about Janet? We saw the button missing from his back pocket. Harry took a picture of it for proof. Shouldn't we tell the Sheriff's police about that? Now that Detective Thomas is dead maybe someone under fifty will take over, someone not old enough to have been involved with these people." I pointed to the list.

"Unless they're the son or nephew protecting their family."

"Or a mother or daughter or sister."

"Oh cripes. I can't think straight." I leaned my head back on my shoulders and stretched my arms out on the table. Harry took the cue and started rubbing my shoulders. I felt a slight movement on my cast and realized Ric was doodling with the colored markers.

What would someone think if they walked in now? The only two men I've ever loved ministering to me at the same time. You're a lucky duck, Gracie girl. I know.

I leaned my head against Harry's stomach and let him knead the tension from my body. He worked around my burned shoulder. I let my chin droop to my chest while he massaged my neck. Harry kissed the nape of my neck.

"What you need is to get into bed and get some sleep."

I wanted to argue but my eyes and mouth were happy to stay closed. It was too much effort to open either. I heard Ric's voice. "She looks like she's out."

Harry pulled the chair back and gently pulled me up. "C'mon, darling, one foot at a time." I let him guide me through the house to the stairs, up the stairs to the bedroom. "Just kick off your shoes, there's my girl and slip under the comforter. I'll be back to check on you in a jiff; going to tie up some loose ends with Kramer than send him packing." He leaned and kissed my forehead, then straightened and tucked my short hair behind my ears to move it off the bandage.

I opened my eyes in the darkened room and drew comfort from familiar surroundings. My shoulder pinched and I shifted on to my right side. I noticed the picture Ric doodled, an angel with dark hair wearing a purple robe and yellow wings. In the fading light the robe looked black.

ᔑ 47 ᔐ

My conversation with Bart Guilfoyle stayed brief and, I suspected, disappointing for him. He asked the same questions different ways until I finally admitted that things were starting to come back, impressions, snatches of conversation and that if I remembered anything solid I would call him. He'd seemed satisfied. I held his gaze while I lied through my teeth, confidant that he didn't know about my eyes, which I'm sure gleamed purple through our entire conversation.

Wednesday morning, I took the opportunity to get my hair trimmed and now the ends barely brushed my jaw line. She'd cut the back shorter than the sides to blend into the clump of hair that almost burned to my scalp. I looked like a little Dutch girl. Harry tried to cheer me up but I felt like a pudgy little kid with a bad haircut. He'd called it sleek and chic. Finally, he'd stopped and hugged me. I felt his shoulders jerk before he spoke, 'we could always go hat shopping'. He burst into laughter and I couldn't help but join in.

Sitting across from Marisol, I placed my order. We'd decided to eat at Panera on Route 59. Walter sat a discreet distance away.

"Cute hat."

"Thanks." I felt for my lost hair. "I feel naked without my hair."

Marisol smiled. "I felt the same when I went from middle of my back hair to this." She smoothed the short fringes of her hair with her fingers. "Somehow I didn't think the bureau would take a pony-tailed agent seriously. Kept assigning me to high school undercover. Even got asked to prom."

Our food came and we both knew our next conversation would be serious. I explained the brainstorming we'd done on Sunday while she took notes. Since then Ric had found Tinucci. He lived in Seattle, but visited town since Thanksgiving, spending time with relatives. We'd found two Randolphs; cousins who'd been raised down the street from the Henrys. They admitted being friends with Janet. They'd buried their cat in one of the crates from the garage. The other Randolph on the list lived in DeKalb, but stopped by last week on his way to visit an old priest who was ill. As Ric had been about ready to hang up, Randolph asked, "Did they find the other crate too?"

That was Monday and, as of yet, the search for the other crate resulted in nothing except a collection of junk. Ric asked another Boy Scout troop, Dick Tressalt's Troop 16 to bring his scouts out to provide camouflage for the young looking 'parents' with curly wires extending from their ears down their shirt collars who searched along side the scouts. They'd stopped the search and pulled the boys out of the woods well before dark. They picked it up again today but used only the troop trailer and the scoutmaster for cover. The schools, out for a two-day teachers' institute, were in session and the boys were back in school.

I told Marisol what I knew then asked, "How did you get hooked up with Agent Guilfoyle? Had you worked with him before?"

"Never met him. He got wind of the investigation after the crate turned up and offered his services. He knew the area and the people, great cover so the brass brought him in."

"The way he acted, you know 'my partner won't mind' and the comment about his tamale ration, I thought you'd known him awhile."

She shook her head and laughed. "That surprised me, my comment, I mean. I had told him about my mom's tamales and promised him some for Christmas. I guess I was feeling grateful for his help.

As for his background, I checked his file and he was never a field agent per se. I mean he worked in the local office as a desk jockey. He came on board with the Bureau right after college in the late fifties, actually ran the motor pool. Took an early out with partial pension and opened up his dealerships. I think he still has contracts to supply vehicles for this location. The debacle in the woods was his first field assignment. Not that it was his fault."

Marisol's statement hung in the air. "You sound unsure."

She laughed. "Now who's psychic? It's nothing, his inexperience, age maybe. I mean, if I'd been him, the minute an agent wasn't where they said they'd be when they said, I'd been out there in a heartbeat."

Marisol shrugged and sipped at her iced tea. "Amateur. Probably couldn't run in the robe."

"Guilfoyle was pretending to be a Wicca?"

Marisol giggled. "That would be one big-ass Wicca." She burst into laughter. She hurried to explain. "He's too big to be a believable woman. We hid him behind the mounds but he was in a black robe to blend better with the ground and to provide a reason for him to be there if he'd been discovered by one of the Sisters; he could have claimed he was spying on us."

I did a one-eighty and asked, "Are you psychic or is that part of your cover?"

Her smile flashed across her face but her eyes stayed serious. "I am Wicca. The FBI doesn't care about your religion. I am psychic to a thirty-two percent accuracy model. That means that sixty-eight percent of the time I am inaccurate or incomplete in my evaluation."

We chatted easily knowing that our time together was winding down. "I'm scheduled for a final de-briefing this afternoon. I'm going to stop and say goodbye to Bart on my way in and tomorrow I leave for some R&R. My cover has been compromised so I get a vacation and reassigned. Another agent will pick up John Henry's case."

Marisol grabbed for the check. "Expense report." She waved her credit card. We hugged at the table. I'd probably never see her again. "With that percentage in mind, I want you to know that I see you with a little boy in your life."

I don't know if she was waiting for me to ask questions. I didn't want to tell her that the sixty-eight percent won out; Will was in my life already. I smiled and nodded.

"Take care of yourself, Grace."

"Keep the Faith." I smiled. Don's expression meant so much to me. I watched her leave then sat down to finish my coffee. Walter joined me.

I dawdled over my cup; killing time before our next stop. We were off to see Don. I'd arranged to visit him at his home. Dad and Jan were meeting me there.

I refused another refill and Walter and I left for Villa Park. The radio was tuned to the local news station. I half listened to the top stories and commercials while Walter followed the directions Phyllie gave me when I called. They lived near the library. I leaned back against the seat and replayed my conversation with Marisol. I'd learned at a young age that if I gave my brain a chance to sort and file the stimuli I experienced, I encountered less 'jitters.' The mid-day traffic noises and the steady movement of the car on I-88 calmed me. I felt us exit through the toll at Midwest Road and I continued to let the drone of the radio provide background for my thoughts.

'Remember, compadres, mosey on down to Black Bart Buick where the good guys wear black hats.'

"Cripes!" I lunged against my seat belt. Walter instinctively put out his arm to stop me.

"Was ist falsch?"

"Everything's wrong. We have to go to the dealership, the one on the radio, Black Bart Buick. Do you know where it is?"

"*Ja*, but I am supposing to take you to Villa Park."

"Walter, Marisol is in danger. We have to go to the dealership."

"Mr. Harry tell me take you were he say. I am sorry, Missus Grace."

I pulled on his thick arm. "Please, Walter. We have to help her."

"We almost at where I must take you. There we talk next trip."

I knew he wouldn't budge. I strained forward against by seatbelt praying we made each light, scanning the address once we turned on Ardmore. The library was on my right, so we were to turn on the first street on the left. The car barely stopped, I jumped out and ran to the door. I realized how crazy this would sound but I didn't care. My dad's car wasn't in the driveway or on the street; we were a little early. I had to find Harry. I rang the bell.

Don answered the door. He looked good except for the sling that held his bandaged left hand immobile. His forehead gleamed with salve and his hair looked trimmed.

"Grace, come in. Phyllie's out picking up a few snacks for us. She's been spoiling me."

He moved aside and I rushed past him. "Can I use your phone? It's an emergency." My face must have matched my voice. He led me into the kitchen and pointed at the far wall.

I dialed our house, no answer. Ric's number, same result. *Where are you guys?* Stupid of me not to know where they were. They knew my schedule. *Walter! He will know.*

I hung up and ran back into the living room. Walter and Don stood talking quietly about me; they stopped as soon as I entered the room. "Walter, where's Harry? I have to find him."

Walter looked uncomfortable. "He not telling me this time."

I believed him. The last time Harry didn't tell Walter where he was going was to protect him from being charged with aiding and abetting a fugitive. So what was Harry up to that he wouldn't involve his 'handler'? He must have left Walter out of the plan so he would focus on me and not worry about Harry.

I had no proof of what I thought; the police wouldn't listen. *The FBI. Her people. They'd listen.*

I ran back to the phone and dialed 4-1-1. *Maybe she's there. Maybe I'm way off base.* I dialed the number and waited through two rings. I cut off the operator right after she said, 'Federal.'

"I'd like to speak to Marisol Nunez, agent Nunez. It's an emergency."

"There is no one by that name here. Are you dialing correctly?"

"Yes, you're the FBI aren't you? I know she's coming down there to debrief. She's in danger."

"Yes, ma'am. You should call the police with your concern."

Translation—maybe you should stop bothering us. Black Bart indeed. I sounded like someone they'd have on their watch list.

I hung up. Every fiber in me wanted to scream but I knew I'd lose any chance of getting help if I acted like a nutcase.

The doorbell rang and the back door opened at the same time. Dad and Jan came in the front door while Phyllis Craig, carrying a sack of groceries, entered at the back. *Oh gee, the gang's all here.*

Before anyone could hug, or even say hello I launched into what I thought sounded coherent. "I can't find Harry or Ric, the police will think I'm nuts and the FBI already does. We have to help her."

I looked from face to face. Stern expressions settled on each. "Please, we're wasting time."

"Honey, slow down."

"I can't. She's in danger, I know it."

"Call her at the dealership. If she's there you can tell her your thoughts. If she's already left, then there's no problem."

I could do that. I dialed information again and called.

"Black Bart Buick where the good guys wear black hats. May I help you?"

Stay calm, Gracie, stay calm.

"Yes, I'm trying to reach my friend who is meeting with Black, uh, Mr. Guilfoyle. Her name is Marisol. Could you connect me to his office?"

Good, calm, polite, sane.

"I'm sorry they're just pulling out of the lot. Can I take a—"

"Whose car are they in?"

"Mr. Guilfoyle's."

I took a chance. "His plate says 'Black Bart' doesn't it?"

"Yes. Excuse me, can you hold for a moment?"

I hung up with a plan that formed in a moment of desperation. One more call.

"Forest Park Police, what is the nature of your emergency?"

"Bart Guilfoyle is in terrible danger. He just left his dealership There's a bomb in his trunk. There's a woman in the car with him. She has a gun. He's in a black 1992 Buick, license plate Black Bart."

"May I have your name please?"

"You don't need my name. He's in danger. The bomb is set to explode at," I looked at the clock, "three-thirty. Hurry."

I didn't watch enough to television to know if they could tell where the call originated. I didn't know what else to do. If the police didn't find her, I knew he'd finish the job he'd started Friday night.

They'd followed me into the kitchen and listened to my last call. Five pairs of eyes stared at me with the same expression of disbelief.

"Gracie, they can arrest you for that."

"Not if I'm right."

"Honey, you said Thomas called him 'bigs'. Bart was never 'bigs'. Only Bigelow was called 'bigs'. Marisol vouched for Bart."

My father's face pleaded with me to listen to him.

Could I be wrong? I'm not being stubborn. I'm right.

"Not exactly, Mike." Don's voice interrupted. "You'd already left the troop when this happened. Remember the kid whose nose Bart broke because he called him 'Iggy'?"

"Yeah, St. Louie wasn't it?"

Don nodded. "He must have had a death wish this one night, 'cause he called Bart 'Iggs' real soft like while Bart walked past him as the color guard did the flags. Anyway after the SPL calls 'two' Bart shoots over to him and grabs him by the throat yelling 'whadya call me, you little wop?' St. Louie either thinks fast or it just came out that way but he croaks out, 'bigs, I called you bigs'. Black Bart thinks about it and gives St. Louie one last squeeze for good measure and lets him loose. Bart liked the name, puffed up a little, and grinned. Bigelow had already left the troop. I dropped out not too much after that meeting. It's possible Black Bart became the new 'bigs'."

The doorbell rang and we followed Phyllis into the living room while she went to the door. Two men, one in uniform, the other in a suit stood in the doorway.

The one with the Villa Park Police uniform spoke. "Hello, ma'am." His eyes swept the room behind her. "May we come in?"

Phyllis seemed frozen, one hand on the doorknob the other on the edge of the door. Don moved up. "Of course, officer. Come in. How can we help you?" He gently nudged his wife.

"I'm Officer Delewski and this is Detective Walsh from the Forest Park Police. Someone placed an emergency call from this number to that department. Did one of you make that call?" They stepped through the doorway but not much closer to us. I noticed the little strap across the top of the officer's holster was unsnapped.

So much for wondering if they could trace a call. I stepped forward. "I made the call, my name is Grace Marsden. I have reason to believe that the man in the car is going to kill his woman passenger."

The detective spoke. "The caller said there was a bomb in the vehicle and that the passenger was armed. Is this another call?"

"No, the woman is armed but she's supposed to be. She's an FBI agent. The man, Bart Guilfoyle, is the killer. I thought it would be faster to say there was a bomb than to try and explain."

"So there is no bomb and the armed passenger has a permit to carry a weapon. Is that correct?"

"Yes, but the man is still a killer."

"Has he been charged?"

"No, he hasn't been charged, no one knows he's the killer. We all thought it was Evan Bigelow."

His eyes widened and his face turned hard. "Making a false report can carry jail time. Are you accusing the mayor of Forest Park of killing someone?"

I didn't like the look on his face. For that matter, I didn't like the look on any of the faces staring at me. The heat moved up my neck until it felt like the tops of my ears were on fire. My mouth moved but no sound came out and my fingers latched on to the yarn tied at my waist. I plucked at the strands using all my energy to delay the overwhelming feeling to turn my back on the room and tie knots.

"Mrs. Marsden, are you refusing to answer my question?"

I'm certain my eyes were pansy purple.

"Stop badgering her and she'll answer your questions." Jan Pauli wrapped one arm around my shoulders and pulled me toward the kitchen. "Let her get a drink of water and sit down for heaven's sake." We walked into the kitchen and she whispered, "Pull yourself together, start at the beginning, and tell them what you told us." She squeezed my shoulders. Phyllis rushed in behind us and poured me a glass of water. I sat down at their table and sipped at my water, counting sips between each deep breath until I drained the water. Jan bought me the extra time I needed to lay out my story in a manner that wouldn't land me in jail.

I looked at the detective. "Okay, let me explain."

He held up his hand. "This is a serious charge. I'd like you to come with me to the station."

My newly found calm skipped and sank like a flat stone on a wave. Before I could answer several voices complained. In the end it was decided that Dad and I would drive with Detective Walsh while Walter followed with Jan, Don, and Phyllis.

I clung to Dad's hand the entire drive. Detective Walsh occasionally looked at us through the rear view mirror. He'd taken North Avenue to Harlem and when he turned on Madison Street, places I normally visited and enjoyed, Circle Theatre and Centuries and Sleuths, held no joy when viewed from the back seat of a police car.

When he turned on Des Plaines I figured we were close. His radio squawked numbers and suddenly his dashboard light went on, and we sped passed the police station. I turned in the seat and sure enough, Walter had gunned the Rover and was keeping pace. *Oh, cripes, we were all going to jail.*

The car turned quickly onto eastbound Roosevelt Avenue. Flashing lights drew our attention and he skirted around stopped vehicles. Several police cars and unmarked cars with strobe lights on their dashboards sat parked at angles in a car wash parking lot a few blocks away from Black Bart Buick. He stopped the car and turned to both of us. "Stay in the car. Shots have been fired. I may owe you an apology, Mrs. Marsden."

He disappeared around the front of the car sprinting toward the police who crouched behind their vehicles. Suddenly Walter's figure loomed next to the window. I thought he'd come to check on me but he kept moving. What was he doing? Then I saw the Roadmaster in the lot–distinctively Hannah's car with her mini Union Jack flying from the antenna. *Oh my God, not Hannah, not the babies.*

48

Pop. Pop. Pop. I threw myself into my father's arms praying that the three shots I heard hadn't found three people I loved. I buried my head against his chest and soundlessly mouthed the same words over and over, 'pray Lord keep them safe.'

He pulled my shoulder up and I raised my head. It was over out there. I could see Bart Guilfoyle walking across the lot with his hands held above his head. Marisol walked behind him holding a gun to his back. An ambulance siren pierced the air and my heart pounded while I watched a man being escorted from the car wash by the SWAT police. He held a bloodied handkerchief to his forehead and leaned heavily against the uniformed officer who was guiding him to the ambulance. Another siren announced another vehicle–the Cook County Coroner's. *Please God let them be all right.*

The police had stopped Walter at the line but now he ran forward shouting something back at us. Hannah and Gertrude walked out each holding an infant. Walter swooped down on them taking charge with one ham-hock arm around each. He walked them toward us. A man in plainclothes moved to stop him but Marisol waved him back.

Dad and I rushed out of the car and followed them to Walter's Rover. Don, Phyllis, and Jan were out of the vehicle and waiting with open arms to take the babies and hand blankets to Hannah and Gertrude. Jan and Phyllis climbed into the Rover and snuggled their new charges. Walter helped Gertrude into the front seat and leaned in talking to her. Hannah, wrapped in a blanket slouched against the front bumper staring back at where she'd been.

I slipped my arm around her shoulders. She shivered and I knew it wasn't from the cold air. "We were the last vehicle. Al had waved me in and the wagon started forward. Out of nowhere this man wearing a ski mask stopped the track and told us to get out. He made Al back the car out and then lock us in the office. I heard the shots but couldn't see anything. We could have been killed." I worried about her going into shock and wondered if Walter's idea to circumvent the paramedics was a good one.

Marisol waved me over. "Be right back." I squeezed Hannah's

shoulders. Her color looked better.

"You can take them home. The attendant told us what happened before he went to the hospital. We don't need their statements."

"Thanks Marisol." I started to leave.

"Whoa, hold up a minute. Why would you tell the police he had a bomb in his trunk and that I was armed and dangerous?"

Her face split into a grin.

"I never said 'dangerous' just armed."

"I owe you again, Grace. How did you know?"

"Pieces of conversations and events get stuck in my head and if I give it time, it sorts itself out. I'm not always even close, definitely lower than thirty-two percent. For about three days I had everyone thinking it was the mayor."

I smiled expecting her to laugh. Her dark eyes narrowed. She nodded toward a gurney carrying a closed black bag. "The Honorable Evan Bigelow. You weren't that far from the truth. I promise I will fill you in, the least I can do but I have to process my 'partner' and that means reams of paperwork. I'll see if I can't stop in tonight." She turned and was absorbed by the dozens of police personnel working at the scene.

I returned to the Rover and told them the news.

"Why was the mayor here? Was he trying to reason with him when he was shot?"

"No. He was one of the bad guys." I waved my hands to stop the questions. "That's all I know. Let's get everybody home." Dad drove Hannah and the babies, while we followed behind him. Next stop, Villa Park. Don asked that we call him when we knew the story.

He shook hands with my father. "Mike, the last time you and me spent some time together with just the guys was at the Jamboree in '79 when that tornado ripped through the campgrounds and those scouts got electrocuted in their tent. Last Friday came close. I think we need to keep the ladies with us at all times, keep us out of trouble and the good Lord smiling down on us."

Jan and Phyllis nodded as one. "Let's try for dinner this Friday night," Phyllis suggested.

Jan shook her curly head. "No one cooks. What about the Terrace Restaurant?"

"Perfect. I'll make the reservation, seven o'clock okay?"

Jan and Phyllis sealed the deal while Dad and Don wondered what happened. I started to hug my dad goodbye. "You're about thirty minutes too soon." He looked at Walter. "I'll take her home. You take

Gertrude home, she looks a little wobbly."

He was right, her normal pink cheeks were pale and her face seemed pinched and worried.

"I promise Mr. Harry I keep her with me, keep her safe." Walter's stern expression seemed ready for a tug of war. Gertrude's lips compressed and she held in a small sob. Walter's head snapped round and back like an animal caught betwixt and between.

"Walter, you're a good man and a great friend to my daughter. I'm her father. Do you think I'd let anything happen to her? Take your lady home."

He ducked his head in acquiescence "*Danke.*"

At last we were on the road to Pine Marsh. Jan drove over the bridge and turned right. I wanted nothing more than to relax and unwind. I knew Marisol would call when she could and I was hoping for quiet time before Harry came home from where ever he'd gone.

I left Dad and Jan downstairs chatting about houses. "Jeannette there's nothing like a home for investment. I don't know that condos sell well these days."

Was Jan condo shopping or had I missed the beginning of their conversation? I didn't care. I ran hot water in the Jacuzzi and slipped under the bubbles before the tub filled all the way. This was how I sorted through the whirlwind ideas that caught and stuck in my mind. My brain needed unengaged time to find the pattern and pigeon hole the data. What couldn't be filed gave me the jitters and I found that I braided, knotted, and stressed more.

The music from the stereo came on. Only Harry knew to do that. I wasn't ready for explanations and recriminations. Dad must have filled him in because, I snoozed under my blanket of fragrant bubbles until the water temp cooled and the scent of Hyacinth faded. Only then did I sense someone was in the room.

Harry sat in the chair near the bed totally engrossed in whatever he was reading. Within the last year he'd taken to using reading glasses for small print. The dark frames gave him a studious look. I kept my head still only moving my eyes to enjoy his image. He must have sensed me. "Hullo, darling. I've been setting here prepared to come lift you from the waters if necessary." He put down his reading material and glasses, and came and sat on the bottom step.

"I doubt you would have seen me slip under with your nose in that book. What is it?"

Harry's eyes gleamed with excitement and I realized it took great restraint for him not to have rushed in and waved it under my nose.

"It's John Henry's case book. Kramer and I convinced Randolph Randolph that he wanted to relinquish the crate he removed from the woods after he watched his cousins and Janet Henry burying it."

"No wonder all those hours of searching turned up zip."

"We checked his alibi for Friday night. It wasn't him. After listening to your day I know we've found the three compadres."

"Why'd he have the crate? Why'd he ask if you'd found the other crate? Was he part of the gun running?"

"We should have taped his confession but then the authorities would have our conversations too."

"That wouldn't be good?"

Harry moved up a step. "Lean forward and I'll do your back." I followed directions and relaxed under the gentle bristles.

"Mr. Randolph needed persuading. He acted quiet rude and coarse when we asked him a few innocuous questions. At one point, the gent yelled, 'I don't gotta tell you shit.' Kramer grabbed him by the shirtfront and said something like, 'tell me here or tell me on the way to the hospital but you're going to tell me.' Now Randolph is all wild eyed and looked to me to be the 'good cop'. I tell him, 'Sorry mate but I'm in the country illegally. Cops don't even know I exist."

I sat up and water rolled over the top of the Jacuzzi. I couldn't help laughing at his description. "So now you're Hutch?" Although in my opinion far more handsome than David Soul.

"It was either him or Cagney," he deadpanned. More sloshing as I laughed harder. "Let's get you out of there before you flood the place." He reached for my bath towel and helped me step out. "*Mmm.* If I didn't have so much to tell you and if a half dozen people weren't coming here in thirty minutes…"

"A half dozen people? Why?"

"The denouement of course."

I hated when he flipped French at me and then it dawned on me. *Cripes I majored in English lit–denouement.* Then I understood. "Marisol called?"

He nodded and smiled. "She'll be here to tell all. Then there's Kramer, your dad and Jeannette, who have never left, and Thomas's replacement on the case." He looked down at his hand and held it open. "Okay, only five but with me and you that's seven. You're dad's preparing snacks. I'm going to open up some wine, any preference?"

"Geez, Harry this isn't a party. Somebody died today."

Harry wrapped his arms around the towel and me. "Of course

it's serious. Sorry, darling, just dark humor." He kissed me before he released me. "Go on get dressed. We'll take this up later."

Forty-five minutes later we assembled at the dining room table. Jan left after she helped my dad prepare a banquet of snacks. Her daughter was visiting and she'd hardly spent any time with her. They were golfing again tomorrow.

We asked Marisol to go first.

"You understand that what is said in this room tonight must stay here. I don't want anything to jeopardize the case against this creep." We nodded and she began.

"The American version of *Brennan Infantry Grenadiers* began with the fathers and uncles of the men involved today. They'd been indoctrinated from early on to hate authority and those who fought against their cause. Bigelow, Thomas, and Guilfoyle were directly involved in the cover-up of the original theft. The night of the camp-out when agent Henry was killed, the boys were in the woods. Thomas had lost interest in scouts and even though he was a couple of years older than the other two he was in the woods at the dumpsite with beer. The other two were on the campout. Bantonini was molesting both young men. They vied for his favors, spying on the other boys, even repeating what they heard at home. The only secret they shared was the one thrust on them by their family.

The night that Agent Henry fought with Bantonini, the two boys stood near enough to hear what John Henry threatened. They wanted to protect Bantonini and so they followed Mr. Henry deeper into the woods. He spotted them following him and confronted them suspecting what had been done to them. At this point I have only Guilfoyle's word for how this went done since, conveniently, his compadres are deceased. He claims they denied that anything like that ever happened and they walked away from Henry to hook up with Thomas at the dumpsite. Guilfoyle swears that Thomas started drinking without them while he waited for one to sneak away from camp, while the other one stayed with Bantonini. He been surprised to see them both and they explained why. Along with the beer, Thomas toted around a pistol showing it off to whoever would be impressed. He got it in his head that they should teach Agent Henry to mind his own business. They ran after him. He handled them at first trying to talk to them, slow down their anger but Thomas was out of control. He waved the gun at Henry threatening to shoot him. Guilfoyle doesn't think he would have but they never found out. He says they heard some low chanting and Thomas lost his focus. That's all the time Henry needed to disarm Thomas and pocket the gun. He heard the chanting too and said something about getting the scouts out of there. Thomas tackled him around the waist pinning his arms. When Henry went down, he hit his head. Bigelow came up with the idea to carry his body to the street and have Thomas run him down with his car. The chanting spooked them and they didn't return for the beer. Bigelow and Guilfoyle went back to the campout. Bigelow pulled rank and he spent the night with Bantonini. Guilfoyle was angry and wanted to hurt someone so when he saw the boys with the Ouija board he guided the message that Specs' dad was dead."

Marisol stopped. She sipped at the wine that Harry poured when everyone sat down.

"What happened to Thomas?"

"He went home, waited a few days and then brought his beater into Bantonini's auto repair shop saying he'd hit a pole. No one suspected him, since he'd been the rookie cop who assisted in the investigation. If Bantonini did, he kept quiet to avoid police scrutiny."

"That's not the version I heard Thomas tell on Friday."

"Remember Grace, Guilfoyle's account is suspect but we can't prove it didn't happen the way he says it does."

"Father Briscoe really thinks Guilfoyle turned himself around."

"To some extent he did. He became a college graduate and a successful business owner. From the outside looking in he looked like he beat the odds. I'm sure Father feels he succeeded with him. It's not until you get a glimpse of the inside that you realize how deep the sickness went."

"Who was out there with Thomas? Guilfoyle or Bigelow?"

"Based on the other agent's timeline and what we got from the youngsters we nabbed, Guilfoyle had enough time and opportunity to slip away meet Thomas, kill me, get back in time to sound the alarm and pretend to search for me. However, we think it was Bigelow. Not only because Guilfoyle says it wasn't him but because of the circumstantial evidence."

"Bigelow was at the chamber fundraiser at the Chaney Mansion that night wasn't he?"

"At first that alibi held for him but we checked and he came in after the ribbon cutting. He made a big deal with the photographer about shooting another ribbon shot to make sure that one got in the paper but in checking with the honorees he hadn't been there at the earlier ceremony. That puts him in the woods at the right time. He's wearing a tux, which could spark Thomas' question of why are you dressed up? We found a tassel from a formal shoe near the woodpile. We were getting a warrant to search his home for the shoe based on what you heard and the report from one of the attendees who remembered commenting to the mayor that he smelled woodsy like a campfire. According to her account he roared with laughter and told her how he'd stopped by Oak Park River Forest High School, on his way to the mansion, for spirit night at the school. Told her he must have stood too close to the bonfire. 'Can never court those voters too soon' he'd confided and totally charmed her."

"Sounds like great interviewing and long hours." Dad complimented her.

"This comes from an entire team checking everything anyone said. By the way, there was no bonfire that night. The fact that Grace heard Thomas call him 'bigs' tipped the scales toward Bigelow."

I interrupted. "I found out today from Don Craig that after Bigelow left the troop other kids called Guilfoyle 'bigs'."

"Wouldn't matter, Grace. Thomas left the troop before either of the other two. He'd only refer to Bigelow as 'bigs'."

"I heard the commercial where he says *compadres* and uses that cowboy accent. The man with Thomas used an accent on and off."

"According to our interviews, Bigelow used an Irish brogue for effect–been doing it for years." She shook her head. "The long and the short of it is that Guilfoyle will confess to passing on information he gleaned from working at the Bureau about any activity concerning the munitions theft or the investigation of Agent Henry's death. He admits he was in the woods when Thomas tackled Henry and accidentally killed him. He denies being the third man. Without something more conclusive, I'm afraid we don't have much.

Guilfoyle gave us a bone on Bantonini. The night of that campout after Guilfoyle tricked Specs, he went to Bantonini's tent to tell him what he'd done to curry his favor. The tent was empty. He went back to his tent. In hindsight he thinks Bantonini and Bigelow were already practicing black magic. It seemed to him that every time they went camping on a weekend with no moonrise expected Bantonini chose Bigelow. Keeping that old grudge in mind, he planted the note in Hannah's truck when it was in for service to cast suspicion on Bantonini for anything that went wrong in the woods.

"You mean this guy could get off?"

"He's been pretty clean since he opened his dealerships. A good attorney could argue that he struggled with a fanatical father, an abusive trusted adult, and bad associations and overcame the odds, not unscathed but a productive member of society."

"Whose side are you on?" Ric's voice sounded bitter.

"I'm just telling it like they're going to."

"What about kidnapping you?"

"I can't prove he kidnapped me. When Grace called the bureau they of course denied my existence, I'm undercover. They did page me because of the threat. Protocol is to page the partner as well. Our pagers both went off and the code on the display ordered us to call in. Bart made the call at his desk. I know now that they relayed the warning verbatim. He told them I was sitting in his office and he'd drive me in. He told me about the threat. I went out to my car to get my briefcase and I think Bart placed a call to Bigelow. He most likely told him that I could identify him from the woods and that he would set me up for him."

"He had to have ice water in his veins to think that calmly and quickly." Several heads nodded at my dad's comment.

"We won't be sure about the call until we can check the phone company records. When we drove out of the lot he asked if I'd mind if he took a quick run through the car wash. He pleaded a later appointment and he wanted a clean car. Bigelow was waiting when we pulled into the bay. Bart started through the cycle and the door behind us lowered. I pulled my gun and told him to stop the car. I had my door opened when I noticed the attendant unconscious on the cement. I yelled at him to get down certain that we'd been ambushed."

Marisol stopped and breathed deeply. She'd been close to death twice in one week. The dark circles under her eyes exposed her fatigue and tension even though her voice didn't.

"The driver's window shattered and I saw the look on his face. In that moment I believe he shifted his planned homicide from me to Bigelow. I don't know if Bigelow was a bad shot or if he'd set up Guilfoyle. He pushed me out of the car, shifted into gear, and drove down the guts of the car wash. I heard three more shots. By the time I reached him Bigelow was dead. Guilfoyle denies he did anything more than follow instructions to bring me in to safety. Until we follow up the loose ends with phone records and his later appointment we have nothing on him. We'll get him and I hope sooner than later."

Dad stood. "I need a break. I can't believe you can't nail this creep. Affirmative mumbles all around. I stayed seated to give Marisol's words time to sink in. *He could go free. If he wasn't the one who tried to kill her did he deserve to go to prison? Wonder how she really feels.*

"We'll get him Mr. Morelli. That's all I have anyway. We might be able to close the case on the gun theft. Most of weapons have been accounted for. Guilfoyle told us where we would find the few cases that never made it to Ireland. Again, according to Guilfoyle, Bigelow wanted to continue arming the *B.I.G.* but his father and their contact in the grenadiers both died within months of each other. He blustered about continuing the good fight but he didn't know how and by then he'd achieved some success in politics and didn't want to risk it. As for Agent Henry's death..." She shrugged. "It could have happened the way he said."

Marisol stood up and gathered her papers. "I still have a flight out tomorrow. Good night everyone. Good luck."

I walked her to the door. "Marisol, can't you tell if he's lying? I mean can you sense the truth?"

"Doesn't work that way. But I'm pretty sure about what I told you." Her dimpled smile lifted my spirits. "Take care of yourself."

I watched her walk to her car wondering again what makes a young woman want to become a 'G-person'. I smiled at my politically correct usage. Everyone was again seated with a refilled plate or glass. Dad filled my wineglass.

Thomas' replacement, Detective June Arroyo, took the lead. Her solid figure and above average height inspired confidence that she could hold her own with a bad guy. Two different Hispanic women who used different styles of law enforcement to reach the same goal. Marisol's speech was unaccented while Detective Arroyo spoke with a flavor of an accent that became more noticeable when she ended statements in an upswing.

"I'm here because my boss got a call from his boss to accommodate you people with an explanation of our investigation of Robinson Woods and Edward Bantonini Sr. One of you has a friend in high places." Her voice was flat and short. "Since re-opening Detective Thomas' case files on those subjects we have found some discrepancies. It is apparent to us that Detective Thomas attempted to take the lead on all calls to the woods and that he under reported events. The department has re-interviewed and investigated only a few of the reports but we can see that any information directly linking Bantonini to the rapes was not included."

"So Thomas protected Bantonini who conveniently forgot about the bodywork he did on a rookie cop's beater car." Ric's comment tied up that loose end.

"Exactly. We are in the process of talking to all the rape victims to see if we can connect him directly."

"Has anyone mentioned his fingers? When I grabbed at the hands around my throat, the fingers on one hand felt weird. I thought he wore gloves but then I saw his hand and the fingers have no nails."

She jotted down the note. "I'll cross check this with their statements. Details like this will help us nail him. Another thing we discovered. Thomas left out total descriptions of the victims but now we think there is a pattern. The victims are Caucasian with fair skin, dark hair and light eyes."

I felt the chill move up my spine like a frozen rolling pin stretching across my back and shoulders. All eyes looked at me.

"Were all these women abducted? I thought it was random." Harry reached for my hand.

"We thought so too and that's the profile we were following. It seems at least two of the five victims were brought to the woods and raped there. The other three were in the woods." She looked down at her notes. "One woman at about three in the afternoon. She was kept somewhere until dark, and the other two were in the woods closer to dusk. People are always stopping to photograph Chee Chee Pin Quay's grave hoping to catch the ghost Indians on film." She shook her head in disgust and mumbled, "Dead is dead."

"Grace's attack was one of chance. She was there, she fit the profile?"

Detective Arroyo nodded. "We believe that was it. I've looked at Mark Hanley's report about Bantonini's obsession with you, Mrs. Marsden. It's true that he never sent those two after you, but he made it plain that whoever could deliver you would be special to him."

"Damn freak." Harry's hand slammed down on the table. "You nail this bloody bastard or I'll do it myself."

"I'll disregard your comment Mr. Marsden because I am in your home and this is upsetting news, but be assured of one thing, I do it by the book." Her stern voice and hard expression gave me the willies. Harry held her gaze until she reshuffled her papers.

"Now that we know his preference, we will be using a policewoman who fits the profile to trap him." She looked at me. "I am advising you to stay put, don't go into the area and don't be alone until we catch him."

The three men around the table nodded for me.

"Why do you think he picks women with those features? I mean isn't there usually a reason?"

"Good question, Mr. Morelli. We don't know, but Hanley suspects it has some connection to the women in his life. His mother was pure Irish with those features. Bantonini married a girl just like mom. We've dug around and found that his mother died when he was an adolescent and his father, Guido Bantonini, straight off the boat, split his time between ignoring and beating his young son. We have nothing that even hints that he molested his son. Edward enlisted under-age with his father's blessing. Before he shipped out he married his high school sweetheart. He was gone almost two years, when he returned he found out his wife's been cheating on him and that he's a daddy. He knows Eddie Jr. is his because of the finger thing."

I interrupted. "Quigley has the same thing only not all his fingers. Don Craig told me he saw his hand at a campout."

"It wouldn't surprise me, the stuff we've been gathering. I'll check it out."

"What happened to his wife?"

"She died in childbirth. Records don't indicate anything out of the ordinary, except that she died. There was one odd note in the file scribbled in the margin of the baby's death certificate, 'no digit anomaly'. The baby was male."

"You think he knew she'd died giving birth to someone else's baby?"

She shrugged. "Who knows what twisted him." She tapped her notes. "If this Quigley turns out to be Bantonini's issue that means that he was doing Mrs. Quigley when he was a mere lad and a newlywed."

"Talk about a double-standard. Was that Mrs. Quigley dark haired and—"

Arroyo nodded her head.

I felt a pressure on my shoulders like hands pushing me down. My brain started the synapse that turns me topsy-turvy. I slipped my hand out from under Harry's and fingered the yarn on my belt. The conversation wore on around me; I heard snatches but my mind retreated to an orderly place and I liked it there.

"That is what the department has. I've fulfilled my order, don't expect anything further until we apprehend Bantonini and that you can watch on the news."

My mind clicked in on her tone. *Whew. She is royally pissed off at having to report to us.*

"What about John Jacob and Janet? Who killed them? Their mother needs closure." The pressure lifted from my shoulders.

Arroyo glared at me. "My instructions were to apprise you of our information on Bantonini." She stood up, "That being done, I'll say goodbye."

Harry walked her out. When he returned, Ric took the lead. He held up a sheaf of papers.

"These are photocopies of the case journal we found in Randolph's possession. We turned over the journal to Agent Nunez tonight and by now I'm sure the FBI is interrogating Mr. Randolph. When we spoke with Randolph's cousin he'd mentioned a second crate. The children found two empty crates in the woods near the Robinson house where Chee Chee Pin Quay's granddaughter lived. They had been reading a story in school about a Viking warrior and how he was honored in death. The kids' pet cat died and they wanted to do a funeral pyre. They convinced their friend Janet Henry to help them. They got cold feet when they thought about setting a fire in the woods and decided to bury the crate. Janet had the idea to use the other crate to honor her father and brother. She filled the crate with items she'd taken from their effects: her brother's cowboy hat, his favorite Zane Grey novel, his spare set of glasses, her father's journal, one of his pipes, his Marine pin, and a small American flag. She asked Randolph to break the links on John Jacob's I.D. bracelet so she could bury half and keep half. He said he smashed it with a rock in a couple of places and pieces flew off. They didn't know a piece landed in the other open crate. She kept a piece and put the rest in the crate. We've confirmed with Mrs. Henry that John wore a bracelet. The piece we found in the cat's crate matches what was in the crate in DeKalb."

"The rest of the bracelet has been a pin that I've seen on every piece of clothing Janet wore. I wondered about the significance of the silver bar but I never asked."

"I don't understand why this Randolph character kept the crate all these years."

Harry answered, "We didn't either. I think the FBI might get it out of him. Maybe he thought he could use the journal against someone. It doesn't really name names, just suspicions and accounts of surveillance. He mentions seeing 'monk like figures in the woods' and hearing 'chanting and drums' during the night. He spent several nights hiding in the woods hoping to catch the grenadiers moving the crates. He suspected that they were cached in one of the sheds near the Robinson home but never spotted any crates."

"He was close. When the Robinson home burned down they

found a deep root cellar with a tunnel that led to the closest shed."

We all stared at Ric. "It was in the papers when it happened. Hadn't thought about it until now."

Harry continued, "According to Randolph he followed the kids to the woods and watched his younger cousins and Janet carefully pack the treasures they'd lugged into the two crates. He'd become suspicious when he noticed his cousin with a shovel. He watched the kids struggle to dig two holes. The first one for the cat crate was deeper. By the time they started on the second hole they were tired and it was getting dark. It was easy for Randolph to uncover the crate."

"So when I told Janet about the troop finding the crate, she rushed out there to look for the one she'd buried." I thought about what I'd said and realized I'd sent her to her death. I bolted from the table and ran upstairs. I heard chairs pushed back in haste.

"Grace!"

"Let her go. She needs to sort this out."

How can I sort this out? It's my fault she's dead. I curled up on the window seat and pressed my head against the cool pane. *No peace for any of us.*

49

I woke up in bed and lay there reviewing the conversations. I am responsible for Janet's death was the only thought I kept hearing in my mind. The bed shifted and I knew Harry leaned up on an elbow.

"It's not your fault." His low voice held little comfort. "Grace?"

I rolled over and closed my eyes and my heart. I knew what I'd done. I wouldn't budge from bed that day or the next. I wouldn't take Dad's call or Tracy's. They both came to visit but I wouldn't come down. Food, even coffee held no appeal for me. I knew I was sinking into a morass from which there might not be escape but I couldn't stop the feeling that I was a pariah to those around me: injury and death followed me or called to me. Cold bones drew me to them. Was I psychic like Marisol? In my case psycho.

Harry kept me apprised on any news. This morning he'd bought me tea and toast. Marty dropped off little blue pills for depression. Each time Harry presented drink or food two little pills were in a Dixie cup on the tray. He didn't insist, just offered. Today, he'd brought Elmo up with him. "Ort's been asking to see his mom." I knew Harry was reaching out to me *His mom, right. You missed your chance to make me a real mom. And Marisol's stupid prediction.* I let the kitten snuggle down next to me but I didn't touch him.

"We've found out something about the trousers Bantonini wore at the court of honor. One of the scouts told Will there'd been an accident with the candle wax before the ceremony and that Bantonini went into the troop wardrobe, donated clothing from older scouts, and found those trousers. He'd commented to one scout that they were a little big but with his belt it should be okay. When he came back from changing, one scout told him about the missing button on his backside. He laughed and said, 'better a missing button on my butt than a suspicious stain on my front'. The boy laughed and gave him a high five. Will told me the story. The trousers with the wax are either in the locked troop closet at St. Edgar or at the cleaners. Be interesting to know how many people have a key to that closet."

Maybe interesting for him but I didn't care. He could tell. "Gracie, please, talk to me, talk to someone."

I turned away and I heard him put the tray down on the night-stand. He spoke from the doorway. "I'm going to Will's meeting to-night. Walter will be here."

I slept on and off thinking of nothing except the look on Janet's face when I told her about the crate. *I should have seen that some-thing was wrong, terribly wrong.*

Harry tried to tell me about the meeting when he got home. "I asked one of the moms about getting uniform shorts for Will for summer camp hoping she'd direct me to the troop wardrobe. Seems several people have keys, Bantonini, the assistant scoutmaster, Ken Ward, the wardrobe mistress Julie Nieves, the school custodian, Pete, and Father Briscoe. Who knows how many more that never turned in their key? I looked in the closet and the pants with the missing button were in there in a plastic bag with a note about the button pinned to it. I don't think that Bantonini killed Janet."

I waited. Silence. I guess he figured he'd be wasting his breath. I wondered if that's how my dad felt when my mother slipped into the grip of depression. Maybe they were sharing strategies.

"You've probably forgotten that you promised Will another horse day this Saturday. He was talking to the scouts at the meeting. By the time I arrived a few of the boys were vying for best friend status so they could go riding.

"Mary Quigley is taking Tim out of the troop; tonight was his last time. Will's going to miss him, they're good friends. The Quigleys have put their house and her studio up for sale. They're moving to Wisconsin. Saturday will be the last time Will spends with Tim.

"If you can't be up for it, I'll understand but I don't want to spoil it for Will. I'll ask Devin to work with them. They're back from holi-day, you know. Barb's been asking for you, anxious to show off her pictures, I'd wager. Think you'll walk in the morning?"

Is this the plan, ask stupid questions and hope for an answer?

"Your dad mentioned he'd be at the cemetery Saturday. Wanted to know if he should pick you up?"

My mom's birthday was Saturday. We always went to the ceme-tery. I'd never missed in five years.

Harry turned on the radio when he left the room. The station played light rock and little news. *'Only ten shopping days left to Christmas.'*

I rolled over and tucked my head under the pillow. *Christmas! Another set of problems. Who gets Will? Who gets Harry?*

I knew it was Saturday because Harry told me.

"Listen, darling, Lily is bringing Will and Tim over at two. She's got an appointment until one. That should give Devin plenty of time to wear them out. I'm going to zip out for a bit and pick up more Papaya juice for you. It's one-thirty. I'll be back in a jiff." He leaned down and as he'd done each day of my self-imposed bed rest kissed me on the forehead. "I love you." I heard him leave.

For some reason Papaya juice seemed to be the only fluid I could drink. I couldn't stomach coffee or tea.

My father brought over *pizelles* and Marty sent more pills. I saw them on the nightstand. These pills were oval and yellow.

I could pretend to take them and hide them until I accumulated enough. Enough for what? You know. Tell me Grace, enough for what? Suicide.

The word in my head reverberated throughout the room like someone had shouted it. The stone weighing on my heart lifted and the funk I'd been wallowing in went with it. That'd I'd even thought about suicide scared me straight. I flipped off the covers and leapt out of bed fearful that the cotton strands might hold me in. Three steps toward the door and I realized that bed rest, except for the slow occasional trip to the bathroom, and starvation except for papaya juice robbed my balance and strength. I stumbled and sprawled across the carpet breaking my fall with my good hand and both knees.

"*Ouch.*" *Damn, it feels good to feel.* I stood up slowly and walked into the bathroom. The mirror reflected a haggard face with dark circles, matted hair and several zits around my chin. *Great, a pudgy Dutch girl with zits.* Only I wasn't pudgy anymore. I wasn't curvy either. I started the shower and avoided looking in the mirror while the water warmed.

I let the water run over my head and body before I shampooed. I didn't care about wetting the cast–I'd deal with that later. I wanted to feel clean and fresh. I scrubbed and rinsed and started feeling better.

"*Yeow*. Damn that plumbing." I pushed the knob in.

My heart froze in the next instant. *Harry's gone; he couldn't have made it back in time. Relax. Burglars don't break in to pee. Somebody flushed.*

I pulled clothes on over my wet skin and stepped out into the bedroom. I heard a muffled pounding but before I could get to the landing something heavy and dark fell over my head. I fought against the material but was lifted off my feet and carried down the stairs. Young voices shouted from a distance.

I recognized Will's voice.

"Stay away, run," I screamed through the dark folds. I knew we'd moved outside by the change in temperature. My struggles lessened as the debilitating effects of my fast took over. He lowered me into something and immediately tied a rope around me. I heard metal slam and I realized I was in the trunk of his car. The motion told me he was driving. I felt the left turn on to the bridge and right turn out to the main road. I knew without seeing we'd be on I-88 headed east for the 290 and Robinson Woods.

Harry is probably already back. He'll know how to find me. He'll come to the woods. What if he's not headed for the woods? What if he's taking you somewhere else?

The drone of expressway ended too soon for us to have reached the woods. We were in stop and go traffic. He wasn't headed for the woods. I felt the lightheadedness overcome me and fought it. Part of the problem was the material blocking my breathing. The rope he'd tied wasn't that tight. I wiggled it up around my shoulders until I could flip the cloth over my head. I'd banged my arms against the trunk but I could breathe easier. My head swam with the exertion and I gulped air until I could see without dots in my vision. Not that I could see much in the dark. I had no idea how long we'd be moving but I knew it would be up to me to free myself.

Light seeped in and I could see a little. I reached for the latch and pulled against it. I didn't know much about cars. I thought you could open the trunk from inside; guess they worked like refrigerators. The situation overwhelmed me and I feared I'd get my death wish. The only thing to do was to wait and surprise him when he opened the trunk.

I lay in the cold trying to build my strength and courage. The lighter glow through the rear lights comforted me in the dark like a nightlight for a kid. *They're made out of plastic. If I can break one someone might notice. Oh God, dear Lord let a cop be behind us.*

I felt around me and under me for something to use to break out the light. Nothing. *How could there be nothing. This is a guy's car. They always have something. Geez, Louise.*

I had something, my hands and feet. I didn't think I could punch my way through the light but maybe I could kick it out if I could get some leverage. I tried not to think about what the jagged plastic would do to my bare foot. Instead I focused on turning on to my back and pushing myself toward the front of the car to get my foot in position. One more push should do it. "*Ouch.*" My head made contact with something hard and pointy. I reached over my head and pulled a slim jim from behind me. *Thank you, thank you.*

I scooted and turned to get back to the light. "God, please let this work." I punched the plastic orb. Nothing. I was not going to end up trapped in here. Now more than ever I wanted to live. My brain set the pattern. *Tap. Tap. Punch!* The metal bar cracked the plastic.

Tap. Tap. Punch! It went through, unfortunately all the way through out of my hands and onto the street under us. No matter I could break off enough plastic to get my hand through. I pulled my sweater down over my fingers and pushed through the plastic edges almost to my elbow. I waved my arm hoping someone was behind us, praying they'd call the police or force him to stop. I heard a car honking and we slowed down but not to stop only to turn. We were moving slowly. Maybe traffic was backed up. We made several soft turns. Where were we? I regretted losing the slim jim; I'd planned to hit him with it when he popped the trunk. We moved slower, more curving turns but no stops.

Like when I was a kid asleep in the car while we drove out from the city. I always started to wake up when I felt the slow curves. We were in the cemetery.

I remembered the crypt he'd stood at with the wreath. And now, in slow motion in my head I could read the ribbon, *'Mother'*. I shook so hard my teeth cracked against each other. No way would he get me inside that crypt. He'd have to kill me to do it.

The car stopped. I pulled my arm in and got on my back with my legs coiled. My hands were flat on the bottom ready to support me. I decided that kicking him when he lifted the trunk lid would be my best chance. The spirit lost to me these last few days filled my heart and head. Even my sense of humor returned and though I was scared silly I whispered, "Feet don't fail me now."

I heard the key in the lock. The trunk lifted enough for a finger hold. I imagined his deformed fingers slipping underneath and almost closed my eyes. Higher, higher. I'd calculated when I could kick without hitting the curved part. *Little more, little more.*

"*Aarrgh!*" My scream and kick exploded and I felt solid flesh give against my feet. I heard the explosion of air from his lungs and the thud when he hit the ground. I didn't count on catapulting myself part way out and I collapsed onto the trunk hook. The pain shot up my back into the base of my skull. My legs went numb. *No! Get up, move damn you. Move.*

The tingling told me I wasn't paralyzed, but I'd lost precious time straddled over the trunk with my feet dangling. I heard honking in the distance. Was it in the cemetery or on Harrison Street?

A hand gripped my ankle. I screamed and kicked, but the grip held. He yanked and the pain across my back took my breath away. He twisted my legs and pulled, flipping me. My shoulders cleared the lip, my chin catching briefly, then bouncing down the bumper. I put my hands down just in time to save my face from crashing on the pavement. I tasted the blood in my mouth and felt the wave of nausea that followed. I fought the darkness that moved over me, not certain if it came from the robe he wore, or from my brain shutting down. In the swirling fog I heard an angry voice shout, "Let go of her you sick bastard or I'll take your head off," and sirens, beautiful sirens.

I woke up still cold, but not lying on the ground. I opened my eyes and looked down at my mother's gravestone. I'm sitting in the aluminum, folding chair my dad brings when he visits my mom. The voice I'd heard was his. I shifted in the chair and he's there.

"Hi, sweetheart. Take it easy don't move. An ambulance is on the way. So is Harry. Hang on baby girl."

Something was wrong with my mouth and nose I could taste blood and looking down at my chest I was soaked in it. My head snapped up and the pain shot through me. My mouth felt stuck.

"Honey, you're okay. Got a bloody nose and cut lip is all. Close your eyes. They'll be here soon."

Instead, I turned my head and saw Bantonini being led away in handcuffs and ropes. The only noise that would come out of my dry battered mouth distracted Dad from his vigil for the paramedics.

"We got him, Honey. He can't hurt you anymore."

Anymore?

I could barely form the words. "Did he…"

Dad understood. "No, no. Never touched you, I made sure of that." He brandished his grass clippers. "I just moved you here. You were out maybe two minutes. Here's the ambulance."

I had my answer; the rest could wait. The paramedics did a cursory check before they lifted me to a gurney.

I heard the squeal of brakes, a door slamming and leather shoes slapping against the pavement. "Mike, where is she?"

Harry's voice filled me with joy. I'd been so miserable to him these past days. I hadn't wanted to die leaving those hours as our last. The paramedics waited. I saw him, in a blur, rush around the end of the ambulance and stop cold. In his eyes I saw that I'd suffered more than a bloody nose and cut lip. And then I saw the pain and anger and finally the tenderness.

He held my hand on the way to Elmhurst Memorial. I could see the tears in his eyes and started to wonder how bad I looked. He cleared his throat. "We have got to stop meeting this way." I tried to smile for him but I couldn't feel if my lips moved. *Oh man, Dutch girl haircut, zits, and broken face.* I squeezed his hand and slept.

The darkness posed no threat; I felt no fear. I woke in my room and knew the moment I opened my eyes I was safe.

"Hey there, welcome back." Tracy smiled at me and her voice woke Harry, in the chair. She backed away.

"Grace." All the love I'd doubted, all the care I could ask for, in one word. I felt my eyes fill with tears and then I felt the fullness of my mouth and nose.

Tracy stepped into my line of vision. "Let me explain about your nose. You'll be okay, breathe through your mouth. Your nose is broken and packed to help it heal. Your bottom teeth bit through under your lower lip. It's been stitched and there's soaked gauze between the stitches and your lower teeth. Your hands are shredded but not broken, your wrist is broken, again, and the small of your back has an indentation the size of Marcie Campbell's engagement ring."

In spite of the shock at her inventory of my body, I started to laugh, "*Oww.*"

She nodded, "I know, it hurts when you laugh."

"*Oww.*" I tried to use my hands to scoot up in bed. "Gaw, daa hurse."

"Let me help you up." She faced me and put her hands under my armpits. "Okay, on three you push with your feet. One, two, three." I pushed and felt myself lifted to the top of the bed. Harry was ready with two pillows to tuck behind me.

"Han kou."

Tracy couldn't hide her smile. "I think we can take out the gauze. You've slept into Sunday; should be enough time." She gently pulled down my lip and removed the gauze. My tongue found the stitches immediately and rubbed back and forth. "Do I have to put this back?"

I felt like a little kid. "No."

"The more you worry at it the longer it'll take to heal. You're not a dog licking his wounds."

"Okay." I swallowed and made a face. "Yuck."

"I brought you some flavored sponge sticks to get that taste out of your mouth. You can gently brush your top teeth tomorrow. Stay away from the bottom for a day or two. I gotta run, kiddo. Wanted to be here when you woke up to explain to you in words not sobs and sappy expressions." She air kissed next to my head.

Harry stood and hugged her. "Thank you ever so much, Tracy." His voice sounded husky with emotion.

"See what I mean." She winked at me and left.

Harry sat down on the edge of the bed. He gently lifted the strands of hair caught in the salve on my cheek and tucked them behind my ear. "Want some juice?" He lifted a glass with a straw.

"Anything but papaya." I smiled and then remembered Will. "Is Will all right? He was shouting. I can't believe I forgot about him. Is he all right?"

"Calm down. He's fine. He'd locked himself in the bathroom and pounded on the door to get your attention."

"Good. I heard him yelling and I was afraid Bantonini hurt him."

"He's downstairs now. Wanted to make sure you were on the mend. Would you like to see him?"

Does he really want to see me or is Harry prompting him?

"Darling, if you're tired I understand and so will he. He'll be back next weekend, time enough to visit."

"No, I want to see him, only not like this. Help me get up."

Harry pulled back the covers and helped me out of bed and into my robe and over to the window seat. I tried to finger comb my hair but both hands were stiff and the new cast on my right hand went further up to my elbow and further down on my fingers.

Harry brushed my hair and squared off the bed covers before he went down to get Will.

I fidgeted with the belt on my robe. I heard him in the hallway. I hoped Harry warned him about my face. He stopped in the doorway and when I looked up, he rushed toward me and stopped short, looking embarrassed.

"I'm glad you're okay. I was really scared when I saw that man going upstairs. I could hear you in the shower."

I motioned toward the other half of the window seat. He sat down and curled his legs under him.

"Thank you for warning me. I think you saved my life." He blushed up through his fair roots. I saw Harry's expression and looked back at Will. "Didn't you tell your dad?" He shook his head.

"Tell me what?"

"Will knew I was in the shower and he flushed the downstairs bathroom. I knew you weren't in the house. I threw on some clothes and was coming down the stairs when Bantonini threw something over my head and carried me out."

I thought for a moment on how to proceed. I didn't want to frighten Will. "I don't think I could have fought back as well as I did if I wasn't wearing heavy jeans and a sweater."

Harry looked at Will with even more adoration. "When I came in, you were in the living room letting Tim out of the priest's hole. I thought you'd locked yourself in so you could yell for Grace."

"That too. I knew she'd never hear me from inside there."

"How did both of you get in?"

"Mrs. Quigley drove us out because mom got hung up in a meeting. She didn't want to talk to either of you so she dropped us off and left. I know where you hide the key. Dad told me, just in case. I let us in and we were in the kitchen when we heard a noise in the living room. I thought it was you and I almost called out, then I saw Elmo's hair sticking up like he was scared. Tim and I saw the guy with his back to us. He moved into the dining room and I took Tim through the living room to the fireplace. I opened the panel and he got in. I was going to get in too, but then I heard the shower go on and I knew you were home. I cut back through the living room and that's when I saw him at the bottom of the stairs. It looked like he'd stopped when he heard the shower; with one foot on one stair like he'd been taking a step. Anyway I thought maybe he was a burglar and would leave when he knew someone was home. It's like he stood there forever, thinking. When he started walking up the stairs I ran into the bathroom and flushed. Then I locked the door and started yelling and pounding."

He blushed. I wondered if Harry had been as shy at this age.

Harry crouched next to his son. "You were very brave and very smart. I owe you for saving Grace. I wasn't here to do it. I'm glad she could count on you." He pulled Will into his arms and ruffled his hair. Will squirmed out of his embrace.

"Dad." He pushed his hands away, but his grin matched his father's. He abruptly turned to me. "Your dad was cool. Uncle Ric told us what the police told him when he got to the cemetery."

Uncle Ric? That would frost Harry's cupcakes.

"He tied Mr. Bantonini's father up like a turkey ready for stuffing. That's what a copper told him."

"Police officer," Harry corrected.

"Uncle Ric calls them coppers and he's going to be one again."

I caught a hint of hero worship. This went beyond frosting.

"But the best was what you did. Your dad said he was cleaning up your mom's gravestone. He was kind of praying, too."

I swallowed when I thought of the miracle that put my dad thirty feet away from me in my most desperate time. I looked at Harry. "We always go in the morning around the time that she died. Why was he there at that time?"

"Your brothers were there in the morning and stopped in at your dad's. He made lunch for them and then went to the cemetery alone."

"What changed your mind about getting up?" I recognized Harry was using speech shorthand in front of Will. I thought for a moment.

"I thought about the alternative and didn't like it?"

He nodded and rubbed my ankle.

"I wanted to go to the cemetery to visit my mom. I guess I didn't miss it."

Will, who waited patiently, interrupted. "Your dad said he wouldn't have even turned around except he heard this weird noise. He saw this man in a black robe on the ground and a woman hanging out of the trunk. The man pulled you, only your dad didn't know it was you, out of the trunk and your dad stopped him. He said he didn't even recognize you until he helped you get up. Then he said he almost dropped you."

He laughed at the story. Harry and I smiled for his sake.

"Will, your mum's going to be here any minute. Best get your things together. School tomorrow."

"Yuck."

"I'll be right back. Just see him out."

I stared out the window, wondering how little boys could become so damaged that they grow up twisted. Two of the raped women were abducted during the day. He'd taken them to the crypt until dark and then brought them to the woods.

How awful it must have been for my father to discover the woman he was saving was his daughter. Would have been more awful if he hadn't been there.

The phone rang. From this angle I couldn't tell which line; it didn't matter I wasn't jumping up to take any calls. Harry came up a few minutes later bearing a bowl of French Vanilla ice cream with sprinkles. He sat across from me and offered a spoonful. "Baskin Robbins. I know you're a strictly vanilla kind of woman but I thought we'd go all out for the occasion so I took the liberty of ordering 'frog' vanilla and adding sprinkles."

I knew that look. He was making light remarks, working up to bad news. The small pink spoon fit easily between my lips and the luxurious feel and taste of creamy vanilla distracted me for a moment. I opened my mouth like a little bird looking for another worm and the pink spoon hurried inside my mouth. I let the cool blob linger on my tongue before I swallowed.

"Who called?"

Harry lowered the spoon into the bowl. "The sheriff's police had been keeping Bantonini under surveillance. We, Kramer, Walter, Peterson, your dad, Don Craig, and I, had our own tag team. Our concern was that they'd slack off after a few days if nothing happened. That's what happened. Yesterday morning, Peterson met up with one of officers he knew leaving Bantonini Jr.'s house. They were on the street for a few minutes. He told Pete that Senior had pulled up and unloaded two boxes from his trunk. His son came out to help him and they'd been inside ever since. Pete set up anyway. Kramer was set to relieve him at two p.m. At one o'clock Pete had called Kramer to check in. Kramer called here to update me. We thought he was in Forest Park visiting with his son.

"Kramer arrived early and became uneasy after a few minutes. Pete hadn't known about the alley. They went up to the house together and found Bantonini Jr. alone."

Harry paused and glanced out the window. I knew he felt guilty that he'd left me alone. I leaned forward and opened my mouth signaling for more ice cream. A vague smile flitted across his face as he fed me another spoonful.

"I'd come home and found the boys terrified and screaming about the man who'd taken you. I must have missed him coming out." He looked down into the bowl.

"You couldn't know. You were trying to help me. They'd told you he was in Forest Park."

His hands twitched and I thought he was going to fling the ice cream across the room.

"Doesn't matter. I left you and Will in danger."

I knew he had to work that though on his own, like I had with Janet's death. "And the call?"

"Bantonini's dead and his son is in jail for his murder."

⮞ 50 ⮜

I thought I'd be shocked but I sat still thinking *'the sins of the father are visited upon the son'* and then the son kills him.

"Gracie?"

"I'm okay. How?"

"When Kramer found Bantonini alone, he confronted him about where his father might be. According to Pete he confronted him several times with the back of his hand. Bantonini kept mumbling about boxes. He'd become suspicious of the boxes his father had asked to store in his basement. He borrowed his car and left about an hour after he arrived.

Junior went downstairs to search for the two boxes he knew were down there, they'd been hidden so well. That's where Kramer and Peterson found him, dazed and staring into boxes filled with human hair and women's panties."

"The trophies." Harry nodded. I shivered and tried to stop from thinking how close I'd come to contributing to that box. Harry rubbed my arms and shifted me so I could lean against him inside his arms.

"Bantonini realized that his father was going to try and frame him for the rapes. He gave Ric the idea that he might be at the cemetery. Ric called it in, hoping squads would cover both locations and called to warn me, but it was too late. He told me about the cemetery. Peterson went to the woods and called Walter to join him there. I tried to call your dad, but he wasn't home. I left for the cemetery and got a call from the police on the scene that they'd found you alive."

"He never killed his victims."

"We don't know what he was planning. According to Hanley he'd become obsessed with you. The son told us his father mentioned you once as the woman with eyes the color of heather, just like his mother's. You might have been his last victim before he disappeared. He had a passport and over five thousand dollars on him. Bantonini rode with Ric to show him the grave. The police were already there. A motorist had stopped a Hillside squad and told him the strange story of seeing an arm protruding from the rear light of a car that turned into Mt. Carmel Cemetery. Smart girl. They were the first to find you. A Sergeant Wollenberg had to subdue your dad as they say.

I'd love to read his report.

The doorbell rang and I knew the Morellis were on our doorstep. I didn't have the entire picture but this was a good place to stop. I knew I was safe. I knew the troop would be disbanded and those boys would be safe.

Harry brought everyone up to me: Mike, Marty, Glenn, and Dad. The Morelli men; though Dad always said I got into as much trouble as the boys, it was like he had five sons. I assured them, as best I could in my condition, that with cosmetic surgery and time for my hair to grow, I'd be good as new.

"I like your hair short. Looks very nineties." Marty's wife Eve wore her hair cut up over her ears and shaved close above the nape.

"Maybe I'll bob my nose to match my hair."

"Hey, that's a Morelli nose, the only obviously Italian part on you. Leave it alone." Laughter healed like no other medicine, including Marty's pills. Harry passed around the *pizelles* and coffee. I couldn't take the heat from coffee so he made me iced coffee.

Dad grew serious. "You heard what happened?" I nodded. He explained to my brothers. "Jr. came into the police station with everyone else. Someone had taken my account, while Bantonini Sr. sat in another room waiting for transport to Cook County. The skuttlebut was that he'd admitted to the rapes, but wanted to trade information about Janet Henry's death for a better deal. About that time, Cook County police showed up and while they walked him through the station, his son jumped up, pulled a knife, and jabbed his father in the neck. The old man collapsed and died five feet away. Before he died, he pointed at his son and said, 'button'. The guy's dying and all he says is button. That won't get him through the Pearly Gates."

"Maybe not, but he might have been trying to do one decent thing and tell us who killed Janet." Everyone looked at me like I had two noses instead of one swollen one.

Harry shook his head. "More than likely he wanted revenge on his son. Remember, he already tried to frame him for the rapes."

"Anyway, Moochie goes crazy, screaming for his priest and reciting the Scout Law while they're cuffing him and leading him to a cell. That was weird to hear the Scout Law recited while they read that Miranda spiel.

"What was he wearing?" Another round of odd looks from my family.

"A class B shirt and his uniform pants. The troop was supposed to help at Carnival Day. Why?"

"Maybe senior wasn't the person wearing the pants with the missing button. Maybe he was pointing to the pants not the person."

"You may have something. I'll call Arroyo."

Harry left the room to place the call.

"What's going to happen to the troop?"

"What Bantonini had been planning all along. Father Briscoe, who by the way says hello to the girl with the purple eyes and hard questions, filled in the little that he knew. Bantonini took over from his father to protect the boys. He wouldn't let any relatives of the previous scouts participate. He couldn't trust that the damage his father had done to their fathers or brothers hadn't carried over. He knew what his father was doing with the Satan cult but he kept trying to protect him, the boys, himself. He made sure whatever he told Father Briscoe was always in confession.

Bantonini Sr. was a sick pervert who ruined the lives of most of the boys who stayed with him when he ran the troop. Junior was trying to run the troop into the ground not giving anyone a chance to take it over. Briscoe, knowing what the old man had done, joined the troop as an advisor. He knew this Bantonini wasn't molesting the boys, knew he lived with the torment of what his father had done, torn between trying to help a father he wanted to love and protecting young lives. He couldn't step down and take the risk that his old man would step up to run the troop. He'd already talked to Dick Tresselt with Troop 16 and they were prepared to transfer the boys

That's going to happen sooner. Whoever wants to transfer will be in Troop 16 before Christmas."

Harry stepped back into the room. "Seems Kramer had the same thought when he saw how Bantonini pointed. Arroyo said it took them a while to get owners to open up on Sunday but they determined, through cleaner marks, that the pants with the missing button belonged to Guilfoyle. They picked him up a few hours ago as he was preparing to take a trip. He's admitting to finding her dead body in the woods and to dumping her trying to make it look like an accident. He'd meant to stage the scene better but when he lifted her the jacket slipped down and he lost his grip. He knew the FBI was already involved and didn't want closer scrutiny. He claims she was already dead under a branch that had fallen from the wind. The autopsy did concur that the fatal blow was to the top of her head and there were traces of bark in her scalp but no way to prove if they came from a branch hitting her or her landing on one in the well."

"This guy is like Crisco. He admits to the lesser crime and slips his head out of the noose. He's gonna walk on this too, isn't he?"

"He'll do jail time, but not for anyone's murder."

I felt the anger and frustration building. I hated for them to leave on such a dark note.

Harry spoke up. "I can't do anything about that but I can get Will out of there. He's transferring to Goodrich Elementary after the holidays and joining Devin's troop in Woodridge. I have it on the best authority that it's a fine troop. The current scoutmaster was the cub master for the pack at Goodrich and he's been at the helm of Troop 562 for about a year. You'll like this, Mike. He has four sons to get through to Eagle. Should be with the troop awhile. And it gets better. After sons one and two, his daughter was born."

Dad laughed and pointed at me. "Another fourteen year plan. You know Harry it's only one hour a week. Thinking about getting involved?"

"Oh yes. I will be Paul Riggs' new best friend. At the minimum, an assistant scoutmaster."

My dad and brothers applauded and hooted. "James Bond meets Lord Baden-Powell."

Harry took the teasing. He let them wind down and then signaled time to go. Each kissed me goodnight, carefully avoiding salve, packing, and bruised skin. The top of my head seemed the safest spot.

So, Will and Lily will be our neighbors. Easier for Harry. What about me? Maybe this is what Marisol meant about seeing a little boy in my life. He'll certainly be here more. Lily is buying Mary's studio to set up a retail location for her work. Harry and I will be home more than she. Guess that's it. He'll be in my life. He saved my life. He must like me.

The thought filled me with happiness. Harry's son liked me. From there we could move on to love. Harry returned and sat down next to me. "A farthing for your thoughts."

I loved his sense of humor. I loved him.

Suddenly, in the midst of calm a terrible thought occurred to me. Harry noticed the shift. "What's wrong?"

"Does anyone believe the bizarre coincidence that three people from the same family could die by accident in the same woods? According to Guilfoyle–"

The room plunged into darkness. An eerie sensation pricked the back of my neck and I knew evil stalked me.

Harry lifted me from the window seat and tucked me on the floor in the corner beyond the bed. He opened the nightstand drawer and removed the gun. He pulled the phone off the stand and placed it in front of me and whispered, "Call 911, and take this." He'd taught me the basics of handling a gun. I felt the rough handle and gripped it. "The safety is off. I'll call out when I come back. If you don't hear me, shoot. Don't let him walk in." He squeezed my shoulder. "I'll be back. I love you."

My hands trembled; I feared I'd shoot Harry's retreating back. I put the gun down and lifted the receiver. No dial tone. I heard a noise and picked up the gun. Silence. My ears strained to hear the slightest sound as I held the gun straight, arm pointed at the door. My thumb brushed against the safety. *Off, one two three. On, one two three. Off, one two three.* The cadence comforted me and I relaxed my grip.

Pop.

A single frightening sound and then silence. No outcry, no thud. Awful silence. *I have the gun. Harry's unarmed.*

I knew what he told me, but I also knew he needed this gun. I gripped the nightstand and struggled to my feet. I'd barely been able to hold the gun properly with two hands trying to aim and fire with my left hand would be futile. I made my way to the landing, listening for any noise that would guide me to Harry. The hairs on the back of my neck warned me against trusting the soft footfalls I heard on the carpeted stairs.

Oh my God. Harry's hurt.

I crouched near the top of the stairs afraid that movement now would alert him to my presence. I might catch him by surprise. If I couldn't push him down the stairs I still had the gun.

Cripes. On off on off. Great. I couldn't tell if the safety was on or off. I heard another sound lower on the stairs. My heart lifted with the thought that Harry was okay.

Beams of light sliced through the darkness and shouts broke the silence. I picked out the voices familiar to me; my father and brothers, seemingly originating from several points. The beams played across the room and up the stairs. In a shaft of light I saw a form on the stairs halfway to the top.

"Douse the lights," Harry shouted and immediately I heard another *pop.* He'd fired at the voice below him, at Harry. The lights went out and I heard movement. Feet rushing through the living room toward the stairs. I wanted to warn them to stay away. Then something moved behind me. The current of air from the door opening brushed past me. Someone had come up the back stairs to the second floor, trapping me between the gunman on the stairs and whoever was sneaking toward me. *Does he know I'm here? Maybe I can surprise this one too, trip him. My brothers know this house. What if it's one of them? Or Harry coming to protect me. Bumping into me in the dark could surprise the wrong person.*

I struggled with the dilemma until two sounds reached me, another set of feet rushing through the corridor behind me and the *popthud* combination of a bullet hitting the railing above my head. In the next instant, Harry pulled the gun from my hand and he pushed his body in front of me to block the danger. I heard someone else behind me. "Get down," Harry whispered. Too late. Three shots rang out above me. I heard a cry almost at my shoulder. I started to rise when Harry yanked my arm. "Stay down." The whisper marked his position and another bullet hit the post he crouched behind. The vibration skittered along the soles of my feet.

Harry scrambled across the opening and crashed into the opposite wall drawing another shot. It hit somewhere behind him. I heard a low moan and wanted to crawl to his side but I knew I might draw his attention and worse more bullets. Harry had the gun and now the sides would be even. *The safety. Was it on or off?* I had to warn Harry.

A noise from below distracted me, drums beating a steady tattoo like the tom-toms in the woods. *Is the noise in my head? Am I losing it?* The gunman heard it. "No, get away," he whispered, his voice pleading. The drumbeat continued. The whispered sound of *Chee Chee Pin Quay, Chee Chee Pin Quay*, barely audible filled the air. Shots rang out again and again until I finally heard, *click, click, click*.

In that instant, beams of light flickered up the stairs and four men pinned Bart Guilfoyle on the stairs. "Up here, someone's hurt. Hurry!"

"Go, Dad, we've got him." Mike shouted.

"Glenn, phone's dead. Call 911 from my car."

It was Marty who lay moaning inches from me, as I crawled toward him in the dark. "Marty?" I felt his foot and then the beam from Dad's flashlight swept across both of us.

He crouched on his knees, pushing the flashlight into my hands, reaching for his son. "Where are you hit? Our gazes raked his body for blood and Dad's hands gently touched him looking for injury.

Marty pushed his hands away and struggled to sit up. He reached into his inside jacket pocket and pulled out dad's spotter, smashed and misshapen. We both let a whoop.

"He's fine. The bullet hit the flashlight."

Dad helped him to his feet, left him leaning against the railing, and walked down the stairs. "Shine that light on this chicken-shit." Without warning my dad punched Guilfoyle, snapping his head back against the wall. "BIG guy? You were crapping in your pants when you heard the drums. You always were afraid of the bogeyman BIG guy; afraid the dead Indians would get you for desecrating the chief's grave."

Guilfoyle struggled against the arms holding him, until he heard Harry's dead cold voice. "Let him go boys. Let's see how brave he is when someone else has the gun." Guilfoyle stood perfectly still.

Shouts and lights echoed through the kitchen in the form of Ric and Peterson. With all the light it seemed like high noon on the stairs.

"Sheriff's police are right behind us. He walked out, some damn clerical error. They checked his house and business. I got the idea he'd show up out here. He kept asking if you remembered more about that night. I think he was afraid you'd remember something incriminating about that night, about Agent Henry or John Henry. He would have come after you sooner or later. Getting arrested must have pushed up his timetable. Lucky you had the extra help. Mike, how the hell did you and the posse find out?"

"We were leaving and he passed us coming in. I saw the dark Buick, got a feeling. The further we drove the stronger the feeling. We turned around and rushed in after we heard a shot fired."

Dad faced Guilfoyle. "I never trusted you. But why come after Grace? Jesus, first that freak and now you." My father punched him again and I heard his knuckle crack against bone. He pulled back his hand and shook it to ease the sting. Blood poured from Guilfloyle's nose saturating his shirt.

Peterson had waited downstairs to direct the police. More flashlights trained on the bloody sight.

"What happened to him?"

"Tripped in the dark, Officer."

"Yeah, looks like it. We got it from here." They manhandled him down the stairs and I hoped out of our lives.

Harry and I refused Dad's offer to spend the night with him until Com Ed could repair our connection. We waited for the police to take our statements and walk the crime scene. The Morelli men stayed, fascinated by a ritual that I'd experienced too much over the last year.

Finally my dad and brothers followed the last technician out of the house, promising to come back tomorrow.

Harry found as many candles as he could and set them up on the window seat. The effect swayed my mood but not to romance. In the flickering light with Harry's arms around me I could relax my mind and let my senses float toward the light. I could feel the steady rise and fall of his breathing. The room glowed brighter and an icy current swirled around the flames and across the room to slide across the bedcovers toward us.

I felt no dread, no threat. The candle flames peaked in a blaze and then settled. The chilly air retreated, cold bones at peace.

Meet the author:

Luisa Scala Buehler grew up in the town of Berkeley, IL, a suburb of Chicago. Her parents made the decision to sell their home on the west side of the city. The small bungalow on Victoria Street was perfect for her family: two parents, older brother, and an uncle.

Her first exposure to a public library was the small "volunteer" library located in the basement of a grocery store on Taft Avenue. It was there she discovered Nancy Drew. Luisa realized that this would be her career; not girl detective, but girl mystery writer. About that time, her family subscribed to the Sunday paper and Luisa found another fascinating role model in the comic pages, Brenda Starr, reporter!

Luisa attended Proviso West High School in Hillside, IL where she immediately joined the newspaper staff. Her advisor suggested she try another release for her writing when she continually failed to meet deadlines for the tabloid. Her articles were stirring but they never made it to press on time.

Luisa joined the volunteer Docent program at Brookfield Zoo in 1987 to pursue her interest in animals. An earlier idea, to write children's books seemed to fit with her duties at the zoo. She answered questions from zoo-goers concerning animal habitat, behaviors, type of food, and the number one non-animal question, *where is the closest restroom?*

After submitting her writing for five years without gaining publishing success, Luisa put the novel away and took up the position of Webelos Leader with her son Christopher's Cub Scout pack. She continued to write, starting her second mystery. She continued in scouting as her son bridged over to Boy Scouts by becoming a trained leader for Troop 562 in Woodridge, IL. In 2002, she signed a publishing contract for *The Rosary Bride.*

She lives in Lisle, IL with her husband Gerry, their son Chris (Kit), and family cat, Martin Marmalade. In her spare time, Luisa loves to garden.